STRIPPER BOAT

LYLE CHRISTIE

This book is dedicated to all who have faced adversity in terms of health, work, relationships, or even a really disgusting public restroom, and now desperately need a FUCKING literary, if not FUCKING literal, break from this crazy thing we call

life.

•Please excuse the use of profanity and be warned that there will be more to follow, as well as some traditional humor, bathroom humor, and a goodly amount of spirited sexual encounters, though it will all be delivered tastefully and with the intent of conveying a deep, rewarding, and soulful catharsis.

STRIPPER BOAT

MANTASY INC.

WWW.LYLECHRISTIE.COM

LYLE@LYLECHRISTIE.COM

BOOK DESIGN AND LAYOUT: CHRISTOPHER IMLAY

COVER DESIGN: CHRISTOPHER IMLAY & LYLE CHRISTIE

EDITORS: THOMAS RAINWEATHER • KATHERINE GUNDLING

PROOFREADERS: KRIS CHRISTIE • EMINENCE TUPPLE • LORD SAMUAL SWIFTBUTTOCKS

ISBN-13: 978-1-949386-21-9

BOOK FIVE IN THE

MANTASY SERIES

CHAPTER ONE: PROLOGUE
Water Foul

It was a little after eight p.m. as the sixty foot Hatteras motor yacht cruised along the city front, with its passengers enjoying a world class view of the twinkling lights of the San Francisco skyline. The people aboard were out here for a bachelor party, and the man at the helm, Daniel Hedwick, was the son of the owner of the yacht. He was also the best man and normally would have had his father's captain aboard to pilot the vessel. Unfortunately, the captain had a propensity for giving Daniel's father detailed reports of his son's activities, so, tonight, Daniel decided it would be best to keep his potential depravity on the down-low by piloting the boat himself.

To make sure his best friend's bachelor party was particularly special, Daniel had brought aboard a literal boatload of food and alcohol, and he had hired four extremely capable strippers to serve as the night's entertainment.

The groomsmen, as typical of twentysomething males, had already devoured all the food and were now gazing out at the view and power drinking in anticipation of the show that would soon begin. Daniel, drink in hand, was looking particularly happy as he set a course that would take them around the lee of Alcatraz before heading north across the bay to anchor just off the town of Sausalito.

The evening had started out rather pleasant, but storm clouds coming in from the west were kicking up the wind and waves, and it was sending sea spray up over the bow. Daniel eventually had to turn on the wipers, though he wasn't concerned, for they were in the relative safety of the San Francisco Bay, and the big Hatteras was a seaworthy vessel that could easily handle the conditions.

Daniel's best friend, and the evening's obvious guest of honor, came over and stood beside him at the helm.

"Dude, this is seriously awesome," he said.

"As your best man, it was the least I could do to give you a proper send off, and I'm not exaggerating when I say that you're going to shit your pants when you see the entertainment. In fact, it just might make you reconsider getting married."

"Let's hope so," the groom responded, as they clinked their glasses together and took a sip of their drinks.

Just then, the lights dimmed, and music started playing on the yacht's sound system.

"The show's starting! You better go take a seat and get

ready!" Daniel said, with a knowing smile.

The groom went and sat in the chair that had been strategically placed for him, and, a moment later, a stunning Asian woman in red thong underwear and matching bra came strutting into the center of the room. She made a seductive pass in front of all the groomsmen then walked to the temporary stripper pole that Daniel had installed for the party. She leapt onto it, threw her legs into the air, then did the splits before sliding down to the floor and rolling onto her hands and knees. It was an athletic move and hinted that the girl had probably been a gymnast. She crawled over to the groom then leaned back and snapped open her bra to expose her breasts, which she shook back and forth in front of his eyes.

All the men in the room started cheering, especially Daniel, whose attention was now completely off the task of steering the yacht, and, instead, was focused entirely on the girl. She stood up and straddled the groom and dry humped him for a brief moment before returning to the poll and dropping down into another full split. At that exact moment there was great grinding noise, and the yacht abruptly came to a halt, sending everyone tumbling onto the floor. Daniel immediately turned his attention back to the helm and throttled back the engines.

"Dude! What happened?" the groom yelled, as he stood up and ran over to join him.

"We went aground," Daniel said, sounding panicked.

"What the fuck do we do?"

"I'm going to try and back off," he said, putting it in reverse.

He gunned the engines, and the boat started inching backwards, but, as it came free, it was obvious the bow was riding a little lower in the water.

"Go below and see if there's any damage!" Daniel said.

The groom disappeared down the stairs to the lower level, and, when he returned a moment later, the three other strippers were with him. Standing beside him was a brunette in a sailor's outfit, a redhead in a cowgirl costume, and a blonde in a gold bra and matching thong underwear, and all of them had worried expressions on their faces.

"Dude, we're seriously taking on water," the groom said.

"Call the Coast Guard," the girl wearing the little sailor outfit said.

"No, we're not calling the Coast Guard," Daniel responded nervously.

"Why not?" the same girl asked.

"Because I'm drunk, and I'll get arrested."

"OK, so what do we do?"

Daniel took a moment to think then appeared to have an idea.

"Fuck it! We'll lower the dingy into the water, and I'll take us ashore myself."

"Will it fit everyone?"

"I don't know, but there's only one way to find out."

They headed out to the back deck, and, in spite of the wind and rain, Daniel and his friends managed to lower the fifteen foot Zodiak rigid inflatable over the stern and into the water, where its air-filled rubber sides kept it from being damaged as it banged against the Hatteras's hull.

"All right, let's get the guys aboard first so they can help the girls climb down into the raft," Daniel said.

"Wouldn't it be easier if the guys lowered the girls from up here?" the girl in the sailor's suit asked, as she was obviously not too thrilled about Daniel's plan.

"No, because if they fall, the guys will be able to catch them."

"Fine," she said.

Daniel went first, and then the other guys followed him into the raft, and it was looking as though it was going to be a tight squeeze, but everyone would be able to fit. A good sized wave rolled through at that moment, and the raft pitched sideways and looked as though it might capsize. It recovered shortly thereafter, but Daniel, who had already started the engine, was looking panicked as he took in the scene.

"Untie the lines!" he said.

"But, what about the girls?" one of the guys asked.

"Yeah, what about us, you fucking asshole!" the girl in the sailor suit yelled from the deck of the Hatteras.

"It's too dangerous. The waves are getting bigger, and we're going to capsize if we stay here. I'll take these guys ashore then come back for you when the raft is less top heavy. It'll only take me ten minutes at the most, I promise," he said.

"No fucking way!" the girl responded.

"Untie us!" Daniel yelled.

The guys manning the lines, unsure what to do, followed his orders and untied the raft, allowing it to drift free, whereupon Daniel put it in gear and headed away from the boat and towards the San Francisco waterfront. The four girls stood at the railing and watched as the bachelor boys disappeared into the stormy night, and, thirty minutes later, there was still no sign of Daniel, and worse still, the storm was growing in intensity. Just then, a series of especially large waves rolled through, and the boat lurched and began sliding deeper into the water.

"What the hell are we going to do?" the blond girl wearing the gold bra and underwear asked.

"Yeah, I think this fucking boat is about to go under," the redhead in the cowgirl costume added.

"We could swim to Alcatraz," the Asian girl suggested.

"Too dangerous. Those waves would tear us apart when we reached the shore. Fuck it, I'm going to radio the Coast Guard," the girl in the sailor suit said, as she headed back inside the boat.

The girls followed her to the helm, then she reached up and clicked on the VHF radio and turned the dial until it was on sixteen—the designated channel for emergencies.

"Mayday, this is the..."

Suddenly, the entire boat went dark, which meant the sea water had flooded the engine room and killed all of the electronics. The girls screamed and started to panic, but their unofficial leader, the girl in the sailor suit, told them to stay on the back deck while she went downstairs to try and find her iPhone. Without light, she was forced to operate from memory, and she was able to feel her way down the stairs and to the stateroom on the lower level where she and her fellow strippers had left their things. The water was now up to her knees, but she soon found the room and managed to feel around the bed until coming across her jacket. In the left pocket was her iPhone, and, ultimately, their only hope of survival. She pulled it out and used the flashlight feature to make her way back upstairs, where she opened her browser and immediately did a search for the Coast Guard's number. She found it, hit dial, and it took three rings before a guy picked up on the other end.

"Coast Guard Station Golden Gate," the man said.

"Hello, I'm on a vessel that went aground, and we are sinking and need immediate assistance!"

"Can you give me your location and a description of the vessel, ma'am?"

"We're just off of Alcatraz, and we're on a sixty foot powerboat."

"Do you have a life raft?"

"No, it just left."

"Excuse me, ma'am, but I'm not sure I understand."

"The assholes who own this boat left on the life raft about thirty minutes ago—without us!" she said, angrily.

"Roger that, ma'am. I will contact the appropriate authorities immediately."

"Appropriate authorities? I thought you were the appropriate authorities."

"Only in cases of extreme distress."

"Well, let me tell you something. This fucking boat is definitely in distress, and the lucky fuckers to arrive first are going to find four really fucking hot and grateful strippers if they can get their asses out here before we sink and die!"

The girl in the little sailor suit was obviously smart and knew exactly what to say to get the young guardsmen to get off their asses and get out there as soon as possible.

"Roger that, ma'am. Help is on the way."

The guardsman she had been talking to quickly gathered his boat crew and waited until he was halfway out the door before making a quick call to his friend who captained a vessel assist boat out of Sausalito. That friend, a man named Greg, answered on the second ring.

"Dude, you're never going to believe this one!" the guardsman said.

"What's up, Adam? Did someone call for help?"

Adam went on to explain the situation, and his friend listened in rapt attention before responding.

"Don't worry, I'm just off Angel Island and can be there

in a minute," Greg said.

"Unless we get there first."

"Loser buys the beer."

"Fuck that, winner buys."

"Yeah, I suppose that's only fair," he said, before they both hung up and turned their attention to the task at hand.

Meanwhile, the girl in the sailor's suit joined the others on the back deck, and they all huddled beneath the roof to take refuge from the storm while they waited for help. The yacht shifted once again and dropped ever lower into the dark turbulent waters of the bay, and the girl in the sailor suit walked to the railing and stared into the deluge of wind and rain, and, off in the darkness to the north, she thought she could see the lights of a boat heading in their direction, and she prayed with all her heart that they would arrive in time.

CHAPTER TWO
Wet Work

It was eight forty-six p.m. on a stormy December night, and it was by all accounts a terrible time to be out on the San Francisco Bay. The rain was coming down in buckets, and a strong westerly blowing in off the coast was kicking up a ferocious chop and making for a decidedly uncomfortable ride. That generally wouldn't have been too much of a problem had I not been sitting on the tiniest of toilets in the smallest of bathrooms, where I was taking an unplanned dump aboard my good friend Greg's thirty-five foot Protector Yacht. Greg was the captain of a Vessel Assist boat, the new marine version of AAA, which came to the aid of stricken mariners, thus alleviating the Coast Guard from all but the direst of sea based emergencies. He had called me earlier in the day and asked if I would like to go on a ride-along tonight, as the weather would supposedly be lovely and, should any emergencies arrive, I could fill in for his usual crewman dimwit Dave, who was home with the flu.

Greg had been trying for nearly two years to get me to join him on one of his nightly forays because of my background as a United States Air Force Parajumper. He figured, rightly so, that my former occupation as a hybrid between a Navy SEAL and a medical corpsman, would make me the ideal crew. Now, what had started out as a beautiful calm night under a full moon had quickly deteriorated into a personal nightmare. Rough waters and extricating the bowels were two things that should remain mutually exclusive, and, for me in particular, it was a disastrous combination. I made a point of never doing anything more exciting than a number one when I was out and about in the world, and therefore couldn't believe that I was currently in the middle of a number two—on a bouncing boat no less. I had eaten a sanwdwich before leaving home and never imagined that the extra pressure on my innards might induce an emergency deuce. That is, until the feeling arrived five minutes ago as we crested a particularly large wave, and I found myself clenching my butt cheeks together as I ran down below and entered Greg's head—so to speak.

The boat was bucking the incoming waves, and the water sloshing around the bowl was making an unpleasant experience even more unpleasant. As I tried to get comfortable, I looked down beside me and was surprised to see that Greg kept a full accompaniment of magazines in a rack beside the toilet. Two thumbs up for Captain Greg, as I was on the cusp of release and therefore desperately in need of reading material. I rifled through the various magazines, which all turned out to be adult in nature, and settled on a two month old *Playboy Magazine*—something I hadn't seen since the internet had begun its unintended assault on print media. Oddly, a gentleman's magazine wasn't my preferred entertainment, as taking a dump in my world was more about reading than gazing at beautiful naked women. I had no problem with nudity, but should it incur unplanned blood flow to my gentleman region, it became a logistical nightmare because even a semi hardened member sent my urine flying high and potentially beyond the bowl, and, needless to say, a full-blown erection negated any ability to pass urine, thereby sabotaging half of the reason that I was here in the first place.

I therefore turned past the air brushed beauty on the cover and let the magazine open to its most natural fold point, the centerfold, then, disregarding a long male tradition, I proceeded to turn the page over and read the supposedly hand written details of the girl in question, who, in this particular instance was Miss October. This section had always been one of my guilty pleasures because of the cheesy Miss America Pageant kind of sensibilities often portrayed, and it seemed particularly ridiculous to place a giant nude spread of a beautiful woman then counter balance it with a bunch of contrived details that were most certainly put together by a marketing department rather than a twenty something beauty queen turned Playmate.

With everything in place, it was time to set my eyes to

the words on the page and let loose a mighty dump. As it turned out, Miss October, real name Fiona Blake, was from Woodside California, and was the second of two children. Her parents were both high school teachers, and she had supposedly attended Santa Clara University and earned a bachelors degree in sociology as well as a Masters in the same subject. She enjoyed hiking, biking, and guys who weren't afraid to get wet. She loved horses, as all girls did, and her favorite family pet was a golden retriever named Petunia. Her lifetime goal was to use her education to join her older brother's foundation, which organized aid for underprivileged peoples around the globe. Cue the applause and the tears. What an incredible load of shit and likely no more meaningful than what I was currently dropping into the toilet below.

Regardless, the story of Miss Blake, however ridiculous, was doing its part in making an otherwise unbearable dump bearable. Unfortunately, the tiny porcelain bowl was awash with both solid and liquid, and it was time to flush and clear the breach before the next salvo. I hit the small rubber coated button that resided just to the right of the toilet paper holder and instantly heard a sound more akin to a garbage disposal or high powered blender. Boat toilets, unlike their land based brethren, were a world unto themselves and definitely a counterpoint to the glamour of yachting. The electric ones, like the one I was currently on, flushed by utilizing a pump and macerator unit that was noisy as all hell. Worse still, the aforementioned process generally relied on water from outside the boat, and that meant that a tube went from the sea to the toilet. In theory, this wasn't a big deal except for the simple fact that seawater was alive with all manner of life, and, when that life reached a darkened hose inside a boat, it died and created an awful lot of rotting material and, ultimately, methane. So, flushing a marine toilet brought with it a great swath of odor generally far worse than anything that may have come out of a person's bowels.

There I sat, literally up to my nose in onerous odor and decided I needed a perk. The second salvo was about over, and that meant I would treat myself to a quick glance at Miss October. I turned over the page, and there before me lay the massive spread of a blue eyed goddess. She was of course beautiful, long legged, lithe, and had long brown hair and ample breasts, though I had to wonder how much was real and how much was Photoshop. I suppose that would just have to remain a mystery, as she likely lived off in Los Angeles, where she was in actual truth pursuing a career as a model-actress. Suddenly, there was a loud banging on the door, and I heard Greg just outside.

"Finn! Hurry up!"

"Shouldn't you be driving the boat," I yelled over the din of the droning engines and pounding sea.

"You've gotta pinch it off and get up here! We've got an emergency and you're not going to believe it!"

"OK, give me a minute, you fucker."

"Why? Are you whacking it to one of my Playboys?"

"No, I'm whacking it, thinking about you in your fucking overalls."

Greg, for some inexplicable reason, always wore dark blue overalls when he worked. Needless to say, I wasn't a fan of overalls—generally on men or women.

"Well put the hammer down and get your ass up here," he said, before stomping back up the passageway to the helm.

Greg left, and I gave it a final glorious push, making sure that I had indeed cleared the baffles. Satisfied that I was empty, I wiped, flushed, and washed my hands before joining Greg up at the helm. He was giddy as a schoolgirl as he steered his vessel and kept his eyes fixed on the churning sea ahead.

"OK, what's got you all excited?" I asked.

"Stripper boat!"

"Excuse me?"

"A stripper boat!"

"I still don't understand."

"Apparently, a boat full of strippers hit Little Alcatraz and is sinking and needs assistance."

"No shit?"

"No shit!"

Greg's face was glowing in the red light of his instrument panel, and his smile was stretching from ear to ear, making me think that this was clearly one of his lifetime dreams finally come true. I suppose it made sense when you considered the nature of his job. His usual clientele probably consisted of boozed up day sailors, and, while a few of them might be attractive females, most would be dressed in foul weather gear and looking haggard from a day in the wind and saltwater spray. So, what could possibly happen that would be as exciting for Greg as rescuing a boatload of scantily dressed women? Not much, I imagine.

Ahead, I could see Alcatraz Island and, in turn, its little brother of sorts—Little Alcatraz—a collection of rocks lying about ten yards off the northwest corner. It had been the site of many maritime disasters and originally had been called Paul Pry Rock, which was named after the steamer that struck it on December 22, 1862. Now, it would be infamous, at least in my mind, as the location for the shipwreck of a boatload of strippers. There were no other rescue vessels in sight, not even the Coast Guard, so it appeared that we were first on the scene, which I suppose meant more fun for us—and especially Greg.

As he steered in closer, I could see that the vessel in question was a white sixty foot Hatteras, and it was a beautiful and sea worthy motor yacht that could generally only succumb to disaster by the fault of an act of God or a particularly negligent captain. It was listing heavily to starboard, with its bow pointed towards the Golden Gate, and that meant that they had been coming around the island when they struck Little Alcatraz. Now only a boat length away, I could see four scantily dressed women screaming and frantically waving from the stern of the beleaguered vessel. I could understand their concern, as the thought of going into the cold, dark waters of San Francisco Bay on a stormy December night would be daunting to say the least.

"So, how are you going to work it?" I asked Greg.

"My vessel draws a lot less, so I'm thinking we can come alongside and offload the girls first then deal with the Hatteras second."

"Girls first. I like your thinking."

Greg smiled and throttled back as he kept his focus continuously moving between his GPS chart, depth gauge, and the stern of the Hatteras—a feat made considerably more difficult by the rain, wind, and current.

"It looks like we'll be fine. The Hatteras is between us and the rocks, so we have plenty of water."

"Well then, let's get those girls off—no pun intended," I said.

Now that we were side to side with the stricken vessel, I could see the tears and frantic expressions on the girl's faces and had to wonder where the hell everyone else had gone. Perhaps they were down below manning the bilge pumps and dealing with the damage to the hull.

"Vessel Assist, is everyone all right? Are there any medical emergencies that I need to call in?" Greg asked.

"No, we just want to get the hell off this boat," the girl in the sailor's suit yelled back.

"Are there others aboard?" Greg asked.

"No, just us," the same girl said.

"That's odd," I said.

"Very," Greg added.

I moved to the aft rail and saw the violence of the wind and waves firsthand as it brought the two boats crashing together—the only things keeping us from taking damage being the massive rubber pontoons that extended the entire length of Greg's vessel. On a break between waves, I reached out and got a hold of the first girl's hands. She was a pretty blond wearing a sparkling gold thong and tiny matching top that barely covered her massive, likely augmented breasts. She was quite a sight this cold night on the bay, and I could imagine Greg grinning behind me as he watched the rescue unfold. A wave hit just at that moment, and I used its momentum to lift her up and onto our boat and down into the cockpit before turning my attention back to the other girls. They were eagerly waiting to abandon the Hatteras, whose deck was sinking ever deeper into the waves. I still had three more people to save, and we were running out of time.

I reached for the next girl, who was a pretty redhead dressed in a cowgirl costume, and she too was sporting some very ample breasts. They weren't as big as her friend's, but they certainly made an impression. During a break in the waves, she managed to cross the void and make it into my arms. I returned for number three, a beautiful Asian girl wearing a matching red bra and thong underwear, and saw that she, like her friends, had also very likely been in the company of a plastic surgeon. At least if she went in the water, I was pretty sure that she would float. She was frantic and practically clawing at me, and her long manicured nails were digging into my forearms as she reached across. A small wave hit, and again I used its momentum to lift her up and into the cockpit of our boat, where she took a seat with her friends beneath the bimini top. One more girl to go, and the most critical part of the rescue operation would be over.

I moved back into place and finally got a good look at the last girl. She was a brunette, beautiful by all accounts, and unlike her peers, seemed fairly calm in the face of adversity—probably the reason she had been their unofficial leader and spokesperson. She was dressed in a tiny sailor outfit that consisted of a blue thong and a tight white shirt tied in a knot just below her ample bosoms. In the chaos of the moment, I couldn't be sure if they were real or fake, but my professional opinion was that they were home grown and certified organic. She moved to the rail and took hold of my hands, but a sudden set of waves came crashing in and slammed the two boats together before pulling them violently apart. The motion caused the girl to slip off the other boat's deck, and it left her dangling from my arms between the two vessels, where she was in danger of getting crushed. Greg hit the port throttle to get some distance between the Hatteras and us while I tried my best to hold onto her. Our hands were wet and slippery, and, when a large wave rolled through, it pulled her from my grip, and she fell backwards into the dark turbulent waters. She popped up a moment later, but the current was already taking her away from the boat and towards the rocks.

"Girl overboard," I yelled to Greg.

"Shit, we have to get her before she gets pounded onto those rocks."

I grabbed a life preserver and a line then tied one end to a cleat on the stern and jumped over the side. It wasn't a particularly smart move because it now put two lives in dire jeopardy, but we didn't have much choice at the moment with the treacherous rocks of Little Alcatraz keeping Greg from moving his boat any closer towards shore.

Fortunately for the girl and me, this wasn't my first sea born rescue operation. In fact, I'd performed many of them across the world, both as an Air Force Parajumper and later as a member of the CIA's Special Activities division. Of course, none of that mattered much when you hit the water and instantly felt that bone-chilling cold shoot straight into your soul. But, it was in moments like this that the training kicked in, and you had to turn off the pain and shock and focus on the task at hand—namely a girl in dire distress who was drifting farther away and getting closer to hypothermia with every second she spent in the water. I swam hard, and the current helped me reach the girl, whose teeth were already chattering uncontrollably as she struggled to keep her head above the crashing waves. I slipped her into the life preserver then waved at Greg. He left the helm and started pulling us in, which was no small task, as he was up against the current, the waves, and the wind. Seeing him struggling, I threw my legs back and kicked along, and the added momentum allowed us to reach the side of the boat, where Greg had unfolded the boarding ladder. He reached down and took hold of the girl while I helped push her from below, and soon we managed to get her up and into the cockpit, where she joined her poor huddled friends beneath the bimini top.

"Permission to come aboard," I yelled.

"Get up here, you idiot!" Greg yelled.

I climbed the ladder and felt greatly relieved, as the air now felt warm compared to the icy waters of the Bay.

"Finn, can you take the helm a minute while I go below for some towels and blankets?"

"Sure," I said.

I took hold of the helm, put her in gear, and idled against the current and wind and felt extremely relieved to be out of the weather. I took a moment to look at our beleaguered passengers and realized that their makeup running down their cold, wet faces, made them look a bit like a family of waterlogged raccoons. Still, they were busty and beautiful water logged raccoons. Greg appeared a moment later with an armload of towels and woolen blankets, and the girls dried off and cleaned up their faces. The towels were now stained with makeup and would be a complete loss, but I doubted that Greg cared, as he had at last experienced his dream rescue. Now that the girls were mostly dry and looking a lot better, he passed out blankets then looked at me with a sad grimace.

"Sorry, I only had four," he said.

"It's OK. You can share mine," the girl I had just rescued

from the water, said.

"Thanks. It'll be a lot warmer with two of us under it anyway. It's standard cold weather survival technique to combine body heat."

I moved over and sat down on the seat, and she threw part of her blanket over me and snuggled up tight against my body.

"I'm Fiona, by the way—and this is Stacy Tease, Daphne Pumps and Tiger Wells," she said, between quivering lips.

"Are those real names or stage names?" I asked.

"Well, Stacy, Daphne and Tiger's are stage names, but my name is actually Fiona—Fiona Blake."

I saw Greg's head turn so quickly that I worried it might snap free from his body and land in my lap. I was wondering what the hell the big deal was when realization suddenly dawned. She was Miss fucking October, and it was obviously by some bizarre twist of fate that the girl who, only minutes ago, I had glanced at on the page was now sitting beside me on a boat in the middle of the San Francisco Bay. I looked at the cold, wet woman, and all my thoughts about Photoshop were quickly put to rest, as Fiona, regardless of her miserable situation, was indeed just as beautiful in person as she was in her pictorial.

"I'm Tag, and this is Greg. It's nice to meet you, though it's too bad it had to be under such terrible circumstances."

"No shit. I can't thank you guys enough," Fiona said.

"No problem. It's what we do," I said, smiling at Greg.

"It's what I do. Finn just happened to be riding along

tonight," he said.

"Well, lucky for me as it turned out. I don't know what might have happened if he hadn't jumped in the water and saved me."

It became quiet as we considered the gravity of that statement, but Greg, being the conscientious vessel assist captain, soon spoke up and broke the silence.

"So, just to be sure—there aren't any other people still aboard?" he asked.

"Nope—just us."

"Where did the others go?" I asked.

"The assholes left in an inflatable about thirty minutes ago."

"You've got to be shitting me! Why in the fuck wouldn't they take you with them?"

"The guy in charge was a cowardly piece of shit and was worried our presence would make the raft too top heavy."

"So, they fucking left?"

"Yeah, though the asshole did promise to come back after dropping off his friends."

"And broke that promise, obviously, though he at least called for help."

"Wrong again. This was a bachelor party, and the very same asshole who crashed the boat was worried he'd get in trouble for drunk driving, so he refused to call for help. I managed to do that myself after they deserted us and didn't come back."

There was a great gurgling rush of air, and we all turned

to see the Hatteras slip deeper under the water until only its aerials and radar tower were still visible above the surface. Who the hell would abandon passengers on a dark stormy night like this? A group of cowards I suppose and one that I looked forward to meeting in the near future. What they did was criminal and tantamount to attempted manslaughter, so I would see to it that the little chicken shits got a little payback.

"There's nothing more we can do for the boat, so I guess we need to get you girls somewhere warm and dry. Where do you live?"

"In the city, but none of us drove. The bachelor party bus picked us up at our homes and delivered us to the boat."

Fiona was still ice cold and needed some serious warmth, and she needed it soon. The fastest way to get her core body temperature back up would be to get her into something like a hot bath, and, fortunately for her, I had a brand new Jacuzzi back at my place that would do the trick.

"How about we go back to my place to warm up, then I'll figure out a way to get you all home from there," I suggested.

"Great idea," Fiona said, moving ever deeper into my arms.

Greg looked over and shook his head.

"Always the hero, Finn—always the hero."

CHAPTER THREE
Boob Stew

Greg throttled up his boat and soon had us rocketing across the stormy bay at twenty-nine knots. The spray from the waves and torrential rain blanketed the windshield, but we remained dry and protected beneath the bimini top until eventually reaching the relative safety provided by the hills of Sausalito. The channel speed was five miles per hour, so Greg stayed out in the middle of Richardson Bay until we were almost to Strawberry before slowing down, turning west, and heading for my houseboat. Fortunately for us, the tide was high, and he was able to slip right up to the dock below my place, so that I could offload our passengers. I jumped off the boat, tied it up, and went to the stern to make sure everyone got off safely.

"Greg, you coming in?" I asked.

"Would love to, but I have to get out of here before the tide goes out."

"Well, feel free to swing back by if you want."

"Thanks, maybe I'll see you later. Good night, ladies."

They all said good night and thanked Greg once again as I untied his boat and gave him a shove off the dock, so that he could motor off into the dark, rainy Sausalito night. I turned and led my guests up the ramp and onto my deck, all the while helping Fiona navigate the slippery wooden planks. She was walking OK on her own, but she was still very cold, and I could now tell that her situation was a little more critical than I had originally thought. I unlocked the door and told everyone to make themselves at home while I got Fiona into my Jacuzzi.

"What about us?" the Asian girl named Tiger asked.

"Well, you're more than welcome to join us. It's just that Fiona is extremely cold and at risk of hypothermia, so I want to get her body temperature up as soon as possible," I said.

"Oh," she said, sounding concerned.

I went to the Jacuzzi, slid off the lid, and, without bothering to properly undress, carried Fiona into the water. At first she gasped in pain, as the heat felt more like a bunch of needles, but gradually I was able to ease her into the water up to her neck, and she at last exhaled a great sigh of relief. The other girls climbed down into the Jacuzzi, and the water level rose visibly and almost reached the rim. It was a virtual boob stew, and now I could smell an assortment of all of their various perfumes and cosmetics mingling with the water and rising in the steam cloud that swirled into the night sky. I reached over and took hold of Fiona's hands to get an idea of her temperature.

"Oh good. You're warming up," I said.

I started to release her hands, but she kept a firm hold and apparently didn't want to let me go just yet.

"Holy shit that was scary," she said.

"Yeah, there's nothing like falling into dark, cold water in the middle of a storm. I'm just thankful I was able to reach you."

"Yeah, me too," she said, as she looked into my eyes and smiled.

Another ten minutes went by, and everyone was starting to feel human again, so I decided it was time to ask if any-one would like something to drink—perhaps water, juice, or alcohol. Fiona was the first to speak up and requested alcohol.

"I never drink on the job, but since we're obviously done for the night, I could sure use a cocktail," she said.

"Sounds good to me," Tiger added.

"Hell yeah," Daphne and Stacy said, at exactly the same time.

"OK then. I'll be back in a second."

I headed inside and decided that I should probably get a fire going to warm the place up. Once the flames were crackling and burning bright, I went up to my room to put on some proper swim shorts. Looking more appropriate for a dip in the Jacuzzi, I went back downstairs, grabbed towels, five glasses, and a bottle of Soft Taco Island rum. I walked back onto the deck but left the towels under the lip of the roof where they would stay dry from the rain. I rejoined the girls who, with the exception of Fiona, had all decided to get naked. I had never really thought about what strippers did in their spare time but apparently it included stripping. Looking around, I realized that my evening had suddenly become the ultimate male fantasy, except that it wasn't exactly my fantasy. I liked naked women as much as the next guy, but I had never really had a thing for strippers, and, by strippers, I wasn't referring to the women but rather the job. I had known too many guys, and one friend in particular, who were almost pathologically obsessed with strippers and strip clubs and visited them sometimes on a weekly and even daily basis.

I don't know where the cutoff is in some men's brains that they get so desperate for female attention that they would be willing to shove five-dollar bills in a girl's g-string until they've maxed out their daily ATM disbursement. Worse still, the vast majority seemed to believe that they could be that stripper's Prince Charming—the rare man who would win her love and rescue her from a life of ogling customers, poles, and lap dances. The sad reality was that those lonely men were walking, talking cash machines to the girls—nothing more.

Interestingly, I remember a particular night many years back when one of those very same stripper obsessed friends and I were en route to a bar in the city, and he said that we should instead go to a strip club—his reasoning being that we might actually see an eight or a nine. What rational person wants to blow a hundred dollars in fives to watch an eight or nine dance, when he can go into an actual bar and perhaps talk to and take home an actual woman—regardless of her numeric designation. Of course, this also calls into question the rating system and how exactly said male rates himself according to that system.

As for the rating system, it seems inherently flawed to any person with a half a brain and an ounce of moral character, because it doesn't take into account personality, and how much can you learn about a person when the only communication is ogling and the transfer of bills to a g-string. Clearly, a numerical value system in this context is therefore not as intelligent or financially prudent as meeting a woman in an open field situation such as a bar or cafe, where a more accurate rating and real connection can be attained.

Better still, what can we assume about the man that upholds such a measuring tool of the opposite sex? He's got to be shallow to say the least, but it also calls into question in my mind how he rates himself. Psychologists have long studied how the sexes interact and much of their research has shown that people tend to gravitate towards individuals of similar attractiveness. While it would make sense in theory, I've found in practical application that men, especially drunk men, greatly overestimate their own rating. I've seen many guys, barely a three in terms of looks or personality, falsely believe that they could take down what they called a ten. Of course, most, if not all, ended up going home alone, and the only ten to ever touch their genitals would end up being the sum total of all their fingers.

But where did all that philosophizing about strippers and stripping leave me at the moment? Ultimately, in a tub full of strippers, but at least that term was now a mostly accurate physical description of my current guest's state of undress. My internal ramblings came to an end, and I handed each of the lovely ladies a cocktail then held up my glass to toast.

"To a wonderful night on the bay," I said.

Everyone laughed, clinked their glasses together, then took a sip of their drinks, and their faces lit up the moment the elixir touched down on their palates.

"Wow, is that good!" Daphne said.

"No shit!" Stacy added.

"Where do you get this rum?" Tiger asked.

"It's from a little place in the Caribbean called Soft Taco Island."

"Oh, sounds exotic," Tiger said.

"It is," I responded with a knowing sigh.

With the addition of cocktails, everyone was getting as warm on the inside as they were on the outside, and it was a nice way to finish up a particularly stressful evening. The more the girls drank, the more they spoke of their unusual occupation—that is, everyone except Fiona, who remained mostly quiet aside from the occasional sigh or nod.

Just as I poured round three, the most unusual and un-expected conversation to arise was on the topic of breast augmentation. To be or not to be—a double D. I had no trouble with breast augmentation or cosmetic surgery in general as long as it was done tastefully and gave the person in question the proper boost to their self-esteem. But, in the world of stripping, more breast volume literally translated to higher earnings. Daphne, who had originally been a natural C cup, decided to get boosted to a double D and instantly doubled her nightly revenue—and that was during the post operative months where she was unable to do anything more than wander around the stage gathering money. In spite of being a consummate boob lover, I couldn't help but think it was perhaps a sad testament to the state of male stupidity, but, at least to these girls, it meant a higher quality of life.

"So, I'm curious. Which kind of implants did you all choose to go with? Saline or Silicone?"

"See if you can guess," Stacy said, with a giggle—and a jiggle.

I looked around the tub at the various boobs, all of which were hovering at the surface.

"OK, but I'm going to need to turn off the jets and have all of you stand up then slip back into the water."

"Nice try," Fiona said.

"No, I'm serious—it's for science. I promise."

"Why turn off the jets?" Tiger asked.

"The bubbles have a tendency to reduce the buoyancy of the water which might skew my little test."

All the girls, including Fiona, stood up then settled back

into the water.

"OK, then. Saline, saline, saline, and natural," I said, pointing at Fiona last.

Each girl smiled and acknowledged that I had guessed correctly.

"Very good. You obviously know your boobs. Do you meet a lot of women with augmented breasts in your line of work?" Fiona asked.

"No, it's really just simple science and reasoning. Silicone is a lot less dense than water and tends to be very buoyant, which means breasts containing silicone implants would tend to float higher in the water, likely the tops of the breasts breaching the surface. Saline is slightly less buoyant than silicone but more buoyant than standard water so the breasts would float right around the surface."

"And what about Fiona? How could you tell while she was still wearing her top?" Daphne asked.

"Elementary, my dear Daphne. You see, she refrained from any kind of comment throughout our discussion, so I took that as sign she had no opinion on the matter one way or the other—and was therefore most likely un-augmented."

"So, what is it you do again, Tag?"

"I'm a private investigator."

"Makes sense," Tiger said.

"So, you're like *Magnum P.I.*?" Daphne asked.

"You've seen that show?"

"Yeah, I love it. I watched the entire series while it was

on Netflix."

Funny, every time I mentioned my profession someone almost always brought up *Magnum P.I.*, but the actual truth was that *Magnum P.I.*, fictitious though he may be, filled many childhood television hours and was definitely a factor in my choosing to go into this profession after leaving government service.

"Well, that's basically me, except I'm here instead of Hawaii and no red Ferrari."

"Is it exciting work?" Stacy asked.

"Yeah, do you get into shootouts and car chases?" Tiger asked.

"Normally I would say no, but my last major case pretty much had both."

"Cool! Can you tell us about it?" she asked enthusiastically.

"Well, I managed to keep a deadly Chinese spy ring from stealing high tech software."

"Sounds dangerous," she said.

"It was, but thankfully it worked out in the end, and I nabbed the bad guys."

"So, how long have you been in this line of work?" Fiona asked.

"Oh—about five years."

"And what did you do before that?" she asked.

"I worked for the Government."

"Doing what?"

"Government stuff."

"Can you be more specific?"

"Oh, you know—background checks and boring stuff like that. Why do you ask?"

"I was just curious how someone gets into your line of work."

"There are lots of ways, but my path was kind of unusual. Most Private Investigators are ex-cops who are looking to make some extra money on top of their pensions."

Just then, Tiger lifted her hands out of the water and looked at her fingers.

"I'm starting to look like a prune," she said.

"Me too," Daphne and Stacy added at the same time.

I was starting to wonder if those two might be related in spite of their difference in stature and hair color.

"You know that your skin getting that prune-like appearance is an evolutionary advantage," I said.

"Really?" Tiger asked.

"It gives you extra grip when you're hands are wet and slippery," Fiona interjected.

"I see you read the same article."

"What can I say—I'm a sucker for science nerd factoids."

"Me too."

"Well, useful as it may be, I suspect it's about time for me to get out of the water," Tiger said.

"I've got towels over by the door if you want to dry off and head inside. There's a fire in the fireplace, so feel free to get comfortable and make yourselves at home. Speaking of which—how do you want to handle getting home? I'm a little buzzed to be driving, but I'll happily pay for an Uber if you're in a hurry or need to get home. Of course, I'm about to make dinner, and there's going to be enough to feed a small army, so you're all welcome to eat, drink, and spend the night, and I'll drive you home in the morning.

"Sounds good to me," Fiona said.

The other girls looked at each other then nodded their approval, so I guess I had an adult slumber party on my hands that none of my friends would ever believe. Tiger was first to leave, and she stepped from the tub and wasn't the least bit shy about being completely nude. The other two girls followed, and soon a trio of busty and beautiful naked women were making their way across my deck and into my humble abode, thereby leaving Fiona and me alone. I had been in a tub with four women, three of them naked, and now left alone with the only clothed one, I was suddenly feeling a little uncomfortable and wondered if perhaps it might be the inklings of some kind of mild attraction—at least on my part, anyway.

"So, I see you didn't go full commando like your friends."

"No, not my style—and they're more like acquaintances, as I only met them tonight. Honestly, I don't usually do this kind of work."

"Oh."

"Why do you sound so surprised?"

"Its just that I—um—well."

"What?" she asked.

"On the way out to get you guys tonight, I briefly glanced at my friend's Playboy collection and couldn't help but notice that you just happen to be Miss October."

She smiled a little bashfully.

"Yeah—there is that, but it's part of a much larger, sadder story."

"Sad? I thought you looked amazing."

"Thanks, but I'm not talking about the pictures. I'm talking about why I did them. Why I'm doing all of this—least of all that sleazy fucking bachelor party, which I only did because those idiots said they would pay me ten thousand dollars to have a real Playboy playmate come strip for them."

"Believe me, in spite of the indignity, you're definitely worth every penny."

She smiled again, but this time she followed it up with a sigh.

"You're too kind—but everything I've done or am doing is all for a much greater good."

"Is it anything you feel comfortable talking about?"

"Well, not usually with a stranger, but I suppose that you did save my life tonight."

"Good, then tell me your story. What events drove you onto the centerfold of Playboy magazine and ultimately onto a boat full of assholes and strippers."

"Well, this might sound a little trite, but I desperately needed the money."

"Understandable. Everyone needs money, and sometimes they need it even more than usual."

"It's more complicated than that."

Complicated! I smiled to myself. There was my word again—a word that I had loathed for almost five years having heard it from every client who walked through my door. That all changed, however, a few months back when I at last found myself in an uncomfortable predicament and, with nowhere else to turn and in dire need of its all encompassing meaning, spit out the words—it's complicated.

"How much more complicated?"

She paused for a minute to gather her thoughts then looked deeply into my eyes, as she was probably wondering whether or not she could indeed trust me.

"I needed the money to help my brother," she said, after a moment.

"What kind of trouble is he in? Financial, legal, or something worse?"

"I guess you could call it legal."

"Here in California?"

"No, far away on a tropical island in the western Pacific."

Interesting. About four months ago I had been at an all time low, both financially and professionally, when a beautiful stranger showed up on my doorstep and hired me to rescue her sister from an exotic Caribbean island. It turned out to be a life changing event, however, and now it made me wonder what kind of trouble this beautiful woman's brother had gotten himself into.

"Care to elaborate?"

"My brother Mark created a foundation called Globo-Care after graduate school."

"I've heard of it. He goes all over the world helping people—kind of like Bono."

"Kind of, but without the band, cool sunglasses, and leather pants."

"Good for him. Leather pants give you sweaty balls."

"Oh, do you have a pair?"

"Balls? Why yes I do, though I like to keep them nice and cool by not wearing leather pants."

She laughed at my stupid attempt to twist her question around, then we sat for a quiet moment and sipped our rum.

"So, your brother must be a really good guy to do what he does. Most people in the world just want to use their education to make a lot of money."

"Not Mark. After getting his MBA from the Wharton School of Business, he turned down endless six figure job offers to put together Globo-Care. At the time it was no easy task, as he had to create a business model then find sponsors in order to grow it into the multinational aid entity that it is today. And, now, he's literally improved the lives of millions of people all over the world by providing food, education, medical care, and even positive political change in rare circumstances."

"Which I'm guessing may have played a role in his current predicament?"

"Absolutely, and now he's in prison and awaiting trial on

a trumped up charge of sedition for inciting unrest."

"Ouch! That can't be good."

"Definitely not, and the foundation has already used up everything it can on his legal fund, so I'm trying to make up the difference."

"And since your parents are both school teachers, I imagine they can't help much either."

"How do you know about my parents?" she asked, looking surprised.

"Your personal detail page behind your centerfold."
She laughed.

"Oh, that's right. I guess I should be honored that you actually bothered to read it."

"Let's see—you went to Santa Clara University, have a BA and a Masters in Sociology, and you enjoy hiking, biking and..."

"Men who aren't afraid to get wet," she said, finishing my sentence.

We shared a smile at the recollection of our moment together out on the bay, and it carried on an unusually long time before we both looked away.

"Actually, the detail page is my guilty pleasure. Truth be told, I thought it was all bullshit created by some marketing department."

"No, it's all real—at least it is in my case, and, of course, this entire soap opera had to go down just when I was about to join my brother in his work at the Foundation. I know it's going to sound cheesy, but I really had hoped to use my education to help people who were less fortunate."

Yet again, her detail section was alarmingly accurate, and I had to wonder if perhaps all my mockery over the years had been misguided.

"So, speaking of money—did you and the girls get paid tonight?"

"No, we were supposed to get paid at the end of the booze cruise, but we hit that fucking rock, and the next thing you know the groom and his buddies were in the dinghy and heading back to the city."

"What a bunch of assholes."

"Yeah, and the only contact information I have is the best man's cell phone number—which just happens to be in my phone—and, as I lost it when I went in the water, it's somewhere on the bottom of the San Francisco Bay."

"Don't worry, I'll find them and see that you get paid."

"It's OK, I can handle it. I don't like to burden other people with my problems."

"It's not a burden, and it's just like you just said. Sometimes it's about helping people who are in need."

She smiled and took hold of my hands.

"Thank you, Tag. You're an unbelievably nice guy."

"It's the least I can do, though I wonder if you wouldn't mind telling me a little more about your brother's predicament. Perhaps I might be able to help with that too."

She shook her head and frowned.

"That would be nice, but I seriously doubt it. I mean— he's being held on an island on the other side of the world for God's sake."

I smiled.

"Well, strange as it may seem, I have some experience in that area."

CHAPTER FOUR
Clothing Optional Slumber Party

Fiona looked ever so slightly conflicted as she thought about the sincerity of my offer, but she soon relaxed, took a long sip of her rum, then proceeded to tell me all about her brother's unfortunate situation. The Globo-Care Foundation, which had enjoyed a great deal of success in countries from South America to Africa and Asia, finally managed to run into trouble on the small, formerly Dutch Island of Malkarta. It had first been settled by the Portuguese in the early fifteen hundreds, but its abundant natural resources such as nutmeg, cloves, and mace soon brought it to the attention of the ever expanding Dutch trade empire. They took it over during the spice wars in the early sixteen hundreds and held it for the next three hundred years before deeding it over to the De Vries, who were a distant branch of the royal family of the Netherlands. Unlike the rest of the Dutch provinces which became part of the Republic of Indonesia in 1950, the De Vries family managed to keep Malkarta a sovereign island nation and absolute monarchy, though they still maintained strong political ties to their Dutch parent country.

At the moment, Malkarta had a strong agricultural industry that was generating over a billion dollars a year in revenue, yet it also had one of the top ten poorest populations of any island nation on earth, as the majority of the money obviously went directly into the De Vries family's deep coffers. Globo-Care arrived in 2016 and had been making steady progress in bringing education, medical care, and a real sense of optimism to the population of 155,000 people. With optimism came hope, but hope could also be the seed of change, and that was something that the powers that be preferred not to exist. They needed an uneducated captive workforce in order to keep their profits high and their expenses low, so, with Globo-Care bringing hope to the citizens of Malkarta, it was only a matter of time before Fiona's brother, the virtual face of change, incurred the wrath of the De Vries. It started with cease and desist orders, but it eventually led to his arrest and imprisonment, and he was now awaiting trial in what would most certainly be a kangaroo court.

"You're raising money for his legal defense fund, but do you think he can actually get a fair trial?" I asked.

"What else can I do?"

"You could try to put pressure on the De Vries by bringing in Amnesty International."

"I tried, but they just have far too many people in worse situations to worry about."

"What about the State Department?"

"Another dead end."

I took a sip of my drink and thought for a moment.

"You could always stage a daring rescue operation."

"Yeah, sure—with all the extra money and resources I have."

"Obviously you'd use your feminine wiles."

"So, I just wiggle my boobs at them, and while they're distracted I grab my brother and run?"

"I can guarantee that I'd be distracted."

She smiled.

"Sorry, Tag, but my options are pretty limited at the moment."

"Yeah, but in all seriousness, I might be able to help."

"I appreciate your enthusiasm, but first I need to deal with the bachelor party assholes."

"Don't worry about them. Tomorrow, we'll find those assholes and get your money. When that's done, I'll make a few calls and see what I can find out about your brother. I have a friend who might be able to help."

She looked at me, and I could tell that she desperately wanted to believe me, but behind her beautiful eyes was doubt. Of course, I could understand her skepticism, as it was rare, if not impossible, to find people who were willing to go out of their way to help someone and least of all a stranger. I knew the feeling, as I myself had suffered some tough times, financial and otherwise, and only persevered with the help of my family and friends.

"You ready to head inside?" I asked.

"Yeah."

We stepped out of the Jacuzzi, slid on the cover, and headed inside, where it was nice to be out of the rain and cold. Stacy, Daphne, and Tiger were still naked, and now they were stretched out in front of the fire as they sipped rum and inadvertently made my living room look like the set of a rather racy R-rated movie.

"Oh sorry, I should have gotten you girls something to wear."

"No problem, we're used to being naked."

"Well, I'll go look for some extra clothes in case you change your minds."

"I'll go with you," Fiona said.

We left the girls and headed upstairs to my spare closet, where there were some clothes left over from my ex girl-friend Melanie, who, after breaking up with me, had never bothered to pick them up. The clothes would likely fit the girls but be a little snug in the chest region. Melanie had some seriously plentiful bosoms, but the girls easily outmatched her by at least a cup size. As I grabbed some clothing items, I noticed Fiona had an unusual smile on her face.

"What?" I asked.

"You're not a cross dresser are you?"

"No—they're leftover from an ex."

"Oh, sorry."

"I'm not. She was a bitch."

"Aren't they all after you break up?"

"Not necessarily, but Melanie was for sure."

Fiona walked around the room then paused at the window to look out at the stormy night.

"I bet you have an amazing view when the weather is nice."

"I do, and it's part of the trade-off for living on the water."

"What are you losing?"

"Certain things—a yard or a traditional garage for example."

"I think it's worth it."

"Thanks, I do too."

We headed downstairs, and I laid the clothes on the coffee table.

"These will get you home tomorrow, but do you need anything to sleep in?"

"If you have an extra T-shirt, that would be fine for me," Tiger said.

"We're good. We sleep in the nude," Stacy said, answering for both her and Daphne.

"I take it you two are pretty close," I said.

"Yeah, we're roommates."

"And practically sisters," Daphne added.

"Alrighty then, I'll be back in a second."

I'd found that women had rather sticky fingers when it came to clothing, so I decided to head down to the dresser of doom, where I kept a bunch of extra T-shirts that I still hadn't bothered to throw away or donate. Fiona again came with me, and I was getting the feeling that she preferred my company to that of the other girls, which I suppose made sense, considering that she had only met them this evening. She paused at the bottom of the stairs with a slightly uncomfortable expression on her face.

"You OK?" I asked.

"Yeah, but all that delicious rum is really making me need to pee. Is there a bathroom down here?" she asked.

"Next door over."

She headed into the bathroom while I went through my drawers and grabbed three extra large T-shirts. Daphne and Stacy apparently didn't need one, but I grabbed each of them one just in case. As I finished up, Fiona reappeared and once again looked at me curiously.

"What is it this time?" I asked.

"I was just admiring your very manly bathroom."

"Oh yeah, the walls of shame adorned with mementos of an unusual life."

"So, you were also in the military."

"Yeah, obviously before I worked for the government."

"What branch?"

"Air Force, I was in Pararescue."

"Is that special operations?"

"Yeah, it is, actually, but our main objective was rescue

operations."

She smiled.

"So, you weren't kidding earlier when you said you had some experience in rescuing people from faraway places."

"No, though I still think using your boobs as a distraction is a legitimately decent rescue plan."

"Jackass," she said, giving me a playful hit on the arm.

Often, actions such as touching someone's hand or engaging in some horseplay could be subtle signs of flirtation, but I was probably just kidding myself. She was Miss October, after all, and I was Mr. Nobody. We went back upstairs and joined the girls to find they had decided to give each other massages—as girls often did when left to their own devices. The difference, however, was that they were naked, and it was all I could do not to take a picture and text it to my friends, as they would never believe the story without actual proof. Unfortunately, or fortunately depending on your perspective, I was a gentleman and therefore refrained from taking any pictures.

"Is anyone hungry?"

"Oh, hell yes—I'm starving. We never got to the food," Fiona said.

"How about pasta Bolognese?"

"Sounds delicious!" she said, excitedly.

I walked around the counter that separated the living room from the kitchen and started pulling out all the ingredients for my famous Bolognese. Fortunately, I had bought all the makings earlier in the day and had already planned on making it tonight, though at least now I wouldn't be dining alone.

"Need any help?" Fiona asked.

"Sure. Can you peel the garlic?"

"Of course."

I handed her the garlic then set to work preparing the meat, which consisted of grass-fed free range ground beef and two spicy pork Italian sausages. I put the burger into the pan then squeezed the sausages from their casings and mixed the two thoroughly together as they cooked.

"I see that you like to cook. Do you get that from your mom or your dad?" Fiona asked.

"Both actually."

"You're lucky. My mom is the only one who cooks, as my dad can barely manage toast."

"So, do you like to cook? I didn't see anything about that in your bio."

She smiled.

"Yes, I do as a matter of fact."

"Well then, do you want to put your cooking skills to work and chop up the onion?"

"Sure," she said, grabbing it and expertly cutting it into small chunks.

I took the chopped up onions and placed them in a pan with some olive oil and let them cook for a few minutes until it was time for the garlic. I squeezed several cloves with my hand press then added it to the mix, and the smell of it cooking was tantalizing as it filled the kitchen.

"I didn't get to read your bio, so maybe you could tell me a little about yourself," Fiona said.

"I take it you didn't see my spread in Playgirl? I was Mr. October."

"Sadly, I missed it."

"Too bad. It was pretty amazing and done in a private investigator theme."

"Were you posing in a Sam Spade style trench coat with a Maltese Falcon statue in front of your manhood or was it *Magnum P.I.* inspired with you wearing a pair of tiny satin eighties style shorts as you lie across the hood of a red Ferrari?"

"Neither. Instead, I was sitting on a breakfast table that was piled high with unpaid bills, and an obese house cat that I rescued was sitting in my lap as a kind of feline merkin."

"Nice. Maybe I can order a back issue."

"No need. A few more cocktails and I'll go grab my neighbor's cat and give you a proper reenactment."

"So, the neighbor's cat is the one in question?"

"Yeah, and it ended up being quite a case."

"You'll have to tell it to me some time."

"I will, but it'll take a while, so we'll probably have to do dinner as well."

"I'd like that," she said, in a sincere tone.

My heart leapt ever so slightly, and then we spent a few quiet minutes watching the food cook before Fiona started up the conversation anew.

"So, are you originally from the Bay Area, or were you a transplant?" she asked.

It was a good question, as it seemed that most of the people I met here were from other parts of the country.

"I'm a native San Franciscan—born and raised here, though I also lived in Lake Tahoe for a time."

"And what about college?"

"That was also here in the Bay Area."

"The Bay Area is a big place. Care to elaborate?"

I had gone to Stanford but generally made a point of trying not to name drop unless people actually asked. I hated those types who were so proud of their school that they put stickers on their back window or had those equally smarmy alumni license plate holders. College was over, and it was time to stop living in your past glory and get on with your life.

"Stanford."

"Well la-dee-daa."

"You went to Santa Clara, and that's not exactly blue collar."

"True—but I had a scholarship."

"Me too. Swimming."

"Mine was academic."

"Beauty and brains. Typical."

The onion and garlic were now cooked enough that I could add marinara, Italian seasoning, red wine, beef broth, and a dash of Worcestershire sauce. I followed that up with some chopped up Swiss chard and a handful of fresh parsley then turned my attention to the meat. It was done cooking, so I drained off the excess fat into the sink then added the meat to the pot. *Perfetto*, as the Italians say.

"Holy shit does that smell good," Daphne said, from the living room.

"It's the onion and garlic. Speaking of which, I'm gonna make some garlic bread as well."

I put the water on for the pasta then ground up some more garlic and mixed it with some feel good grass fed butter and olive oil and spread it on the sourdough bread and stuck it in the oven. By the time I was done with that, the water was boiling, and I dropped in the spaghetti noodles then leaned back against the counter and took a moment to sip my rum.

"So, assuming you get your brother out of jail—what then? Join Globo-Care and help save the world?"

"Well, that was the plan, but I'm not so sure anymore."

"Yeah, the world can still bite you in the ass—even when you're trying to save it."

I used a fork to snag a piece of spaghetti, tasted it, and decided the noodles were just about ready. Any longer and they wouldn't be al dente, which was the Italian phrase for firm. I drained the noodles, grabbed the garlic bread, and then proceeded to dish up dinner by placing it all on my dining room table. The girls came over looking hungry as hell, and they were practically drooling as they regarded the Italian feast before their eyes. Fiona and I sat beside each other while the others spread out around the table.

"This looks amazing," Tiger said.

"I certainly hope so. Now go ahead and dig in, ladies!" I said.

"Wait, we have to toast first," Fiona said

"To Tag, our hero and host."

"And to the first topless dinner party I've ever had. May it not be the last," I added.

We all clinked our glasses then started eating dinner, though the girls were obviously hungry, as they dug into their plates like wild rabid dogs.

"Tag, this is seriously the best pasta ever. Are you married? Because if not, I'd like to propose right now. A man who can cook like this is too good to let get away," Tiger said.

"Well, thanks for the compliment, but sadly I'm already married to the twins here," I said, holding up my hands.

The girls chuckled but quickly turned their attention back to their plates and continued to eat in a harried frenzy. Daphne, in her haste, spilled some sauce on her boob and proceeded to lick it off, which I suppose was one of the key benefits to nude dining—no stains on your clothes and easy clean up. At that moment, there was a knock at the door, and I excused myself to go have a look through the peephole. Standing outside was a policeman named Jack Chin, who also happened to be a fairly close friend, and I opened the door to find him standing there with the world's biggest shit eating grin on his face.

"What's up, Jack?"

"Oh nothing. I just got off the phone with Greg, and he told me all about your little adventure out on the Bay tonight."

"How nice of you to be so concerned."

"Yeah, sometimes its scary how much I care. Now, is there any chance that your lovely ladies are still around? I was hoping to get a little information, as it's possible that the boat was berthed here in Sausalito."

"Wouldn't that be lucky for you?"

"It would."

"Well, you're in luck. They're still here. In fact, we just sat down to a late dinner. Why don't you come in and join us?"

Jack was a bit of a ladies man, so I imagined that this incident report was probably going to be the highlight of his night—if not his year. I led him in to the dining room, and he stopped dead in his tracks and looked so surprised that I feared his eyes might pop out of his head.

"Motherfucker," he mumbled.

"What was that, officer?" I asked.

"Nothing."

He leaned in and whispered in my ear.

"You didn't tell me that they were naked."

"Technically only three of them are."

"But—why?"

"I just have this effect on women."

"Dude, seriously now. What the hell's going on?"

"Well, all they had on when we rescued them were their

stripper outfits, but they decided to go full commando when we hopped in the Jacuzzi."

"Jacuzzi? Seriously?" he asked with a smile.

"It's been quite a night."

"No shit, and this is possibly the best call I've taken in my entire career as a policeman," he said.

The girls all looked up from their plates as Jack approached the table.

"Hello, ladies, I'm sorry to intrude, but I was hoping to get a little information about the incident tonight."

Jack looked down at the table and saw the plates of food.

"Oh sorry, I didn't realize you were eating."

"Yeah, that's what I meant when I said we had just sat down to dinner," I said.

He gave me a scowl.

"Please—feel free to finish up, and we can talk afterward," he said.

"Are you hungry, Jack?" I asked.

"I am as a matter of fact. I forgot to bring dinner, and, as you know, the only place still open in town is the Seven Eleven."

"Have a seat, and I'll grab you a plate."

Jack sat down and did hid best to try and not stare at his dining companions' substantial breasts, and he was about sixty percent successful while the other forty percent was spent unintentionally ogling.

"I'm Jack, by the way," he said, introducing himself to the girls.

I handed him a steaming hot plate of pasta, and he officially joined what would probably be his first and only mostly nude dinner party. Once everyone was done stuffing their faces, Fiona helped me clear the table while the others went into the living room to give their account of the events of the night. Jack, in spite of the tendency for his eyes to wander, listened intently to the girls' accounts and managed to maintain more professionalism than I would have thought possible. Finished, he at last stood and said a reluctant goodbye, as he was likely headed back to the station to recount the night's events. Either that or he would sneak off to some dark secluded spot and pound his pork.

"All right, another round of drinks, and I guess we should figure out our sleeping arrangements," I said.

I refilled everyone's glass, and Fiona gave yet another toast.

"To Tag, a good man and an excellent host."

We proceeded to enjoy the fire and sipped our drinks until everyone grew tired and officially decided it was time to call it a night.

"I figure Stacy and Daphne can share a room since they're already roommates. Tiger can take the other downstairs bedroom, and Fiona can have the extra one upstairs."

"Sounds good," Tiger said, grabbing a T-shirt from the stack and heading downstairs.

Daphne and Stacy followed sans T-shirts, so I guess it was true that you could lead a horse to water but couldn't make it drink. That left Fiona and me alone in the living room, and I poured a small half shot in each of our glasses before leading her upstairs into her bedroom, where she looked around and appeared happy with her accommodations.

"Oh, follow me, I have a brand new toothbrush for you as well," I said, stepping into the guest bathroom and opening the top drawer, where I happened to have a number of brand new toothbrushes that I'd recently gotten from my dentist.

"Thanks!" she said.

"I suppose I should probably give one to the others as well."

I grabbed three out of the bathroom then paused at the door.

"Nighty night, I'll see you in the morning," I said.

Before I could leave, she came over and hugged me.

"Thanks, Tag—for everything."

"No problem."

She let go and smiled and looked as though she wanted to say something, but she remained silent. I headed downstairs and knocked on Daphne and Stacy's door, and, when Daphne appeared, I handed her two toothbrushes.

"Oh, thank you, but you didn't have to get us each one," she said, smiling appreciatively.

"Let me guess—you could have shared one."

"Yep."

"Well it's all about the amenities here at *casa de* Finn."

"It sure is," she said.

"Well, nighty night, girls. There's toothpaste in the top drawer, so don't forget to brush your teeth before bed, because I'll check your brushes, and if they aren't wet, I'll have to give you both a time-out, and if that doesn't work we'll move on to spankings," I joked.

"Promise?" Daphne asked.

"Yes—because plaque is not a laughing matter. Now, nighty night," I said, as I left them and headed over to Tiger's room.

I heard running water and realized she was in the bathroom, so I knocked, and she opened the door, and I noticed that she had taken off her remaining makeup and now looked, in my opinion, better, as it gave her a more wholesome appearance.

"Oh God, I was about to get in the shower, so now you're seeing me without makeup."

"Trust me, you're just as beautiful, if not more so, without it. Anyway, here's a toothbrush, and there's toothpaste is in the top drawer. Need anything else while I'm here?"

"Could you wash my back?" she asked.

"Only if I get to do the front as well."

She opened the door all the way and stepped aside to make room, and I couldn't help but smile.

"I was just kidding," I said.

"I wasn't."

I regarded the beautiful woman before me and was

sorely tempted to take her up on her offer but decided that I had best retreat before I got into any hot water—both literally and figuratively.

"I'd really love to, but, in the interest of remaining a gentleman, I really should pass."

"Well, I'll be here all night in case you change your mind."

"Good to know."

"Oh, and my real name is Andrea, by the way."

"Nighty night, Andrea."

"Nighty night, Tag."

I turned and walked back up to the main floor to make sure that I had turned off the stove and closed the screen to the fireplace. It was kind of a nuisance, but such were the joys of an obsessive compulsive personality. Did I turn off the stove? Did I lock my car? Should I have showered with the hot girl in my downstairs bathroom? All were good questions, and all would continue to haunt me as I went up to my room, undressed, and stepped into the shower for a quick rinser before bed.

The cascade of hot water felt good, and it gave me time to process such an eventful evening. The last couple of months since my Chinese spy ring case had been fairly uneventful, with the only thing of interest to fill my time having been the extremely beautiful Cherry Poppins. We'd met during that very same case and ended up having a fairly serious relationship until she headed off to China for an undetermined amount of time while she helped a large overseas corporation open up a major hub here in America. Her departure left me living a quiet northern California life, and the only thing filling my days had been the personal renovation of the bottom of the building I had recently purchased. I rented out the second and third floors but converted the bottom floor into a massive garage and man cave. Now that I owned four cars, I needed a place to keep them, and it was an added bonus that I took in a little over twenty grand a month in rent from the tenants. Thus, my daily existence of putting up wallboard, picking out paint, and finishing up construction had taken a drastic turn for the better when Greg called earlier this evening. Who would have thought that I'd end up as the host of a stripper sleepover, with the culmination being that the lovely Miss October was bunking in the very next room?

Life certainly could change quickly and sometimes even for the better. I had actually been hungering for a new client, some adventure, and perhaps a little travel, and in one fell swoop I had potentially discovered all three. Better still, I was hopeful that I might be able to help Fiona with her brother, as it wouldn't be my first time rescuing someone from an exotic island, though it was entirely possible that I might be able to solve the entire affair with a phone call to the right person. I had a close personal friend in a fairly high place, and he owed me the greatest of favors, so tomorrow I was going to give him a call.

I stepped from the shower, dried off, then brushed my teeth and put on a T-shirt and some pajama bottoms before slipping into bed. Lying there in the quiet of the night, I could hear the water running and thought about my lovely houseguest and the fact that she was naked and showering on the other side of the wall. It was odd to hardly know someone yet already have seen her naked body, and I imagined that it must be a weird life for centerfolds—your body already known but your mind a complete stranger.

At last, I turned off my light, closed my eyes, and listened to the storm as it raged outside and brought with it a deluge of rain that was clattering on the skylight above my bed. Of course, I could also feel the storm, as each gust would buffet my houseboat and cause it to rock ever so gently back and forth. This was one of the unique experiences of living on the water—you truly felt the weather, and now it was as though mother nature herself were lulling me off to sleep. My conscious mind was fading, and I was just starting to dream about a warm blue sea when I heard a knock on my door. I opened my eyes and saw a figure standing in the shadows of the doorway, and I wondered if it was Andrea coming to make good on her offer.

"What's up?" I asked.

"Can I come in?"

Gulp.

CHAPTER FIVE
Breast Friends Forever

The stranger at the door was, in fact, Fiona, and I had to wonder what was so important that she would come calling at this late hour. Actually, it was strange how many times in recent history that I had a female guest in the adjacent bedroom only to have them migrate over to my room in the middle of the night. I'd had three beautiful women in that room, and not one had bothered to do so much as pull down the covers. At least if this encounter followed the usual trend then I might not have much cleaning up to do in the morning, so, perhaps, sharing a bed was the first step in a greener more environmentally friendly lifestyle.

"What's up?" I asked.

"I was wondering if it would be OK if I slept in here with you?"

"Sure, climb on in, but I have to warn you—I sleep in

the nude."

"Good, so do I," she said, sliding off her underwear and slipping out of the T-shirt.

"Wait, I was just kidding."

"Too late now. Lose the pajamas. I'm not going to be the only naked person in the bed."

I pulled off my clothes and threw them on the floor as she slid into the bed and cuddled up to me. I was already feeling a tad bit awkward, but then she upped the sexual tension when she slid her leg over mine and pressed her bare breasts firmly against my chest, which also left her sweetly scented hair draped down over my shoulder.

"I hope I'm not intruding too much, but it's been a hell of a night, and I could use a little company."

"Couldn't we all."

Feeling her breath tickle my neck made me remember back a couple of months ago to when a beautiful female client had joined me in the same way, only the night had ended with some rather epic sex. Of course, back then I had been particularly vulnerable after a shitty break up and was ripe for the picking. Tonight, however, I had more resiliency, as I'd had plenty of female companionship in recent months and therefore hoped to maintain my professional demeanor—or so I hoped. She abruptly rolled onto her side and pulled me with her into a spooning position that placed her in my arms. I tried to keep my hand in the safe neutral zone of her side, but she took hold of it and placed it directly on her left breast, whereupon her nipple slid between my middle and index fingers. Sweet mother of God! How could any man be placed in the presence of such tempting flesh and remain pure of heart? But, I was an adult, and this was yet another challenge, so I would remain calm in the face of adversity. That is—until she decided to wiggle her lovely backside against my man parts and leave me unable to coax Tag Junior down from his rapid growth spurt. In mere seconds he was in full boner mode and had burrowed between her legs, where he now lay cozily nestled against her warm lady parts.

The odd thing was that she made no effort to move and instead cuddled up to it as though it were the family pet. I remained true to the course, however, and tried to ignore the fact that my boner was hard and unflinching, and my hand was on her breast with my fingers gently cupping her nipple, which was equally hard and seemed as though it were trying to say hello in its primitive *mammarian* language. As if that weren't enough, she wiggled her butt, and it made Tag Junior slide once again against her vaginal opening, and I could feel it was warm and possibly even wet. Fuck—now I was even harder, and it made me realize how particularly embarrassing it could be to have a boner, and the experience was suddenly making me feel more like an eighth grader during his first slow dance. It was, therefore, time to be the better man, and that meant closing my eyes, giving Fiona a gentle squeeze, and doing my best to fall asleep in spite of the woman cradling my hard-on. It would end up taking fifteen minutes and twenty two hundred sheep, but I eventually drifted off to sleep with Miss October, warm, safe and mostly unmolested in my arms as I bid farewell to consciousness and entered the world of dreams.

I awoke the next morning to find Fiona still in my arms, though my boner had subsided to a semi as it lay nestled cozily between her legs. The rain had let up, and above me through the skylight I could see the clear blue sky of a beautiful California winter day. As I carefully slid out of bed, Tag Junior sprung free from between Fiona's thighs, and the whip like action made him strike his two very sensitive and immediate neighbors with a dull slapping sound. Keeping any cries of discomfort within the confines of my inner voice, I threw on some shorts, then ventured into the bathroom to brush my teeth before heading downstairs to make some coffee. I reached the kitchen, and all was quiet with nary a stripper in sight. I put fresh coffee and water in the machine and hit the button then patiently waited while the heavenly aroma filled the kitchen. Once it finished brewing, I filled two cups, added cream, then headed back upstairs and set her cup on the table beside the bed. She slowly opened her eyes and smiled when she saw the coffee.

"Morning," she said.

"Morning."

She sat up and took a sip of coffee before cradling the warm mug between her breasts. This was actually the first time that I had gotten to see her nude in the plain light of day, and she was by all accounts as beautiful as she had been on the page.

"Thanks for last night," she said.

"No problem. I wasn't about to let someone drown on my watch."

"I wasn't talking about out on the Bay. I was referring to right here, and the fact that you didn't make a single move on me—not even when I did my best to tempt you."

"I did get that boner."

She smiled.

"Yeah, but you didn't do anything with it."

"Well, call me a pussy, but I like to know that a woman actually wants to have sex with me."

"You didn't think that was an invitation?"

"I wasn't sure—you'd had quite a night, and I didn't want to take advantage."

"I'm not sure that I could have been more obvious."

"Seriously?"

"Let me recap. I wandered into your room, stripped naked, then joined you in bed and placed your hand on my breast and your hard penis between my legs, where I all but put it in my vagina."

"Shit—I feel kind of stupid now."

"Don't, because now I respect you a lot more. Most guys would have done anything to be where you were last night, but you *weren't* most guys. You were better, though, if you had responded to my advances, I would have fucked you to high heaven."

"I suddenly don't feel better."

"You are, and it means that you're not just helping me to get laid. You're a sincerely nice guy."

Interesting, this was a *damned if you do, damned if you don't* moment, and I suppose that last night had inadvertently been a kind of test. Sure, she would have had sex with me and given me the night of my life, but I was a better person for abstaining. Life was way too complicated.

"What if I had died of blue balls in my sleep?"

"Then I would be guilty of necrophilia right now."

"Funny."

We sipped our coffee, talked, and enjoyed the morning, but it was time to at last get ready, as we had a busy itinerary for the day—namely getting Fiona and the girls their money from the asshole bachelor boys. Fiona thankfully headed next door to the guest bathroom to get ready while I headed into my own, more than ready to expunge my bowels from a wild, though sex-free, night. I made sure the door was locked, then grabbed my iPhone and took up residence on R2-Pee-Poo, which was my pet name for my recently purchased Japanese Toto toilet. It was a state of the art bathroom accessory and delivered everything my heart could ever desire from a toilet. It had a heated seat, bidet function, and a dryer, though with some creative redirecting of the water jet, you could get some pretty decent penile stimulation. Sadly, that only lasted as long as the penis remained in its downward flaccid attitude, which was something stimulation would soon change, thereby making my toilet a bit of a cocktease. I suppose that if I never managed to find the right girl, I would make some minor modifications to the sprayer attachment and end up dragging this little fucker down the aisle to make it my lovely porcelain bride.

I turned on the seat warmer, or bun warmer as I called it, and I had to admit that it was a particularly soothing way to start the morning. Sure I missed familiarity of the plastic seat of my downstairs toilet, but, with company about, I was relegated to my lofty personal commode. Oddly, in spite of this being the master bath and technically the nicest toilet in the house, I generally used the toilet on the main floor, because it was closer to the kitchen—the place where I usually drank my coffee.

So, as I sat upon my new and exciting throne, I searched the web for any stories about the boat wreck last night and found a link on my local news page. I clicked on it and soon was looking at a picture of the boat and its owner—a man named Robert Hedwick, who also happened to be one of San Francisco's elite investment bankers and a major player on the world financial stage. I read on and learned that it was his son Daniel who was actually using the boat at the time of the incident. Young Daniel had been hosting his best friend's bachelor party when the weather had supposedly hampered their visibility and caused them to strike

Little Alcatraz. There was no mention of the other passengers or the fact that the assholes had saved themselves and left the evening's entertainment to die on the boat. Ten seconds on LinkedIn and I learned that Daniel worked for his father at the aptly named Hedwick Corporation. With that fact, I put both his name and the company's name in the Google search bar and soon found a news story featuring young Daniel. In it, he was describing what it was like to work for his father—and, more specifically, to have an office just down the hall from one of the country's best and brightest minds in high finance. Bingo! I had all I needed to know, so this was going to be fairly easy and possibly a little fun. Still, I decided to do another search, though this one was of Daniel's social media accounts, and I quickly found some juicy photos that I thought might come in handy. Now, I had only one last chore to complete—namely a phone call to a good friend, and I pulled up his number, dialed, and surprisingly heard him answer on the second ring.

"How the hell did you know I was in town?" he asked.

"I didn't. What the fuck are you doing here?"

"Speeches, bullshit, and fundraising—same ol' same ol'" he said.

"Well good. Where are you and when can we meet?"

"I'm staying at the Clift Hotel, and I'll be free after two. What's the occasion? Are you horny and looking for a quick hook up?"

"I have an exciting new client, and she could use your help."

"So, she's horny and looking for a hookup?"

"No, but when you see her, you'll wish she were."

"Why? Is she hot?"

"She's Miss October."

"Yeah right—I'll see you at two. Fuck you," he said.

"Fuck you too," I responded, hitting the end button.

Satisfied that I had completely emptied my bowels, I set down my phone, flushed, and stepped into the shower. Five minutes later, I was dry and getting dressed in a power suit for credibility instead of my usual black stretchy skinny jeans. I met Fiona in the hall, and together we headed downstairs to the kitchen.

"What do you usually eat for breakfast?" I asked.

"Eggs or Irish Oatmeal. How about you?"

"Same, but this morning I'm thinking about a scramble with broccoli, onions, cheese, and nitrate-free bacon."

"And homemade whole grain waffles on the side?" she asked.

"I wish."

I threw the bacon in the skillet, then grabbed some of my feel good free range chicken eggs that I'd gotten at the local Farmer's Market and set it all on the counter with the various other ingredients. Next, I put the wheat bread in the toaster and turned my attention back to the bacon. When it finished cooking, I cut it up and threw it and the other ingredients together in a cast iron frying pan with a little milk. After some vigorous stirring, the breakfast was cooking away, and the smell was apparently enough to rouse the other girls, and they appeared a moment later looking sleepy and slightly hungover. Daphne and Stacy were still wonderfully topless, though Andrea, the girl formerly known by the stripper name of Tiger, was wearing a T-shirt. The three of them took a seat at the table, and I handed out coffee and received three appreciative smiles.

"How'd you all sleep?" I asked.

"Good, but alone," Andrea said.

"Great," Stacy and Daphne said, at the same time.

"Well, I have good news. I know where your best man from last night works, so we're going to go see the little fucker and get you all your money."

"How the hell did you find all that out so quickly?" Fiona asked, looking surprised.

"I'm a detective."

"And a good one, apparently," Andrea added.

I dished out breakfast, and everyone dug in, and it was interesting to see that strippers, unlike models, apparently ate like lumberjacks. I suppose it made perfect sense when you took into account the physicality of their job—namely pole dancing, which was an activity that was so physical that it had become an exercise fad. Each girl finished her plate, two pieces of toast, and even had second helpings of coffee. With breakfast finally over and everyone properly sated, the three late risers hit the bathroom to freshen up. Forty-five minutes later, everyone was ready to go and looking far more subdued in Melanie's clothing.

We walked up to the parking lot and continued on about

fifty yards to my building. We entered my man cave on the bottom level, and, when I flipped on the lights, the girls all gazed around in awe at the bizarre collection of cars, bikes, weapons, and gear that lined the walls.

"This is like a museum of masculinity and more or less puts your bathroom to shame," Fiona said, with a laugh.

"Yes indeed, and you haven't even seen the bronze casts of my penis on the back wall."

"Seriously?" Andrea asked in an enthusiastic tone.

"No."

"Too bad," she said.

"Yeah, but you will find my collection of Star Wars and GI Joe action figures over there."

"Sorry, I'm afraid I'm not as interested in those."

The girls were quiet a moment as they mulled around the room looking at my mementos of manitude, but Fiona, however, was looking only at my cars.

"So, which one are we taking?" she asked.

"Well, since there are five of us we only have two choices—the Subaru or the Range Rover. Anyone have a preference?"

"Which has heated seats?" Andrea asked.

"Range Rover."

"That's the one then."

I motioned for the girls to climb into the Range Rover while I went to a panel on the wall and hit the button to open the garage door. As it slid open, I gazed around at the contents of my man cave and still found it strange to see so many cars, as not long ago I had been a one-car man, with my only vehicle being my beloved Subaru WRX STi. That all changed, however, after the recent accumulation of wealth had allowed me to live a little and thus buy three more glorious automobiles. The first new member of the herd, a Porsche 911 Turbo, had been a necessary purchase after my Subaru was rendered temporarily out of service from a brief gun battle on the Golden Gate Bridge. The other two, the Mini Cooper S and the Range Rover, were bought purely for fun. Now that I had a stable of automobiles, two of which were fancy name brands, I was officially a real Marin County asshole and had the toys to prove it.

I walked over and joined the girls to find Fiona had claimed shotgun and taken the front passenger seat while the others had piled into the back with Daphne riding bitch in the middle. I started the car and pulled out of the man cave, hit the remote garage button, and soon we were heading south up the Waldo Grade—a steep and winding section of Highway 101 that probably would have terrified the shit out of someone from the midwest, as their roads tended to be flat and straight. We passed over the top of the hill and went down through the rainbow tunnel to emerge into what I considered to be one of the most spectacular views of both the Golden Gate Bridge and San Francisco skyline. A long sweeping turn later, we were on the bridge and rolling along with the steady flow of traffic.

"So, I saw your pictures in the downstairs bathroom and was wondering what exactly you used to do in the military?" Daphne asked.

"He was in special operations," Fiona said, before I could answer.

"Wow! Did you ever kill anyone?" Stacy asked.

"Yeah, but I saved a lot more than I killed."

"Were you stationed in Iraq or Afghanistan?"

"Yeah, both, as well as a lot more places I'm not allowed to mention."

"So, how does an ex-special operations soldier turned private investigator afford all that shit back in your man cave?" Andrea asked.

"Good question, and the answer is that I got really, really lucky with a recent case."

"I wish I could get that lucky," Daphne said.

We crossed the Bridge and decided it would probably be wise for everyone to stop at their respective places and get proper clothes before we confronted the unofficial leader of the bachelor boys. First up was Andrea, who lived just across the street from the Presidio. She turned out to be pretty business savvy and owned a large triplex, whose two additional units probably rented out for a hefty profit in this part of the city. She was apparently wisely spending the thousands of dollars that men tucked in her g-string. Good for her.

Next stop was Stacy and Daphne's place, which was a large luxury apartment building on Russian Hill that was formerly a hotel. All the units had been converted into condos, and they were now privately owned, though the girls were still only renters but had the first option to buy should the owner ever decide to sell. Twenty minutes later, they reappeared and looked nice, if not a little racy, in their tightly fitting Bebe dresses and high heels. Last was Fiona, and she had an apartment in the Laurel Village area, which was the final stop for San Franciscans before they got pregnant, berthed their brood, then made the northern migration to Marin County and its top notch school districts. She returned to the car after only ten minutes and looked very respectable in black leggings and a micro puff jacket. Now that everyone was dressed and ready, it was time to ease on down the road to the Hedwick Corporation's office building.

CHAPTER SIX
Conan the Golfer

We drove down California Street then parked in a garage and walked the rest of the way over to Pine Street, where the Hedwick Corporation's San Francisco headquarters was located. The building, as expected, was a monument to the company that owned it, and its exterior was modern looking yet classy with its marble, glass, and stainless steel facade that stretched well up into the city's towering skyline. We entered through glass doors and were immediately greeted by a security man, whose gaze quickly left me and fell upon the girls, who were quite a sight for any man's sore eyes. He directed us to the main reception desk, and we went over and met with yet another security man.

"How can I help you?" he asked, as his eyes, like those of his associates, went straight to the girls.

"The name's Finn, Tag Finn, and we're here to see Daniel Hedwick," I said.

"Do you have an appointment?" he asked.

"No. It's official business," I said, flashing a State Department ID that I still had from a case a few months back.

I had gotten it while doing a job for the CIA, but I kept it around for moments when I needed a little official credibility. Of course, there was no reason the State Department would be investigating anything like this, but people were usually enamored enough with credentials not to question its validity—hopefully anyway. The man got on the phone and talked to someone, probably Daniel's assistant, and told him, or her, that there was a man from the State Department and four particularly attractive women here to see Daniel. After a moment, his expression changed, and he looked uncomfortable as he hung up.

"Mr. Hedwick's assistant will be down in a second to speak with you. In the meantime, would you like to wait in the guest lounge?"

"Sure."

The runaround—just as I had expected. The man stood and led us past the elevators to a large room with an espresso machine, bottled waters, and a number of trays of pastries and fresh fruit. We all took a seat on the plush leather couches and were relegated to sit and wait. This building was like a veritable castle, and Daniel was the prince who falsely believed its glass and stainless steel ramparts would protect him from the world at large.

"Do you really think you can get us our money?" Daphne asked.

"Absolutely, though if I can't, I'll give it to you myself."

"No you won't. You've been too nice as it is," Fiona said.

"Believe me, I can afford it—and it's the least I can do considering it's the holidays."

"No."

"Yes, but don't worry, fuckhead Hedwick will pay up."

Fiona cleared her throat and looked over my shoulder, and I turned to see a mildly attractive, though stern-faced, woman standing behind me. She was tall, well put together, and every bit the professional woman she appeared to be, and I was fairly certain she had just heard how I had referred to her boss.

"Hello, my name is Cynthia. I'm Mr. Hedwick's personal assistant. How can I help you?" she asked rather coldly as she eyed the odd group of people assembled in the room.

"We need to talk to Fuckhead."

"I'm sorry. I don't know to whom you're referring."

"Oh, then perhaps you know him as Daniel, or Dan, or Little Danny, but fuckhead is a little more accurate at the moment."

She cleared her throat.

"So, what do you want with Mr. Hedwick?"

"Obviously, we need to speak with the fuckhead."

"Will you please stop referring to Mr. Hedwick by that name?"

"No—not until he's made amends."

"I might as well tell you right now that a meeting is never going to happen."

"Really? Because I believe that it is," I said, pulling out

my Sate Department ID.

She looked closely at the picture, crossed her arms, then looked back up at me.

"Mr. Hedwick is extremely busy," she said.

"And about to go to jail for attempted manslaughter for a little maritime mishap he was involved in last night—in which case, he'll have a lot of extra time on his hands, and you won't have a job."

She looked at me a moment and tried to get a read on how serious I might be, then pulled out her phone and walked around the corner, where she was probably calling her boss. That was the opening I was hoping we might get.

"Let's go," I said, as I set off towards the elevators.

"Where?" Fiona asked nervously.

"To Prince Fuckhead's office, of course."

A group of people had just exited, and the door was still open as we piled in. I hit the button for the top floor, and thirty floors up, only ten before our destination, the elevator stopped, and the doors slid open to reveal a lone man. He was young, likely fresh out of college, and standing there wide eyed in shock.

"Going down?" he asked timidly.

"Sorry, but we're going up—something I suspect your penis is also doing at this very moment," I said.

"What?" he said, looking confused, having completely missed my stupid joke.

Fiona hit me in the arm, so I decided to answer properly.

"Yes, we're going up, but feel free to ride along," I said.

He stepped inside and immediately violated proper elevator etiquette when he continued to face his fellow riders rather than turn and face the door. He was breaking from common courtesy and accepted social norms, but who could blame him for staring unabashedly at the veritable wall of feminine beauty. He wiped a bead of sweat from his brow then reached in his pocket, where he was likely making room for the semi that was brewing in his properly pressed grey suit trousers.

"So, do you all work here?" he asked, after mustering the courage to speak.

"No, we're just visiting, as we've been hired by the HR department to conduct a seminar on sexual harassment in the workplace."

"Oh," he said, before abruptly turning around to face the door.

We exited on the fortieth floor and left the youngster alone with only his memories to keep him company. Now, we were officially in the dominion of the one percent, and before us was a grand foyer adorned with marble floors and rich mahogany walls. We ventured on and reached the hallway that encircled the entire floor then cut left and worked our way around the building until finally finding young Daniel's office just up on the right. He had a large smoked glass door, and we passed through it to find the little fucker standing there with a putter in one hand and his phone in the other. I called him little, but he was actually a bit larger than your average bear, and stood about six foot two and looked as though he regularly went to the gym. Regardless of his height or build, however, his actions on the water last night meant he would forever be a little piece of shit in my eyes.

"Oh wait—they're right here," he said, looking surprised as he hung up the phone.

"Technically, you're trespassing and shouldn't be up here," he said.

"Technically, you're a cowardly little piece of shit who shouldn't be up here either—so what say we put all that aside and sit down and have an amicable chat, resolve our little problem, and we'll be on our way and out of your finely quaffed hair."

"Excuse me, but I own this building, so I'll be giving the orders here."

"Your father owns this building."

"Same difference, so if you don't leave now, I'll call the police, and you five will be going to jail."

"At least we can warm up your cell for you."

"I don't know what you're talking about."

"You don't remember being out on the Bay and leaving these girls to die on a sinking boat while you and your fellow members of Delta Sigma Chickenshit took off in the inflatable? I find that hard to believe."

"What do you want?" he asked.

"Just for you to pay the girls what you owe them."

"Who are you? Their pimp?"

"No, I'm just a friend."

"Well, friend, the thing is, the show had only just started when we hit that rock, so, the way I see it, they didn't earn the money."

"Well, the way I see it—you're own incompetence cancelled the show, and as you've now committed a grievous crime tantamount to involuntary manslaughter, paying the girls what they're owed is about the easiest way to keep you and your good name out of jail let alone the news."

"Fuck you. You can't threaten me."

"Perhaps you remember a cruise ship called the *Costa Concordia?*

"Yeah, so?"

"Well, the captain of that vessel faced some major charges, among them, abandoning his ship as well as multiple counts of manslaughter. You could end up in the very same boat—so to speak."

"I didn't get anyone killed."

"Yeah, because I rescued them after you left them to die, and that's close enough in my book."

"Look, asshole, I'm done with you and your fucking bitches, so it's time for you all to leave."

"If you call them bitches again, I'm going to seriously consider fist-fucking your shitty overprivileged little face."

Fiona spoke up nervously.

"Tag, it's not worth it. Let's just go," she said.

The door burst open, and Cynthia walked in looking harried and out of breath.

"I'm sorry. They snuck past me when I left to call you,"

she said.

"It's OK, Cynthia. They're leaving now," he said.

"No, Cynthia, we're not."

"Yes, you are."

"Look, junior, no one's leaving until you pay the girls what you owe them."

I could see his face turning red, and the veins in his neck were starting to bulge, so it would appear that Prince Fuckhead was getting angry. He obviously wasn't used to having someone defy him in his father's castle, and I was pretty sure that he was close to his breaking point. He glanced at the putter in his hand and suddenly raised it over his head and slammed it onto his desk. The girls screamed and stepped back, but I had a different strategy. When you had someone with a bat, a club, or in this case, a putter, there were two options. The first was to stay the fuck away while the other was to make sure you were close enough to move inside the arc of the weapon should the fuckhead holding it decide to take a swing at your head. I went with option number two and moved forward until I was only a step away from Prince Fuckhead.

"Get the fuck out of my office!" he screamed, sending little flecks of spittle flying from his mouth.

"Sorry, but we can't leave until we resolve our little business matter."

"You're fucking dead!" he bellowed, as he swung the putter at my head.

Interesting, I had never been attacked with a golf club

before and suspected that such encounters were usually relegated to the dominion of a golf course—most likely the green, as it was the place of greatest pressure and therefore most conducive to explosive violence. I would imagine the first such encounter probably occurred in Scotland sometime during the fifteenth century, and a man in bright clothing, likely named something like Fergus, might have missed a putt and had his golf buddy, a fellow named something like Angus, deliver the tiniest of wise cracks at his misfortune. This would have resulted in the two coming to blows, and the brightly colored golf clothing, flying tufts of grass, and flailing arms would have been just the kind of spectacle van Gogh might have put on canvas. This was speculation but by no means an idle fantasy, for I was familiar with golf and human nature, and I'm pretty sure it could have happened—especially since I too had often felt that kind of rage and slammed a club or two into the ground after a particularly bad shot. Of course, I never swung at a fellow player regardless how much he or she might have deserved it.

So, here I was, facing the fury of Conan the Golfer, and I had nothing but my wits, a six handicap, and a lifetime of martial arts to back me up. I continued forward inside the arc of the putter and shot out both of my hands and caught his arm at both the wrist and bicep then redirected it down, so that the golf club thudded harmlessly into the floor. My next move was to snake my left hand in and around his putter hand and pull back, thus trapping both his hand

and the putter against my body. With the weapon safely secure, I twisted my hips counter clockwise and slammed my right elbow straight into Daniel's solar plexus, and he buckled over and let out a gasp of pain. I quickly followed up with a right chop to the side of his neck, and this meant I had just hit two major targets in rapid succession, and, while the first blow knocked the wind from his lungs, the second traumatized the nerves in his neck and invoked the baroreceptor reflex. This made his brain slow blood flow through the carotid arteries, and it created a mild paralysis that left his body pliable enough for me to shove him backwards into a nearby bookcase. Cynthia was in shock, but she still managed to let loose an ear piercing scream as I manhandled her boss, though I don't know what she was getting all excited about, as it wasn't as if he were swinging his putter at her head—at least not this particular putter, though, judging by what I had seen of their relationship thus far, I imagine she had come in contact with his other putter—his flesh putter—and she probably let him play a few holes after one too many drinks at a company party.

"Sorry, but it looks as though you didn't make par, so if you don't calm the fuck down, I'm going to be forced to play through—and by that I mean ram my knee up into your fucking balls," I said.

Just then, a tall, fit looking grey haired gentleman of about sixty entered the room and looked confused as he gazed at all of us.

"What the hell is going on in here?" he asked.

"Mr. Hedwick, that man just attacked your son!" Cynthia said, excitedly as she pointed at me.

Daniel, still holding the putter in his hand, was starting to recover from the shock of our little exchange and angrily tried to break my grip on his arm so that he might try to swing at me again.

"Daniel! Relax and put that putter down immediately!" the senior Hedwick yelled.

"It's a smart move, Daniel, especially as you're now facing an obvious bogie," I added.

Daniel didn't like my joke much, but he acquiesced and dropped the putter as his father closed the door and regarded everyone in the room.

"Now, will someone please explain what the hell is going on in here!"

I turned to face the senior Hedwick.

"No problem, Mr. Hedwick. My name's Finn, Tag Finn. I'm a private investigator, and I'm sorry to tell you this, but your son here has been a very, very, bad boy."

Hedwick senior obviously knew that his son had experienced trouble on the Bay last night but had no idea that his brood had put four lives in imminent danger. I, therefore, recounted the events of the previous night as well as Daniel's putter attack, and the elder Hedwick listened intently though with a hint of sadness on his face when he finally responded.

"People, I would like to sincerely apologize for my son's actions, and may I say that I am utterly ashamed."

"Oh come on!" Daniel complained.

"Be quiet, and let me talk," the senior Hedwick said.

He looked around the room and made sure to look everyone in the eye as he spoke.

"I tried to teach my son to be a good man, and deep down I sincerely hope there's one in there, but last night's actions make me think I may very well have raised a coward and an asshole."

"Dad! You can't be serious," Daniel whined.

"I am, Daniel, and you've disappointed me."

"But, you don't understand—it was rough out there, and I'd had a few drinks and wasn't thinking clearly. When we hit those rocks, I just panicked. I thought I was doing the right thing when I loaded up the raft."

"With only your friends?" Fiona asked.

"I was going to come back for you and the other girls."

"Bullshit. You didn't even call the Coast Guard. We spent nearly thirty minutes on that boat until I finally called them myself," Fiona said, angrily.

"I don't understand how you could do that, Daniel," Robert said, sadly.

Daniel thought for a moment before responding.

"Well, one of the groomsman hit his head when we went aground, so I thought it was more important to take him to the hospital."

"Nice try, but I'm afraid your Instagram account paints a very different picture of the rest of the night. You didn't go back for the girls, because you and the rest of those assholes decided to salvage the night by going to a fucking strip club," I said, as I brought up the pictures I'd found in my earlier search.

The senior Hedwick stepped forward and looked at the pictures, and I could see a little piece of his soul die in that moment. No one wanted to see that their son was a complete piece of shit.

"Disgraceful," Robert muttered.

"Come on, dad—you know how it is," Daniel said, in a plaintive tone.

"No, I don't, because the people on that boat, all of them, were your responsibility, and right now you're just lucky that no one got hurt or killed, as your life as you know it would be over. What you did was a criminal offense, and, worse still, it makes me doubt your humanity."

Robert Hedwick was a good man, and now he looked sad as he faced the reality that his son was, by all accounts, a total asshole and a possible sociopath. Interestingly, I'd found that assholes like Daniel often exhibited that trait, not because they were born without empathy, but rather because they never developed it during their overprivileged childhoods.

"I will personally write each of you a check for what you're owed plus any damages that you see fit to add. All I can ask in return is that you let me deal with Daniel privately, so that we can keep this a family matter."

I looked at the girls, and they all nodded their approval.

"No problem, that's all they really wanted. I'm sure we

can all agree to keep this little story to ourselves."

"Here, come with me to my office."

The senior Hedwick and the girls went ahead, leaving me with Fuckface the Barbarian and Cynthia, who was quietly comforting her boss by rubbing his neck.

"Just so you know, Daniel, we all face adversity in life and get scared, but it's how you deal with it that makes you a man. If you had been even a little sorry and, least of all, nice, this would have gone down a lot differently," I said.

"Why don't you just go with those whores and get your money," Cynthia said, with a sneer.

"I'm getting the feeling that you don't like those women."

"They make money by selling their bodies."

"And you make money by selling your soul. Which do you think is worse?"

I walked outside then joined the others in Robert's office, which, not surprisingly, was a lot larger and nicer than his son's. He went to his desk and took out his checkbook and wrote each of the girls a check in the amount they specified but paused when he got to Fiona.

"So, how much do I owe you Miss Blake?"

"How do you know my name?"

"I've been a loyal Playboy subscriber since I was eighteen and still have every issue. Who could possibly forget the lovely Miss October?"

Fiona blushed and averted her eyes.

"Yeah, well..."

"Well nothing. You should count yourself lucky. A lot of incredible women have bared all for Playboy Magazine. So, how much were you supposed to get paid?"

"Your son and his friends promised to pay me ten thousand dollars," she said, looking uncomfortable.

"That's ridiculous!"

"Yeah, I suppose it is."

"Ten thousand is far too low for Miss October," he said.

"Um, excuse me?" she said, sounding a little shocked.

"Mr. Hedwick, I think it's important you know that she didn't do it for herself. Every cent she earns is being used to help her brother," I interjected.

"Oh, is it for a medical condition?" he asked, sounding concerned.

"No, it's legal, and it's rather complicated. I don't know if you've heard of my brother Mark Blake, but he's the founder of Globo-Care, and he's run into some trouble with his latest aid project."

He nodded and slapped his hand on his desk.

"Of course, it was in your centerfold bio, and, believe it or not, I already know about Globo-Care, as my company has donated a fair amount of money to your brother's foundation."

"Small world," I said.

"Indeed, and do you mind telling me about what's happened to Mark?"

Fiona explained the sad tale of her brother's difficult situation, and, when she finished, Robert appeared to think for a minute as he looked down at his checkbook. A moment later, he filled out a check and slid it across to Fiona.

"I hope this helps," he said.

She picked it up and read the amount and looked shocked. I glanced at as well and saw that it was for fifty thousand dollars. The elder Hedwick was not only honorable but generous.

"I can't accept this!" Fiona said.

"Is it not enough?"

"It's too much!"

"It's for a good cause, and, besides, it's nice to know that those bio sheets are actually accurate."

"I know, right?" I said, nodding, having learned the same lesson only the night before.

"No, I'm serious. I can't accept this."

"If you don't take my check right now, I'll just give it to Globo-Care directly—so why not save me the time."

"I'm sorry, but I just can't accept it," she said, putting it back down on the desk.

Robert picked it up and placed it back into her hand.

"It's just money to me, but in your hands it can do something good. Now, please take it and help your brother. He can't help anyone as long as he's locked up in a cell."

Robert had an excellent point, and Fiona finally conceded and slipped the check into her pocket.

"I can't thank you enough for your help, Mr. Hedwick," Fiona said.

"Call me Robert, and, believe me, it's not a problem. Now, as for you, Mr. Finn—are you owed any compensation in this affair?"

"Call me Tag—and no, I'm just here to help."

We shook hands and said goodbye to the better half of the Hedwick family and headed down to the lobby and out onto the street.

"So, where can I take you girls?" I asked.

"I think we're going to stay downtown and do a little shopping," Daphne said.

"How about you, Andrea?"

"I think I'll join them," she said.

I exchanged contact information with the three girls, then we hugged and parted ways, thus leaving Fiona and me alone.

"Where to now?" Fiona asked.

"We're meeting a friend."

"Oh really, and who might that friend be?"

"You wouldn't believe me if I told you."

We began the relatively short walk to the Clift Hotel, and Fiona reached out and took hold of my hand, and we moved through the throngs of people and looked like just another happy couple out doing our holiday shopping.

CHAPTER SEVEN
High Friends in High Places

We arrived at the Clift Hotel about ten minutes later to a great deal of hoopla, as news crews and all number of official looking people were occupying the lobby. Upon reaching the main desk, we were greeted by a woman named Susan, who was doing her best to remain calm and composed as she weathered the storm of activity.

"It's busy here today, Susan," I said.

She looked confused for a moment and probably wondered if perhaps we might know each other, until recognition dawned that I had merely looked at her name tag. It was an interesting phenomena that people wearing name tags often forgot they were wearing them, and, similarly, people talking to people wearing name tags rarely looked at them, so, I took a great deal of pleasure in actually learning and using people's names. It was a silly habit, but it served in generating a much quicker emotional connection to a stranger in a shorter amount of time. Susan relaxed and smiled as she responded.

"Yeah, that's how it is when we get a VIP. How can I help you?"

"We're here to see Sasquatch."

The woman looked surprised, then took a minute to look us over, as though she might doubt the sincerity of my request. Fiona too gave me an odd look.

"Your name?" Susan asked.

"Tag Finn. He's expecting me."

She gazed at her computer screen, typed something, then looked up and smiled a second later.

"Oh, yes, sir. I'll tell him you're here."

She got on the phone, and, shortly thereafter, an attractive blond woman in a business suit arrived.

"Hello, Mr. Finn. My name is Sandra," she said.

Judging by the suit and earpiece, she was obviously Secret Service, and I was also fairly certain I had seen her before.

"Hello, Sandra," I responded.

She smiled and led us to the elevator.

"So, how do you know Sasquatch?" Sandra asked.

"We're old friends from our service days in Afghanistan."

Recognition crossed her face, and she looked embarrassed.

"Oh, of course. I'm sorry—Tag Finn. I should have remembered you. We crossed paths in Switzerland a couple months ago."

Fiona gave me a questioning look.

"Sasquatch? Switzerland? I don't understand."

"Long story," I said.

"Sounds like it."

I paused for a moment and gazed at Sandra until I finally realized that she had been one of Sasquatch's Secret Service contingent in Switzerland.

"Ha! It was the airport in Zurich!" I said.

"That's right. Good memory, Mr. Finn, though now I'm head of Sasquatch's detail."

"Congratulations, and please call me Tag."

"Tag it is, and I must say, I really am surprised you remember me."

"I never forget a beautiful woman with a gun."

Sandra smiled, pressed the button for the top floor, and, when we reached our destination, we exited and were led to the hotel's premier suite.

"Sasquatch is a code name, by the way," I said, to Fiona.

"For who?" Fiona asked.

"You'll see."

Sandra opened the door, and we walked in to see my friend sitting at a table where he was probably about to order lunch. He instantly stood and came over to greet us, and Fiona looked at him as though she were staring at a ghost.

"What the hell?" she whispered under her breath.

"Finn, you son of a bitch! I thought you were fucking with me on the phone," he said, as his eyes fell on Fiona.

"Nope, she's real," I said.

"Miss October—Fiona Blake! It's an honor to meet you."

"Fiona, this is one of my oldest, dearest friends, John Matheson."

"Yeah, I recognize the vice president of the United States," she said, nervously.

"So you've heard of me?" he asked.

"Of course. It's an honor to meet you, sir," Fiona said.

"Call me John, and the honor is all mine."

Fiona looked to me, unsure how to refer to the vice president of the United States.

"I just call him Sasquatch."

"Technically it should be Yeti, but Finn is too much of a stubborn asshole to acknowledge that fact. Now, more importantly, have you guys eaten, because I was just sitting down to lunch."

"You buying?" I asked.

"In a manner of speaking, though technically, it's on the United States taxpayers."

"So, it's more or less on us."

"Yeah, if you actually paid your taxes. Any idea what you want to eat or should I just send for the children's menu? I hear the chicken tenders kick ass."

"Nice try, but I will be ordering from the adult's menu, so no small portions for me, which obviously means that your penis is not on the menu."

"Yeah, but only because it's more than even the three of us could possibly eat."

Fiona looked a little taken aback by the sudden turn to

penis jokes, and, when John saw her expression, he gave her his best politician's smile.

"I'm just a regular guy under all the pomp, circumstance, and good looks, but the truth is that Tag and I have been talking this way to each other ever since our time together in Afghanistan. I don't suppose you know that he saved my life over there?"

"No, but now that means there are at least two of us in that club," she said.

"Seriously?"

"Yeah—last night he plucked me from the cold, dark waters of the San Francisco bay after the boat I was on hit a rock and sank just off of Alcatraz, but I doubt it's as exciting a story as yours."

"Hey, all life and death stories are pretty fucking exciting—especially to the people who experienced them."

"True," she said.

"I don't suppose you were lucky enough to end up with a catchy nickname like Sasquatch?"

"Thankfully not, as that wouldn't have been too flattering a name for a woman."

"Yeah, but at least it would have been more geographically correct, and if Finn weren't such a stubborn dumbass, he'd have called me Yeti, as it would have been more appropriate for Afghanistan."

"So, why Sasquatch," Fiona asked.

"That was obviously a reference to my enormous penis."

"No, it was a reference to his large body and minimal

intelligence."

"Which doesn't matter when you have a giant penis."

We had descended to penis jokes, which, along with fart jokes, was the lowest common denominator of male interaction and inexplicably occurred when men were left to their own devices. John, hoping to end this conversation on a win, turned and led us over to the table, so that we could take a seat and look at the menu. He decided upon a tuna sandwich on whole wheat with a salad on the side, so I decided to screw with him by ordering what he could not.

"I'll go with the burger and fries."

"Dude, seriously? Fuck you," he said.

Fiona looked confused.

"His majesty the vice president is watching his red meat intake, but what he doesn't know is that the burger is made with grass fed beef and, therefore, actually would have been good for him, as it has the desirable ratio of omega three to omega six fatty acids and also contains the cancer fighting ingredient conjugated linoleic acid."

"Oh big words—somebody obviously went to college," he said.

"John here, with his life of privilege, made his man servant go to his classes for him at Yale. All he really knows shit about is golf, polo, and women—and when I say he knows about women I mean that he knows they have boobies and, more importantly, innies rather than outies."

"Guilty as charged. So, Fiona, what would you like for lunch?" John asked.

"The chicken Caesar salad."

Sandra, who was standing nearby, got on the phone and called in our order.

"Anything to drink?" Sandra asked.

"Coffee and water for me," I said.

"Me too, and can I use your bathroom?" Fiona asked.

"Absolutely. It's right in there," John said, pointing towards his bedroom.

She stood up and excused herself from the table.

"You finally got a *Playboy* centerfold into your bedroom," I said.

"Very funny."

Once the door closed, he leaned in toward me.

"Goddammit, Finn—I really thought you were fucking with me when you said Miss October."

"I know, and I wasn't sure who was going to look more surprised—you or her."

"Definitely me. It's far more exciting to meet a playmate than the vice president."

"Agreed."

"Holy shit is she hot! Have you slept with her yet?"

"Yes and no."

"Meaning?"

"We slept in the same bed together, but we didn't sleep together in the biblical sense."

"Is this you coming out to me? Should we hug and I tell you that I've always known?"

"It wasn't the right time—she'd had a hell of a night."

"Yeah, but then you could have had a hell of a night—together!" he said, groaning and looking frustrated.

"Look, Mr. blue blooded bachelor, you need to get out of your womanizing mindset, settle down, and meet a nice girl, so that you can run for president one day. I'd hate to always think of you as my asshole under achiever friend."

"Maybe Miss October would be interested in sharing a life in politics."

"I guess you didn't read her bio on the back page."

"What bio? They have writing in *Playboy?*"

"Yeah, lots of it, believe it or not."

"I must have missed it, as I was too busy looking at the beautiful girl. The one who is currently sitting on my toilet."

"Maybe you could go in and smell the seat when she's done."

"Would that be weird?"

"Not really—considering you're the vice president of the Unites states and a full blown ass kissing politician. If you ask me it's only a subtle deviation from your usual target."

"Excellent point."

Fiona reappeared and took a seat at the table.

"So, what have you two been talking about in my absence?" she asked.

"World peace," John and I said, at exactly the same time.

"Nice try," Sandra said, from the other side of the room, where she had apparently been listening to our conversation.

Fiona eyed us curiously and looked as though she didn't entirely believe our response, but John and I remained steadfast in our resolve and stared back as innocently as possible under the ever penetrating radar of female intuition. Thankfully, lunch arrived, and we turned our attention to eating and talking, or, more accurately, John talked—mostly to Fiona. He asked her all about *Playboy* and what it was like be in the most famous men's magazine of all time. He also asked her about her childhood, where she went to school, and whether or not she wanted to continue doing pictorial work. Annoyingly, he was particularly charming and won Fiona over with the tenacity of a sperminator robot, and, watching it all unfold, made me realize that he really needed to give up his single man's mindset and settle down, or he could kiss the presidency goodbye, which would end up wasting all the precious energy I spent saving his life.

We finished lunch, and our talk thankfully turned to more serious matters—namely Fiona's brother. She explained his predicament, and John, who was actually a very nice guy underneath all of his pomp and apparent girl-craziness, listened intently and waited until she had finished her story before responding.

"I actually know all about your brother and his work. He's made some amazing progress in countries that we really thought were beyond hope, and, as for Malkarta, if I'm not mistaken, we have some kind of deal brewing with them, so I'd be happy to make some inquiries and see if I can help."

"How long are you in the Bay Area?" I asked.

"Until tomorrow—why?"

"I'm thinking about dinner. I have someone that I want

you to meet."

"Profession?"

"Lawyer."

"Hair color?"

"Brownish blond."

"Bra size?"

"High C, maybe low D."

"I'm in."

"You guys are pigs," Fiona said.

"Oh, we're just kidding around—and besides, Finn had me at high C," John said.

CHAPTER EIGHT
A Twist of the Blade

John was probably telling the truth when he said that I had him at high C, but I let it rest, as he had agreed to help with Fiona's brother. We finished up lunch and let John get back to his political rabble rousing, which consisted of shaking a lot of hands, kissing a lot of ass, and making a lot of promises to his party's supporters in the Bay Area. Fiona and I left, but not before checking in with Sandra, as anyone who dined with the vice president had to be properly vetted, so I needed to give her the name of our fourth dinner guest, her address, and the name of the restaurant where we would be dining. Finished with all the busy work, we left the hotel and walked the three blocks back to the garage where I had parked the Range Rover. I used my ticket stub to pay at one of the little kiosks, then we headed up to the car and drove to the exit, and I paused, as I was unsure where I should go.

"So, what now? Is there any place that you need to be at

the moment?" I asked.

"Not really. What's the story with dinner?"

"I was hoping to go on a double date."

"Am I one of the dates?"

"I certainly hope so."

"And who's the other?"

"A friend who was recently divorced. I think she would be perfect for John, and he really needs to settle down if he hopes to become president."

"Jesus—do you realize that you would be friends with the president of the United States?"

"Fucking A! Why do you think I'm dragging his ass to dinner?"

I pulled out into traffic, and we made our way back to Sausalito, whereupon I stopped at one of our local coffee shops to fuel up on caffeine. There were four cafes in town, with two of them corporate and two of them independent, and I chose one of the independents, as the coffee was free trade, and it was conveniently right off the main road. We parked and walked in to find the usual end of day crowd sitting and working on their laptops, and each and every one of them had their ear buds firmly wedged in their ears as they sat there completely oblivious to the rest of the cafe's patrons.

We stepped up to the counter and ordered two cappuccinos to go, and, as we stood there waiting for our order, I felt a rush of cold air and turned to see the door open, and there was my infamous ex Melanie and her yacht club guy boyfriend. Melanie was the lovely bitch who had the indecency to break up with me by phone from her new boyfriend's yacht—after they had sex, of course. I then went through a several month dry spell in which I seemed to constantly run into her and the yacht club guy, and I never once had a woman on my arm to ease the psychological blow to my self-esteem. Starting a few months back, however, I had the incredible fortune to continuously run into Melanie while I was in the company of particularly attractive women—and it seemed to keep happening over and over. It was, of course, petty and a little childish to relish such experiences, but then being human was often petty and childish, so I decided to accept fate and enjoy every moment of discomfort that I now dished out to Melanie—wrecker of men.

The two of them strolled over, ordered, then stood beside us, and both quietly played with their smart phones as they waited. Melanie eventually looked up from her phone and saw us, and her eyes nearly dislodged from her head when she spied Fiona. Of course, that was nowhere near as dramatic a reaction as her boyfriend, who, after appearing to recognize my beautiful companion, looked as though he was on the verge of cumming in his pants. Melanie could see that she was beautiful, but her boyfriend was obviously a Playboy subscriber and therefore knew that the girl beside him was a centerfold—a mythological being for a man and a veritable unicorn.

He tried his best not to stare or drool but managed

to do both, and suddenly I had a newfound empathy for women in Fiona's position. Sure, they became an instant celebrity, and many had rocketed their fame into exciting careers, but those same girls also had to contend with male attention that bordered on pathological. While the proliferation of porn on the Internet lessened the effect of the physical version of Playboy magazine as an avenue of the nude female form, most males of a certain age would always hold it in high regard. It was almost like your first girl, except that she would never exist anywhere except on that page, where she was only an arm's length away from that obligatory box of Kleenex.

Yacht Club Guy was just such a man, and now he was seeing his first real life unicorn, or, in this case, Fiona Blake—Miss October. Melanie might be a bitch, but she was also a psychologist by profession, and she therefore understood human behavior well enough to see that her boyfriend was infatuated with the woman she believed was my girlfriend. Awesome.

"Oh hello, Melanie and Yacht Club Guy," I said.

I'd never actually bothered to learn his name, so I kept it simple and called him what he appeared to be—a yacht club guy. He was around forty-five, wealthy, a little thick in the middle from too many yacht club meals, and almost always wore khaki Dockers, top siders, and a dark blue sweater. Of course, the cherry on the hot fudge sundae that was his fashion sense was the captain's hat, which he apparently wore religiously, as I'd never seen him without it. Melanie had said he was some kind of important investment banker, but his true love was supposedly sailing. I, however, got the distinct impression he never used his boat for anything other than entertaining the ladies—as had been the case with Melanie. So, to me, he was Yacht Club Guy, or depending on my mood—Yacht Club Fucker.

"Hello, Tag, who is your new lady friend?" he asked in his Ivy League, better than thou tone.

"This is Fiona Blake," I said, saying her name very deliberately by pronouncing each syllable and vowel perfectly.

Yacht Club Guy's face flushed upon hearing the name, thereby confirming that his earlier summation had been correct, and that she was indeed Miss October. He roughly shoved Melanie out of the way and offered his hand.

"Hello, my name is Reginald, but you can call me Reggie," he said, to Fiona.

"Or Yacht Club Guy," I added.

He scowled at me before returning his attention back to Fiona.

"It's very—very nice to meet you, and might I say that you look very familiar," he said, giving Fiona the subtlest of winks.

"Is there something in your right eye?" I asked.

He turned his attention back to me for a second.

"Um, what?"

"I said—is there something in your right eye? I saw you blink kind of strangely, and I was worried there might be something in it."

Namely the visage of a beautiful Playboy centerfold I said, to myself.

"No, it's fine," he said, as he returned his full attention back to Fiona.

I saw that Melanie was looking particularly agitated, so I decided to stir the pot of her emotional turmoil.

"Melanie, since Yacht Club Guy forgot to introduce you, I'll do the honors. This is Fiona Blake. Fiona, this is Melanie," I said.

Fiona smiled and offered her hand, and Melanie tried her best to appear friendly as she reached out to take it, but she looked more as though someone were handing her dog shit.

"Well, Mel, and, Yacht Club Guy, it's been nice seeing you two, but we have dinner plans with the vice president of the United States and really need to get going."

"Very funny," Melanie said.

"I'm serious."

"Nice try."

"Swing by the Buckeye tonight, and you'll see," I said, before we walked outside and took a seat in the Range Rover.

I looked through the window of the cafe and saw both of them watching us, and Melanie looked particularly confused—obviously because of the Range Rover. When we had been dating, I had one car, and it was a silver Subaru WRX STI which she had found to be particularly embarrassing because of its enormous rear spoiler and front hood scoop. It was about the most un-Marin car a person could drive, but that only made me love it all the more, and Melanie's disgust with it even went so far that she'd actually make me park it well away from any restaurants or parties we attended. Thinking back now, it was hard to believe that I hadn't been the one to initiate our breakup, as the car was only one of the many sore spots of our six month relationship, with the worst being how she treated waitstaff. Apparently, and perhaps because of some deep seated childhood insecurity concerning her own worth, she took a great deal of pleasure in torturing the service industry by burdening them with an undue amount of extra work that included complaints such as my food is too cold, my food is too hot, and the ice in my ice water is too large. Who in the world actually sent back water because they wanted smaller ice? I would be so embarrassed at the end of a meal, that I'd tip the waitstaff double just to try and make amends, and, mind you, pouring out that kind of money hadn't been easy, as my work was erratic, and paychecks were few and far between.

Thankfully, my life had moved on for the better, and I now had plenty of money and no connection whatsoever to Melanie. I did, however, take a great deal of pleasure in slowly divulging to her, generally by divine intervention and chance meetings, that my finances and love life had taken a major turn for the better. I gave the Princess of Evil a final wave and a smile, which she, of course, didn't return, then I pulled out into the light afternoon traffic and headed north towards my place.

"So, what's up between you and Melanie?" Fiona asked.

"She's the ex whose clothes I loaned you guys last night."

"Oh, the bitch."

"Yeah, the bitch who broke up with me to be with Reginald the yacht club guy."

Fiona looked confused.

"But why?"

"Money. He had it, and I didn't."

"You're right. She really is a bitch."

"And then some."

We continued driving for a moment, then Fiona suddenly looked over at me with a concerned look in her eyes.

"Shit, am I dressed nicely enough to dine with the vice president?" she asked.

"It won't be your clothes he's looking at—and, besides, it's not like he's the president or anything. He's really just a lackey."

"He's the second most powerful man in the world."

"He's the second most powerful lackey in the world."

"I'm serious."

"Well, you were fine for lunch."

"Lunch is different."

"Do you want to go shopping before dinner?"

"Would you mind?"

"Not as long as you show me everything you try on, and no hiding in the dressing room."

"Deal."

CHAPTER NINE
Shopper's Paradise

We drove past the turn to my humble floating abode and continued north onto Highway 101 with our destination being the Village—one of the two primary malls in Southern Marin. The holiday shoppers were out in force, and the freeway was clogged with traffic, but we were fortunately a twosome and took advantage of the carpool lane until merging back over and exiting in Corte Madera. The Village was, of course, jammed, but we managed to find parking in one of the generally overlooked parallel spots that resided directly in front of the shops. We exited the safety of the Range Rover and ventured into the great abyss that was holiday shopping.

Around us hustled and bustled a cornucopia of people, and, looking at my fellow shoppers, I noticed something particularly interesting—they were all oddly agitated. People were supposed to be happy during the holidays, so happy, in fact, that they would band together with their neighbors and go out into the cold winter night for some joyous caroling. But, this wasn't exactly the case in Marin County, where its entitled populace, in spite of its vast wealth and mostly crime-free existence, seemed to be particularly stressed. While it was generally a year round phenomenon, it seemed most prevalent during the holidays. Peace and joy were fine as long as you didn't get in their way when they were trying to get a little shopping done or make it to their spinning or yoga class. Delay during any of those events was a sure fire way to get shoved, elbowed, or rundown by a shopping cart or SUV.

We reached the Apple Store without incident, and I paused to gaze in at one of my great temptations. I loved Apple products and silently cursed Steve Jobs for his brilliance in creating such an enticing retail environment, but today was about getting Fiona ready for tonight's dinner, so my tech geek side would have to wait. We continued on to Banana Republic, a place I usually avoided in favor of their outlet, but we were on a tight schedule. Entering the store, I watched as Fiona, like most of the women I had known, took to shopping the way men took to porn. I could imagine that for some, the experience was so pleasurable that it might border on orgasmic. Fiona wasn't quite so extreme, but she adapted quickly and went into hunting mode, and her eyes scanned the racks while her brain instinctively made millions upon millions of micro calculations with an efficiency that would put even the fastest super computer to shame. Color, fabric, style, and fit were just a few of the variables swirling in her mind as she moved through the racks with determined efficiency. She looked at a pantsuit and a little black dress then moved on, and, after sizing up about eight more outfits, at last settled on the second thing she had looked at—the little black dress. Fucking women. I knew exactly what she would end up choosing, but I knew that my opinion would be moot until she had finally eliminated all the other possibilities without any input from me.

"Dressing rooms?" she asked, looking at me.

"Right this way," I said.

We went to the dressing area, and she left me outside to wait, and I joined a group of men that included three husbands, one thirtysomething boyfriend, one twentysomething boyfriend, and two tween boys. In spite of the various age and relationship status differences, the one great commonality they all shared besides gender was that they were all fucking around on their phones. I took mine out and officially joined the herd when I scanned Facebook and then Instagram to see what in the hell the rest of the world was doing at the moment. As expected, it wasn't much, and the majority were mostly posting about what they were eating or who they were eating with, so it was the same ol—same ol. Just as I clicked off my iPhone and put it away, Fiona emerged from her dressing room.

"What do you think?" she asked.

Suddenly, every single pair of eyes turned away from their phone screens and focused on Fiona.

"Holy shit," the two tweens said, at the exact same time,

which made me wonder if they recognized Fiona as Miss October—either in one of their father's Playboys or possibly even on the Internet.

"I'll second that," I added.

Fiona, as I'd already seen in her Playboy spread, had quite a figure, but there was just something about how the right dress fell on a woman's curves that made them all that much more appealing. It wasn't an accident that we wrapped the Christmas presents, as it added a sense of mystery and made unwrapping them all that much more thrilling. Fiona looked exquisite and would have been a welcomed gift under any man's tree and seeing her standing there was really bringing out the holiday spirit—in my pants. Merry Christmas, penis.

"So, it's a yes?" she asked.

Everyone nodded—literally everyone.

"Good, now I just need some stockings and the right shoes."

She went back in to change then emerged a moment later, and we left the dressing room area under the watchful gaze of all those in attendance. At the last moment, I hazarded a brief glance back at the onlookers, and the two tweens smiled, then one of them held up his phone to show that he'd taken a picture. The other mumbled something under his breath that sounded a lot like Miss October, so perhaps print media wasn't dead after all.

I followed Fiona, and she grabbed a pair of stockings, then we got in line at the counter.

"What about the shoes?" I asked.

"I didn't see any that I like, so I'm going to try Nordstrom's."

"Good call," I said, recognizing that they would have the kind of variety that would guarantee success.

I slapped my card on the counter before Fiona could pull out her wallet.

"I don't want you paying for me. You're already doing enough as it is."

"It's not often that I have been in a position to pay for little things like this, so, I'd really like to be able to do this for you."

"You're helping my brother. That's what's really important."

"Exactly, so spend your money on him, and I'll take care of this. It's really not a problem," I said, as I nodded at the saleswoman to run my card.

The girl had me sign the little screen then placed the items in a bag on the counter.

"Fine, you can pay—but, just so you know, it makes me feel like a whore," Fiona said, as she turned to leave.

"I wouldn't feel like a whore," the girl behind the counter said.

"I'll keep that in mind. Happy holidays," I said, turning to follow Fiona.

She was outside and trucking along at a good clip on her way to Nordstrom by the time I caught up to her.

"Wait, slow down, whore!" I said, as I came up alongside

her.

"Not funny," she said.

"Look, I have been in your shoes most of my life, and it's only by a miracle that I have any financial security at the moment, so, that being said, I think you should swallow your pride, leaving room for dinner, of course, and let someone do you a fucking kindness."

She stopped and looked at me for a moment, before the faintest hint of a smile finally formed on her pouty lips.

"OK, Tag. I'll concede that I might have a bit too much pride at times, so, this once, I'll swallow it and let you buy me some fucking shoes—some very, very expensive fucking shoes."

"There's nothing wrong with swallowing every now and again."

She smiled and punched me in the arm, and we continued on into Nordstrom's then veered left to the women's shoe department. Interestingly, it was about six times the size of the men's—obviously because it was about six times as crowded, though we of course just happened to come during one of their massive yearly sales, and it wasn't pretty. Hordes of women were moving about the racks with the tenacity of a horde of locusts, so I decided to stay safe and moved to the side and took a seat with the other men, who stayed ever vigilant to intercede should a confrontation flare up between two women desiring the same pair of shoes. Never ever get between a woman and her shoes. I made a visual check on Fiona's whereabouts then pulled out my phone to kill some time and suddenly realized that I hadn't yet called John's potential dinner date. I found her number, hit the send button, and two rings later heard a familiar voice.

"Hey, Tag, what's up?" she asked.

"What are you doing tonight?"

"Nothing yet. Why?"

"I have someone that I'd like you to meet, so it'll be a double date."

"He better be a decent guy, because I've had bad luck with the online dating scene lately. The last asshole that messaged me for a date had a picture of himself dressed up as Han Solo on his profile. Seriously—who does that?"

"As a Star Wars fan, I kind of have to give the guy some credit."

"It might have been different if he had looked like Harrison Ford, but he looked more like Chewbacca."

"Hairy?"

"Yeah, he had one of those giant fucking hipster beards, which I can't stand, because they trap food and spit and eventually end up smelling like a hobo's taint."

"You can rest assured that he's smooth shaven and doesn't have a beard or smell like a hobo's taint."

"Is he a loser?"

"Define loser?"

"Does he have a job?"

"Yeah, but he's only the number two guy at his firm."

"A job is enough. What does he look like? Tall, dark and

handsome?"

"Yeah, and then some."

"OK, deal—but don't let me down."

"I won't. Shall we pick you up at seven?"

"Sure. What's the dress code?"

"We're going to the Buckeye, so semi-dressy."

"Got it. See you at seven."

I hit the end button and smiled. John was going to shit his pants when he saw his date, and his date, in turn, was also going to shit her pants when she saw John—assuming, of course, she decided to wear pants. As I put my iPhone back in my pocket, Fiona appeared with a pair of black leather semi-high heels.

"What do you think?"

"I like them."

"Good—now, we can go."

We went to the counter, and I dropped my card on the light grey formica and again signed the little electronic screen. The shoes were four hundred and ninety nine dollars—on sale, so I guess Fiona was going all out to test the sincerity of my offer. We left Nordstrom's and worked our way back through the endless parade of shoppers, and I found it odd how many people dressed up to go to the mall. Who were they trying to impress—the sales people or the other shoppers? It was like an interactive runway show, only the crowd were the models, and the intended audience was their own vanity. This all begged the question that if they were dressed so nicely, then what in the hell were they doing here? The last thing these people needed was more clothing.

We finally reached the car and left the land of retail and headed back to my place to get ready for our exciting date with Sasquatch. I headed into my bathroom while Fiona used the guest one next door. I realized that the cappuccino was doing its job, and that meant I'd need to take a maintenance dump to get through the evening. It wasn't by any means an emergency, and I could probably hold it, but I liked the idea of having the ol' digestive system free and clear for the evening ahead. I grabbed my iPhone and dropped onto R2-Pee-Poo and began ejecting the remnants of what I assume was breakfast. Once the entire operation was completed, I set down my iPhone and wiped, only to discover that it was unnecessary, as I'd taken what I called a teflon dump. A teflon dump was so clean and perfect that no residue remained, thereby negating any need for further toilet paper. It was a rare and coveted event and perhaps an omen of good things to come as well as a sign that John would have good news for us tonight. Still, I hit the wash button, and the soothing jet of water pelted my backside to make sure all the nooks and crannies were as clean as could be. Next came the dry cycle, then I dismounted, flushed, and stepped into the shower, soaped up, and rinsed off before exiting and toweling dry. I put on deodorant, face cream, cologne, brushed my teeth, and headed out to the bedroom to put on a white dress shirt with a black suit, though I left out the shoulder holster and pistol, as I didn't want to spook the Secret Service.

Dressed and ready for the evening, I headed downstairs and poured two small glasses of premium Soft Taco Island rum, and, a moment later, I heard footsteps coming down the stairs and looked over to see Fiona looking spectacular. I had already seen her in the dress, but now she had pulled it all together with the hair, shoes, and just a touch of makeup and some luscious red lipstick.

"Wow, I wouldn't have thought that it was possible for you to look even more beautiful."

"Thanks, you look nice too," she said, with a smile.

I handed her a glass then held mine up to toast.

"Here's to Sasquatch having some good news about your brother."

We clinked glasses and sipped our rum and enjoyed the quiet until my phone rang, and I looked down to see that it was his majesty the vice president calling. I hit accept and answered in my usual jovial tone.

"What do you want, fucker?" I asked.

"I'm outside. Interesting place—I take it this is how the other half lives?"

"Half? More like most."

"Quaint, but have you ever thought about spending any of your vast quantity of money to buy a real house?"

"I like being a man of the people."

"Well then, man of the people, drag your trashy ass out here and let's go eat."

CHAPTER TEN
Revenge is Best Served with Filet Mignon

Fiona and I made our way up to the parking lot to find a black Cadillac limousine and two sedans waiting at the entrance to the gate. The back door of the limo was open, and Sandra was keeping vigilante watch.

"Hello, Mr. Finn and Miss Blake," she said.

"Hello again, Sandra."

"Your place is amazing. You're lucky to live in such a beautiful area," she said.

"Thanks, can you repeat that for Sasquatch?"

"I would if I thought he might listen."

We entered the limo and took a seat across from John to find him sipping a martini and looking very vice presidential—vice being the operative word. Sandra joined us a moment later then closed the door and spoke into her mic that we were clear to go. The limo and its entourage of chase cars pulled out of my parking lot and headed north onto highway 101. John's blind date lived in a beautiful house out on Strawberry Point, which was an area that was once thought to be a poor man's Tiburon. Tiburon was the next peninsula over, and it stretched all the way out to Belvedere, which was yet another exclusive enclave of Marin's *über* wealthy. Over time, however, Strawberry grew in popularity because of its closer proximity to highway 101, and that lessened the commute into the city by a good twenty minutes. Now, it was as posh and snobbish as any other hamlet in Marin and boasted spectacular views of the San Francisco Bay.

We turned onto Century Drive and soon came to a stop in front of a massive terra cotta colored home which sat on the very end of the point. The house had thankfully been part of the divorce settlement and was now at last a happy place. I looked out the window and saw John's date appear from her front door, and she was looking drop dead gorgeous in a red dress and matching high heels. Sandra opened the door and greeted Jessica, and she looked more than a little baffled by the size of our entourage, and, with only one foot in the vehicle, she started in on me with a sassy comment.

"What is this, Finn? The fucking prom?" she asked.

"More like homecoming," John said, as he leaned forward to introduce himself.

Jessica turned her gaze to John, and, upon recognizing the fact that he was the vice president of the United States, suddenly looked as if she had just sat on a porcupine or perhaps even shit her pants, though it would be impossible to tell, as they were basically the same look.

"John, this is Jessica—Jessica—um—Thurman," I said, after a brief pause.

I had almost called her by her married name Jessica Green, but, thankfully, I corrected myself at the last second. That wouldn't have gone over well and was still a bit of a sore subject. I looked over and saw that John was already in love, and his eyes were ablaze with longing, and his perfectly whitened teeth were aglow behind a smile that stretched from ear to ear. Jessica held out her hand and looked equally smitten, so I had to wonder if I might have actually called this one correctly.

"I'm John Matheson," he said.

"It's OK, I know your name, sir, and I'm sorry about the little slip of the tongue just now. Somebody didn't bother to tell me who we would be dining with tonight," she said, giving me an annoyed look.

"Please, call me John, and I like a woman who can make good use of the word fuck," he said, taking her hand and offering her a seat at his side.

"Well, thank you, John."

I introduced Fiona and Jessica, and they exchanged the usual pleasantries, and soon we were on our way to the Buckeye Roadhouse, which was probably the best, although priciest local restaurant. It had once been a quaint little family owned German style Hofbrau, but, after new ownership and a major facelift in the eighties, it had become one of Marin's busiest nightspots. We pulled up in front, and Sandra and another agent accompanied us into the restaurant, which, as usual, was particularly crowded. We managed to squeeze through the waiting people, and more than a few gave us a double take as they recognized John and possibly Fiona. We reached the hostess stand and were greeted by a pretty girl with long dark curly hair and spectacular composure, considering the large number of people she was currently facing—let alone the fact that she had a last minute reservation by the vice president of the United States. She immediately introduced herself then led us to our table, where she handed us menus and asked if we would like to start with any drinks. John ordered a bottle of wine, and, a short time later, our waitress appeared and allowed his majesty the vice president to do the obligatory smug taste test protocol. John rolled it around in his glass, had a sniff, then took a sip before finally nodding his official approval for the waitress to fill our glasses. Once she was finished, I held my wine aloft and looked to the others.

"What shall we toast to?" I asked.

"New beginnings," John said, smiling at Jessica.

Everyone clinked glasses and sipped the wine, which turned out to be particularly delicious and a sign that the vice president was at least good for something. Jessica caught my eye and gave me a smile, so I think she was pleased with her date. Of course, I had already been secretly pondering that they might make a nice couple but never imagined having the luck to actually get them in the same place at the same time—considering that John lived in Washington and Jessica lived here. On a more personal level, I sincerely believed that each of them deserved to meet a special person and hopefully settle down, and, just as that thought passed, Jessica looked at me and shook her head and smiled.

"What is it?" I asked.

"Now I get it. Number two guy at his firm. Very funny, Finn," she said.

John laughed.

"Yeah, he seems to take a lot of joy from that fact."

"It's not exactly a bad thing to be the number two guy at your firm," Jessica said.

"Thank you, at least somebody appreciates me," John said.

"Everyone needs at least one admirer," I added.

"So, John, how the hell did you and Finn meet?"

"Afghanistan, and Finn, believe it or not, saved my life," John said, his voice turning serious as his mind traveled back to that painful episode.

He went on to tell Jessica how he had dropped off a SEAL Team on a mountain top in Afghanistan, but, when it turned out the landing zone was overrun with Taliban, he went back in for a pickup, and his helicopter was hit by a RPG. He was forced to crash land, and the violence of the impact killed his crew and broke both of his legs in the process, and, as he lay there trapped in the wreckage, he was sure, in his heart of hearts, that he was going to die on that mountain—cold, alone, and thousands of miles from home. That is, until he heard my voice come out of the darkness.

"And what did the ever charming Finn say?" Jessica asked.

"You look like shit, John."

"Couldn't you have said something a little more heroic?" Fiona suggested.

"He really did look like shit, so I was just being honest."

"Yeah, but I nearly cried when I heard him speak those words to me that night, and, even now, I still practically cry whenever I repeat them, because that asshole managed to carry me on his back for seven kilometers while the Taliban tried their best to kill us. The only reason I'm alive today is because of fucking Finn," John said, sounding a little choked up.

"Quite a night," I said.

"Yeah, and in some ways, it was worst and best night of my life," John added.

"How do you mean that?" Jessica asked, sounding intrigued.

"You never appreciate what you have—your life, your friends, your family—any of it—until the moment when you might lose it all, and suddenly, everything that is important in your life comes into perspective."

There was a moment of silence while everyone sipped their wine and pondered John's words. Most people would thankfully never experience anything like that, but it really gave those who did a new appreciation for life. I looked across at John, and he gave me a knowing smile. It was easy to forget the craziness of that time, but it never left you completely, and the only ones who understood your experience were the ones who were there. Ironically, there was often nothing like combat to cement the bonds of humanity, and it was stranger still to think that John and I lived in completely different worlds, but, ultimately, because of our shared experience, were closer than brothers—which is also probably why we enjoyed giving each other so much shit.

Our waitress returned and asked if we wanted to start with any appetizers, but everyone was hungry and ready for the main course, so we decided to order dinner. I went with the filet mignon, and Fiona chose the same, which I found surprising, as I would have thought of her as the gentle chicken and salad type. John went with the pork chop, and Jessica got the Petrale sole. All in all, they were all good choices, though it was hard to go wrong at the Buckeye. You paid a pretty penny, but you got a good meal for your money.

John also ordered another bottle of wine, and, in the meantime, he and Jessica talked in depth and seemed to be enjoying each other's company. I had a feeling that was going to be the case, in spite of the fact that I hadn't actually known Jessica all that long. Sure, I'd known John since my days in the service, but I only recently met Jessica when her husband hired me to follow her and get proof that she was having an affair with her personal trainer. She was indeed having an affair, but it was in response to her husband's infidelity, and he turned out to be a major league asshole. I gave him back his money then warned Jessica of her impending divorce, and now she was a free woman with a sizable settlement. Unfortunately, her boyfriend, a guy I nicknamed Tarzan, was a bit commitment phobic, and apparently preferred relationships with married women, so, Jessica was soon single. A couple months later, we reconnected, and, after a mostly innocent though wild night of private room karaoke, we became good friends.

The wine and food arrived, and we ate, drank, talked, and enjoyed a lovely evening. Once the plates were cleared and the diners properly sated, it was time to get to the real business of the evening—namely Fiona's predicament.

"So, Sasquatch, any news on Fiona's brother?"

"What's happened with your brother?" Jessica asked Fiona.

Fiona quickly explained her brother's predicament, and Jessica reached across and took hold of her hand in a nice show of sympathy.

"Oh my God, I'm so sorry," Jessica said.

John cleared his throat and was looking a bit self-satisfied.

"Well, I have good news," he said, smiling smugly.

"What is it?" Fiona asked expectantly, the anticipation obvious as she leaned forward in her chair.

"Apparently, the number two guy can actually get something done. Malkarta has agreed to release Mark as long as he leaves the island immediately and unconditionally agrees never to return without the express written permission of the monarchy. I've already made some calls and even secured the Vandenberg jet, so you two can leave tomorrow, pick him up, and be home in time for Christmas."

Fiona's eyes filled with tears as she jumped up from her seat and went around the table towards John. He stood up to greet her, and he was nearly knocked down by her enthusiasm when she leapt upon him and delivered a bear-like hug as she thanked him profusely. He appeared to be genuinely touched, so I figured it was an excellent opportunity to give him a little shit.

"Up in your ivory tower it's probably hard to imagine, but this is what helping people feels like in person," I said.

"Really—and do all your clients have such strong arms?" he said, looking a little surprised as he gazed at me over Fiona's shoulder.

"I think you meant to say big boobs, and yes they do."

"Then I clearly chose the wrong occupation."

"No, you definitely didn't," Fiona said, as she let go of John and came over to me.

I stood up, and she hugged me as well, though I also got a kiss on the cheek. John thankfully saw it and gave me a frown and a little shrug.

"Honestly, I think she hugged me a little harder—but whatever," he said.

Fiona sat back down and couldn't stop smiling as she gazed at me.

"See? I told you that I had a friend who might be able to help," I said.

"Tag, you're a miracle worker, and I will seriously owe you for life."

"Don't worry about it. Helping people is what I do."

"Yeah, when you're not laying on the couch and crafting little animals with the lint you harvest from your bellybutton," John said.

"The very same lint that I used to make you a Teddy Bear last Christmas."

"Well, you'll be happy to know that I love that little guy just as much as if he were made with the lint harvested from my own bellybutton."

Jessica cleared her throat and interrupted our man banter in the hope of changing the subject away from bellybutton lint.

"So, what exactly is this Vandenberg jet?" she asked.

I smiled as I thought about the good times I'd had aboard the flying fortress of fornication.

"It's just the private jet of the Vandenberg Corporation. They loan it out on occasion to the government in return for special favors," John said.

"Must be nice," Jessica responded.

"Oh—it is," I said.

I refilled our wine glasses with the remainder of the wine and held mine up to toast.

"To Sasquatch, may his generosity and exceptional moral character take him to the White House one day—as the president," I said.

Everyone clinked glasses and sipped their wine, all the while relishing such a nice moment amongst friends both new and old. I suddenly realized that all the food and wine was making for an incredibly uncomfortable bladder.

"If you ladies don't mind, I need to excuse myself to go take a horse piss."

"Do you need me to come along to help you get your pee-pee out your pants?" John asked.

"Yet another excuse for you to touch my privates."

"Like I need one."

"Do they always talk to each other this way?" Jessica asked Fiona.

"From what I've seen, I'd have to say yes."

"I'll be back," I said, standing up and feeling the full weight of all the food and drink that I had consumed.

"I'll join you," John said, also standing and patting his stomach.

"Oh, are you two sneaking off so you can gossip?" Fiona asked.

"Yeah, I suspect John probably wants to talk about Jessica's boobs."

"Really?" Jessica asked.

"Guilty as charged," John responded.

We left the girls and ventured towards the men's room, with Sandra leading the way and all eyes on the his majesty the vice president. We entered the baño and found it empty except for the unusual fact that Sandra had followed us in and was now standing by the door.

"Do you always have to accompany Sasquatch into the bathroom?" I asked.

"Yeah, sadly."

"I imagine that could get a bit awkward."

"Absolutely."

"I think of her as my number two wingman," John said, saddling up to one of the two urinals.

I walked past and was about to enter the standard stall when John spoke up.

"What? Are you too good to piss next to the vice president?"

"No, I was just giving you some breathing room."

"My dick's not that big. Come on, don't be such a pussy."

"Hey, I know how you get when you pull that fucker out."

"Seriously, dude—do you still have your bathroom issues?"

"What do you mean?"

"The public restroom thing. You know—the fact that you won't use a bathroom anywhere but home."

I glanced at Sandra and saw that she was smiling and trying not to laugh.

"Yeah, mostly, but that doesn't include peeing."

"So, pee."

"I will," I said, as I continued towards the stall.

"Not in there, Frodo. Right here next to me."

"If I'm Frodo, then you know that makes you Sam the fat hobbit."

"Sam the fat hobbit with the giant dick."

"You mean the average dick that only looks giant because it's on a hobbit."

"Whatever, Frodo—now, man up and get over here."

I begrudgingly came back and saddled up to the urinal beside John, pulled Tag Junior from my pants, and stared at the pee spot—the mythological place on the wall directly in front of my eyes that all men looked at when standing beside another man in a public restroom. The theory was that it made it very clear that you were not checking each other out and therefore eased the tension of peeing in close proximity to others. There was even psychological research on this very subject that discovered that the closer men were to each other when peeing, the longer it took for them to start urinating. Bearing all that in mind, I stood and tried my best, but no urine would come out. I realized, however, that the problem wasn't necessarily John, but also that I desperately had to fart but didn't want to do so in front of Sandra. I couldn't release one without the other. Fuckinzee.

"I don't hear anything," John said.

"Focus on your own shit."

Another long moment of silence passed and still no flow.

"Maybe you should get your prostate checked."

"Maybe you should fuck off."

"Wow, strong language. Do you kiss your mother with that mouth?"

"No, I kiss yours."

"Look dude. I'm serious about your prostate. I could check it right now. Only take a second," John said, holding up two fingers.

"Hell no, you've got hands like a farmer."

John started peeing, and I heard a great healthy stream

and thought about nudging him with my shoulder but knew that he'd just turn the flow on me. Instead, I decided to wait him out, and soon he finished up without so much as the tiniest freep, the definition of which being a gaseous release so small that it didn't even qualify as a fart. He zipped up and moved to the sink to wash his hands.

"OK, Frodo, we'll be outside, so you're free to let her rip," he said, as he and Sandra walked out the door.

With the door open, the loud clatter of the restaurant temporarily filled the restroom, and I decided it was a perfect time to let loose my simmering flatulence. It blew from my backside with unbridled fury, and the violence of its passage became more apparent when the door closed and brought forth a quiet that allowed the deep bellowing tone of my fart to echo off the hard tiled walls and floor. I had just pushed out the final aftershock when a figure appeared beside me in a captain's hat. Fuck! It was Yacht Club Guy, so I was guessing he must have slipped in as John left, and now he was giving me a rather sour look. Apparently, he wasn't too excited about my fart, but I suspect he might have just been a tad bit jealous.

"Oh hello, Yacht Club Guy. I just made you something very special. Sorry, I couldn't wait until Christmas to give it to you."

"How thoughtful," he said, casting me a scornful gaze before turning to stare at his own pee spot.

I finished urinating, washed my hands, then headed out of the bathroom knowing full well that if Yacht Club guy was here then so too was Melanie. It turned out that she was patiently waiting directly outside for her man, but her gaze, however, was focused on a particularly important and famous person—namely John. I joined him, keenly aware that Melanie was now watching us very intently.

"All done! I went pee-pee like a big boy!" I said.

"Did you remember to wash your hands?"

"I sure did," I said, holding them up at John.

John and Sandra then exchanged some quiet words and looked a wee bit concerned.

"What is it? They don't look clean enough?" I asked.

"Your hands are fine, but we are curious about the woman behind you with the staring problem."

"What about her?"

"Sandra was getting a little concerned that I might have a stalker," he said.

"Oh, that's just my ex Melanie, and the dude in the sailor's hat who just exited the bathroom is the guy she left me for," I said, pointing at Yacht Club Guy.

"Ouch. That must have hurt."

"Only the first two months. After that I started sending him thank you cards."

"Interesting. So, is Melanie a threat?"

"Only if you decide to date her."

"Good to know, though I can't help but wonder why she'd leave you for Yacht Club Guy? It obviously wasn't because of looks."

"In case you haven't already guessed, it was about money."

"So, does Melanie know that you're now worth a bazillion dollars?" John asked extra loudly.

"Assuming she's listening as intently as I think she is, then yes," I responded, desperately wanting to kiss John for his incredible insight and timing.

We turned and walked back to the table and left Melanie in probably the most depressed state of her adult life. She was a money grubber and a social climber and just realized that she had failed miserably at both. Live, learn, and be as nice as possible to all the people you meet, because you never know where you or they might end up.

We rejoined the ladies and decided to share two double chocolate layer cakes. I usually didn't order dessert, but the night, thanks to John, was officially a celebration, so why not splurge? The cake arrived, and we tried to be polite by eating daintily, but soon it was a veritable battle with Fiona quite nimbly nabbing the last bite. She was nice enough to split it with me, and, after we finished up, John paid the bill. With dinner officially over, we exited the main dining room, and this took us past the bar, where I spied Melanie and Yacht Club Guy. I smiled and waved but got no response, which was actually the response I was hoping to elicit, as it meant that she was quietly brooding over tonight's revelations. The man she cheated on, who didn't make enough money for her expensive tastes, was now a multi-millionaire and close personal friend of the vice president of the United States. It didn't get any better than that—or worse from Melanie's perspective.

"She's actually very attractive," John said.

"Not on the inside, sadly."

We exited the Buckeye, bypassed the valet's station, and entered the limo, which was idling at the edge of the parking lot. Once inside, John looked at us expectantly.

"What now?" he asked.

"After dinner drinks with the proletariat on my shitty houseboat?"

"I'd love an after dinner drink with the proletariat on your shitty houseboat."

"It's settled then," I said.

Sandra got on her radio.

"It looks like we're going to Finn's shitty houseboat for drinks with the proletariat," she said.

CHAPTER ELEVEN
Handy in the Bedroom

We made the short trip back to my place and settled into the living room. Jennifer and John sat on the couch while Fiona and I took up residence by the fireplace, where I soon had a glowing fire filling the room with soft light and warmth. I brought up a Pandora music mix on my Apple TV, and, now that we had the mood, it was time for the drinks. I went to my bar and returned with a bottle of Soft Taco Island rum and four glasses then filled each one with rum and handed them around before taking a seat beside Fiona.

"John, do you own a Han Solo costume?" I asked.

"Sure. Doesn't every man?"

"Very funny, Finn," Jessica said.

"To new beginnings and drinks among the proletariat," I said, holding up my glass and smiling at Jessica.

We drank and talked well into the night, and I was pretty damn sure at this point that I had chosen wisely in uniting John and Jessica. The interesting part, however, would be to see if their budding relationship lasted past this evening. John was a bit of a player by nature, but deep down, I knew he was ready to be a one woman man. I know his father would be thrilled, as he had actually called and confided in me only a month previously that he was worried John might never reach the presidency if he didn't fall in love, settle down, and get married. History had actually showed that the elder Matheson was correct in his assumption, as only two presidents had been bachelors—James Buchanan and Grover Cleveland, though the latter married during his first term. But, more than just wanting to be president, I think John wanted to find someone special. Sure, it was fun to be a dick swinging bachelor, but, ultimately, it was an empty existence. I knew the feeling all too well, as I had yet to find the right girl at the right time. People were all on different cycles of life and finding someone on your same cycle only seemed to get harder with time.

Eventually the night came to an end when John and Jessica departed, and, while John was supposedly just dropping Jessica back at her house, I suspected other things were on the itinerary, though I'd have to wait until morning to find out. My house was now very quiet with Fiona and me finally alone.

"Long day tomorrow, so I suppose we should get some sleep," I said.

We headed upstairs and retreated to our respective bathrooms to brush our teeth before meeting in the doorway to my room, where we spent an awkward moment with neither of us sure what to say until I finally broke the silence.

"Do you want to stay in here or the guest bedroom?" I asked.

"Here," she said, as she strolled in and undressed before my eyes and slid into bed.

I stripped down and joined her, and she immediately cuddled up to me and wrapped her long leg over mine. We lay there in the silence of the night, and the wind outside whistled as it blew through the rigging of the nearby sailboats. Suddenly, she leaned over and kissed me, and soon thereafter her mouth opened, and her tongue darted in to meet mine. I was caught off guard but quick enough to respond in kind, and soon I was up to speed, and my heart was racing and my head spinning. I was smitten with Fiona, but our union was of such a precarious nature that I wanted to tread lightly.

Fiona, however, seemed to feel differently, and what started as a simple spark was soon a blazing fire. Our mouths were entwined, and it was only a matter of time before our hands were exploring each other's bodies, and Fiona came across my manhood, which had already set up camp and had made a hell of a tent under the blanket. She ran her fingers up and down its length then encircled the tip between her thumb and forefinger before starting anew.

Not to be outdone, I too ventured forth and used my finger tips to tease each of her nipples to life. It took hardly a moment before each was fully erect, and I moved my hand south over her stomach before cresting over a small rise to find a lush valley, where the slightest touch made Fiona's heart race. We were firmly embroiled in a foreplay fiesta, with Fiona stroking my mantool and I gently caressing her lady trigger. The passion was growing in intensity, and our breathing was harried and our efforts more urgent, until she suddenly pulled back and gazed at me with her face contorted into a strange combination of uncertainty and longing.

"Fuck me, I can't do this," she said.

"Wait—I'm not sure how to interpret that statement. Do you mean the first part or the second?"

"Both—er, fuck—I mean the second part. I'm sorry—I don't know how to explain it."

"It's OK, I find it particularly comforting when a woman suddenly pulls away from me in a moment of passion."

"It's not what you think. I mean—I really want to have sex with you, but…"

"But you're in love with Yacht Club Guy?"

"Don't be stupid. The thing I'm trying to say is that I'm worried that sex will feel like some kind of compensation for you helping me with my brother, and I want it to be purely because it's something I want to do."

"Well, it's definitely something I want to do."

"Me too, but all of this is just a lot to process right now.

I mean fuck—you really know how to sweep a girl off her feet. First you saved my life and then you get your friend the vice president of the United States to get my brother freed from prison. I mean, how is a girl supposed to deal with all that?

"By being happy, hopefully."

"Oh, I'm happy all right, but the problem is that I've always solved my own problems, so I'm not comfortable with the idea of needing help from people. It's like I told you at the mall. I don't want to feel like a whore."

"What if all the people across the world that your brother helped felt like whores?"

"It's different."

"Not really—everybody needs help at some time in their life, and it doesn't make them whores."

"Fuck—I'm a massive pain in the ass, aren't I?"

"No, you're more of a pain in my balls—but it's OK— I'm used to dealing with it."

"I'm sorry."

"Don't be. There's nothing wrong with waiting until it feels right."

Fiona dropped back down onto my chest and snuggled up alongside me.

"Will you be able to sleep with that massive boner?"

"Yeah, I'll be fine. How about you?"

"I think I'll be fine too."

"Then we really should get some sleep, as we've got a big day tomorrow."

"Yeah, I guess so. Good night, Tag."

"Good night, Fiona."

We lay there in the quiet of the night, but, as I tried to fall asleep, Fiona reached out and felt my boner.

"Still hard, I see."

"Yep."

I reached down and placed my hand over her lady parts.

"And you're still a wee warm," I said.

"Yeah, and a bit moist."

"Would oral sex be crossing the line?" I asked.

"Probably, but I could really use it."

"There's always the Dutch rudder."

"Or sixty-nine, but wouldn't that count as sex?"

"Not sure—it's mutually beneficial with both parties giving and receiving."

"OK, fuck it! I have an idea. Sit up and face me," she said.

We both sat up and knelt on the bed and faced each other in the dim blue light of the partial moon.

"We're gong to masturbate together. Now, follow my lead," she said.

She reached down and began making slow deliberate circles of her clitoris, and I sat there feeling a bit awkward as I watched.

"You can join in anytime," she said.

"I was taking it slower, thinking I might finish sooner."

"I doubt it, and you should also feel free to cum on my chest."

"Seriously?"

"Yeah."

"Lovely—I think your boobs will provide some excellent encouragement."

I took hold of Tag Junior and, as I set to work matching Fiona's pace, she used her other hand to caress her nipples. It was a lot of visual stimulation, and it was bringing me closer to release while also making me feel even more desperate to make love to the Fiona. The frustration gradually grew as I drew nearer to release, and I could see in Fiona's eyes a similar longing until it all came to a head, and she spoke.

"Oh my God! I want you inside of me right now."

"Wait—I'm confused—are you violating our mutual masturbation agreement?"

"No, well, yes. I mean no. I'm just saying what I'm thinking out loud. Oh fuck, I'm gonna cum."

"Me too," I said, frantically.

Just as she began to climax, she leaned close and kissed me, and the move was so startling that it sent me over the edge as though she had passed me a metaphorical sex baton, and sweet release came shooting forth from my manhood. At last, we stopped, and she wrapped her arms around me and held me tightly as our heartbeats slowly dropped back down to normal.

"I guess we should clean up now," I said.

"Yeah, you made quite a mess. You should have cum on my chest."

"In the heat of the moment, I unfortunately forgot."

"Oh well, maybe next time," she said.

We got up, and I grabbed a towel from the bathroom and cleaned up the bed, then we jumped in the shower for a quick rinser. Clean and feeling the mellow oncoming of post coital relaxation, we adjourned to the bed but were careful to avoid the wet spot. It meant both of us crowding to one side, but I was happy to get as close as possible to my lovely houseguest. We assumed a spooning position and settled in for yet another night of cuddling.

"So, is that something you do often?" I asked.

"Nope, first time, and it was pretty fucking erotic actually."

"It was—though a little frustrating. It's hard to see someone that I want to touch so badly—and not touch them."

"I agree, but that's what made it so exciting."

Fiona steered my hand over her breast, and her substantial nipple slipped between my fingers and made for a perfect fit as I drifted off to yet another night of glorious sleep beside the beautiful Fiona Blake.

Morning came, just as we had the night before, rather abruptly and without mercy, and the light was spilling in through the blinds that I had forgotten to close. I looked at the clock and saw that it was eight seventeen in the morning, so I slid out of bed, brushed my teeth, took a massive horse piss, then headed downstairs to make coffee. When the pot finished brewing, I filled two cups, added cream, and headed upstairs to find Fiona was awake and sitting up in bed, with her bare breasts serving as a lovely reminder of the night before. It was a tad bit chilly, and her nipples were looking particularly pokey and, like the eyes in certain paintings, seemed to be following my progress as I walked to the bed and handed her a cup of coffee. She took her first sip then smiled and cradled the warm mug to her chest.

"Coffee in bed? I may never want to go home."

"I believe it's a tradition after experiencing your first mutual masturbation session."

"Speaking of which—what the hell was the name of that weird sex act you mentioned last night?"

"The Dutch rudder?"

"Yeah."

"Well, according to the movie *Zack and Miri Make a Porno*, it's when two people reach across and direct the other person's arm while masturbating. That way, you're technically still only touching yourself."

"So, what kind of movies do you watch?"

"Awesome ones, obviously."

"Well, that one sounds like a porno."

"Only in name, but in reality it's actually a sweet romantic comedy."

"Seriously?"

"Yeah."

"And what other kinds of movies do you watch?"

"All kinds, though I'm especially drawn to anything by Wes Anderson, Paul Thomas Anderson, Judd Apatow, Spielberg, Lucas, J.J. Abrams, Kevin Smith, Taika Waititi, and Kevin O. Russel in spite of the fact that he can supposedly be kind of a psycho on set."

Fiona nodded her approval, but then it would be hard to argue against any of those filmmakers, as their work was universally beloved. We continued to enjoy the morning by sipping our coffee and chatting about our various interests until Fiona segued to the day's events.

"So, what exactly is the plan today?"

"Pretty straightforward. We get dressed then pack and head off to the Western Pacific on the Vandenberg jet."

"I've never been on a private jet."

"Then I'm afraid you haven't truly lived. It's fucking amazing and a far cry from flying commercial."

We finished our coffee then retreated to our respective bathrooms to get ready for the day. I shaved then made a quick run downstairs for more coffee, as the extra caffeine was a sure way to be guaranteed a perfect dump. I heard the water running next door, and that meant Fiona was already in the shower, so I decided to live dangerously and skip closing the bathroom door. Instead, I set my cup on the sink, grabbed my iPhone, and then hit the heater button for R2-Pee-Poo. He heated up incredibly quickly, so it only took a second before I was dropping down into his loving embrace. There was nothing quite as soothing and proactive as a warm toilet seat, as the heat just had a way of opening up the back door and making everything flow smoothly. An old school standard toilet had no such conveniences, and the cold could have a tendency to close the body down and trap the torpedoes before they could leave the submarine—so to speak. Of course the pivotal detail in this scenario was that the heating had to be a mechanical feature, because a warm toilet seat in the old days meant that someone had just vacated it, and that made the experience a bit unappealing. Therefore, the most luxurious number two entailed an electronically heated toilet seat like the one in my beloved R2-Pee-Poo.

"Pee poo-pee poo-pee poo," I said, in a little robot voice as I got comfortable on the luxuriously warm seat.

"What was that noise you just made," Fiona asked, as she suddenly appeared at the open doorway to the bathroom.

Startled, I jumped off of R2 and moved with the swiftness of a circus performer being shot out of a cannon. Fiona, however, was completely unperturbed and continued to stand there and smile at me.

"What noise?" I asked.

"That little robot sound—pee poo-pee poo."

"Oh nothing. I call my toilet R2-Pee-Poo and imagine him saying that to me when I sit down."

"Then you're obviously a Star Wars fan."

"Isn't everybody?"

"I guess so—some obviously more than others."

"Yeah, anyway—what do you need?" I asked, my heart still pounding as I stood naked beside my toilet now feeling like an even more awkward version of C3Po—the only difference being that I had genitals and the ability to take a shit that was more than nuts, bolts, and gear oil.

"You didn't need to get up on my account. You could have just continued with what you were doing."

"Very funny. I'm not getting anywhere near that fucker with you right here in the room."

"Why not? It's a perfectly natural bodily function. Everyone does it—even centerfolds."

"I know, but I can't. It's my Achilles Heel. Indiana Jones has snakes. Superman has kryptonite. Ironman has alcohol and women, and I have the bathroom."

"That's sad."

"Why?"

"Because you have to use a bathroom every day. It would be a very limiting way to live."

"Fuck—I never thought about it that way. I hope you're happy that you've not only interrupted my dump—but brought my lifelong eccentricities into great moral and practical question."

"It wasn't my intention."

"So, what did you want?"

"Shampoo," she said, walking closer.

"Oh, right here," I said, reaching into the lower cupboard and grabbing a bottle.

"Thanks."

"No problem, and that brand really makes my hair shiny and clean."

"You're joking, right?'

"Look at my beautiful fucking hair."

She glanced at my hair, frowned, then turned her gaze down into the toilet, but thankfully I hadn't released so much as a breakfast sausage. That's it—from here on out, I needed to be more vigilant and always, always close and lock the fucking door.

"Feel free to blow Santa out of the chimney now," Fiona said, as she turned to leave.

"And the elves—maybe even the reindeer."

"I stopped listening at elves."

She left, and I locked the door and headed back to the toilet and was about to sit down when she tried the knob then knocked again. I walked back over and unlocked the door.

"What's up?" I asked.

"You don't need to lock the door."

"I do, and you coming back and trying to open it is proof of that fact."

"You fucking just jacked off in front of me last night. I think I can deal with you taking a shit."

"No."

"Seriously?"

"Yeah, but I'll think about it. I really will."

"You will be a happier person if you can get over this."

"I'm afraid it's time to get ready, and, more importantly,

you're wasting water," I said.

She nodded disapprovingly as she walked out and at last left me free to continue. I closed the door, locked it, and returned to R2-Pee-Poo.

"Pee poo, pee poo—ooooooh," I said, with the last note descending into R2-D2's signature sad tone.

I sat, took a sip of coffee, and, as Fiona suggested, blew Santa, his elves, and at least one reindeer out of the chimney. What the hell did I eat yesterday? I had my iPhone beside me but refrained from using it, as I was still a little too rattled to enjoy any digital entertainment after Fiona's unplanned intrusion. I finished up and flushed the entirety of the North Pole down the toilet, then unlocked the door before getting into the shower. Five minutes later, I was out and drying off when Fiona reappeared with a towel wrapped around her midsection and one around her head. She used my deodorant and face cream, and it was yet another bizarrely intimate moment for two people residing firmly on the fringe of a non-intimate relationship. This, of course, made me think back to the female guest who hired me to go rescue her sister from Soft Taco Island. Ironically, she had used sex to get me to help her while Fiona was avoiding sex because I was helping her. Fuck, none of it made sense, but at least I was getting out of the house for a little excitement.

We got dressed and headed downstairs for breakfast and, unlike the previous morning's scramble, went slightly healthier by choosing eggs, toast, and Irish oatmeal. Done, we cleaned up, bagged the trash, then brushed our teeth one final time before loading up and heading to the car. This time, I decided to give Fiona a little test and see how she reacted to my Silver Hornet. That was my pet name for my silver 2005 Subaru WRX STi, and its name was a direct homage to the Pink Panther movies and, more specifically, Inspector Clouseau's winged silver Citroen. Mine, like his, had an enormous wing, but it was definitely not a piece of shit and, quite to the contrary, was the most affordable super car a person could buy. For thirty grand it had race car performance and Subaru reliability, though the only drawback was the scorn it elicited from fellow Marinites, who wouldn't be caught dead in anything less than a BMW, Audi, or a Mercedes. So, Fiona's reaction in my choosing this car over the Range Rover, Mini Cooper S, or the Porsche would tell me a lot about whether or not she had superficial tendencies. My initial guess would be that she was beyond such personality flaws, but it would be an interesting experiment nonetheless. We dumped the garbage, set the alarm, and said goodbye to my quiet little slice of paradise on the water.

CHAPTER TWELVE
Everything but the Kitchen Sink

We were traveling to the tropics, though I wasn't sure if we were doing a quick turnaround or spending a couple days, and that meant we might actually have a little down time to hit the beach and do some snorkeling. That part of the Pacific was, like Hawaii, a tropical paradise, so naturally I'd love to get in the water. To that end, I figured I might need a few things—namely my dive mask, snorkel, and fins.

I kept the majority of my man goodies in my man cave, so we walked over to my building, but, as it was primarily a work trip, I also decided I might as well bring a pistol. My main gun stash was a large hidden closet back on my houseboat that I called my man room, but the one here was kind of its bigger twin brother and included a full length indoor firing range. After opening the secret door, a bookcase on hinges, I grabbed a pistol and a silencer, which was probably overkill—both literally and figuratively, but it afforded me the comfort a child might get from a teddy bear, only my teddy bear was made in Germany and fired 9mm bullets. I pondered grabbing my HK 94 submachine gun or perhaps an M4 Assault Rifle but abstained, as I realized that this was by all accounts a diplomatic mission, and there was little or no chance that I'd need that kind of firepower. It looked as though I was going to do it James Bond style, and that meant I only needed a girl and a gun. With the final bit of my packing complete, I gazed towards my cars.

"I'm thinking about taking the STi for our trip to the airport. Any thoughts?" I asked.

"Sweet! I love that car."

"You know about the STi?"

"I'm a gearhead."

I regarded her a moment.

"Really?"

"Really," she responded.

"Do you watch Top Gear or The Grand Tour?"

"Both, though it still bothers me that the BBC fired Jeremy."

Fiona, as it turned out, was into cars, which, of course, was now sending copious amounts of blood flowing into my gentleman region.

"Would it be weird if I whipped out my wiener and started masturbating?"

"After last night? Not really."

I decided to forego the whacking and instead threw our things in the trunk then opened the garage door.

"Do you want to drive?" I asked.

"Hell yeah," she said, as she got in on the drivers side and immediately placed one hand on the wheel and the other on the gear shifter.

"Nice! You've got the short shift kit."

"Of course. I'm a man."

I jumped in on the passenger's side, and she started the Silver Hornet and eased her out of the garage, and we drove out of the parking lot then turned right onto Gate Five Road.

"I've had some additional work done, so you'll want to be a little gentle with the gas pedal."

She looked over and delivered a peculiar smile, and I wasn't quite sure how to read her expression—until she put the hammer down and sent me flying back into my seat. The wheels chirped for a mere second before the Subaru's advanced all-wheel drive system properly placed the power on the road and sent us barreling forward like the fucking Millennium Falcon making the jump to light speed. She reached the intersection and made a hard right turn and sent the back end out before expertly counter steering and bringing the car quickly back in line. Holy fuck! Fiona could drive.

"OK, that's it! I'm going to pull my dick out and start masturbating right now."

"Be my guest, but you might want to finish up quick. On

a nice day like this, there's bound to be a lot of tourists out on the bridge."

"Not a problem. A couple more turns like the last one, and I'll be done."

She smiled then cut over into the left turn lane and downshifted using proper heel-toe technique that set my heart aflutter.

"You always drive like this?" I asked.

"Sometimes, but right now I'm just fucking with you. Of course, I do come from a family of gearheads, and my dad had my brother and me racing karts as soon as we could walk. My brother quit in high school, but I continued all the way through college."

"Do you actually have your own cart?"

"Yeah, got it in kit form and built it with my dad."

"Where is it now?"

"Stored at the racetrack—that way I can go up anytime and get some laps in."

"Why didn't you put that in your bio?"

"Gotta hold something back to keep me interesting."

"Don't worry about that. You're plenty interesting."

"Even with my clothes on?"

"Especially with your clothes on."

We made the tight right hand turn onto Highway 101, and Fiona again put the hammer down and flew through the gears and rocketed up the Waldo Grade before eventually easing off the throttle and bringing us down to a cool sixty nine miles per hour—the number reminding me of last night and bringing yet another surge of blood to my gentleman region. Soon, we were across the Golden Gate Bridge and working our way to Fiona's apartment in Laurel Village. We found a spot on the cross street then headed around the corner and into her apartment, which resided on the top floor. Fiona opted that we take the stairs rather than the rickety old elevator, and I was pretty sure it was decisions like that which allowed her to maintain such a fabulous figure.

We reached the top floor and entered her one bedroom apartment, and I was surprised to see it was sparsely furnished and looked as though she hadn't been living in it for very long. She saw my expression and answered my question before I even asked it.

"Yeah, I know. It's a little sparse, as I moved here two months after graduation and didn't imagine I'd be here all that long."

"Well—at least it's easy to keep clean."

As she left the living room, she gestured for me to follow, and we entered Fiona's bedroom, which was a place I was particularly curious about, because it would hopefully offer some more insight into her personality. In high school, this piece of personal space was about posters and music, but later in life it was more about pictures and artwork. I looked around the room and was relieved to see that Fiona had at least managed to create a semblance of life, and there were pictures of her and her family and even one which showed her in some exotic place with her brother.

"Wow, is that Rwanda?" I asked.

"Yeah, I spent the summer before graduate school working with my brother. I take it you've been there?"

"Yeah, I went there once for work."

"As a private investigator?" she asked.

"No, this was while I was working for the government."

"Oh, so what were you doing there?"

"Rescuing an American aid worker who had been kidnapped."

"Sounds exciting."

"Fairly."

"Interesting—were you by chance in the CIA?"

"Me? A spy? Hardly," I said, laughing.

"Yeah, you—the guy with the man cave full of all kinds of questionable firearms, who just also happens to be the best friend of the vice president. Seriously now, what else do people in the special operations do after they leave the military?"

"Besides scrapbooking, knitting, and trouser tenting?"

"Yeah besides those things."

"I wouldn't know."

She let the subject drop, but I was pretty sure that she knew exactly what I had done after leaving military service. It was an awkward subject, and one I wasn't legally supposed to speak of, yet it was the first question everyone asked. Fiona pulled a flower print suitcase from her closet and started opening drawers and pulling out clothes, and I started to worry about how much she was packing, considering the fact that our trip would probably be nothing more than an overnight excursion. She grabbed pants, shirts, dresses, shorts, and skirts, with the latter two being the only things she would likely wear in the hot tropical climate of Malkarta. Next, she moved on to more exciting stuff like underwear, bras, and bathing suits, and, as she was stuffing a tiny white bikini into her suitcase, a pair of lacy thong underwear fell to the floor.

"Victoria's Secret?" I asked, as I picked them up.

"Target."

"Nice. I like a choosy shopper."

She nabbed them from my hand and placed them in her suitcase.

"Done?" I asked.

"No I have to pack my toiletries and makeup now."

"Seriously?"

"Of course."

She went to the closet, pulled out a smaller case that matched the larger bag, then went into her bathroom. There, she opened the medicine cabinet and ran her hand across the shelves creating a great avalanche of beauty supplies that fell into her bag. She dropped the case, closed the door, and I heard her backside hit the toilet seat. A moment later she flushed and reappeared. Apparently, she peed, though it could easily have a been a number two, considering women had the magical power to do either bodily function in the same amount of time.

"Have a nice pee?" I asked.

"Actually, I pooped."

"Bullshit."

"You're right—but I could have and would have if I had needed to."

"Again, I say bullshit. There's no way you'd do it with me right outside."

"Wouldn't be a problem."

I thought a moment.

"Well, I suppose you are safely at home in your own bathroom."

"Still, that wouldn't even make a difference. When you gotta go, you gotta go. It's part of being human."

"So's masturbating, but we don't do that around other people," I said.

"What about last night?"

"Excellent point, but I think we can both agree that was a special circumstance."

She took the smaller bag and jammed it into the larger suitcase, which I now had to sit on so that she could zip it closed. We headed downstairs, and the journey down was far more arduous than the one coming up, because I was now toting a bag that weighed more than me after a Thanksgiving dinner.

"Sweet Jesus! It feels like you packed your entire apartment into this fucker!" I said, with a grunt as we reached the second floor landing.

"John said you carried him seven kilometers. What's three flights of stairs with a tiny little suitcase? Don't tell me that you're suddenly turning into a pussy."

Perhaps it was time to keep the past to myself, as it set the bar a little high for my current day exploits. After much effort, we reached the car and loaded her suitcase in the trunk, and I could have sworn the back end dropped a few inches, but it was probably just my imagination. This time, I got behind the wheel, because I knew the easiest way to get to the private terminal at SFO. We drove back to Park Presidio then passed through the short but winding stretch that traversed Golden Gate Park before turning right in order to avoid one of the city's worst traffic nightmares. It was called 19th Avenue, and it was a crowded section of highway with timed lights that seemed to work better at slowing traffic than moving it through the city. Instead, we headed down to Sunset Avenue, which was like the Autobahn in comparison, and the perfectly timed lights allowed us to quickly reach Highway 101, where we headed south at a cool seventy-nine miles per hour. As we reached Daly City, I spied the ultimate siren song of salt, sugar, and grease, and there, just off the freeway was an In-N-Out Burger and a Krispy Kreme donut shop. They were the ultimate temptation and even more so after the consumption of alcohol, which had a tendency to lower impulse control and increase the desire for salt, grease, and sugar.

"You ever make any late night stops there?" I asked, pointing at the mecca of guilty pleasures.

"Of course. I eat really healthy almost all of the time, but you just have to splurge once in a while."

Great mother of all things sweet and greasy! First cars and now junk food. If this kept up, ejaculating in my pants was going to be a clear and present danger. Fiona was a woman among women and was rapidly turning into a male fantasy come to life. I smiled to myself, adjusted the crotch of my pants to make room for Tag Junior's growth spurt, then turned my gaze to the road ahead. The Highway 380 cutoff came into view, and I merged onto it, and, five minutes later, we were pulling in and parking in the private air terminal. A short distance away, the Vandenberg jet still looked as majestic as ever as it sat out on the tarmac. It was a converted Boeing 777 that afforded more luxury than most five star hotels, and I was therefore more than happy to know that it would be our home for the next fifteen or so hours. I pulled my bag out of the trunk, followed by Fiona's, which was a backbreaking task, but at least the fucker had wheels, so it could roll the rest of the way to the plane. I clicked the lock button on the Silver Hornet's key fob, then we made our way out to the jet.

"So, which one are we flying on?" Fiona asked.

"The big one with the tan guy standing next to it."

"Holy shit! That's as big as a commercial jet."

"That's because it essentially is a commercial jet, and that beauty over there happens to be a Boeing 777, or, in pilot speak, a triple seven.

"It's huge!" she said.

"Yeah—technically it's four feet longer than a 747, and, more importantly, it has been outfitted to be a hell of a lot nicer inside than your average five star hotel."

"Cool—so, who's the guy?"

"Brett. He's one of the pilots."

"He's handsome."

"Seriously?"

"Yeah, but I was just making an observation, so don't get insecure. You're also very handsome."

"Does very mean I'm more handsome than he is?"

"That would depend on his personality."

"Well in that case, I'm definitely more handsome."

We walked up and stopped before the man with the tan.

"Hello, Brett, you're looking as tan as ever," I said.

"Thanks. Who's your guest?"

"Fiona, Fiona Blake," I said, curious if Brett would recognize her from Playboy.

"Holy shit! Miss October! It's very nice to meet you," he said, his smile ablaze and his teeth blinding me with their unnaturally white brilliance.

"Nice to meet you too," she said, smiling back.

Suddenly another voice came from the plane, and I looked up to see Tatyana coming down the boarding stairs. She was one of the regular pilots, and she was looking as beautiful as ever with her stunning brown shoulder length hair, pale green eyes, and curvaceous figure. She came straight up to me, wrapped her arms around my back, and kissed me on the lips just long enough to make me feel particularly uncomfortable. She finally stepped back and turned her attention to Fiona.

"Hi, I'm Tatyana, and I'm one of your pilots. It's nice to meet you."

"Nice to meet you too," Fiona said, looking ever so slightly uneasy.

"Come on aboard, we'll be ready to leave soon, and we have a special temporary crewmember for this flight," Brett said.

"Is it a she?" I asked.

"Yep."

"Beautiful as usual?"

"Yeah," he said, with an unusual tone in his voice.

"Meaning?"

"You'll see," Brett said, with a sly smile.

"What does that mean?" I asked.

"Well, she's Mr. Vandenberg's favorite employee, serves as his personal chef, and usually travels with him everywhere he goes."

Oddly, all of the Vandenberg employees that I had ever met all looked as though they had stepped off of some kind of magazine cover. In fact, it was my private joke that he hired models then trained them for whatever position he had available, so it stood to reason that the temporary crewmember would very likely be just as attractive as the others. Tatyana and Brett headed up the stairs, and that left Fiona and me alone on the tarmac.

"So, it would appear that you obviously know Tatyana pretty well."

"Um—well—sort of. It's kind of a long story."

"Yeah, I imagine it is, but it's a long way to Malkarta, which is more than enough time to tell me all about it."

CHAPTER THIRTEEN
The Flight of the Phallus

We walked up the stairs and entered the Vandenberg jet, and I could already hear the word man-whore coming up in conversation. That term had been used by a lovely Vandenberg employee named Estelle to describe my wild exploits during the course of my particularly exciting Soft Taco Island case, and some of those exploits just happened to have taken place aboard this very jet. It was kind of an unfair nickname, however, as I had spent the majority of my life as a very happy one woman man until that case had unknowingly thrust me into a world of wine, women, and wonderment. Needless to say, I was back from that short foray of fornication, but life had a funny way of coming around full circle—in this case with Tatyana. We'd never officially dated, mainly because of geography, but we had shared a very lovely and intimate shower on the jet while en route to Europe—a fact that might in some way bother Fiona.

But, should it bother Fiona? That was an interesting question, and one to which I did not have an adequate answer, as I had absolutely no idea where we stood. On one hand, she was merely a pro bono client, while on the other hand she was a potential love interest—though that was probably up for interpretation. Were we even dating? It was hard to say, as thus far we had only engaged in a little kissing, a brief moment of heavy petting, and some mutual masturbation. Complicated? I'd say extremely complicated, and I certainly never imagined that we would be traveling together on the fucking Vandenberg jet, where I had more than a few skeletons in the closet.

We followed Tatyana and Brett down the passageway and into the main salon, where Fiona gazed in wonder at the luxurious appointments of the jet. The room was adorned with all the trappings of a luxury home, and on one end there was a massive dining table while on the other there was a lounge full of leather sofas custom upholstered in the Vandenberg corporate colors of white and navy blue. Residing along the middle wall, and likely the most important accouterment, was the bar, which was a place that I had spent most of my time on this wonder of the skies. Fiona walked around the entire space and gazed in wonder at the extreme level of luxury.

"And to think I've never flown in anything more exciting than coach," she said.

"Yeah, it's a little overwhelming at first. Just wait until you see the staterooms," I said.

"Speaking of which, we weren't sure how many you needed," Brett said.

I looked at Fiona, as I wasn't sure how to answer.

"Two, I guess," she said.

I suppose she didn't want to give anyone the wrong idea about our relationship, though Brett, of course, smiled at this news, as he was obviously excited that Miss October might be single. This, however, made me wonder where Yvonne his girlfriend, or perhaps ex-girlfriend, might be at the moment.

"Where's Yvonne?" I asked.

"Working on Vandenberg's new yacht. He has a new sister ship to the Sozo that he's keeping over in the Mediterranean full time."

"So, you two are?"

"Broken up, sadly," he said, his smile growing ever so slightly larger.

Lovely—Mr. Tan and Teeth was back on the hunt, and I suddenly hoped that he would be flying the first leg of the trip.

"Here, let me show you to your room," he said, as he picked up Fiona's bag and tried to smile in spite of the obvious strain.

"Ahhh—always the gentleman. Careful you don't give yourself a hernia," I said, grabbing my things and heading to my usual room.

Fiona and Brett walked to the end of the passageway while I stopped and turned left at the first door, and the experience felt as though I were stepping into a time capsule. I hadn't been in this room in at least four months, but it still looked exactly the same. In the corner was a personal coffee machine and a mini fridge while in the center was a California king sized bed adorned with the obligatory navy blue Vandenberg V in the center of the white bedspread. I placed my suitcase on the floor and went into the bathroom, which was more akin to a five star hotel with its fine granite counter tops and large Jacuzzi tub and shower. Ah—the Jacuzzi. Though it was empty at the moment, I still remembered it full, topped with bubble bath, and sporting a very beautiful girl named Tiffany. It was during my month of madness, so yes we did experience a very awesome night of passion. Now, however, she was working aboard Vandenberg's massive super yacht Sozo and dating the captain, who was a good guy, so I wished both of them well in their new relationship.

I set my small bag of toiletries on the sink and left my cabin and headed back out to the lounge to grab a sparkling mineral water from the bar. I always followed the same rule when flying—proper hydration before dehydration, and if all went well, a little fornication, or at least that's how it had gone four months ago. I had a feeling that this flight might be a bit different, and I'd be lucky if I even got ahold of my own privates for some traditional masturbation, let alone some mutual masturbation with a lovely partner.

More troubling, however, was that I now had to contend with the tan menace, who was just dying to move in on Fiona. Still, I was a pathological optimist and was therefore always hopeful for a happy ending—so to speak.

"Oh sorry, I would have gotten that for you," I heard a woman say from behind me.

I turned to see the mysterious other crewman and was mildly surprised. Contrary to Vandenberg's apparent penchant for hiring skinny runway model types, this woman was more full figured, or in art terms, Rubenesque. The Flemish Baroque painter Sir Peter Paul Rubens had inadvertently created the expression with his propensity for painting beautiful full figured women—such as the one was standing directly in front of me. She was indeed full figured, beautiful, and sporting a head of lustrous long red hair that fell well below her shoulders. She was wearing a tight pantsuit instead of the usual short skirt and blouse, and it made a lovely point of showing off her curvaceous bottom and rather large breasts.

"Oh, no problem, I can help myself. I'm Finn, by the way. It's nice to meet you," I said.

"Nice to meet you too, Mr. Finn. I'm Rose—anything you need, feel free to ask."

"Anything?" I asked, raising an eyebrow.

"Almost anything, as I'm afraid I'm engaged," she said, as she gave me a flirtatious wink and flashed me her engagement ring.

"Then my first request is that you call me Finn or Tag—

no Mr."

"Finn it is."

"So, Rose, what brings you aboard the Vandenberg jet?"

"A favor. Mr. Vandenberg needed someone to fill in on this flight, so I volunteered, as I thought it would be nice to go somewhere warm and tropical and get a break from the cold."

"No shit. This has been a bitch of a winter."

"Fucking A," she said, using a touch of unexpected profanity as she sat down beside me.

Brett and Fiona appeared a moment later, and they were chatting away, which meant he was probably talking abut the Naval Academy, whitening toothpaste, or his favorite cocoa butter tanning oil, as those were generally his favorite topics.

"I understand that you already know Biscuit," Rose said.

"Um — Biscuit?"

"Yeah, Brett. Fluffy white on the inside, golden brown on the outside."

"I don't get it," Fiona said.

"Think of a tanning bed as an oven," Rose said.

Fiona scrutinized Brett for a moment then laughed out loud. I too laughed, happy to hear that someone else found Brett's penchant for serial tanning to be peculiar.

"Can I hug you now, Rose?" I asked.

"If you think you can handle it. I'm a lot of woman — too much for some men."

"I'll risk it," I said, as I stepped forward and hugged her

and felt that she was as strong as a bear.

"Ah, wonderful, you two are bonding, so now I'll be hearing everything in stereo," Brett said.

"Or surround," Tatyana said, as she and the other pilot Wendy appeared from the front of the plane.

Wendy introduced herself to Fiona then gave us a brief update as to our flight plan and arrival time in Malkarta. She also told us that she and a new pilot in training named Jim would be taking the first shift, with Tatyana and Brett doing the return leg. Lovely. That left the tan menace free to put the moves on Fiona for the next fifteen or so hours, though I was at least pleased to have a new and interesting ally in Rose, which might make for a more tolerable flight.

Wendy excused herself to head back to the cockpit while the rest of us prepared for takeoff. Brett annoyingly grabbed the seat beside Fiona, so I sat between Rose and Tatyana and, when I looked over, the fucker was smiling at me as though we had just shook hands and were now engaged in a duel, with the prize obviously being Miss October. What a prick.

The jet's powerful engines spooled up, and soon we were rolling along the tarmac and making our way out across the airport to wait in line with a number of commercial airlines. We passed the main terminal and sat for only a few minutes before making the sharp left turn to prepare for take-off. A moment later, Wendy came over the intercom.

"Welcome to Vandenberg air. We are cleared for takeoff, so please remain in your seats until we have reached our cruising altitude, and I have officially declared it is safe to move freely about the cabin."

The massive engines throttled up, and the big jet vibrated until the brakes were finally released, and we began accelerating down the runway. The terminal and surrounding buildings were flying by ever faster, and the g-forces were pressing us back into our seats until we at last left the ground and started climbing into the sky. I looked out at the view below and watched as South San Francisco gave way to ocean as the plane angled slightly west and continued ever higher into the bright blue sky. Five minutes later, Wendy came over the intercom and told us we were now free to move about the plane. Let the party begin.

Rose was the first to leave her seat, and she headed off into the passageway that lead towards the front of the plane. I stood up and went for the bar but again chose another sparkling water, as it was still way too early in the day for alcohol. Brett stayed right where he was—next to Fiona, while Tatyana followed me and took up residence on the adjacent stool. She was wearing the usual Vandenberg uniform and really was looking every bit as beautiful as I remembered, and her large green eyes felt as though they were drawing me in like a moth to a flame.

"So, how have things been, Finn?"

"Good. How about you?"

"Good, though perhaps a little lonely. It's hard to have a normal life when you're always flying all over the world at a moment's notice."

I hazarded a glance at Fiona and noticed she was watching my interaction with Tatyana.

"Yeah, I understand. I've been there myself," I said, returning my attention to the beautiful woman in front of me rather than the one being romanced by the life size Naval Academy Ken doll.

"Have you talked to Lux at all?"

She was referring to the woman I had rescued from Soft Taco Island. That same woman also happened to have been one of the early loves of my life but had ended up marrying my good friend from the Air Force—a man named Cornelius Wallace, who I called Corn.

"No, she and Corn have been going to therapy. I figured it was best to stay well out of the way of all that until they worked through their issues."

"Probably a good idea."

"Yeah."

"Any new love interests?"

I looked at Fiona and was unsure how to answer. Tatyana saw my gesture and smiled before lowering her voice.

"Are you two boning?" she asked.

"No."

"You sure? Because there seems to be some real sexual tension between you two."

Fucking Tatyana was like a bloodhound when it came to sexual tension and could smell it a mile away.

"Honestly, I don't know. Our whole situation is a little complicated. She's not very comfortable with people lending her a helping hand, and that's kind of keeping things platonic for the moment."

"That sounds frustrating."

"And mildly confusing."

"Brett certainly seems to be making some headway."

I looked over and saw that he had placed his hand on her knee, which she had annoyingly refrained from swatting away. Fuck. I really thought that she was smarter than to fall prey to the man with the tan.

"Ultimately, she's just a client and free to do whatever she pleases."

"Apparently."

"I'm going to go to my room and chill out."

"Want some company for moral support," Tatyana asked.

I looked over and saw Fiona laughing at something Brett said, and it made my answer simple.

"Love some," I said.

Tatyana and I stood up and headed to my stateroom then stretched out on the bed beside each other, though we did so without actually touching. Still, I could smell her perfume drifting across on the plane's air conditioning system, and it was filling my mind with all manner of olfactory memories of our brief, though exiting, time together. It wasn't long before those memories were sending sharp jolts of electricity down to my penis, but I kept Tag Junior in my pants and my thoughts idling in neutral.

"So, how are things—really?" she asked.

"Actually they're mostly good. Work is a little sporadic as usual, but, as I'm now financially stable, I'm slowly adjusting to the idea that it's OK."

"You should enjoy yourself. You've spent your life devoted to your country and helping people, so take the hit. You've earned it."

"I'll try, but that's enough about me. I want to know how your life is aboard the jet."

"Well, it's fun to always be going to new places, but it's starting to get old. Most days I have no idea where I am when I wake up."

"There's something to be said for waking up in your own bed," I said.

"And not alone," she added.

Tatyana yawned and shifted closer until she was snuggled up to me, and her soft breaths were tickling my ear.

"Tired?" I asked.

"Yeah, we just flew in from Europe, so I didn't get much sleep and could use a little nap to get through the rest of the evening."

"Me too. Had a crazy couple of nights."

"I'm sure you did."

She closed her eyes, as did I, and I realized we were sharing what was perhaps our most innocently intimate moment together. It was one thing to have sex with someone, but it was an entirely different matter to platonically snuggle and share some quality downtime. I lay there with those thoughts drifting across my mind as the low droning of the engines and the slow movements of the plane lulled me off to a glorious afternoon nap.

I awoke two hours later, saw the beautiful woman at my side, and had to take a minute to remember I was aboard the Vandenberg jet and napping with Tatyana—which was a weird, though comforting, feeling. I slid out of bed and looked at my watch. It was almost six, and that meant it was cocktail hour and probably time to get up, so that I would still be able to sleep later tonight. Tatyana felt the movement and opened her eyes and smiled.

"Thinking of taking a shower?" she asked.

I smiled as I remembered the time we had made sweet love in that very same shower.

"Why—are you feeling dirty?"

"Always, and speaking of which—do you still have any of that delicious rum?"

"Four bottles."

"Pour a lady a drink?"

"Of course."

I dug into my bag and pulled out a bottle then filled two glasses before handing one to Tatyana and sitting back down beside her on the bed.

"To a fellow member of the mile high club," she said.

We clinked glasses then sipped and enjoyed the rich flavor of the rum until our reverie was interrupted by a knock at the door.

"Come in," I said.

Fiona walked in and immediately froze when she saw Tatyana sitting on my bed.

"Oh, I'm sorry. I didn't mean to intrude."

"You aren't. We were just having our first cocktail of the evening," Tatyana said.

"Yeah, here I'll get you a glass."

"That's OK. I—think Brett is looking for me."

She left, and Tatyana looked over at me.

"Sorry—I hope I'm not causing any trouble."

"You're not—technically."

We finished our rum then headed out to the main salon to find Brett and Fiona looking at an iPad. The tan menace was smiling and using his fingers to zoom in, so I was guessing he was showing her pictures of himself.

"That's me freshman year!" he said, excitedly.

"Oh God. Naval Academy pictures? Seriously?" I asked.

A moment later, Rose strolled in and immediately looked over Brett's shoulder.

"So, this is pre-tanning salon. Interesting. You know you're teeth don't look as white when you're not so tan."

He ignored her comment and turned his gaze back to me.

"Where have you two been?" Brett asked, obviously hoping to change the subject.

"Hanging out and having a drink," I said.

"For two hours? It must have been a hell of a drink."

"It was," Tatyana said.

"So, are you going to share any of that precious rum I've heard about?" Rose asked.

"Of course, my princess of the skies, and every comment about Brett, his tan, or his teeth is another refill," I said, holding up the bottle.

Rose went to the bar for a glass then returned and held it in front of me. I filled it then clinked glasses with her, ever curious how she would react to the rum. She took a sip, and her eyes immediately rolled back into her head, and she gasped.

"Holy shit, I think I just came. That shit is better than cunnilingus," she said.

"Oral sex in a bottle."

"Where is ours?" Brett asked.

Begrudgingly, I went to the bar and grabbed two more glasses, filled each, then handed them to Brett and Fiona before holding up mine to toast.

"To friends," I said, eyeing Fiona.

Everyone drank, and quiet descended upon the room, until Rose stood and headed behind the bar to the entertainment system. She pressed a button, and music filled the air, thankfully lightening the awkward mood.

"Anyone getting hungry yet?" she asked, as she returned and took a seat next to me.

"I'm always hungry," I said.

"Good, because I've got a hell of a dinner planned for tonight, and it's not for the timid of appetite."

"Oh, is it your vagina?" Brett asked with a little chuckle.

"It sure is, but don't worry—I'll be serving your dinner around back at the take-out window."

"Bam! One point to Rose for giving Brett shit—figuratively and literally!" I said, reaching over and filling her glass with another splash of rum.

Rose and I enjoyed a nice laugh while Brett proceeded to frown as he sipped his drink in defeat. Giving and taking shit was its own unique art form, and some people were a lot better at it than others. This almost made me feel sorry for Brett, as underneath his tan womanizing exterior and brilliantly white teeth beat the heart of a decent guy—some of the time, anyway. Right now, however, he was in full dick swinging bachelor mode, and his mind was focused on a new exciting prize, which, unfortunately, made him an object of great scorn. Another round of drinks was poured, and Brett excused himself, probably to brush his teeth. Either way, I finally managed some alone time to talk to Fiona, who annoyingly brought up the topic of Tatyana.

"So, were you guys an item?" she asked.

"Not exactly."

"Meaning?"

"We had one little fling a long time ago."

"And how long is a long time ago?"

"Four months."

"So, basically—yesterday."

"No, it's been like a third of a year."

"Nice try."

I had to remember that women's calendars worked differently than men's and varied by the situation. A fling with Tatyana four months ago was basically yesterday. Apply the same amount of time to the age of a pair of shoes and they would be ancient and desperately in need of replacement. It wasn't logical, but ultimately that didn't matter, because women were more emotional creatures—a fact that was both a good and bad thing depending on the situation. If you were feeling beaten down by life, the love of a good woman might be all that you needed to persevere. But, make a small mistake, such as forgetting a birthday or anniversary, and that empathy turned to rage and eventually spite.

"I don't exactly see you thwarting Brett's advances."

"He's nice, and, besides, we're just talking and enjoying each other's company."

"Yeah, I can see that."

"See what's happening? Romantic entanglements make things complicated, and now you should understand why I want to leave sex out of the equation and keep our business just that—business."

"So, last night was just business?"

She thought for a moment, and I could see the turmoil behind her beautiful eyes.

"Last night was a mistake."

"That's fine. I told you from the beginning that I was helping you with no ulterior motive. No strings attached. Feel free to ride biscuit until both of you are covered in his gravy. It's none of my business," I said.

She reached over and picked up a magazine while I turned my attention back to my drink, which was my most loyal companion at the moment. Shit—was that our first fight? How could that be when we weren't even dating? Tatyana reappeared and said something to Rose, who stood up and left us, apparently to prepare dinner. Brett too came back, and he was smelling unusually minty as he took a seat next to Fiona and struck up yet another wonderful conversation. I grabbed a tabloid magazine off the table and quickly learned that all the same trouble prone celebrities and reality stars were all in just as much trouble. It wasn't exactly entertainment, but it kept me busy for the forty minutes until Rose appeared to tell us dinner was ready. We all moved to the dining table and gazed in wonder at a feast fit for a king. Before us lay baby back ribs, mashed potatoes, steamed kale, corn on the cob, and freshly baked green chili corn bread.

"If you don't end up getting married, I'm officially proposing, Rose," I said.

"Two ways into a man's heart—pants and mouth."

"Indeed."

Everyone, obviously unafraid to get a little dirty, dug in, as ribs were finger food and therefore came with a bit of a mess. It was worth a few extra napkins, as Rose's rib recipe was delicious, and, instead of smothering them in barbecue sauce, she had seasoned them with a dry rub and baked them until the meat was falling off the bone. It was literally heaven on earth, and I ate until I feared I could no longer get up from the table.

"Rose, I want to personally thank you for the best dinner I have had in a long time."

"You're welcome, Finn, and I think you should know that I substituted cornbread for biscuits at the last minute fearing Brett wouldn't eat one of his own."

"You've just earned another glass of rum."

"Excellent, shall we adjourn to the lounge to enjoy dessert and some of your delicious rum?" Rose asked.

"Absolutely, but would I be sacrificing any of my dignity if my bloated stomach were to force me to drop to the floor and crawl my way over?"

"None whatsoever. I'll see you down there."

CHAPTER FOURTEEN
A Bumpy Night

Now that everyone was properly full, we rose from our seats and headed for the couches, which made me realize that my joke about crawling wasn't too far from reality. I was full and feeling the effects of a large meal weighing heavily on my body as I dropped back down onto the supple leather sofa. Again we formed into our original cliques, with Fiona and Brett on one couch, and Tatyana, Rose, and I on the other. In order to dull the awkwardness, I poured more rum, and we sat and ruminated while digesting our incredible dinner. Brett decided to try and get Fiona alone by suggesting a tour, and he and Fiona stood and headed forward and exited the main salon.

"So, I take it that you and Fiona are, or were, an item of sorts?" Rose asked.

"No, technically she's just a client."

"But you like her."

"Maybe."

"Maybe?"

"Well, we've only known each other three days."

"Yeah, but I've seen people fall in love in the space of a glance," Tatyana said.

"True."

"Have you had sex?" Rose asked.

"No, not officially."

"Meaning?"

"Meaning we haven't had sex."

"That sounds vague—as though your hiding something," she said.

"Um—well—we had a night of mutual masturbation."

"No shit? You masturbated in front of each other?"

"Yeah."

"Jesus, that's almost more intimate," Tatyana said.

"Really?"

"Hell yeah—to feel comfortable enough to do that in front of someone is pretty major, which begs the question of why she's ignoring you and hanging out with Biscuit," Tatyana said.

"Excellent question, and I believe that the answer is related to what I told you earlier."

"That she's not very comfortable with people lending a helping hand?"

"Yeah, and to that end, she doesn't want to complicate our relationship with sex."

"Complicate it with sex? Hello! Isn't that one of the main reasons we have relationships—for the sex?" Rose asked.

"Yeah, but she thinks that because I'm helping her, sex will feel like some form of repayment, which, in turn, apparently makes her feel like a whore."

"Jesus, I'm glad to be out of the dating scene and engaged to an awesome guy," Rose said.

"Yeah, I bet. Who is the lucky fellow?" I asked.

"Doug—my sexy stock broker."

"And you left him home while you flew off to paradise?"

"No, he's at a convention in Florida."

"Do you worry when he's away?"

"Hell no. I'm more than enough woman for Doug, and he knows it. I'm telling you—I would probably break a normal man's dick—and not because of my substantial curves. I know that I'm a big girl, but the real deal is that I have a magical vagina. I fuck hard and take no prisoners, but the man who can take the punishment experiences a heaven like no other."

"Well, let me know when you're single."

"I will."

I held up my glass to toast.

"To Rose's magical vagina. May it not break Doug's dick—nor his heart," I said.

We clinked glasses then sipped the rum and let the smooth elixir warm our hearts and minds, and, as we finished our glasses, Rose stood and smiled.

"Time for dessert," she said.

"Does it have anything to do with your vagina?" I asked.

"Sadly no, but the night is young, and your rum is making me pretty horny, so you never know," she said, disappearing from the main salon.

She returned a few minutes later with a banana cream pie and five plates.

"You have got to be shitting me," I said.

"Baked it special just for tonight."

"Doug must weigh three hundred pounds."

"He's six two, one ninety, and fit as a fiddle."

"I guess your vagina really is magical," I said.

"Yep, every minute your dick is in it, you burn a hundred calories. Every minute your mouth is on it, it's double that. You could burn off that entire pie in about four and a half minutes just by giving me some cunnilingus."

"Well, then keep that glorious lady valley of yours primed and ready, because this cowboy likes his pie," I said.

Brett and Fiona returned, and the two of them were giggling like a couple of love struck teenagers, and it made me remember how quickly life moved on this fucking jet. Oh well, there was nothing left to do but roll with it, which I suppose would likely become a physical reality when I was done eating Rose's pie—so to speak.

I dug in and took a small exploratory bite, and, as had been the case with dinner, I was incredibly pleased with the results. The pie was deadly delicious and would inspire a great deal of exercise in the near future. Still, I was so entranced by its creamy sweet nature and delicious crust, that I wolfed it down and found myself staring at the remaining pie, where I was seriously considering another piece. Rose saw the yearning in my eyes and offered me more, but somehow I managed to abstain, as I knew I had already quintupled my daily caloric intake. Instead, I leaned back in my chair, sipped my rum, and relaxed in the pleasant atmosphere of the main salon—well as pleasant as it got with Fiona and Brett still in the middle of their unending conversation. Seriously now—how much more could he possibly have to say about the United States Naval Academy, whitening toothpaste, and his favorite cocoa butter tanning oils?

The evening eventually came to a close, and everyone said good night, thanked Rose for an amazing dinner, then adjourned to their various rooms for what would hopefully be a quiet and uneventful night. That is, everyone except Brett and Fiona, who remained in the main salon. Being a sneaky and curious son of a bitch I left my door open just a tiny crack so that I could hear whether or not she returned to her cabin alone or with Biscuit. I poured myself a final snifter of rum and took a seat on the bed as I settled in for some improvised surveillance. Hardly a minute had passed when I heard a knock and looked up to see Tatyana at the door.

"Did you know that your door was open?" she asked.

"No," I lied.

"So, a trained former field agent for the CIA forgot to close his door? Nice try."

She came in and filled her glass before taking a seat on

the bed beside me.

"They're still in the main salon in case you're wondering," she said.

"I wasn't."

"Two lies in two seconds flat. Keep this up and you'll be qualified for a career in politics."

Tatyana smiled. Obviously, I was a shitty liar, but maybe that was a good thing, as it helped keep me honest. As I was about to respond to her last statement, I felt something in my eye that was very likely an eyelash. I tried to fish it out but was having no success, so Tatyana, seeing my discomfort, moved in to examine my eye. She placed her hands on either side of my head and leaned in close, inadvertently bringing her lips only inches from mine.

"There it is. Hold still," she said.

She reached her finger over and gingerly pulled the errant lash free.

"Is that it?" I asked.

"Hold still and let me check."

Suddenly my door opened, and there stood Fiona, looking particularly unnerved to see Tatyana in my stateroom yet again. Of course, it was worse this time because it looked as though we were about to kiss. Fucking timing was everything.

"Oh, sorry. I didn't mean to interrupt," she said.

"You're not. Tatyana was just getting an eyelash out of my eye," I said, instantly fearing she would think I was lying.

"Oh, really?" she asked, obviously not believing me.

"Really," I responded, staring back as earnestly as I could, though this probably only made me look even more guilty.

"Whatever, it's none of my business. I was just coming by to say good night."

"Oh, so I take it you're done talking with Biscuit?"

"For the moment."

"Well then, good night."

"Yeah, let's certainly hope so," she said, in a challenging tone.

What the hell was that supposed to mean? Was it a veiled threat, and, if so, it didn't seem very veiled. She proceeded to give me a discerning gaze then turned and left, but I didn't hear the door to her stateroom close, which perhaps meant that she was doing a little counter surveillance of her own.

"That was awkward," Tatyana said.

"It sure was."

Tatyana and I continued to quietly sip our drinks, until she lay back on the bed and sighed.

"Fucking Rose is an excellent cook. Thank God she's only here on a temporary basis or I'd end up being about five hundred pounds," she said.

"No shit. I have no idea how I'm going to burn off all these extra calories."

"I can think of a way," Tatyana said, rolling onto her side to gaze at me with a mischievous smile.

"Me too, but I'm really trying to abstain from my man-whorish ways."

"You know that you trying to be a better man only makes you that much more attractive."

"And blue in the balls. Sweet mother of God am I pathetic. We should be making sweet love, but it just doesn't seem like the right thing to do at the moment."

"You're probably right, though this amazing rum is doing nothing to inhibit my libido."

"It's like Spanish fly in a bottle," I said.

I refilled my glass, sipped my rum, and gazed at the beautiful Tatyana and realized that I was crazy not to take her up on her offer. Truth be told, I had maintained a major crush on her since the moment we first met, but the timing just hadn't been right for anything prolonged or meaningful. Now, here I was with her, but I was pining over Fiona—someone who made it clear that she didn't think it was a good idea for us to be sexually involved. I finished my rum and realized that I was thoroughly buzzed and therefore in dangerous territory, as my inhibitions were weakening with every second that I sipped more rum and spent time in the presence of Tatyana.

"Sweet Lord! What the hell am I doing pining over Fiona? You are more woman than any man deserves," I said, with a sad sigh.

"That's probably just the rum talking."

"If it is, then it's not lying."

"I suppose that's probably my signal to leave you in

peace and go to bed," Tatyana said.

"Probably a good idea."

"Well, good night," she said, leaning in and giving me a hug.

It felt good to hold Tatyana in my arms, and it inadvertently allowed me to smell her enticing perfume as well as feel her ample bosoms pressing against my chest. The hug lasted longer than I had intended, and, as we parted and gazed into each other's eyes, I had the unmistakable urge to kiss her. We hovered in that moment, and my mind was clouded with impure thoughts until guilt and reason overcame lust.

"Well—um—shit. Good night," I said.

"Good night," she said, as she exited and left the door slightly ajar.

I stood up and headed into the bathroom, brushed my teeth, then returned to lay back on the bed, where the solitude of the moment allowed me to ponder my current situation. I realized that I had a pretty decent buzz on and probably should have skipped the final glass of rum. In fact, I was thinking that I should probably snack on something such as a piece of bread in order to help stave off any chance of a hangover. I left my room and made my way down the passageway, through the main salon, and on to the galley at the front of the plane. All was quiet as I slipped in and rustled around through the various cabinets until eventually finding a sourdough dinner roll, which would hopefully slow the absorption of alcohol into my bloodstream. I turned off the light and was about to leave, but I heard someone coming down the passageway, so I ducked back inside the galley and stayed in the shadows. A moment later, Fiona walked by me and continued on towards the front of the plane. I leaned out just far enough to see that she was knocking on Brett's door. The tan menace answered a moment later, and she went inside. Fuck. Why in the hell was she making a house call? Suddenly, the thought occurred to me that I was fooling myself to think that there had actually been something real between us, and perhaps it was time to wake up and put our actual relationship into perspective. I popped the last bite of the roll into my mouth, walked back to my room, then brushed my teeth yet again before sliding off my pants and crawling into bed.

The problem now was that I was too drunk and too aggravated to sleep, and my thoughts kept returning to both Fiona and Tatyana. I had stupidly rebuffed one under the belief that there might be something with the other. I was an idiot and failed to realize that a bird in the hand was always worth more than two in the bush—or, in this case, a single bird in the room next door. I tried to roll over onto my side to find a more comfortable position but nothing seemed to help. I finally gave up and decided to go for a walk around the plane in the hope that it might clear my head—or perhaps allow me to accidentally run into Tatyana. I opened the door, and there to my surprise stood the woman in question, and she was looking sinfully delicious in a sheer robe that was doing very little to conceal a lacy bra and matching thong panties. It was an outfit that left very little to the imagination, which ironically had my imagination in full swing.

"Funny, I was hoping to run into you," I said.

"Hard time sleeping?" she asked.

"Yeah."

"Me too. Want some company?"

"Hell yes," I said, motioning for her to enter my room.

She slithered past me, and just as I was about to close the door, I heard voices in the passageway. I hazarded a glance and saw Fiona and Brett coming from the main salon, so I slipped back inside and listened as they went past and entered her room. It looked as though Fiona and the tan menace decided to have a little sleepover. Lovely. I closed the door and walked back to the bed to find Tatyana was already nestled under the covers, and her sheer robe was on the floor, so she was down to her bare essentials.

"I guess we've officially got a slumber party on our hands!" I said, getting into bed.

"It's only a party if we're naked."

"Is that the official rule?"

"Pretty much," she said, as she reached under the covers and slipped out of her bra and underwear.

She pulled them out from under the covers and dropped them on the floor, and I followed suit by sliding off my boxer briefs and T-shirt. With both of us naked, she snuggled up against me and nestled into the crux of my neck and started gently caressing my chest. I reciprocated in kind, though I kept my fingers safely in the neutral zone that ran from the bottom of her breasts to just below her belly button. Fuck—I was drunk, horny, hurt, but still doing my best to avoid any kind of sexual interplay. Unfortunately, lying next to Tatyana was like being an overeater at an all you can eat buffet, and my desire to feed was deep and primal. Still, I was feeling like a wounded animal, and that meant my motives would be questionable, so I did my best to keep my thoughts focused on puppies, kittens and unicorns—innocent things of childhood abandon that might stave off sexual thoughts and feelings. Annoyingly, puppies became sweater puppies, kitten became cat or, more specifically, pussycat—which, of course, became the shortened version—pussy. Unicorn, because of its phallic horn, became an erect penis, and it, in conjunction with all the other images, wasn't exactly making my life any easier. Fuck—I needed to think about something that was totally unrelated to sex, but then what in the hell was I doing in bed beside a beautiful naked woman? It was an excellent question, and one I should have asked myself long before slithering out of my clothes.

My reverie was suddenly cut short, however, when I realized that I was now sporting a very hard and very obvious boner. Tatyana apparently felt the open space created in the blanket, and, when she hazarded a brief exploration, her hand bumped into the Finn Tower Housing Complex for wayward semen.

"Oh, hello there," she said.

"Sorry about that, but Tag Junior sometimes has a mind of his own."

"Yeah, and apparently he can be pretty hard headed."

"No shit—I think there must also be Viagra in that fucking rum."

"Apparently."

I decided to clear my mind and bring forth my years of martial arts training in which I had learned to put mind over body and redirect and ignore pain, fear, and many of my human frailties. Unfortunately, I could do nothing to quell Tag Junior's libidinous rigidity.

"It's obvious how I'm feeling, but how are you doing at the moment?" I asked Tatyana.

"Horny but surviving. I, of course, would like to make sweet love to you, but I'd rather do so when the timing is proper—not when you're drunk and pining for Miss October."

"I wouldn't say that I'm pining."

"You're pining."

"That's silly. I hardly even know her, and she's probably making sweet love to that fucking tan menace."

"When he wants to, he can definitely bring out the charm. It's only later after you get below his tan surface that you see the insecure douche."

"True, but there's also a nice guy and an excellent pilot under there somewhere as well."

"Yeah, I suppose."

"So, wait a minute. How do you know that she's Miss October?" I asked.

"Fucking Brett was so excited that he told everyone on the plane."

"Typical."

"So, you're not impressed by her Playboy status?"

"I suppose I was at first, but if she hadn't actually turned out to be a nice person, I would already be over it."

We lay there silently beside each other, and, as we shared the occasional awkward glance, it became obvious that there was an ever increasing amount of sexual tension.

"Seriously now, this is ridiculous. We're both consenting adults, and neither of us is otherwise engaged," I said.

"If that's true, then have your way with me right now."

The problem was that I really wanted to, yet also really didn't want to. I was a roiling yin yang of human emotion, with half of me filled with lust, the other guilt, and I didn't know which was stronger. Tatyana obviously sensed the conflict going on behind my eyes and offered a suggestion.

"How about another of your mutual masturbation sessions?"

"I could deal with that," I said, though part of me couldn't believe that I might again get involved in such an unusual sexual encounter.

"OK, sit up and face me. I want us to look into each other's eyes as we climax," she said.

I rose up and knelt across from Tatyana to see her green eyes were glowing, and her full sensuous lips were curled up into a naughty smile as she looked back at me longingly. She began running her fingertips over her nipples, and continued to tease them until they were hard and extended. Next, she slid her right hand down until it came to rest atop what was technically called her mons pubis. I always loved that term, because it gave such majesty to that part of a woman's anatomy by making it sound similar to Mars's tallest mountain—Olympus Mons. The mons pubis might have been smaller and had fewer telescopes focused on it, but for me and many others, it could be a hell of a lot more intriguing than the Martian landscape.

Now, Tatyana was making small circles over her clitoris, and her hips were subtly gyrating in perfect sync, and it instantly reminded me of Fiona from the night before. Fuckinzee! There was nothing more rude than being with one woman while thinking about another, so it was time to take hold of Tag Junior and join in the fun—all the while keeping my thoughts solely on the beautiful Tatyana.

My hand was moving fore and aft, and my excitement was growing with each cycle, and I had a sudden thought about self pleasure and the various names that had come to describe the act. There were so many euphemisms for male masturbation, yet so few for the female equivalent. Men used the terms beat the meat, slap the monkey, jack off, flog the dolphin, and so on, yet what did women call this simple act? I'd heard flick the bean in a funny movie, but that was about it. So, why did this inequity exist? Was it because men spent more time masturbating and, therefore, more time naming their favorite pastime? It was an interesting question, but one that wasn't important at the moment, because regardless of what you called the physical act that Tatyana and I were currently doing, it was incredibly erotic and making me want her all the more.

"Maybe we should just touch each other," I said.

"We can't, as it would ruin all the sexual tension."

"Yeah, but isn't sexual tension, by its very definition, supposed to lead to sex?"

"Interesting point. Perhaps it would be OK to at least touch a little bit."

"Yeah."

She started to reach for me but looked conflicted and stopped.

"Fuck! No, we can't, so we should just keep going."

We continued on, and the longer I watched Tatyana, the harder it became, both literally and emotionally, to avoid actual physical contact.

"How badly do you want to touch me right now?" she asked—her breaths heavy and her breasts wobbling in time with her efforts.

"Very badly."

"Do you want to be inside me?"

"Oh God yes!"

Those were apparently the magic words, for at that exact moment she began to climax, and her moans filled the air as her entire body convulsed in orgasmic release. It was incredible to watch and made me think back to a study I had read that had entailed scanning women's brains during orgasm. Apparently, they tended to disconnect psychologically from their bodies and enter a state of virtual bliss. That was certainly looking to be the case at the moment, as Tatyana's eyes were glassy, and she appeared to be lost in some other plane of existence, but soon she was back in her body and looking at me questioningly.

"You left me out there hanging," she said.

"Sorry, I got distracted watching you."

I was still stroking my mantool but suddenly felt a little awkward, as I was the only one masturbating in the room. Tatyana sensed my uneasiness and leaned back against the headboard and directed me forward onto my knee's so that my penis was now directly in front of her ample bosoms.

"How's this for encouragement?" she asked.

"Excellent. I feel like a kid at the counter of his favorite bakery."

"Well come on then. It's my turn to watch you, so hurry up and cream these puffs!"

Interesting. This was the second time in two days that a woman offered up her breasts as a repository for my manseed, and I had to wonder if semen might have some unspoken medicinal qualities that made the skin look vibrant and beautiful. Perhaps there was even a new product idea in there somewhere. Semen—nature's secret to a younger and more beautiful you. Now available in the easy to access pump version. I set back to work making up a homemade batch of beauty cream, though work would hardly be an accurate description of my actions. Milking my man-cow and watching the beautiful Tatyana stare up at me lustfully was about as good as any chore could be.

"Do you still want to be inside me?" she asked.

"More than ever."

"Prove it. Release the Kraken."

That was about all I needed to hear to blow past St. Peter's Gate and coast straight into heaven and revel in the onset of sweet release. Of course, I was caught off guard when the devious Tatyana suddenly lurched forward and encompassed my shaft between her breasts, then used her hands to press them together like two Christmas hams—thus encompassing my manhood in a valley of slippery holiday pleasure. Shit, did tit-fucking constitute an official sex act, or was it simply a messy end to mutual masturbation? That question would have to wait, however, until I had finished up my gloriously sweet climax. With my man-seed fully plucked from my balls and thoroughly coating Tatyana's lovely chest, I let out a long sigh of relief.

"Sweet Lord! Winter came early!" I said.

"At least it came—and that was quite a blizzard. I take it you're feeling better now?"

"I am, actually, and I'd like to thank you for helping me not be a complete man-whore."

"You're not a complete man-whore, but I'd still rate that exchange as about two on the man-whore scale."

"I can live with two."

"Good, now let's go take a quick shower."

"Excellent plan."

We left the bed and entered the shower and took great solace in the warm rush of hot water. There, we proceeded to clean up before rinsing, drying off, and returning to the bed. I lay back with Tatyana snuggled up against me, and I pondered our unusual encounter. Two women in two days and sex with neither. This was a major turn of events in my sex life, and I could take comfort in knowing that I was mostly steering clear of my man-whorish ways. I closed my eyes and felt the slow subtle movements of the jet as it plied the vast empty skies above the Pacific Ocean, and I soon drifted off to sleep with my thoughts fading into the all encompassing abyss of sleep.

CHAPTER FIFTEEN
The Morning After Could be a Pill

Morning came with the harsh light of reality shining brightly into my room, and my vision was a wee blurry and my thoughts hazy as I turned my gaze to Tatyana. Her breaths were slow and constant, and she looked as peaceful and beautiful as an angel as she slept beside me. I checked my watch, did a little math, and realized that it was early morning, and I was somewhere over the Pacific Ocean. Flying in the same direction as the sun was an unusual phenomenon, but at least it allowed you to gain hours—as long as you didn't cross the International Date Line—in which case you lost about twenty-four. I rose, entered the bathroom, took a well needed horse piss, then brushed my teeth before returning to bed to see Tatyana stir, open her eyes, and look up at me with a big smile.

"That's the first time that we've actually slept together,"

she said.

"Well, not counting the nap."

She stood up, entered the bathroom, and peed before using my toothbrush to brush her teeth. She returned to bed and slid under the covers.

"Wow, quite a night. I hope that you're not going to be in too much trouble with Fiona," she said.

"Hard to say, but it was a nice compromise between need, desire, and remaining true to a woman with whom I have no official obligation."

My thoughts flashed to Fiona, and I wondered what in the hell she and Brett had gotten up to last night. Breakfast was certainly going to be interesting, and I had to admit that all this drama was enough to make me look forward to picking up her brother and finishing up this adventure. It certainly didn't help being aboard this jet, which always seemed to work like a pressure cooker to create this kind of emotional turmoil. I therefore decided to clear my head by going over to the coffee machine to start a pot and enjoy the aroma as it filled the cabin. I took a moment to look out one of the windows and could see a lot of blue water and a smattering of islands, and that meant we were probably getting close to our destination.

The coffee finished brewing, and I poured each of us a cup before joining her back in the bed. I took my first sip and instantly felt better. There was nothing like the first taste of coffee to mend the excesses of the night before. I imagine it was what a smoker felt when they took their first morning drag, though I wouldn't actually know, as I'd never had the indecency to bring a cigarette to my lips.

"Did you ever smoke?" I asked Tatyana.

"Only once, at a party when I was really drunk. Why do you ask?"

"I was just wondering if smokers felt about cigarettes the way I feel about coffee."

"Oh, absolutely. I dated a smoker once—it was horrible. He smoked after everything—sex, food, shitting, you name it."

"Yuck! Smoking after shitting."

"It's not a pleasant combination."

"Definitely not, and it's a terrible way to celebrate a fine dump."

I finished yet another cup of coffee and was soon feeling the rumblings of my imminent morning movement. Of course, that brought up the problem of how I was going to pull it off with Tatyana in my room. Fortunately, Wendy announced over the intercom that we were an hour and a half from our destination, so breakfast would be served shortly.

"I guess it's time to get ready," I said.

"Yeah, so I better get back to my cabin to shit and shower."

"Wow, that's a pretty bold announcement."

"Not really. I shit and shower every day."

"Yeah, obviously, but I was referring mostly to announcing the shitting part. I generally keep that on the down low."

"Well, I don't, as I pretty much need to do it every day, so why hide it?"

"I'm not sure I would mention it to the guy I just masturbated in front of."

"If I can't tell him, who can I tell?" she asked.

"Hmmm—good point," I said, as I thought about her words.

"So, I'm going to get going, so you can get your dump on," she said, as she rose out of bed, with her naked form a tantalizing reminder of the previous night.

She dressed then returned to give me a friendly kiss before heading for the door.

"Have a nice shit," she said, before disappearing from view.

I refilled my cup, grabbed my phone, and headed for the bathroom relieved that I was alone for my special time. After setting my cup on the sink, I pulled up my web browser and silently gave thanks for the fact that the Vandenberg jet had Wi-Fi. I did a quick scan of the headlines and found a story about embarrassing bodily functions. Perfect. What better way to spend my time performing a bodily function than by reading about bodily functions? I grabbed my coffee, took a sip, and set my eyes to the article, relaxed, and released my bounty unto the bowl. The article was a bit more comprehensive than I had anticipated and contained references to dumping, farting, burping, blushing, and even yawning. I had expected the first three but never the last two, so I was pleasantly surprised to have plenty of reading material.

Sitting there, engrossed in the words, I realized that there was just something so cathartic about dumping and reading that transcended what was by all accounts a mundane daily experience. The two just went together like peanut butter and jelly. As a matter of fact, I had spent the entirety my life so desperate for reading material during my dumps that I had read everything from toothpaste tubes to shampoo bottles, and I had never felt quite so vindicated as when I had watched a particular scene from my favorite Farrelly brothers' movie Kingpin. In it, the main character's friend needs to take a dump and asks for reading material, so he hands him a bottle of shampoo. It was proof positive that there were indeed some universal defecation truths in the universe, though I had to wonder where this unusual bathroom pastime fell in the bigger picture of human evolution. Why were defecating and reading so inescapably linked to each other. It seems reasonable that in ancient times a dumper would have been more at risk if he or she extended the length of a dump by the introduction of distractions—least of all something as engrossing as reading. Thankfully, I lived in the modern age, where a long, lone dump was possible without the theoretical intrusion of fellow humans or a hunting lioness. We were living the dream existence, where a person could sip coffee, drop a deuce, and read an interesting and compelling article. At least I believed so until I heard a knock on the bathroom door. Shit. I looked over and saw that I had forgotten to lock it and instantly started to panic. I needed to initiate emergency procedures, the first being to flush the toilet, the second to exfiltrate the LZ and find air freshener. If I could manage those, then I could consider my final option—namely escape. Before I could rise and make a break for freedom, the door opened, and in stormed Fiona.

"We need to talk," she said, stopping only a few feet away.

She immediately placed her hips, and her stern expression and posture were a clear indication she was ripe for confrontation.

"Now?" I asked.

"Now."

"Can I finish what I'm doing?"

"No."

"Seriously?"

"We're going to talk right now."

"Do you know how vulnerable I'm feeling?"

"That's the point."

This was one of my personal nightmares coming to fruition in the most sacred of places. This bathroom was suddenly the north Atlantic, me the Titanic, and Fiona the iceberg that would tear a hole through my side, thereby spilling my deepest, darkest insecurities unto the cold dark waters of my very existence. I even thought about crying but figured it wouldn't help, as she looked pretty set in her current agenda. Worse still, it would only take away from what remained of my crumbling dignity.

"What do you want to talk about?"

"Us."

"Great—fire away."

"How do you feel about me?"

"I like you. At least I did until you barged in here."

"I'm serious. How do you really feel?"

"Before or after you started your new relationship with Biscuit?"

"Right now. I want to know how you feel right now. Forget about Brett."

I looked at the angry, beautiful, vulnerable girl, who would apparently do anything to help her brother, and I suddenly felt sad. Sure, she was an endless pain in my ass, but she was also a pretty amazing person, who was filled with a great deal of empathy for her fellow humans. Of course, that barely balanced my annoyance regarding her budding love affair with Biscuit, though I suppose I should look beyond such trivial matters considering my own recent indiscretions.

"I like you—and yes, I mean that in a romantic way."

"So, why have you been all over Tatyana?"

"Maybe I'm feeling a little put off that you're spending all your free time with Biscuit."

"Did you ever think that I might be doing that because of your whole pre-existing relationship with Tatyana? Face it, you two have been inseparable ever since we came aboard this jet."

"As have you and Biscuit, which means we're in a who

came first scenario—the chicken or the egg."

"Assuming Tatyana is the chicken, then it's clearly the chicken."

"Well if Biscuit is the egg, I'd have to say he came first, especially after you put the whole kibosh on our relationship before we even got here. Remember, it was you who wanted to keep everything on the up and up. No sex—because it made you feel like a whore."

She stood there, quietly brooding for a minute before speaking.

"OK, I'm getting confused by the whole chicken and egg thing, so let me ask you this. Did you and Tatyana spend the night together?"

"Define *spend the night together*."

"Did you have sex?"

"Not officially. Did you have sex with Biscuit?"

"Not officially."

"Did you kiss him?" I asked, starting to feel like a lawyer building a case against a slippery witness.

"Yes."

"Well then, in that case we have nothing more to discuss. Please leave my bathroom."

"Fuck you. Did you kiss Tatyana?"

"Not in a romantic way."

"Bullshit."

"I'm serious, it was technically platonic."

"Really—so, no sex?"

"No, we did not have sex with each other."

She took a second to consider her next question.

"OK then, how about this—did semen leave your body?" she asked, with one eyebrow raised.

Fuck. That was a tricky question.

"Have you ever thought about law school?" I asked.

"No, now answer the question."

"OK fine, yes, but only by my own hand."

"Don't tell me you had another mutual masturbation session."

"I—um—did."

"How could you?"

"I did it for you," and I actually meant that, though I also did it to release a great deal of pressure and angst that was filling both me and my balls.

"That's it. The minute we have my brother out of Malkarta, I'm going to do whatever I can to pay you back for your time and efforts. From here on out, we're all business, and I'm going to forget any misguided feelings I might have felt for you."

"Before you get all high and mighty—why don't you answer the question as to whether or not you and Biscuit spent the night together?"

"Stop calling him Biscuit."

"Answer the question."

"Yes, as a matter of fact. We did."

"Did any semen leave his body?"

She thought for a moment, and a troubled look overtook her features. Hah! Now the shoe was on the other foot!

"Um—yeah, but it's not like it sounds. It's—er—complicated."

"Not really. A penis is pretty straight forward. It only takes a few tugs and voila—man juice."

"Look, we were really drunk and started making out, and the next thing you know, he wants to have sex."

"He or we?"

Again, she thought for a moment and chose her words carefully before answering.

"Him, mostly, as I decided it wasn't a good idea—obviously because of my feelings for you."

"So, how did the semen leave his body? Magic? Was it like Harry Potter? Did he yell out *Semenis Exploderandis* and his balls were suddenly empty and you were covered in Biscuit's gravy?"

"Now you're being childish."

"No, I'm just trying to understand how it is that I'm the bad guy—when you were obviously getting all hot and buttered by the Biscuit."

"I decided to stop what we were doing and go to bed."

"And?"

"And when he thought I was asleep, he jacked off into a pillow case."

"A pillow case—so not on your tits."

"No! Not on my tits!"

"Well, that's a relief."

"You know what? I'm done arguing about this, because I finally see how abundantly clear it is that we are officially ending our romantic relationship."

"How can we be officially ending what we never officially started?"

"It doesn't matter."

"Fine, and now that you've officially shit on my heart—do you mind if I officially finish shitting in this toilet?"

She stared for a long time with the anger still simmering behind her eyes as I sat there virtually trapped on the toilet, wondering how in the hell I had gotten myself into such a vulnerable state.

"I'll see you at breakfast," she said, before finally turning to leave.

"Yeah, and hopefully we're having biscuits and gravy—unless, of course, you're already tired of that."

"Not funny," she said, as she left and thankfully closed the door behind her.

I sat there feeling utterly confused and, at some level, violated. It was one thing to hash things out, yet another thing entirely to invade my space at such a vulnerable time. She knew that I had toilet issues yet used them against me in order to pursue her evil agenda. Women, who were generally the kinder of our species, were truly capable of a great deal of deviousness. Oh well, it was time to accept my fate and go bravely unto the future.

I managed to let loose a final, albeit melancholy salvo, and my brave army of turds dropped down into the still waters of the bowl with nary a splash. I flushed and entered the shower to take solace in the warm embrace of the onslaught of moving water. Like coffee and a dump, a shower was one of my key ways to jumpstart my morning, and it usually left me feeling refreshed and ready for the day ahead. When I finished, I did indeed feel refreshed, though I still couldn't shake the aching feeling in the pit of my stomach that was left after my conversation with Fiona. I swallowed what pride remained, got dressed, and headed out into the main salon to find Rose setting the table for breakfast.

"Need any help?" I asked.

"No thanks. Just relax, I've got it."

"So, what's on the menu?"

"Biscuits and gravy, nitrate free bacon, and fresh fruit, and speaking of biscuits, how's it going between Fiona and Brett?"

"The biscuit is still doing his best to butter her."

"Yuck."

"Yeah, and it looks as though the two of us are very unlikely to be pursuing any kind of intimate relationship."

"What exactly happened?"

"We had an argument."

"About?"

"About the fact that I had another mutual masturbation session—this time with Tatyana."

"Wait, you and Tatyana got naked and masturbated in front of each other and didn't have sex?"

"Nope."

"Holy shit. That would take some serious restraint. I

think in that situation, that even I'd have to fuck her."

"Exactly, and do you know what kind of willpower I showed last night?"

"You are a man among men," she said, as she handed me a mug of coffee then held hers up to toast.

"To the ladies," she said.

"To the ladies."

We each had a sip, then Rose placed her hand on my shoulder and looked at me sympathetically.

"Don't worry, things always work out in the end."

"Hopefully."

"Definitely."

Just then, Fiona and Brett arrived and took a seat at the table, and Brett was smiling so brightly that I decided to put on my sunglasses to decrease the glare. It was also a nice psychological barrier to Fiona, who, while directing an icy affront towards me, made quite a show of acting all chummy with Biscuit. As a person prone to optimism, however, I channeled that into proof that deep down she still cared enough that she felt the need to make me jealous.

The next to arrive was Tatyana, and she said a cheerful hello to everyone then she took a seat beside me. A moment later, Rose returned from the kitchen with a tray fresh fruit, a gravy boat, and a steaming pile of biscuits, which of course brought a scowl from Brett.

"Oh, biscuits—very funny, Rose," he said

"I hope you don't mind eating your own kind," she responded.

"I'll adapt."

As much as Brett hated being called biscuit, even he was unable to resist the delicious looking meal before our eyes, and he loaded up his plate and poured on a heaping helping of gravy. Everyone else followed suit and I managed to easily gobble down three biscuits and even pondered having more but abstained and instead finished with fresh fruit and two slices of bacon. To wash it all down, I had yet another cup of coffee, and I was feeling that I might have one more dump in me before we landed in Malkarta. This time, however, I would lock the door and make sure that I dumped in solitude.

I thanked Rose for another great meal, excused myself, then returned to my room and locked the door before stripping down and hitting the pot, ever eager for the comfort of my porcelain mistress. Sitting there feeling as full as a tick, I realized there was nothing like a belly full of biscuits, gravy, and coffee to give your intestines that extra push for a double deuce. A good dump had always been an omen of a good day ahead, and I wondered if my second dump going undisturbed would counteract any of the bad mojo created by my first one. It was an interesting theory and one that I would put to the test forthwith.

I exhaled, opened my third chakra brown eye and spilled yet another load of precious karma into the still waters of my commode. Considering it was the second dump of the morning, it was unexpectedly fruitful and meant that I would be footloose and fancy free until the following morning. Feeling giddy as a school girl, I leapt from the pot, and stepped into the shower for a brief rinser, as a fresh, clean butthole was always a nice way to start the day.

Clean and dry, I dressed, brushed my teeth, and packed up my things before joining the others in the main salon. Brett and Fiona were on one couch, and Tatyana and Rose were on the other, so I went to the neutral territory of the bar and grabbed a sparkling water. I always liked to be hydrated whenever I was caffeinated.

I had just finished the entire bottle when Wendy came over the intercom and told us that we were on final approach, and it was time to buckle in for landing. I took a seat between Rose and Tatyana and slipped on the belt then made sure it was fastened and snug.

"Anyone here ever been to Malkarta?" I asked.

No one spoke except Tatyana.

"No, but I've heard that it's extremely beautiful and has incredible beaches and world class snorkeling."

"Maybe we'll have time to do a little sightseeing and get in the water," I responded.

"Wouldn't that be nice," she said.

"It sure would, and I could use a little sun," Brett added.

"Yeah, you're tan looks like it might be fading a little."

"Fuck off," he said, casting his gaze down to inspect the tint of the skin on his forearms.

I leaned over, looked out the window, and saw a bright blue turquoise sea and numerous lush green Islands. Wendy came over the intercom again and informed us that we were now on final approach, and that local time was eight fifteen a.m., and the temperature was a blustery seventy nine degree's Fahrenheit. That certainly beat the Bay Area, which was experiencing a miserable cold front and had been dipping into the middle thirties at night.

I continued to stare out the window, and saw Malkarta's southern tip come into view. This was the most populated part of the island and was the location of New Leiden, the largest city, which I assume was named after the city Leiden back in Holland. It contained the airport as well as most of the luxury resorts, hotels, and the Royal Palace. There were a number of towns along the coast as you headed north, but most of the interior was sparsely populated and covered by dense jungle.

The landing gear dropped with an audible thump, and the high-pitched whine of the hydraulics kicked in as the flaps lowered and reduced our airspeed. The big jet made a sharp left turn and angled in for a quick descent to the runway, and the water and ground became more defined with each passing second. Soon, the jet's nose flared up, and we dropped smoothly onto the tarmac, where the brakes and reverse thrusters came on and slowed the plane as it bumped along on the runway. I hazarded a brief glance at Fiona and noticed her breasts were giggling from the movement, and, while it was mildly silly to notice such things, it instantly brought a subtle feeling of heartache bubbling up from my innards. She caught me looking and responded with a scornful stare, so I returned her scornful stare with a smile, but it only increased her scorn.

Men might have been from Mars, but women were clearly from another galaxy altogether. Yes, I had masturbated in front of another woman, but, unlike Fiona, I did not go so far as to make out with that person. Touching tongues seemed to be a hell of a lot more personal to me, and the thought of Fiona and Brett rubbing their lips up against one another was almost enough to make me toss my biscuits. At least I could take solace in knowing that his mouth was clean and mostly free of germs.

The Jet slowed and eventually made a sharp left turn off the runway and headed towards a smaller building that was likely the private terminal. A man in shorts wearing the requisite ear protection and holding orange signal paddles directed the plane to come to a stop, and Wendy's voice came over the intercom.

"Welcome to Malkarta. Feel free to grab your shit and hit the beach," she said.

A better welcome to an island paradise I couldn't imagine.

CHAPTER SIXTEEN
Island of Broken Dreams

I unbuckled my seatbelt and grabbed my stuff before heading towards the front of the plane, where I spent the alone time waiting for the ground crew to move the boarding stairs into place. I heard a clunking sound, then, a moment later, Wendy appeared from the cockpit and opened the outer door. The fresh air was glorious after fifteen straight hours in the jet, and like most tropical islands, it was thick with the scent of fresh flowers and the nearby sea, and the experience instantly triggered my olfactory senses into a state of calm optimism. There was nothing like the fresh air of the tropics to calm the nerves and soothe the soul.

I walked down the boarding stairs and stood on the tarmac and could feel the sun was already hot and making me wish that I had decided on shorts. I wasn't sure when we would be going to get Fiona's brother, so I had dressed a bit more formal in khaki colored slacks and white button up shirt, which I had left un-tucked for better air flow. Now, even in light colored clothing, I was feeling the heat and humidity of the tropics and desperately wanted to tear off my clothes and dive into the ocean. That, however, would have to wait until we spoke with the authorities and figured out the itinerary of our diplomatic rescue mission.

Fiona appeared at the doorway a moment later with Brett a few steps behind, and he was looking ever burdened as he carried her suitcase. At least he was good for something and would save my back by taking over the transport of that monster. He huffed and puffed as he struggled down the boarding stairs, and I couldn't help but laugh out loud when he finally stopped and deposited the suitcase on the ground.

"Biscuit, could you help me with my bag as well?"

"Fuck you," he said.

"Oh, don't be bitter—everything comes at a price," I said, casting my gaze over at Fiona, who had come to stand beside me.

"So, what's the plan?" she asked.

"I'm not sure exactly."

Just then, a white BMW sedan with United States Embassy plates pulled up and parked a few feet away. Shortly thereafter, a fit and tan-looking thirtysomething man with a full head of grey flecked brown hair emerged and walked over and smiled as he held out his hand.

"I'm Tim Stansfield, deputy ambassador to Malkarta,

you must be Tag Finn."

"Nice to meet you, Tim," I said, as I shook his hand.

"Likewise. Welcome to paradise."

"Indeed, you must have a hell of a job here."

"Warm weather, beaches, ocean, and bikinis. Honestly, I have a lot of job satisfaction."

"I can imagine."

"Have you been in touch with the vice president about your itinerary here?" he asked.

"No, but we were just wondering about that."

"Well, the government is ready to release your man, but the paperwork won't be processed until tomorrow morning, so you have a day to enjoy yourselves, and the vice president has instructed me to extend you every courtesy, which means dinner on the United States Government in one of New Leiden's best restaurants.

"I think that sounds like a pretty decent evening."

"Yeah, and in the meanwhile I'll take you to your hotel to get settled in, and then you can do a little sightseeing or hit the beach."

"Even better."

Tatyana exited the plane and came down to join us.

"So, what's the story with you and the crew? You coming along?" I asked.

"Not sure yet. We have to take care of the plane first, then we'll find out where we're staying. Hopefully I'll see you later," she said, giving me a hug and a wink.

Fiona and Brett exchanged a hug, then the tan menace,

of course, tried for a kiss, but she turned her head at the last minute. With our goodbyes concluded, Fiona and I loaded up into Tim's car and left the airport and headed north through New Leiden. It was a beautiful city, and its architecture was definitely the product of its European heritage. Most of the buildings were covered in white stucco, and the streets were narrow, with some even still paved with cobblestones like the great old cities of Europe. We passed through the main part of town and headed towards the coast, where a beautiful blue ocean extended off to the horizon. Tim reached into the glovebox then pulled out a satellite telephone and handed it to me.

"Compliments of the vice president. He had us give you this, so that you could stay in touch and reach him if there were any questions or problems. His direct line is already programmed in."

"Thanks."

"So, are you and the vice president close friends?" Tim asked.

"Yes indeed. We met and fell madly in love while serving in Afghanistan."

Tim laughed.

"Always good to know people in high places."

"I suppose, but I wish the asshole would get his ass in gear and run for president. I'd get a lot more mileage at cocktail parties saying I was close personal friends with the president—rather than his lackey."

"True, but even knowing the vice president is still probably a good conversation opener."

We turned onto a smaller road and drove through beautifully manicured gardens before pulling into the courtyard of an extravagant hotel. It was painted eggshell white and looked more like a European royal palace with its ornate window trims and elegant courtyard. The place buzzed with activity, and people dressed in lightly colored tropical uniforms moved around us with practiced efficiency as Tim pulled up under the main entrance. We came to a stop, and a valet with smooth Asiatic features stepped up and opened the door.

"Welcome to the King William Hotel," he said, in excellent English.

"Thank you," I said, exiting the car and waiting for Fiona to climb out.

Tim stepped out of the car and joined us on the curb.

"I'll be by around six to pick you guys up," he said.

"Sounds good. Any advice for a nice beach?"

"Yeah, the one here at the hotel. This place wasn't built here by accident."

"Nice, we'll see you at six."

"Oh, and the dress code is island chic."

He drove off, and we meandered inside as a valet loaded our things onto a cart before following us into the finely appointed lobby. We reached the stately reception desk and were greeted by a pretty blond girl in her early twenties. She had lovely light blue eyes, tan skin, and the healthy physique of someone who maintained a very active lifestyle—likely surfing given the granules of sand resting on the edge of her scalp.

"Hello, and welcome to the King William Hotel. My name is Nicole—how can I help you, sir," she said, with an Australian accent, which made sense, as we were only a bit north of the land down under.

"G'day, the name's Finn, and I believe we have a reservation," I said.

She smiled and looked down at her computer screen.

"Oh yes, Mr. Finn, we have your reservation right here. You and your friend are staying in the presidential suite."

"No shit?"

"No shit. Apparently someone thinks you're very presidential."

John had booked our accommodations, but I suppose hotels didn't have vice presidential suites, so, in this case, we got the default—the presidential suite, which was fine by me. I thanked Nicole and turned to follow the bellman, who, instead of going to the elevators, took us down a hallway along the main floor.

"So, the presidential suite isn't on the top floor?" I asked.

"No, sir, it sits by itself out beside the beach."

"As it fucking should!" I said, starting to get excited.

He wasn't sure how to take my enthusiasm and smiled shyly as he turned his attention back to the task of pushing the cart. After a brief trek, we reached the door to our suite and paused while he opened it and stood aside and politely waited for us to enter. I stepped inside and almost had to shield my eyes as though I were looking Brett straight in the mouth. Unlike the tan menace's whitened smile, however, this place was warm and inviting. The entire wall facing the ocean was sliding glass doors, and their glorious presence served to funnel sunlight into the main living room, where all of it reflected off the white marble floors and equally white furniture, thus making the experience border on divine. I couldn't help but imagine that heaven must certainly resemble this suite, though my soon to be roommate was definitely not an angel—at the moment, anyway.

I gazed around the room and admired the furnishings, first and foremost being the bar, which sat near the far wall. It had stools for six and was well appointed with a wide array of top shelf alcohols. Presidents apparently liked to drink, but, if drinking wasn't your thing then you'd be equally happy taking up residence on the plush linen sofa or matching chair that sat atop a cozy white shag throw rug. To complete the effect, there was also a fireplace, though I doubt it ever saw much use due to the warmth of the climate. Still, it beckoned to be the setting for two lovers to make sweet passionate love—as long as those lovers weren't Brett and Fiona.

I walked to the far side of the room and paused in front of the wall of sliding glass doors and instantly felt as though I might fill my pants with man juice. Before me lay a tiled patio complete with loungers, gazebo, and a lovely infinity pool and adjoining Jacuzzi. Beyond that was one of the most beautiful white sand beaches I had ever seen, and the water beyond it was smooth and devoid of wave action due to the presence of a reef that curled around from the far shore. Holy shit! This was the single greatest working trip I could ever imagine.

Shifting my gaze back inside the room, I saw that we had a full kitchen as well as five bedrooms. It was a lot of space for one person, let alone a family, so it would appear that presidents traveled with quite an entourage. The bellman placed our things in our individual rooms then rejoined us.

"Is there anything else I can help you with?"

"No, we'll be just fine. Oh, do you accept American dollars for tips?" I asked.

"Absolutely. Euro's or dollars are both equally acceptable."

I slid the bellman a twenty, which I'm not sure was the appropriate amount, but he appeared to be pretty happy as he left, so I'd probably done OK. I left Fiona and had a quick look at my room, which, like the rest of the place, was utterly amazing. It had a massive four-poster bed in the center, and beyond that was a doorway leading to a bathroom large enough for at least six people to use without ever running into each other. Jiminy fucking Christmas — this was the life. I walked over to the toilet and peed and took a moment afterward to wipe the splatters off the rim with a piece of toilet paper. It was a habit that my mother had instilled in me as a child, and I continued it into adulthood. Being a true gentleman, in her opinion, apparently entailed leaving very little of yourself behind.

I headed back into the bedroom and immediately stripped and slipped on my board shorts and a T-shirt before heading out to the patio to check out the scenery in person. Fiona appeared a moment later, and my heart skipped a beat as I spied her looking absolutely divine in a tiny two-piece white bikini. She smiled and walked past me, and the look on her face was a sign that she was aware of my purposeful gaze. We may have been on uncertain terms, but that fact would do nothing to quell my attraction for her and ultimately would be her greatest tool in making me utterly miserable in her presence. Let the battle for my piece of mind begin.

I walked over to a small gazebo on the far left side of the pool and found fuzzy white cotton beach towels. I grabbed two and brought one to Fiona, who thanked me as she took a seat on one of the loungers. I threw my towel on the seat beside her and immediately dove into the pool and instantly felt the last fifteen hours of plane travel dissipate from my body. There was nothing like a dip in cool water to reinvigorate the body and soul, which perhaps harkened back to something buried in our DNA that linked us to the primordial sea from which we originated. There were even studies and a name for it—the mammalian diving reflex. When mammals such as human's were immersed in cold water it reduced their heart rate. For whales and dolphins this meant they could dive longer and deeper, but in hu-mans it just seemed to help us relax and recuperate. Either way, the cool embrace of the water was my personal savior as it enveloped my body and made me feel refreshed and ready for a day of fun and sun. I popped out of the pool and took a seat beside Fiona.

"The pool is nice, but it seems like a shame to waste that beautiful ocean. Do you want to go down to the beach and do some snorkeling?"

"Maybe."

"Maybe? Hello! We're on a beautiful tropical island right now, and tomorrow we'll be back aboard that plane sucking in recirculated air, so we really should get out and enjoy ourselves while we can."

"Unlike you, I didn't bring any snorkeling gear."

"No problem—there's some in the gazebo."

"Do you think it's safe to use?"

"Yeah, assuming its only been used by actual presidents, and not any of their lackey vice presidents."

She smiled.

"You even make fun of poor John when he's not around to hear it."

"Yeah, I'm sentimental that way."

We grabbed the snorkeling gear and headed down to the beach, which was fairly crowded with tourists obviously here to enjoy the sun, sand, and gloriously warm clear blue ocean. We found a spot with two empty loungers under one of the hotel's beach umbrellas and made camp by setting our towels and things on the small rattan table. I instinctively took a minute to do a little surveillance of our surroundings and spied an endless sea of sunbathers. One umbrella away, was a middle-aged couple that had apparently never heard of sunblock, and their expanses of reddened flesh were an unpleasant reminder of the effects of a long day in the sun. Moving my attention farther along the beach, I spied more of their kind, and all of them were baking away under the hot Malkarta sun. Amongst them, however, and sitting close to the hotel's oceanside restaurant, was a man fairly overdressed for the beach. He was wearing khaki pants and a button up shirt and appeared to be looking our way, though he turned his head when he saw me glance in his direction. Interesting. It was unusual for someone to go to the beach dressed in long pants and shirt unless they were a voyeur or an albino. Judging by the guy's formidable tan and apparent singular interest in us, I was guessing he was neither, which begged the question of why we had come under his scrutiny. I stored his face in my memory and returned my attention back to Fiona, who had just pulled out a tube of waterproof sunblock.

"Would you mind putting some of this on my back?" she asked.

"Not at all," I said, grabbing the tube and pouring out a large dollop before rubbing it in—ever careful to lift her bikini straps and make sure all of her skin was adequately covered.

"Want me to get the front as well?"

"No thanks. I think I can handle it."

"You sure? Because it's a pretty big job, and I'm a wizard at getting to all those hard to reach places—like your nipples."

"Oh, do these look hard to reach?" she asked, as she slid her oiled up hands under her bikini top.

"Well, yeah—from here."

She smiled at me then proceeded to continue rubbing sunblock onto her chest while I did the same to my own body, though my eyes stayed focused on her, and my heart rate continued to increase with each passing second. Sure, it was just a menial task, but I took it in as a subtle form of torture, considering I had intimate knowledge of those areas, yet now would probably never again have the opportunity to run my hands or mouth over their soft curves—but such was the cruelty of existence.

I asked if she could get my back, and soon we were both properly bathed in sunblock and ready to get in the ocean. We grabbed our gear and moved to the water's edge, where we slipped on our flippers before turning and backing in until it was deep enough to swim. I spit in my mask, gave it a partial rinse, and slipped my head under the surface to see a surprising amount of sea life this close to shore. It was likely the result of the topography of the bay, specifically its reef, which kept out the larger predators and made this the perfect safe haven for fish.

We moved farther out, and Fiona swam just ahead, and her magnificent backside was the perfect lure to hold my interest until we crossed over the reef and discovered vast schools of colorful fish. This part of the bay was even more dense with sea life, and there were flourishing corals, anemones, and sea urchins covering every inch of the reef, and around them swam more varieties of fish than I could count on all my fingers and toes. Fiona tapped me and pointed out a large puffer fish that was swimming by, and its odd shape was almost comical as it moved along with its tiny pectoral fins looking more like miniature helicopter blades. We moved on into slightly deeper water and came across a massive school of baby tuna that were all swimming in a great swirling cyclone that stretched from the ocean floor to the surface of the water. As we drew closer, they changed course and swirled all around us and enveloped us in a great silvery curtain. Fiona started to get nervous and wrapped her arms around my chest and practically pulled me underwater in the process.

I managed to stay afloat and guide us out of the school and back into open water, where Fiona relaxed but still kept ahold of my hand. We continued on and came upon a large sea turtle, which stayed with us for an unusually long time before diving and disappearing into the reef below. I popped my head up to look towards shore to get a quick bearing then decided to head north, so that we could follow the reef until it turned in and curved back towards the beach. Fifteen minutes later, we were on warm sand and walking along the shore, and I paused to take a look around.

"What's up?" Fiona asked, looking concerned.

"My *scrot-sense* is tingling."

"What?"

"I said my *scrot-sense*—is tingling."

"That's what I thought you said, but what the hell does it mean?"

"It means that I'm sensing some kind of imminent danger, and my scrotum is tingling, which of course is a signal for my balls to climb up and hide in my butthole."

Fiona stared for a long, hard moment.

"Is this something related to a dark episode from childhood perhaps?"

"No, a friend and I were drinking a lot of beer a couple weeks ago, and he came up with the idea that I should give my intuition a catchy name. You know—like *Magnum P.I.* and his little voice or Spiderman and his Spider Sense."

"And you came up with *scrot-sense?*"

"It seemed pretty funny at the time."

"It's funny all right, but in a prepubescent boy kind of way."

"Which is still funny."

"If you were a prepubescent boy."

"Or young at heart"

"And mind, unfortunately."

I decided to ignore her comment and get back to the task at hand—namely scanning for the apparent threat that was making my *scrot-sense* tingle. I, therefore, performed a quick sweep of the crowd and spied the same guy from earlier still watching us, though he had changed spots and had two new friends sitting at his table. He could obviously use a little help with his spy craft, as he should have switched out with a different watcher long ago.

"Someone on the island of Malkarta clearly has an interest in us," I said.

"Did your *scrot-sense* tell you that?" Fiona asked.

"Sort of. See that guy over there in the button up shirt and sunglasses?"

"Yeah."

"Well, he's been watching us ever since we got here."

"Who do you think he is?"

"Judging by the haircut and outfit—some kind of government dink."

"Why would he be watching us?"

"Your brother was accused of sedition, so it stands to reason that they'll be keeping a close eye on anyone associated with him as well."

"What do we do?"

"We go say hello."

"Are you sure that's a good idea?"

"Yeah, what harm could it possibly do to get friendly with the locals?"

We walked up the beach past the other tourists and straight to our guy, whose expression got more and more uncomfortable the closer we came to his table. This was yet more proof that my suspicions were correct, and he tried his best not to look at us, but I purposefully stood directly in front of him and even went so far as to set my wet sandy fins, mask, and snorkel on the center of the table. Looking rather annoyed, he stood up, and I could see that he was young, fit, and about six foot two, which made him approximately an inch or so taller than me. While six two was well above average height for an American, it was about average for a Dutchman, who, along with the Danes, were statistically some of the tallest people in Europe. My young stalker was therefore a fairly imposing individual, though part of that conclusion was based on knowing that he was fresh out of the military, which was something I deduced by his haircut and the youthful confidence he held behind his light blue eyes.

"*Goedemiddag*," I said, which meant good afternoon in Dutch.

"Hello," he responded uncomfortably, while his two friends looked to him for guidance.

I purposefully spoke one of the few Dutch words I knew, because it would instantly confirm my belief that he was local.

"So, are you and your friends from the tourism board," I asked.

"No, and it's definitely not any of your business."

"Well, if you're watching me and my lady friend, then I think that technically it is my business."

"No, it's not."

"I beg to differ."

"Perhaps you should be on your way, as there's no need for you to get yourself into any trouble."

"Trouble? Is talking illegal? Is it now the job of the Malkarta Internal Security Service to enforce silence?"

They stayed quiet, which meant that they were indeed members of the Malkata Internal Security Service, or in short—MISS.

"Fiona. Say hello to three of Malkarta's finest. Maybe if we're nice, they'll let us take a picture with them. Can we get a picture?" I asked.

"No."

"Seriously?"

"Yeah, fuck off."

"It's a good thing you don't work for the tourism board, because, honestly, your people skills need some serious work."

He abruptly stepped back from his seat, and the move sent his chair falling backwards onto the ground.

"Do we have a problem?" he asked, as his face reddened with anger.

"Aside from your attitude? Not really."

He came around the table and squared off in front of me, looking ready for a fight. Before our little exchange could escalate, a voice sounded out from a short distance away, and I looked past my voyeur and saw a distinguished looking man in his upper forties approaching the table. He, like his subordinate, was tan, fit, good looking, and had sandy blond hair, though his age brought with it a few flecks of grey. He was wearing a fine linen suit and held himself with a great deal of bearing and was therefore somebody very important. When he reached the table, I saw that he was wearing a tie clip that had the Royal Dutch Military Academy's seal, and it told me all I needed to know about the man. He was career military, and it was a trait that followed a person into every aspect of his personality for the rest of his life—kind of like Brett and his precious Naval Academy.

"Stand down, Sten," he said.

My stalker instantly obeyed while the man in charge turned his gaze toward us and smiled as he held out his hand.

"I'm General Maas Groot," he said.

"I'm Tag Finn, and this is Fiona Blake," I said, though I was pretty certain he already knew our names.

"Yes, I know who you are, and I'm sorry about the situation with your brother and any suffering this has caused you and your family."

"Well thank you, General Groot," Fiona said.

"Please call me Maas."

"So, what's with the baby sitters?" I asked.

"Oh, sorry about my men. They sometimes take their job a bit too seriously, and young Sten here is still adapting to civilian life, having only recently returned from Afghanistan."

"I understand. I was stationed there myself."

"You were a soldier?"

"Yeah, and while I've been out for a few years, it's still very present in my consciousness."

"Yes, it does indeed tend to linger."

Sten was listening intently, and I saw his expression drastically change from anger to shame as he realized he shared a kind of kinship with the man he had just wanted to punch in the face. All soldiers shared a common bond, especially if they served in the same part of the world, and now Sten and I would likely have a completely different relationship.

"Believe it or not, these men were actually here for your protection. It's not often that the vice president of the United States sends a personal envoy into our midst, so we wanted to make sure that you and Miss Blake were kept safe."

"This is paradise. What could possibly happen here?" I asked.

"Our island is mostly peaceful, but we do have a few incidents of unrest that flare up every now and again. Al Qaeda and some of its Indonesian splinters operate in the islands around us and have attempted a few incursions to Malkarta, and with you being American, you're a particularly enticing target."

"Well, thanks for caring."

"You're welcome, now please enjoy yourselves on Malkarta. I'll see you both tomorrow morning when we release Mr. Blake into your custody."

Fiona and I said goodbye to Maas, Sten, and the others then turned and walked back to our spot on the beach and sat beneath our umbrella.

"He was nice," Fiona said.

"He was, and learning that young Sten is recently back from Afghanistan kind of makes me feel a little guilty for getting him all riled up."

Conversation ceased for a moment, and I found myself regarding Fiona. The air was warm, but her suit was still wet, and the thin fabric was doing very little to hide the fact that evaporation was bringing her nipples out to say hello. She, of course, caught me looking but made no move to cover up, which meant that she was still very willing and able to use my attraction to her as a subtle, though particularly cruel, form of torture.

I turned away, leaned back, and decided instead to stare out at the ocean, as its smooth blue surface would calm my nerves and take me to my happy place. I'd always tried to remain close to the ocean throughout my lifetime, which is why, after leaving government service, that I'd chosen to live on a houseboat. So, now, even thousands of miles from home, I could still find familiarity, and in that, strength—something that I was going to need a lot of if I hoped to survive the next twenty-four hours in close proximity to Fiona.

The sun moved slowly across the sky, and we continued to relax and enjoy the day until I looked at my watch and saw it was a little after five. At that point, we decided to return to the presidential suite to get ready for dinner, and I was also looking forward to a shot of espresso, a quick and unexpected third dump, and a nice hot shower. We entered via the patio, and I went straight to the espresso machine while Fiona took a seat on the other side of the bar. Upon smelling the heavenly aroma of fresh brewing coffee, she put in an order for a cappuccino, so I grabbed two cups and within moments had two drinks hot and ready on the bar.

"Salute," I said.

"Salute."

We sipped in silence, with the cappuccino providing a needed end of day pick me up after a long flight and an afternoon on the water.

"So, will the others be joining us?" Fiona asked.

"I'm not sure. Why?"

"Just curious."

I had to wonder if she was curious about the lovely Tatyana or the tan wonder, and if it was the latter, would she be willing to consummate their relationship just to make me miserable. I suppose that's what I got for helping out a stranger—a trip to the tropics and an epic case of blue balls. At least the cappuccino was starting to work its magic, so it was time to excuse myself and head to my room to strip down and hit the bathroom. I grabbed my iPhone, set my cup on the sink, and hit the porcelain, which was comfortably close to room temperature and therefore a glorious catalyst in freeing the family of fecals that were currently homesteading in my anus. One by one, they all made the brave leap into the water, thus leaving my anus a deserted wasteland—so to speak. I reached over, finished my coffee, then got into the shower to find its warm, wet embrace all the more comforting after an afternoon in the sun, sand, and salty ocean.

First, I rubbed a dollop of shampoo into my hair and

let it soak in while I used the bar of soap to wash the rest of my body. The trick then was to finish up before the shampoo managed to make its way down my forehead and into my eyes. Everything went according to plan and, with everything clean as could be and my penis perhaps a shade cleaner because of the more enthusiastic scrubbing, I turned off the water and grabbed one of the particularly soft white cotton towels and stepped out of the shower. Once dry, I put on deodorant, face cream, and cologne and walked into my room to go through my clothes and decide on something to wear. Tim had said island chic, and now I was wondering what in the hell that meant. Was it a Hawaiian shirt and khaki pants, or shorts and a T-shirt? I went with the former, though I substituted the Hawaiian shirt for a white short sleeve button up shirt and finished the outfit up with some sandals. I hazarded a brief glance in the mirror and decided that I looked like a Miami Beach drug dealer. Perfect.

I left the safety of my room and headed to the bar and made two very light tropical cocktails that consisted of coconut rum and a mixture of pineapple and orange juice. Drink in hand I ventured out onto the patio and saw that the long rays of the end of the day were making for a particularly beautiful sunset, and the distant clouds were already taking on a rich orange color that dissolved into pink at the far off edges of the horizon. I took a sip of my cocktail and sighed as I took in the great expanse of beauty that stretched out before me. The sound of footsteps broke my reverie, and I turned around to find Fiona walking out to join me. Sweet Lord! I felt my breath escape my lungs as I took in yet another picture of beauty, and it was as if Fiona were trying to challenge mother nature herself as she stood there looking stunningly beautiful in a tight lavender colored cotton dress that couldn't have adhered more effectively to her curves had it been painted onto her body. After an awkwardly long and quiet moment, Fiona was the first to break the silence.

"Are you just going to stand there and stare, or are you going to tell me how I look?" she asked.

"I'm not sure there's a word on this earth that could adequately describe how beautiful you look."

"Well thank you, Tag. Did you happen to make me a cocktail as well?" she asked.

"Of course," I said, handing her a drink.

We clinked glasses and toasted.

"To getting your brother out of this God awful hell pit of a place," I said.

"Yeah, I'm starting to understand why he came here."

"Who wouldn't want to save the world if it looked like Malkarta?"

"Yeah, no shit," she said, taking a sip.

We stood in silence as we sipped our cocktails and gazed out at paradise. A warm gust of wind blew in from the east and caused Fiona's dress to billow up just enough to expose the tan upper reaches of her shapely thighs, and the brief show made my pulse quicken and my shaft thicken.

Every person had their physical preference when it came to the opposite sex, and mine was having some shape, and in a perfect world, some muscle tone. Skinny stick figure models just didn't do it for me, so if I had to choose either too big or too thin, I'd go with the former. Fiona, like a gift from the heavens, of course had it all: an athletic physique consisting of long shapely legs, nice round backside, and natural full breasts, which of course is obviously how she ended up as a Playboy centerfold. All these subtle facts combined at this very moment to make my heart ache all the more, and the final frosting on this cake of despair was the fact we were in possibly one of the most romantic of settings yet were, at the moment, nowhere near having a romantic relationship. Or so I believed until she suddenly reached out and took hold of my hand.

"Tag, I really want to thank you for all you've done, and I'd like to apologize for being such a pain in the ass. So, tonight, I hope that I can make it up to you."

"It's OK, don't worry about it. I understand what it's like to be dragged into the craziness of this jet set lifestyle. It can be a little disorienting."

"No, I mean it. Tonight, we are going to have a good time—no soap operas, no bullshit."

Just then, a voice called out from inside our suite, and we both turned to see the man with the tan and teeth, a man now known as biscuit, stepping out onto the patio.

"Good news! Tatyana and the other pilots got plane duty, so I'm free for the evening!"

CHAPTER SEVENTEEN
Vette Moeder

Brett was standing there smiling with his teeth aglow in the remaining light of the day, and I was wondering what qualified as justifiable homicide and whether or not cock-blocking could be used as an adequate defense in a court of law. Fiona looked at me uncomfortably as Brett walked over and took hold of her drink, finished it, then asked if there was more. I pointed at the bar inside the suite, and he left and gave us a brief respite to talk.

"Fuck. How the hell did he find us?" Fiona asked.

"The fucker must have called the Embassy and talked to Tim."

"What do we do now?"

"Kill him, hide the body, though I'm not sure what we can do about the teeth."

Brett reappeared with the cocktail and joined us.

"So, Tim says we are going to a place called *Vette Moeder*, which means fat mother. Supposedly it's the best place on the island and even has three of those Michigan stars," he said.

"You mean Michelin stars," I corrected.

"Yeah, that's what I meant."

"Well, I'm sure it's going to be a lovely evening," I said, suddenly feeling the need for more alcohol.

Thirty minutes later we were in front of the hotel and getting into Tim's white BMW sedan. He was dressed in a short sleeve shirt and khaki pants, so I suppose that I had interpreted island chic appropriately. We drove off from the hotel and headed into New Leiden's lovely city center then turned north onto a road that led up the hillside and wound past a cavalcade of beautiful homes that reminded me of Monte Carlo. The *Vette Moeder* apparently sat high on the mountain and would most certainly have a spectacular view of the city. Five minutes of switchbacks and we at last pulled into its parking lot, where a team of valets opened our doors and welcomed us to the restaurant. The guy on Fiona's side did a double take, though not necessarily because he recognized her from *Playboy Magazine*, but rather because she was incredibly attractive and had exited the car legs first—a sight than no red blooded straight man could ignore.

With everyone out of the car, Tim led us inside, and we were greeted by a polished young man of Indonesian descent. He said hello and smiled to reveal teeth easily as white if not whiter than Brett's, and I glanced at the tan menace and noticed that he too was admiring our maître d's oral magnificence. Brett, sensing my gaze, turned to me and shrugged.

"I know you're just dying to say some stupid insult, so you might as well just spit it out," he said.

"Well, it's technically not an insult. I was merely thinking you might just want to come out and ask our maître d what kind of toothpaste he uses."

Brett shook his head slowly side to side then casually extended his middle finger at me.

"You're only mad because it's true," I said.

Before we could continue our exchange, our host turned and led us all out onto the deck, where we had the premier table overlooking the entire city and surrounding countryside of New Leiden. He asked if we would like to start with any drinks, so I ordered a Mojito, as I preferred to stick with one kind of alcohol. Everyone copied my order, and, soon thereafter, a waiter appeared with a tray full of delicious looking mojitos, and, once everyone had a cocktail in their hand, Tim raised his glass to toast.

"To the release of Mark Blake," he said.

"And a wonderful dinner, compliments of the United States Government," I added.

Everyone clinked glasses and took sips of their Mojito's, and the looks of satisfaction were more than enough evidence to know that I had chosen wisely. I set down my drink and turned my attention to the menu to discover that it was Indo-Dutch cuisine, which was something that I had never tried in my years of world travel. I therefore decided to put my trust in Tim, who went on to order for the entire table. He chose *rijsttafel*, which literally translated as rice table and consisted of rice, dozens of small dishes including *Rendang*, and spicy *sambal* paste. I had no idea what any of it actually was, but it sounded good, and I imagined that our host must know what he was doing.

We ordered another round of drinks, and the conversation soon fell upon Malkarta, which was more interesting politically and culturally than I had been led to believe by Fiona's initial description. The Island, according to its official tourism board, was a peaceful paradise where travelers could experience the Dutch West Indies in style and safety. Still an autonomous state with close ties to Holland, it boasted that it was free of Indonesia's bouts of terrorism and violence that seemed to flare up every couple of years in the form of bombings and minor civil wars. The real story, however, was obviously a little more interesting.

"This part of Malkarta is pretty much exactly like the brochures say—quiet, peaceful, and the perfect spot for a tropical island getaway. Things change, however, when you head north or up country as the locals say. Up there are the unofficial strongholds of the two factions that would desperately like to make some serious changes on the island, with the first and foremost being a change of government. On one end of the political spectrum, you have the Malkarta Democratic Alliance, or MDA, a group of moderates that want better schools, medical care, and, at some point, a freely elected government or parliamentary system to balance out the power of the monarchy. Then, on the other end is the Malkarta Socialist Alliance or MSA. Their name sounds innocuous enough, but they're basically religious extremists with close ties to Al Qaeda, who would like to turn Malkarta into an Islamic military state. Over the last few years, they've been involved in numerous kidnappings and even a few bombings," Tim said.

"Do the MDA and MSA coexist peacefully?" I asked.

"Not exactly. The two factions mostly stick to themselves, with the MDA occupying the northeast and the MSA occupying the northwest."

"And what's the US's official opinion on all this?" I asked.

"Well, we're hoping to put in a Naval base here, so, as it stands now, the US is happy with the current government. The MDA would come in a strong second, assuming that is, if they were OK with the base. The MSA is clearly not on the favorites list and something we are monitoring closely because of their ties to terrorist factions."

"Do you think the sedition charges brought against Fiona's brother are horse shit?"

"Absolutely. The government here obviously wants a cheap, uneducated labor force, because it means lower operating costs and greater profits. This island generates more than a billion dollars a year from its spice manufacturing, and anyone who challenges that, regardless how noble his or her intentions might be, is going to eventually end up in a lot of trouble with the powers that be."

"So, Malkarta is a lot like South America when it was

controlled by the United Fruit Company."

"Exactly, though, in this case, the company is also an absolute monarchy."

Dinner arrived, and we ate Dutch-Indo style by piling rice and food from the various dishes onto our plates to enjoy a cornucopia of flavors and spices. We also ordered another round of Mojitos, and it would have been a truly perfect evening had it only been Fiona, Tim, and me. Unfortunately, Biscuit was in rare form and doing his best to steer the conversation to his time flying fighter jets, and, whenever possible, the Naval Academy, which made me think that Brett was to his alma matter what Mickey Mouse was to Disneyland. I'm all for school spirit, but once you graduate, it's time to move on into adult life—no more stickers on your car, license plate holders, or sweatshirts. The fucking tan menace continued blabbering, and after about ten straight uninterrupted minutes, I almost felt as though I too had attended the Naval Academy. Thankfully, our waiter arrived and interrupted Brett's flow when he asked if we would like dessert. Tim looked around to see if there were any takers, but there was a unanimous groan that all were fully sated. I, however, decided on a Dutch coffee, which, like an Irish coffee, was spiked with booze—in this case, a spiced Dutch Brandy called *Schelvispekel*. As if that weren't already delicious sounding enough, it was also topped with whipped cream and toasted almonds, and, by the time our waiter had left the table, everyone, including the tan menace, had also ordered one.

The drinks arrived, and everyone used that brief respite from conversation to look out at the view and enjoy the sights of New Leiden as it glowed in the fading light of the day. I felt eyes on me and looked over to see Fiona staring, and we exchanged a brief smile. Perhaps things were looking up. Several minutes passed, and everyone finished their coffee, so Tim paid the bill, and we left the restaurant and began the drive back to the hotel. Fifteen minutes later, we thanked our host for dinner, then said good night and adjourned to the presidential suite. The hotel staff had apparently already been there and dimmed the lights in the living room, which made it look particularly romantic and immediately begged the question of what exactly presidents did when they stayed at hotels. If this room were any indication, then it was very clear that they were all fornicating, hopefully with their wives rather than their mistresses or interns. I went behind the bar and made myself another tropical rum drink then took a seat. Fiona joined me a moment later, which would have been rather nice had Biscuit not been following her like an obedient little poodle.

"So, Fi, which room is yours?" he asked.

Fi? He already had a pet name for Fiona? How the fuck did she get a cute little pet name in twenty-four hours? Perhaps she hadn't been entirely truthful about her night with the tan menace. I had officially had about all that I could take and decided to get out and enjoy a walk along the water and perhaps visit the hotel's beachside bar. Anything would be better than sitting here watching Biscuit fawn all over Fiona—or should I say Fi. Fuckers. I said goodbye and headed towards the patio, only to have Fiona race over and catch me at the door.

"Where are you going?" she asked, looking concerned.

"Outside for a little walk along the beach then maybe a brief stop at the hotel bar. I figured you and Biscuit would want some privacy."

"No, don't go. We don't need any privacy."

"No, it's cool. I'll see you later, Fi."

I turned and left via the patio to reach the path that skirted the beach, and I followed it a few yards then stopped and had to ask myself why in the fuck I was walking on a paved path? I could walk on concrete every day back home, so why would I waste an opportunity to walk on the warm sand of a beautiful tropical island? I went back and threw my sandals onto the patio then returned to the beach to enjoy the feel of the sand underneath my feet. Sometimes, walking barefoot could be incredibly grounding, and I could use a little grounding at the moment.

I padded along the sand then made a brief detour into the water and looked out at the view, before turning my gaze to the night sky, where there were millions of stars visible due to the relative lack of ambient light, and, had I not been alone, it would have been the perfect moment to hold my special someone's hand. As things currently stood, however, the only hand I would be holding would be my own, which was all the more reason to go drown my sorrows in drink.

I continued about a hundred yards down the beach to the bar, which resided between the pool and beach and was comprised of a small bamboo hut and a large patio full of tables that were lit by tiki torches. It was serviced by a lone waitress who appeared to be particularly busy, as all her tables were full of thirsty tourists. I took the only open seat at the bar, and it happened to be next to the place where the wait staff picked up drink orders. Having found my spot, I was free to have a look at my fellow patrons, and around me were numerous Europeans, and most, if not all, were fair skinned and speaking Dutch, and nearly all of them were suffering from sunburn. The bartender, a tan Dutch looking man of about forty, came over and put a cocktail napkin down in front of me.

"What can I get you?" he asked, in Dutch accented English.

"Mojito, please."

"Coming up."

While he was busy making my drink, the cocktail waitress appeared and set her empty tray on the bar. Now that she was up close and personal, I could see that she was probably in her late twenties, beautiful, and obviously of Indonesian descent, considering her Asian features, tan skin, and beautiful long black hair. She had a flower just over her right ear, and she was wearing a silk floral print cocktail dress that nicely accentuated her striking figure. As she turned to me, her perfectly pert breasts came into view, but I managed to keep my gaze firmly locked upon her dark penetrating eyes, and I was rewarded with a lovely smile.

"How are you this evening?" she asked.

"Mostly good, and you?"

"Good, though what do you mean by mostly?"

I let out a long sigh then broke it down to two words.

"Girl trouble."

"Ah—but isn't it always?"

"Pretty much."

The bartender returned with my Mojito and asked if I would like to charge it to my room, but the lovely cocktail waitress held up her hand and interrupted.

"No need. This one's on me. This poor guy has girl trouble."

"I appreciate the offer, but I can't let you pay," I said.

"Don't worry. It's on the hotel."

"Well, in that case, thank you."

"You're welcome. I'm Ayu, by the way."

"I'm Tag. Very pleased to meet you," I said, holding out my hand.

"The pleasure is all mine."

The bartender filled Ayu's tray with drinks, and she departed only to return a few moments later with empty glasses.

"Busy tonight," I said.

"Actually, it's busy every night. In this part of the island, everyone is on vacation, so every day is a holiday."

"Ah—paradise."

She smiled.

"I'm guessing you're American?"

"As apple pie."

"You're obviously a long way from home. What brings you to Malkarta? Vacation?"

"Not exactly. I'm helping a friend who got into a little trouble here."

"What kind of trouble?"

"Legal trouble—he was charged with sedition."

"Wait, are you talking about Mark Blake of Globo-Care?"

"Yeah, you know him?"

"Not personally, but everyone here on the island knows of his efforts and subsequent trouble with the government. He was doing great things for the people of Malkarta."

"That's what I've heard."

"So—how do you know him?"

"Technically, I'm friends with his sister."

Friend being the operative word at the moment. She looked around to make sure no one was listening then leaned in a little closer and lowered her voice.

"It's terrible what they did to him, and everyone here knows that it is all a bunch of lies concocted by the monarchy."

"Interesting. I take it that you aren't too pleased with the powers that be."

"No, and neither is anyone else. The people of Malkarta

break their backs working for the spice industry and make only a pittance while the royal family pockets billions and live a life of privilege in their palace. It's criminal."

"It is, and you would think that they could at least afford to divert even a small amount back to the population that has made them so wealthy."

"Yeah, but they won't."

Just then, a great bull of a man came and sat down on the other side of the waitress stand. He was young, probably in his middle twenties, and had the red sunburned face of a man who had spent a long day in the sun. What was it about these Europeans? Did they get so little sun back home in the northern latitudes that they went apeshit when they finally reached the tropics? A certain amount of sun was good, but too much was a one way trip to the dermatologist. What happened to moderation in all things? That obviously wasn't a motto this guy lived by, as he soon ordered a double vodka and a beer chaser, and, judging by the smell of alcohol emanating from his entire being, he had obviously started putting them back long before arriving at the bar. After pounding down the vodka, he began scanning the bar's many females, and, as he lifted up his beer to take a sip, I noticed he was wearing a wedding ring. Married yet still on the hunt. What an asshole.

Ayu returned with a tray of empty glasses, and Mr. Asshole instantly made a very obvious point of checking her out, even going so far as to lean back and take a look at her ass. That was already creepy enough, but he took it to a completely inappropriate level when he reached over and gave it a squeeze. Ayu was so startled that she practically dropped her tray and its contents, but, as she recovered, she immediately moved out of his reach.

"What's your problem?" he asked, in slurred, though Dutch accented, English.

"I'm afraid, sir, that your behavior is inappropriate."

"It was just a little touch on the bum."

"It's still inappropriate."

"Oh, don't be such a bloody cocktease."

The bartender overheard the exchange and joined the conversation.

"Sir, I would greatly appreciate it if you would please keep your hands off of the staff."

"I would greatly appreciate it if you would mind your own business and fuck off."

I'd had about enough of the drunken asshole and decided I should politely intervene.

"Look, I understand your motivation. Ayu is a very beautiful woman, so it's only natural you'd want to have a look, but touching is absolutely out of the question."

Ayu stepped forward and looked embarrassed.

"Oh please, Tag, you don't need to get involved."

"Yeah, why don't you fuck off, friend," he said, reaching over and giving me a drunken shove.

Ayu stepped in between us in an effort to deescalate the situation, but the asshole reached out and grabbed her and pulled her close to his body, so that his face was just inches from hers. She tried to pull free, but he was far too strong and moved in for a kiss. Thankfully, she twisted her head at the last minute, and he ended up with a mouth full of hair rather than her lips. It was a simple defense, but it managed to create the break Ayu needed to wriggle free and step well out of his reach.

"What's your problem?" he asked her.

"That's it. I'm afraid it's time for you to leave," I said.

"I believe I told you to fuck off," he said, pointing his finger directly at my face.

I decided it was time to take a more proactive role, and I grabbed ahold of the asshole's finger then twisted it back until he cried out and nearly fell off his stool.

"Who the fuck do you think you are?"

"Her husband."

"Bullshit!"

"It just so happens I am," I said, as I let go of his finger then reached over and placed my arm around Ayu's waist.

"Oh really?" he asked sarcastically.

"Yeah."

"Then where are your wedding rings?"

"We don't need rings. Our love is enough," Ayu said, leaning over and kissing me.

"Satisfied?" I asked.

"No," he said, stepping closer and getting in my face.

I held up my hands in the usual non-aggressive placating gesture.

"Look here, Mr. Happy Pants, you're far too drunk to

even consider a fight."

"Oh, I take it you're realizing you may have bitten off more than you can chew!"

"Not exactly, but you're very inebriated, and, judging by the wedding ring on your finger, there is apparently some particularly unlucky woman probably wondering where in the hell you are. So, why not cut your losses, maintain what dignity you still have remaining, and go back to where you belong."

He glared angrily and used the moment to size me up, though his eyes were having trouble focusing, as he was obviously grossly impaired by the abundance of alcohol in his system. I also used the moment to size him up, and it was obvious he was bigger than me, but he clearly wasn't smarter, for, if he had been, he would have chosen a much better course of action. As typical of a twentysomething male, his drunken stupidity prevailed, and the asshole conceded to his growing anger and decided to throw a punch at my head. It might have even had a chance of landing had I been extremely drunk, blind, or slow, but I was none of those things, and therefore easily capable of handling his half-assed attack. It was a right roundhouse, the typical angry man's punch, and, in this instance, it was best to step to my right and inside the arc of his arm. Once I was safely off its path, I performed the trusty old block-check-counter, and that entailed redirecting his punch with my right hand and grabbing his wrist with my left, thus freeing up my right hand, so that I could reach around and slam it into the crux of his elbow. This forced him to bend his arm, and I was now able to use my leverage over his shoulder joint to take him backwards and down to the ground. There, I moved quickly and put pressure on his elbow to leverage him onto his stomach, where I pinned him in place by stepping on his shoulder while simultaneously applying hand twist to his wrist. The asshole struggled and spouted various vulgarities, so I decided to add a little extra measure of pain. I leaned down, and, using my left hand, I reached over and dug my thumb into his carotid artery and applied just enough pressure to make him stop talking and remain mostly placated until hotel security arrived about three long minutes later. The two large well-muscled security guys quickly picked him up off the ground and hustled him away, and Ayu came over to me and smiled appreciatively.

"Wow! You're pretty good with your hands," she said.

"Nah—he was just drunk."

"Yeah, but also big and strong."

"And equally slow and stupid."

"Either way, you showed some amazing skills."

"Well, you pick up things when you're a Chippendales dancer and have to fight off a lot of ladies."

"Wait—you mean like Thunder From Down Under."

"No, actually, I'm just kidding."

"Well, to be perfectly honest, I think you have the physique to pull it off, but if you aren't really a dancer, then what do you do?"

"I'm a private investigator."

"Is is a dangerous job?"

"On occasion, but a lot of the time it's pretty boring."

"So, when did you learn your fighting skills?"

"That started as a kid, but it continued in the military and when I worked for the government."

"So, you're basically James Bond."

"More like his lame American cousin."

"You mean his equally dashing American cousin. So, Mr. Bond, I say we forget about tonight's unfortunate little incident and share a drink. Bram, we'll have another round of Mojitos," she said.

He returned a minute later with the Mojitos, and we clinked glasses before taking a long sip.

"I don't get it. Just because I wear a nice dress and serve drinks, these assholes get the idea that I'm somehow on the menu."

"Being a woman is its own kind of curse, and even more so if you happen to be particularly beautiful."

Ayu smiled at my compliment.

"Well, thank you, Tag! I appreciate the compliment," she said, as she leaned over and kissed me on the cheek.

"You're welcome, though I'm only stating a very obvious fact, and giving you an honest compliment is the least I can do, considering you just got molested by a drunken idiot."

"Yeah, and it's one the main things that makes my shit job even shittier."

"The world just has too many assholes."

"True, but at least there are nice guys like you and

Bram," she said.

I had a moment to think about my lovely new friend, and thoughts of our little encounter with that drunk asshole really made me feel particularly annoyed.

"It really isn't fair," I said.

"What?"

"The shit women have to deal with, simply because of their gender. Face it—men and women each make up an equal half of the biological continuum that is our species. We all come from the exact same place—literally, but, we aren't treated the same. You come out with two X chromosomes, and you're facing a completely different world, and that world can be pretty shitty depending on where and even when you're born. Grow up in the wrong country and you could spend your entire life hidden behind a veil and have fewer rights than the average donkey. We don't choose our gender, our race, our sexual preference, any of it, yet we are subject to so much shit and potential suffering because of it. It makes me wonder how in the hell we've even made it this far as a species without completely eradicating ourselves."

There was a long moment of silence, and I realized Ayu and Bram were staring at me.

"What is it?" I asked.

"Do you perhaps moonlight as a women's studies professor in your free time?" Ayu asked.

"Not in the traditional sense, but I do take a lot of interest in women. Do I sound a bit preachy? It must be the

Mojitos talking."

"Well, I like what you have to say, so maybe you should have another."

I smiled at Bram.

"One more round, please."

A minute later, Bram filled our glasses, and Ayu immediately held hers up to toast.

"To Tag! Protector of women's virtue," she said.

CHAPTER EIGHTEEN
Inebriation Altercation Principle

The three of us continued drinking our mojitos until the bar eventually emptied out, and it was time to close up and head home for the night. Ayu counted out her tips, then Bram closed out the register, said good night, and left us alone in the bar.

"Thanks for earlier," she said.

"No problem."

"Which direction is your room?"

"Up the beach and right on the water," I said.

"The presidential suite—aren't you lucky."

"Luck being the operative word. I only have it because of friends in high places."

"Which says a lot about you. Remember, water seeks its own level."

"Now who's philosophizing?" I asked.

She smiled.

"Well, my car is parked on that side of the hotel. Would you mind if I walked out with you?" Ayu asked.

"Not at all. In fact, I'd enjoy the company."

She poured us the remnants of the last batch of Mojito's into our cups then turned off the lights and locked up the little bar. With our drinks in hand, we headed off along the shoreline as a partial moon hung just above the horizon and illuminated the beach and made for a particularly spectacular walk. We stopped about halfway and had a seat in the sand and took a moment to sip our drinks and enjoy the view.

"So, what kind of girl trouble are you having?" she asked.

"Actually, it's incredibly silly."

"Well, just because it's silly doesn't make it any less difficult to deal with."

"I suppose you're right."

"I am, now why don't you tell me about it. Maybe I'll have some valuable female insight."

I took a sip of my drink and gathered my thoughts.

"As you know, I'm here to help Mark Blake, but it's his sister who's the biggest problem at the moment."

"Are you two *together*?"

"Not in any official or meaningful way."

"So, what's the problem?"

"I think we'd like to be together—or maybe it's just me that would like us to be together."

"I'm sure it's mutual. A girl would have to be crazy not

to go for you."

"I'm not so sure."

"Well, believe me—I am."

I had to smile at Ayu's compliment.

"Well, thank you for the vote of confidence, but the problem with us is that our situation is a little—um—complicated. You see, she believes that me helping facilitate her brother's freedom makes her indebted to me."

"So."

"So, she thinks that if we were to consummate our relationship, she'd be doing it out of guilt rather than desire, or, to put it more bluntly, she'd feel like a whore."

"That's extremely ridiculous. Needing and getting help doesn't make her a whore! It makes her human."

"Exactly!"

"Life is too short for that kind of thinking. If you like someone, you should just go for it."

"I can't tell you how happy it makes me to hear you say that!"

"Because it's true."

"Can I hug you now?"

"Yeah, but I will probably have to kiss you, and then you'll have an entirely new girl problem to deal with," she joked.

"It wouldn't be the worst thing I could imagine."

We shared a smile then gazed out to see and listened to the sound of the waves gently rolling up onto the shoreline. She smiled and placed her hand on my knee.

"Things will work out," she said.

"You think so?"

"I do, but, if not, we can always try that hug."

Our lovely moment was suddenly interrupted when we heard voices just down the beach, and we turned to see a group of people walking in our direction.

"Friends of yours?" I asked.

"I'm pretty sure it's the guys who work in the kitchen. Sometimes they hang out after work and have a few drinks."

One of the guys started yelling in our direction.

"Hey, Ayu, who is the *bulè*?"

"Sounds like they've had more than a few," I said.

"It does."

"What the hell is a *bulè*?" I asked.

"It's Indonesian slang for a white person," she said.

"Lovely. Do you know them very well?"

"Only from work. The one yelling is named Gori, and he's the sous chef at the hotel, and he kind of has a thing for me."

The group reached our quiet little place on the sand and stood so menacingly close, that we could smell the alcohol emanating from their bodies like cheap cologne. Gori, their apparent spokesman, stepped forward and cast his scrutinizing gaze directly at me. He was young, probably in his early twenties, and well muscled though a bit on the sinewy side. His most prominent trait, however, was his extremely inebriated state. Young men and alcohol had a direct correlation for trouble that seemed to increase exponentially with the degree of intoxication. It was something I called the Inebriation Altercation Principle, and it concerned the combination of alcohol and youth. Studies that had shown that men generally didn't achieve adequate impulse control until the ripe old age of twenty-five, so, when you took a standard twentysomething mindset and added a lot of booze and perhaps even a little lover's angst, you had a lot of potential trouble—something to which anyone who has ever survived their early twenties can corroborate. It was also likely part of the reason for my earlier trouble with the young asshole at the bar.

"Well? Are you going to tell me who the fuck this *bulè* is?"

"It's none of your business, so why don't you all just be on your way," Ayu said.

"I think we'll stay right here and wait for this *bulè* to get the fuck back to where he belongs."

"This *bulè* is happy right where he is," I said.

"I bet. Another white man come to bang a hot island girl."

Gori could obviously be a mean drunk and clearly didn't like people of the white variety hanging around one of his fellow islanders.

"In my country, interaction with the opposite sex is not just about banging. In fact, we sometimes even talk to girls. It's very rewarding—you should try it."

The guy next to Gori stepped forward. He was short, though buff, and had dark curly hair that made him look a lot like a baby gorilla, and I had to wonder if perhaps the Malkarta zoo might be missing an animal.

"What the fuck did you say?" the baby gorilla asked.

"I said that you should try talking to women. It's a lot more effective than grunting, and it allows you to have more complex and rewarding conversations."

"Fuck you, *bulè*."

"Seriously, guys. I understand you're all a little drunk and angry, but rousting tourists really isn't going to make anyone feel better. It's a large beach, and there's room for everyone."

"Everyone but you," Gori said.

Ayu was obviously getting nervous and stood up and placed herself between me and her coworkers.

"Why don't you all just leave. Can't you see that you're acting like a bunch of drunken idiots?" she said.

Gori shoved Ayu aside, and the move caused her to stumble and fall onto the sand. I immediately stood and helped her up before turning my attention to the asshole contingency.

"Do you know that you're the second asshole tonight to lay a hand on Ayu, but that's OK, because you'll be the last," I said.

"No, Tag, they're not worth it," Ayu pleaded.

"They might not be, but you definitely are."

"No, seriously—don't hurt them. They're just drunk and stupid."

"Who you calling stupid—and what the hell makes you

think he's gonna hurt us. We're going to put this *bulè* in his place," Gori said, angrily.

"I admire your spirit, but, honestly, this is your last chance to walk away and preserve your dignity. Think about how embarrassing it would be tomorrow if it was revealed to your fellow workers at the hotel that a *bulè* laid out you and the entire kitchen staff? That, of course, also brings up a more important question—namely, who's going to make it in to work to handle tomorrow morning's breakfast. If you're all laid up in the hospital, then I'm stuck eating cold cereal, and that's not a good way to wake up in paradise."

"I've heard just about enough shit out of you!" Gori said.

Gori stepped forward and tried to give me the obligatory two handed guy shove—the posturing move that preceded most fights between males of the human species. As I outweighed him by twenty pounds and was ready for the push, I didn't budge an inch. This, of course, served to make him even more angry, as it left him looking silly and impotent in front of his friends. Sensing Gori's distress, the Gorilla decided to move around to my left, where he was probably hoping to flank me and divert my attention. That theory came to fruition when the Gorilla suddenly grabbed me from behind with a bear hug, that allowed Gori to step in and throw a punch straight into my midsection. Thankfully, I was ready and managed to disperse most of the energy with a proper exhale, but that didn't mean I was going to wait around for him to do it again. I rammed both elbows straight back into the gorilla's chest then squatted down and shot out my arms. This made my body wider and broke his grip, and now that I had a little breathing room, I moved slightly left and threw a hammer fist into the gorilla's groin. He grunted, and his head dropped down, and I brought my right elbow up under his chin. If I had aimed for his neck and delivered it with enough power, it would have been a killing blow, but I had been gentle and aimed for his chin, which left the Gorilla dazed and in pain as he stumbled backwards.

Gori was somewhat in shock but aware enough to attempt another punch. He pulled back his arm to throw, but I was quicker and shot a hard front kick straight into his solar plexus that buckled him over, and nicely set him up for the knee that I delivered to his nose. He immediately dropped to his knees and cradled his face in his hands. So far, I had the advantage, but I needed to stay vigilant, because there were more opponents, and that meant assessing the location of my enemies and maintaining a three hundred and sixty degree awareness. This paid off about a second later, when I glanced over my shoulder just in time to see that the gorilla had recovered and was preparing for another attack.

"How about a banana, little fellow?" I asked.

He paused and looked rather confused, and it created the opening I needed to throw a nice right side kick into his stomach. It hit home, but he managed to grab hold of my foot, leaving me balancing like an idiot on one leg. This left me with several options, some involving me dropping to the ground, but, with multiple attackers, it was important to stay on my feet. I therefore hopped up, twisted in midair, and brought my hips around and delivered a jump spinning back kick that impacted the Gorilla's formidable chest and sent him to the ground with the very real potential of having suffered a couple of cracked ribs.

Now was when things would get interesting. I had two men down and five more to go, which meant I needed to take a moment for some quick strategizing. Back in special operations, we learned that when you were faced with superior numbers, one extreme option was to come at your enemy with overwhelming force and extreme violence of action, with the theory being that you would break their resolve and ability to continue the fight. That was all well and good if you happened to be with a proper SEAL Team or an SAS Unit, but I was basically alone at the moment and suddenly facing five angry opponents who had just watched two of their friends get taken out of the game in about three and a half seconds flat. Perhaps my Inebriation Altercation principle was something that I should have applied to myself as well, as I now stood and watched as they banded together and stared menacingly. If they were smart, they would have spread out, but morale was low and they appeared to prefer the relative safety of the proximity of their peers.

Ayu started to move to my side, but I motioned for her to stay out of the way, as I was going to need some room to maneuver and didn't want her getting hurt. Multiple attackers were a tricky undertaking and one of the primary reasons for studying a martial art that dealt with more than one opponent. People were enamored with the whole cage fighting phenomena but often forgot about the fact that it was a one on one match. Grapplers, for instance, were excellent against single opponents but were at a disadvantage if their opponent's friends were nearby and joined the fight while he or she was rolling around on the ground. One of my specialties as a practitioner of Kenpo Karate had always been multiple attackers, and I trained to use speed and power to deliver pin point strikes, throws, and joint locks to critical areas of multitude opponents in as little time as possible. The goal, just like in the special operations, was to quickly take the fight out of your opponents, and, subsequently, your opponents out of the fight.

The nearest guy suddenly pulled out a butterfly knife, did a few quick flips for show, then held it up with the blade pointed in my general direction. Guys loved butterfly knives because of the show that inherently came every time the knife was opened. In reality, however, it was a third world switch blade, and it was inefficient and generally known to cause more damage to the user than the opponent. But, it was still technically a lethal weapon and therefore upped the stakes of our little tussle into a potential life and death situation.

"Five men and a knife against one is hardly a fair fight," I heard from just off to my left.

I thought the voice sounded familiar, and I turned to see my new acquaintance Sten coming to join the party.

"Hello, stranger. Fancy meeting you here," I said.

"Well, it just happens to be a lovely evening to be out on the beach following around a cocky American."

"Lucky for me as it turns out."

"Yeah, it looks like you might need a little help now that they've brought a knife to a fist fight," he said.

Apparently, we had put our differences from earlier aside and were now on the same team. The more the merrier.

"Just so you know, anything we do tonight will drastically effect the hotel's morning breakfast service," I said.

"No problem, there is an excellent restaurant right across the street."

"Well in that case, I see no reason to hold back," I said, bumping fists with Sten.

The two of us squared off with just enough angle to cover each other's backs while our five remaining opponents spread out, with none daring to move until one of them spoke something in Indonesian. It was apparently some kind of call to action, because the nearest guy, the one with the blade, rushed me and attempted to stab me in the stomach. I took a step backward to gain a little space and hopefully lure him in, but his move turned out to be a feint, and he quickly brought the knife up and around, where it was on course to impact my throat. Fortunately, I always kept my other hand up to protect my head, and it allowed me to catch his wrist, but now I had a decision to make. How much did I want to punish him for trying to stab me? The more severe option would be to snap his arm at the elbow like a stalk of celery, but I decided to be nice, however, and instead just rotated his arm slightly clockwise to line up the joints, then used them as a leverage point to drive him onto his knees and kick him square in the face. It was a little harsh, but it left him with the ability to use both of his arms, and that was something that might come in handy when he was preparing tomorrow morning's breakfast. He still had some fight in him and tried to pull free, however, so I twisted the knife out of his grasp then leveraged his elbow across my knee in order to force him around and face down onto the sand. I delivered a quick heel kick to his ribs for good measure, and he finally went slack, thus allowing me to take a moment to have a quick look around. I had three more opponents left in the fight.

The next guy had been watching too much television, and he came in with a high roundhouse kick to my head. He had a pretty good stretch and a relatively decent kick, but it did nothing to stop me from catching his foot and kicking out his standing leg to drop him onto his back and deliver a stomp kick to his groin. He cried out in pain and tried to pull away, but I still had his other foot locked under my arm. I twisted it clockwise and forced him onto his stomach, where a mouth full of sand quelled his complaints as I slipped forward and delivered a sneaky kick up between his legs. It impacted his groin with enough force to elicit an ear piercing scream as well as remove any remaining will to fight.

I looked up just in time to see the gorilla had re-entered the fight, and he was coming in low and hoping for a clinch. I had to give the guy some credit. He had taken a pretty good beating thus far but still managed to come back for more. This time, he was obviously hoping to use his bulk to take me down, but, as he moved into range, I widened my stance into a sprawl and managed to absorb the impact. With his arms wrapped around my waist, I dropped a hard elbow onto his back, then followed it up with several knees to his face that left him dazed and wavering enough that all I had to do was toss him face down onto the sand, where he remained done like dinner.

I took a second to check on Sten and saw that he was just finishing off his last opponent with a nicely executed judo throw. He was obviously good at hand to hand combat and had likely studied martial arts in the service, which now made him a formidable ally and more than capable of holding his own in our little tussle. He joined me, and the two of us turned our attention back to the final opponent and saw that he didn't appear to have much, if any, fight left in him after seeing his friends get decimated. Standing completely alone, he looked petrified as he gazed back and forth between the two of us, and when we made one tiny step forward, he threw up his hands in defeat.

"I don't want to fight!" he said.

"I think he's smarter than his friends," Sten said.

"Definitely, but the bigger question is whether or not he can cook."

"I guess you'll find out in the morning."

The man roused his friends, and soon the seven trouble-makers were rubbing their bruises as they ambled off to at last leave the beach in peace. Ayu immediately rushed to my side.

"Are you OK?" she asked.

"Yeah, that was just a little harmless kitten play."

"Kitten play, my ass! You clearly haven't left any of your exciting life behind."

"Maybe not entirely, but I really am just a boring private investigator these days."

"Who just laid out the entire kitchen staff."

"With help. Speaking of—this is my old friend Sten, by the way. And, Sten, this is Ayu," I said.

"It's nice to meet you, Sten," Ayu said.

"Very nice indeed," Sten responded.

"I don't know about you guys, but I worked up a bit of a thirst. How about we all adjourn to the presidential suite for a victory drink to mend our wounds," I suggested.

"I'm officially off work, so why not," Sten said, enthusiastically.

"Sounds good to me. I've never been in the presidential suite," Ayu added.

The three of us headed down the beach and turned right and walked up the path to the patio and entered the presidential suite. The lights were on, but there was no sign of

Fiona or Brett, so we apparently had the place to ourselves. I had my guests take a seat in the living room while I ventured behind the bar.

"Are rum drinks OK?"

They both nodded their approval, so I made a pitcher of Dark and Stormies, which was my drink of choice during my Soft Taco Island adventure. I grabbed three glasses, the pitcher, and led my new friends onto the patio and handed each of them a cocktail.

"To battles won," Sten said, raising his glass to toast.

"Indeed, and tomorrow we shall take housekeeping. By week's end, we shall control the entire hotel!" I added.

"And by the following weekend, you won't have any food or clean sheets," Ayu said.

We all laughed and clinked glasses, then everyone settled into one of the plush patio chairs.

"I'm really sorry about all the trouble I've brought you tonight," Ayu said.

"It's not your fault—sometimes men and alcohol are a bad combination," I responded.

"Well—men, women, and alcohol," Sten added.

"Good point, and do you mind if I ask where the hell you came from?" I asked Sten.

"Holland."

I was finally seeing that young Sten had a sense of humor.

"No, I'm talking about tonight, obviously."

Sten smiled at his weak attempt at humor.

"As part of your security detail, I was nearby maintaining proper surveillance."

"Proper surveillance, indeed. Thanks for watching my ass," I said.

"You're welcome."

"Anyone up for a relaxing dip in the Jacuzzi?" I asked.

Both of my guests nodded their approval, and, shortly thereafter, the three of us were stripping down and entering the warm waters of the Jacuzzi. Sten and I were already wearing shorts, and Ayu had a bikini on under her dress, so no one was forced to go full commando—though I imagine neither Sten nor I would have minded if our female guest had forgotten her swimming garments.

"This is the first time I've been in the Presidential Suite," Ayu said.

"Me too," Sten added.

"Me three, and I'm finally starting to understand why people run for office."

"No shit. This is more than enough reason to give up your morals and become a politician," Ayu said, with a chuckle.

We finished our first round, and I refilled our glasses, then Sten and I spent a brief time talking about our single most shared experience—namely our tours in Afghanistan. Unlike me, he was newly out of the service, specifically the *Korps Commandotroepen*, or in English, the special forces of the Netherlands, where he had served in the provence of Uruzgan. There, he had been involved with all manner of special operations, a lot of it helping the indigenous people raise their standard of living, with the idea being to make the Taliban irrelevant. There were also a lot of counter insurgency operations as well, so young Sten had seen more than his fare share of death and destruction, which was very likely the reason why he was off on a tropical island enjoying a completely different kind of job description.

"Do you suffer from PTSD?" Ayu asked Sten.

"A little bit, but it's gotten better since arriving here. Less nightmares."

"There's something about the sea and the sand that settles a person's soul," I said.

"Yeah, I'm definitely getting used to this," he said.

"So, Ayu was telling me tonight that there is a lot more discontent here than they put in the tourist brochures. Have you experienced much of the island's darker side?" I asked Sten.

"I've only been here a short time, but I can see that there's an incredible amount of inequality, and, honestly, the people we helped in Afghanistan didn't have it much worse than the people here."

"Yeah, that's why everyone was so excited when Globo-Care came. Mark Blake really was a hero to the people, as this place is still operating pretty much like it did in the sixteen hundreds. Sadly, with the way things are looking, it will apparently continue to do so indefinitely," Ayu said, taking a sip of her drink.

"So, how do you feel about all this? It's got to be a little conflicting being a member of the security service and all."

"It's a beautiful island, but it would certainly be a nicer and more peaceful place for everyone if there wasn't such a divide between the people and the ruling class."

I refilled everyone's cocktail, then we clinked glasses and drank and continued to talk until our little party was interrupted by the sudden appearance of Fiona and Brett.

"Who are your friends?" Brett asked.

"This is Sten and Ayu," I said.

"I remember Sten," Fiona said, as she walked over to join us, though she was mostly looking at Ayu.

"Yeah, we all just got back from a lovely night on the beach," I said.

"You and Sten didn't look quite so chummy the last time I saw you together."

"What can I say, I'm the master of diplomacy."

"Apparently. Well, it's nice to see you again, Sten," Fiona said.

"Speaking of—I suppose I should finish introducing everyone. Our two late arrivals here are my roommates. The attractive one is Fiona, Mark Blake's sister, and the tan man beside her is Brett. And, just in case you haven't already guessed—Brett is a dental hygienist from Phoenix," I said.

"Very funny. I'm actually a pilot, and it's nice to meet you both," he said, instantly turning his full attention to Ayu, where his smile was unusually prominent as he took off his shirt and slipped into the Jacuzzi.

He sat beside her, but, to his dismay, she turned her attention to Fiona.

"Fiona, I want you to know that I am very sorry about what happened to your brother. The people here really appreciate his efforts, and none of us condone what the government has done."

"Well, thank you," Fiona said.

"Do you two want a drink?" I asked Brett and Fiona.

"Love one," Brett said.

"Sure," Fiona added.

I left the Jacuzzi and went inside to the bar, made a fresh pitcher, then grabbed two more glasses before returning to find Fiona too had joined the others in the Jacuzzi. I handed her and Brett a cocktail, refilled the other's glasses, then stepped into the bubbling waters before raising my drink to toast.

"To a better Malkarta," I said.

Everyone drank, and soon thereafter conversation started anew, with Ayu describing the eccentricities of Malkarta and what it was like growing up in a mostly closed society. Her parents had been poor, but they were lucky enough to work for the royal family, and that had enabled them to send Ayu to private school and get a better education than many of her peers. She had even managed to go to college in Australia, and she earned a degree in business, but, because of her Asian heritage, still faced a great deal of discrimination in the local job market. Thus, she was only able to make a living by delivering drinks to drunken tourists at the hotel. This inequity also explained the great deal of animosity that her fellow workers had felt towards me, and I kind of felt bad for beating the shit out of them—kind of.

Overall, the odd assemblage of guests made for an interesting night, especially for Sten, who was still learning about the politics and turmoil that existed in his new home. Fortunately, he was a freethinker and a pretty cool guy in spite of our rather hostile first meeting. The talking eventually diminished as people grew tired, and the night officially came to an end when we all rose from the Jacuzzi and headed inside the presidential suite. We all exchanged contact information, then I escorted my two new friends to the front door.

"Thanks again for tonight," Ayu said, as she gave me a friendly hug.

"You're welcome."

"Any idea how long you'll be here?" she asked.

"Probably leaving tomorrow."

"That's too bad, I would have liked to have shown you the real Malkarta."

"That would have been nice."

"Well, if you stay another day, give me a call," she said.

"I will."

At that point I shook hands with Sten.

"Fun times tonight. Hopefully tomorrow will be a bit less exciting," I said.

"Well, I know breakfast will be," he said, with a laugh.

"Yeah, no shit. Well, I guess I'll see you in the morning."

"Bright and early."

"Preferably dim and late."

"Agreed," he said.

Ayu and Sten departed, and I headed back to the living room, where it was now just Fiona, Brett, and me.

"Well, I'm heading off to bed. Good night," Brett said.

"Good night. Don't forget to brush your teeth."

"I never do," he said, quickly disappearing into his room.

Once he was gone, Fiona and I took a seat at the bar.

"So, how are things with Brett?" I asked.

"They're not. I told him that nothing was going to happen between us."

"I guess that explains why he gave up and went to bed—in his own room."

"What's the deal with Ayu? I got the impression she might have a thing for you."

"Nah, we're just friends."

Fiona reached over and refilled her glass with the remains of the pitcher then smiled.

"I guess it's just the two of us," she said.

CHAPTER NINETEEN
Biscuit of Discontent

I made myself another rum drink and gazed at Fiona, who was quietly sipping her cocktail and looking a little anxious.

"Tomorrow we'll be finished with all this business, and you can get back to your life," she said.

"I suppose, but, in spite of the drama, it really has been fun."

"It has."

I held up my glass to toast.

"Here's to bringing your brother home tomorrow," I said.

We clinked glasses then took a sip of our drinks, and, in the silence that followed, I decided to ask Fiona about her evening with Biscuit. She went on to tell me that she and Brett had gone out to dinner in the hotel restaurant, and he had spent the evening basically putting the screws to her about taking their relationship to the next level. At the end of the meal, and while they shared a piece of cheesecake, she finally told him that she was not interested, and that they would never be more than friends. That was good news to me, though I still wasn't exactly sure how it would impact my turmoil laden relationship with Fiona.

"So, how was your evening?" Fiona asked.

"Eventful."

"Meaning?"

"Well, I had a nice walk on the beach then stopped at the hotel's oceanside bar for a drink and met Ayu. Unfortunately, a drunk customer grabbed her ass, and I ended up needing to step in and defend her honor."

"Seems to be a pattern," she said.

"Apparently."

"Well, that doesn't sound like much fun."

"It wasn't, and things actually got worse when we took a walk on the beach."

"Worse? That sounds like the beginning to a pretty fucking romantic date."

"Yeah, maybe if I hadn't been talking to Ayu about you."

Fiona scrutinized me for a moment as she considered her response.

"Were you really talking about me?"

"Well, I was until the arrival of a bunch of drunk, angry locals."

"What were they so angry about?"

"The fact that Ayu and I were hanging out together, and they were so angry, in fact, that they tried to delve out a little island justice. Luckily Sten showed up, and we delved out a little mainland comeuppance and sent them on their way."

"Jesus! Are you OK?" she asked, looking concerned.

"I'm fine, but don't be expecting much in the way of breakfast."

"Why is that?"

"The angry locals were all part of the hotel's kitchen staff."

"Oh..."

"Yeah, and there's definitely a lot more angst on this island than anyone wants to admit."

"Well, my brother doesn't usually go to happy places."

I finished my drink and looked at my watch and saw that it was twelve thirty-six and therefore about time to go to bed, as we had a lot to do the next day. I was still fairly buzzed, but decided on a final small glass of rum before saying good night to Fiona and heading off to my room, where I undressed and sought respite from the long day by taking a nice hot shower. I stood there with my back to the torrent of water, sipped my rum, and pondered the night's events. Sure enough, that course of thought eventually led to thoughts of the beautiful Fiona Blake. Relationships were often complicated, but ours bordered on ridiculous. We weren't even dating or having sex, yet seemed to have all the problems associated with both of those activities. I could handle some drama, but I would at least like some kind of actual reason. What was it about relationships or, more specifically, sex that made things so complicated? It was a biological imperative and a perfectly natural act that was the key to the continuation of our species, yet humans managed to turn it into one of the great problems of our existence.

I suppose I too fell prey to its call and engaged in all manner of idiocy in its pursuit. Clearly, when you linked the most powerful sex organ, namely the brain, with the other major sexual organs, the penis and vagina, you had a recipe for a lot of drama, suffering, and in the right instances, pure joy. Shit monkeys. I did a final rinse, then stepped from the shower to dry off and brush my teeth. At last ready to call it a day, I left the bathroom to find that I wasn't alone, and, there, lying in my bed, with the covers drawn all the way up to her neck, was Fiona.

"Do you mind if I sleep in here?" she asked.

"Not at all, but I should warn you that I sleep in the nude."

"I know," she said, lowering the covers to reveal her beautiful bare breasts.

My heart started racing, and I threw my towel onto the chair, hit the lights, and slid into bed.

"Any particular reason for this visit?" I asked.

"Yeah, I've finally decided to forget about all my neurotic pride, so I can finally fuck your brains out."

"Couldn't we just cuddle?"

"Sure, if it involves your penis entering my vagina."

"That's the kind of cuddling I was referring to."

"Good, then we shouldn't have any problems."

She climbed atop me and kissed me, and her tongue darted across to greet mine—thus initiating an oral melee of slipping, sliding, and bold attempts to try and gain dominance in the nether region between our lips. Where once we shared frustration and hurt feelings, we now shared desire, and every second our lips remained in contact, my hunger for her became too great to control. I broke free of her lips, but there were so many places I wanted to visit that I felt like a child wandering through a candy store, and I could hardly decide where to go first. I wanted all of her, but, it was important to prioritize. I therefore started by kissing her neck and lingered just long enough to elicit some goosebumps and a smile, before I ventured down to her breasts. This was truly a place that beckoned for my touch, and I encircled her nipples with my tongue until they were hard and taught.

Fiona was overwhelmed with desire and began her own exploration, which entailed running her hands down my chest to my hard manhood. She took hold of it and stroked it as though were Aladdin's Lamp, and her efforts would release the genie—so to speak. He'd be out all right, and a lot sooner than either of us would have preferred, so I needed to make sure one of her three wishes included some super staying power. As I prepared to intercede, she took the upper hand and knocked me onto my back then leaned down and took Tag Junior into her mouth—one hand minding the shaft and the other taking care of the stepchildren. That was certainly the easiest way to get the genie out of the bottle.

Before you could say open sesame, I was on the verge

of sweet release, but Fiona was apparently a master of the flesh sword and knew a few things about handling the blade. She kept me right on the edge of release, and the moment I got too close, she'd slow her efforts before starting anew. This would happen several times before I could take no more and had to use every ounce of will and strength to sit up and roll Fiona onto her back.

"Enough, devil woman!"

"Excuse me?" she asked, with an indignant look.

"Time for a little quid pro quo," I said.

I sat up and kissed her long and hard on the lips then pulled back and took a minute to gaze upon the incredible woman who had been tormenting me for the last forty-eight hours. Fiona was beautiful, and every inch of her lithe body was an invitation for my lips. I knew my destination, but I wanted to take my time and revisit a few places on my journey south. I kissed her neck again then continued on to her breasts to find her nipples were still hard from my last visit. I ran my tongue over each one, and she reached up and ran her hands through my hair as though guiding my efforts.

"I want you inside me right now," she said, breathlessly.

"All in good time."

I left her generous peaks then dragged my lips down across her stomach but paused at the edge of her erogenous zone that had been, until now, officially off limits. I ran each of my hands down her thighs then gently pressed open her legs.

"God's country," I said, aloud.

"This is the body of our Lord, take it and eat it," she said.

"Indeed," I responded.

My mouth was now hovering just above her lady fruit, and my breath alone was enough to make her wriggle in delight. I touched down and plunged my tongue into her essence then moved it up and began lightly caressing her clitoris. She threw back her head and arched her back as I continued to use my tongue to make slow exploratory circles. As she grew more tense, I made the occasional detour inside in order to prolong the pleasure. I continued with this pattern, though I ever so subtly applied more pressure and speed with my tongue, and Fiona began to undulate and rock her hips forward and backward. It wasn't long before she abruptly reached out and gripped the sheets and began to call out as she started into the throws of climax.

"Oh, God, yes, yes, yes—fuck yes! I'm going to cum!"

She came with a great howling fury, and her orgasm continued until I gradually eased my efforts, and she experienced only a few residual tremors throughout her body. She smiled and pulled me up for a kiss then stared into my eyes with a look that was equal parts longing and contentment.

"We're even now, and that means your penis has a very immediate appointment with my vagina."

Fiona took hold of my manhood and guided it into the warmth of her inner delight, and a vocal sigh escaped both of our lips as I pressed forward unto her reaches.

"Why the hell did we wait so long to do this?" she asked, with her eyes unfocused and lost to the intense pleasure.

"That's a very, very good question, and, in the interest of us continuing with this, I'm not going to point out the obvious answer."

"Truly a gentleman," she said, with a smile.

I started pressing slowly in and out, so that I could continue to kiss Fiona. This also allowed me to add a little hip action at the apex of each thrust that made sure her clitoris was properly attended to, and it inspired her to reach up and join my efforts by pulling me tight to her body. We were in a perfect pattern of sexual homeostasis—and time was immaterial as we balanced on the razor's edge between pleasure and release. I wanted to remain in that moment for eternity, but lust eventually overpowered will, and we steadily increased our efforts until our cries of ecstasy eclipsed the sound of our pounding hips.

"Oh fuck, yes!" Fiona called out.

"Oh shit!" I responded.

"Oh, God!"

"Oh, sweet Jesus!"

"Oh, God—fuck me!"

We were pounding away with the fury of wild stallions at full gallop when, suddenly, there was a knock at the door followed by Brett's voice.

"Hello? Tag are you awake?" he asked.

I ignored him, but he proceeded to knock yet again.

"Tag? Is Fiona in there with you?"

We slowed our efforts and exchanged an annoyed look.

"Goddamn cockblocking jet-jockey-motherfucker!" I

muttered to Fiona.

"I'd like to shove that naval academy ring right up his tan ass about now," Fiona added.

"There's no way in hell that he doesn't already know you're in here, and this is a lame and obvious ploy to fuck with us."

"Is your gun nearby? Maybe you could shoot him."

"Fuck! It's in the closet. All we have are our words."

Fiona and I exchanged an annoyed look, then she called out to Brett.

"Biscuit, I don't mean to be harsh, but nothing is going to happen between us!"

"Come on, Fi, if you'd just take a moment to talk to me, I think you'd see that we have a real connection here," he responded.

Fiona let out an annoyed groan before responding.

"Goddammit, Biscuit, you have more connection to that pillow case you jacked off into! Now, seriously, would you please just leave us alone!"

"But, Fi!"

I'd never heard Brett be so persistent, so he apparently wasn't giving up without a fight.

"OK, that's it, Biscuit, if you're really that eager to find a warm place for your dick, then why don't you go shove it in the toaster," Fiona bellowed.

"Do we even have a toaster?" I quietly asked her.

"Yeah, it's in the kitchen."

We didn't hear anything else from Biscuit, so he had apparently left—or stayed at the door to listen, but either way I didn't care as long as he shut the fuck up.

"Oh shit, I just thought of something," I said.

"What?" Fiona asked.

"Assuming the kitchen staff doesn't make it in tomorrow, we would be forced to cook something up in our room."

"You mean—like toast?"

"Yeah."

"Oh well, maybe we'll just have fruit. Now, roll onto your back and hold on tight, because I am going to fuck you so hard your balls might catch fire."

I did as instructed and lay on my back and gazed up to see Fiona looking at me with a sense of purpose in her eyes that was a bit intimidating.

"I must say—a part of me is a little nervous for my balls, and I can't help wondering if we should have a glass of ice water or a fire extinguisher on hand."

"Don't worry—if your balls actually catch fire, I'll just smother the flames with my breasts," she said, with a devilish smile.

"Good enough," I responded.

She started grinding away on me, and the greatest benefit of our orientation was that my hands were now completely free to explore her tempting flesh. Heaven was a word that could be used to describe a lot of situations, but no usage would be more meaningful or accurate than in relation to this exact moment in time. Fiona was atop me, my hands were cradling her breasts, and her nipples were entwined between my thumbs and forefingers. I had found my personal slice of the divine, my Shangri-La, but such moments of perfection were fleeting in this imperfect world, and it was time to face the inevitability of sweet glorious release. Our pace quickened, and it forced me to lovingly keep a firm hold of her breasts in order to steady their raucous movements through the final stretch. The end was officially here, and neither of us could postpone it any longer.

"Oh shit, I'm going to cum," Fiona yelled.

"Oh shit! Me too!"

Together, we put on a great final burst of speed, and our bodies moved in sync like the pistons of a race car's engine as it roared down the final stretch towards the checkered flag. I pulled Fiona down to me and kissed her, and it became the final spark that would ignite our mutual climax. Our bodies and minds became one, and we rode out each successive wave of pleasure until finally coming to rest with our bodies shaking from exertion.

"Holy fucking shit," Fiona muttered, as she collapsed onto my chest.

"You can say that again."

"Holy fucking shit," she repeated.

We were both drenched in a sheen of perspiration and therefore decided to adjourn to the bathroom for a quick rinse. I started the water while Fiona peed, then, together, we entered the large glass enclosure. I grabbed the shampoo and soap then sudsed up my shower buddy from head to toe. She then did the same to me, though she took special interest in Tag Junior, who seemed as though he might have another round in him. We kissed, rinsed off, then dried ourselves before adjourning to the bed, where we spooned like a couple of honeymooners. I closed my eyes and listened to the gentle waves as they rolled up onto the nearby shore. It was hard to believe that I was a world away from home on an exotic island and, better still, had a beautiful woman in my arms. The web of human interaction was indeed complicated and could change so quickly that it was a wonder unto itself when things finally came together and worked out for the better. Even the island of Malkarta itself had played an unlikely role in serving as the final catalyst to lead to tonight's blessed event.

As I pondered our glorious encounter, I remembered Brett's untimely intrusion and couldn't help but wonder what he had gotten up to after being sent on his way. Was he sleeping just outside the door, or was he in his room fastidiously masturbating—one hand stroking his steed and the other perhaps slathering tooth whitener on his teeth. Clearly, the endorphins released from finally having had sex with Fiona were carrying my thoughts to deep, dark places.

"I feel so much better with all the ridiculous shit behind us," Fiona said.

"No doubt, and tomorrow we'll get your brother, and all will finally be right with the world."

"Thanks, Tag, for everything."

"You're welcome, Fiona."

With those final words, I drifted off to sleep, ever hopeful that the day ahead would be even better than the one we left behind.

CHAPTER TWENTY
The Prodigal Son

I awoke at eight thirteen and looked over to see Fiona still sleeping peacefully and looking beautiful in the soft light of morning. Her right breast was uncovered, and I looked at it longingly as I remembered the events of the previous night. She stirred, slowly opened her eyes, and smiled at me.

"Are you staring at my breasts?" she asked.

"Technically, I'm only staring at one of them."

She pulled down the sheet to reveal its neighbor.

"Is that better?"

"Absolutely, as it's kind of like going from mono to stereo."

I reached over and gently caressed their soft curves and secretly wished that I could wake up to such a sight every day. Fiona took hold of my head and pulled me in for a brief morning kiss, then we parted and both rose and headed to the bathroom, where I brushed my teeth and she peed.

Done, we switched places then dressed before heading out into the suite to start the day. Brett was already awake and sitting at the bar drinking a cup of coffee as he gazed at his iPad.

"Aren't you afraid that coffee will stain your teeth?" I asked.

"No, because I always travel with a tooth whitening kit."

"Have you ever thought about marrying a dental hygienist?"

"I have, actually."

We shared a smile, then he pointed at the coffee machine.

"Speaking of—I just made a fresh pot."

Interesting. Brett was being unusually cordial, so perhaps our exchange with him last night had officially enacted some kind of truce in our latest war.

"Thanks," I said.

I went behind the bar and filled two cups and added cream before handing one to Fiona.

"Cheers," I said, holding up my cup.

Brett, Fiona, and I clinked mugs, then I took my glorious first sip of coffee and instantly felt invigorated.

"So, I was going to make us all some toast to go with the coffee but..."

Brett didn't even need to finish his sentence before I remembered Fiona's words from last night and nearly spit my coffee across the room. Brett had turned her late night outburst into a halfway decent quip, and, while it wasn't extremely funny, it was one of those moments where the timing was just right to make consuming any kind of liquid an impossibility. Sure, Brett might have lost the war, but he hadn't lost his sense of humor, and even Fiona had to laugh, though she looked a little embarrassed at having her previous night's words recalled in the harsh light of morning. I finally managed to get my coffee down then smiled at the tan menace.

"Pretty funny, jet jockey," I said.

He held up his cup and nodded at me then gestured at the tray on the coffee table.

"The kitchen had a problem with staffing this morning, so you'll be happy to hear that we at least have a continental breakfast."

"Ahhh—first world problems," I said, grabbing a croissant off the tray.

Fiona also partook, but, in the spirit of practically every woman I'd ever known, she bypassed the pastries and grabbed a bowl of fruit and yogurt. Oh well, those were probably the kind of decisions that helped her stay in such excellent shape. With food and coffee, we enjoyed a light, though decent breakfast, and, once finished, Fiona excused herself to go to her room to get ready for the day. Of course, I knew that she was just sneaking off to do what I was about to do, which was go have a well-deserved morning movement. Now, it was just Biscuit and me sharing some brief alone time.

"Congratulations," Brett said.

"I take it that you're not too upset about Fiona and me."

"All's fair in love and war, my friend."

"Indeed," I said, raising my cup to his.

We clinked mugs, then I finished my coffee and went behind the bar to refill my cup, and I suddenly felt a building pressure in my lower abdomen. It was time to meet up with my porcelain mistress and divulge my deep seated fecal ramblings. I excused myself and returned to my room, where I grabbed my iPhone and dropped onto the toilet seat just in time to take a sip of coffee before releasing my bounty. Meanwhile, I brought up my email and clicked through the various crap, but found nothing particularly interesting and decided that my time on this humble commode was nearly at an end. Before I could conclude my business, there was a knock at the door, and I heard Brett's voice.

"Dude! I'm out of toothpaste," he said, frantically.

"Call room service or go over to the store in the lobby, you jackass."

"Not until I brush my teeth."

"Seriously?"

"Yeah."

"Fuck."

Almost made it. I rose, flushed, and washed my hands before going to the door with my toothpaste. I opened it to find a very anxious looking Brett standing there with his toothbrush in his hand, and I squeezed a little dollop onto the bristles then closed the door and entered the shower, wondering if my encounter with Brett was an omen of a bad day or merely an inconsequential hiccup in my morning routine. Soon, I forgot about him and was smiling to myself as I thought about my night with Fiona. It had been a hell of a good time, though it would certainly be interesting to see how our relationship continued to progress, if at all, back in the states.

I rubbed in the particularly fresh smelling shampoo then soaped up, rinsed, and left the shower feeling refreshed and a little sad that my time in Malkarta was coming to an end. In spite of its obvious problems, it was a beautiful island, and, so far, I liked most of the people that I had met. I put on deodorant and cologne then got dressed and again chose casual island clothing that consisted of khaki pants and an un-tucked button up short sleeve shirt. Finished, I headed out into the living room to wait for Fiona, who arrived about five minutes later, looking lovely in a summer dress. She was also smiling giddily, as she was obviously excited to see her brother.

There was a knock at the door, and I opened it to find our embassy man Tim, and we followed him out to his car and set off for the Malkarta courthouse. A little over ten minutes later, we arrived at our destination to find it resided atop an elevated section of the city, and its location offered an excellent view of New Leiden. The courthouse was also one of Malkarta's oldest buildings, and it was a perfect representation of actual Dutch colonial architecture. In the United States, we had revivalist Dutch architecture, but this was the real deal—created by actual Dutch people, and it showed in the details. The structure was a bright shade of white, two stories, and had a clay tiled roof that extended at eaves which hung out over the sides of the building. Below that were ornate windows that resided uniformly across each level, and in front of the structure was a large well-manicured lawn with a statue of the Island's first founder William De Vries. He was standing and appearing to proudly gaze out at the city below, and we passed by him and pulled in and parked in one of the visitor spaces. From there we headed inside through a large stately doorway and into the lobby, where we had to pass through a metal detector, which was something I found to be a sad testament to the state of affairs in the modern world. Here we were on a beautiful tropical island in the middle of paradise, yet we still had to be afraid that someone might smuggle a gun or bomb onto the premises. Even Malkarta had been brought into the post September Eleven hysteria, which I suppose made sense, considering the terrorism that intermittently flared up in this part of the world.

We continued inside to the information desk and were greeted by a serious looking young man who was busy looking at his computer. He glanced up and said hello, and we responded with a similar greeting along with the purpose of our visit. He turned back to his screen, typed something in, then made a quick phone call before referring us to the second floor. We left the lobby and headed up a grand staircase and were greeted by a representative who introduced himself as Jan Akker, attorney general of Malkarta. He led us into a small conference room, then excused himself and left us alone to wait. Fiona was practically bubbling over with excitement as she reached over and took hold of my hand and smiled. A moment later, Jan returned with General Maas Groot and Mark Blake, who was dressed in civilian attire and looking fairly good considering that he had been incarcerated for the last two months. I could see that he also shared Fiona's excellent genetics, for he was tall, good looking, and had an athletic physique as well as a bushy main of brown hair and strikingly blue eyes. He smiled when he saw his sister, and Fiona, in turn, smiled back, and tears appeared in her eyes as she raced over and hugged the stuffing out of her brother. Eventually she let go and brought him over to me.

"Mark, this is Tag Finn, the person who helped arrange your release."

"Nice to meet you, Tag, and thank you for all your help," he said, as we shook hands.

"No problem. Always happy to help a person in need."

Tim stepped over and offered his hand to Mark.

"Nice to see you again, Mark. I'm glad we were finally able to resolve this," Tim said.

"Me too," Mark responded.

Jan Akker and Maas took a seat at the table and beckoned us all over, and we sat down in front of a small stack of documents. At that point, Jan grabbed the top one and placed it directly in front of Mark.

"The island of Malkarta hereby officially releases you into the custody of Mr. Finn and your embassy representative. Furthermore, your release is contingent upon your agreement that you will leave the island forthwith, never returning without the express written permission of the Monarchy. Now, please sign and date this final release form at the bottom, which states that you acknowledge your charges and wave all your rights under the constitution of the solemn kingdom of Malkarta in return for immediate extradition."

Mark signed both documents, then Jan reached his hand across to Mark.

"You are officially a free man, Mr. Blake."

Everyone smiled and stood up from the table, and Maas reached across to Mark, and the two shook hands and exchanged a rather unemotional nod. It wasn't friendly or unfriendly, which was both interesting and a little intriguing, considering that Maas was head of Malkarta security, and Mark was allegedly a dissident. I would have expected at least a little animosity between the two men. Oh well, I suppose I should just sit back and enjoy the fact that I was able to bring a happy ending to this story.

"Congratulations, Mr. Blake. I'm happy we could finally resolve this matter," Maas said.

"Yes, thank you, General."

"Thank you again, gentleman. I suppose we should be going, as I imagine Mark would probably like to get out and enjoy a little freedom and sunshine," Tim said.

We shuffled out of the room and into the expansive hallway and started walking towards the stairs, with everyone engaged in some kind of amiable conversation. Tim was chatting with Jan, Fiona was chatting with her brother, and I was talking with Maas about Malkarta. The procession suddenly stopped, however, when Mark said that he needed to use the restroom, and he excused himself and disappeared into the nearby men's room while the rest of us waited and continued our various conversations.

"So, I must say that you have a beautiful island here," I said, to Maas.

"Yes, though I was very sorry to hear about your little altercation on the beach last night."

"Eh, shit happens everywhere."

"Yes, I suppose, though we generally try to keep the peace and avoid any major incidents."

"Yeah, angry locals rousting tourists certainly wouldn't do much for tourism."

"Definitely not."

"At least your man Sten was nearby and ended up being a big help."

"Yes, he's a good man."

"He is. Hopefully you have more like him."

"We do, but I believe things will be quieting down soon, as we have some new measures in place that should help mend some of the feelings of discontent between the government and the people."

A moment of silence ensued that made me realize the

man of the hour was taking a long time, and I had to wonder if perhaps he might have needed to drop a deuce. God only knew what his cell's bathroom was like, so it would make sense if he put off his morning movement in hopes of using a more civilized commode. Thinking about the bathroom, I realized that my morning coffee was making its presence known in my bladder, and I decided I should go take a quick pee.

"I'm going to use the facilities, as well," I said, leaving the group.

I walked over and entered the bathroom to discover that it was a fine space for either a number one or two. The walls were brilliant white, the fixtures were modern, and between each urinal were adequately sized dividers. Beyond them, were three premier stalls, and only the farthest one had a closed door. It was also the exact one I would have chosen due to its distance from the door as well as its close proximity to the window. I imagined that it also afforded plenty of fresh air and a spectacular view of the city. I saddled up to the nearest urinal in order to give Mark plenty of dumping room, as men generally liked their space in a bathroom.

"How are the facilities? I imagine it's pretty nice to have a more civilized bathroom," I said, not receiving any immediate response.

Perhaps he was a serious dumper and took this time wholly for himself. I finished peeing and went to the sink to wash my hands and waited until I was completely done before speaking again.

"Well, have a good dump. You earned it."

Again I got no response, and it was starting to give me a bad feeling, so I walked over to his stall door and spoke again.

"Mark? You OK in there? You're not out of toilet paper or anything are you?"

Again, no response, so I dropped down to the floor, looked under the door and discovered the problem. The stall was empty. Fuck. I took out a coin and slipped it into the outer notch of the latch mechanism and twisted it to unlock the door. Thankfully, most public toilets had this feature, and I imagined it was for emergencies like heart attacks, where it would be important to reach someone should they be incapacitated on the toilet. I opened the door and found an empty bowl, and there wasn't even the slightest evidence of a number one or a two. Someone had pulled a fast one, and by fast one I didn't mean a dump. The window was open, and, as I suspected, it did indeed afford a beautiful view of the city. I leaned out and realized there was a ledge that led along the entire floor of the building and just happened to go past a fire escape ladder. Wonderful. The guy who I had flown halfway around the world to free, had just flown the coup—but why? He was a free man, so why in the hell did he pull a runner and jeopardize his release? I left the bathroom to join the others in the lobby, and Fiona was the first to speak.

"Is Mark feeling OK?" she asked in a concerned tone.

"I wouldn't know."

"What's that supposed to mean?"

Everyone, upon hearing our exchange, quietly turned their attention to us, and I gazed at the group of people and delivered my unusual news.

"Ladies and gentleman, I'm afraid that Mark Blake has left the building."

CHAPTER TWENTY-ONE
Man on the Run

We followed Jan Akker back up the hallway and around the corner to his office to find it was well appointed with dark green berber carpet and a massive antique oak desk surrounded by old school leather bound chairs that you'd expect to find in a exclusive gentleman's club. On the walls were paintings of stately looking men who were probably Jan's predecessors. He took a seat at his desk then looked over at us gravely.

"In fleeing, Mr. Blake has drastically changed the nature of the situation and is now a fugitive, which means the authorities can act with whatever force they deem necessary."

"You can't be serious! He's not actually a criminal!" Fiona said, angrily.

"I'm sorry, but now he officially is. In signing that document, he acknowledged his crime and has therefore officially become an enemy of the state."

"That's ridiculous," she said.

"It was the easiest way to bypass the judicial process and quickly secure his release. No one ever imagined he wouldn't leave the island."

"So, what now?" I asked.

"Honestly, I don't know."

"Could we have some kind of grace period for me to find him and get him the hell out of here?"

Jan looked to Maas.

"Perhaps, but how is it that you think you can find him?" Maas asked.

"It's what I do. I'm a private investigator. Finding people is one of my specialties," I said, obviously not including the fact that I also found the occasional lost pet.

Maas stared with his eyes unblinking as he scrutinized me.

"All right, Finn, I'll get you a week to find Mr. Blake, but after that I can not guarantee his safety. In the meantime, however, you'll have any and all the help you need," Maas said.

"Thank you, general. Now, if you'll excuse us, we have a man to find."

I rose and shook hands with Jan and Maas, then Tim, Fiona, and I walked out to the car, and I called shotgun but decided to be a gentleman and climbed into the back in order to give the front seat to Fiona. Tim, meanwhile, started the car then looked over at us.

"Well, where would you like to start?" he asked.

"Not sure, though Globo-Care's local office would probably be a good place."

"I'm not so sure. After Mark's arrest all of the staff were sent home until the situation could be resolved," Fiona said.

"Even so, they might still have some paperwork or relevant information lying around that could be useful."

Tim pulled out, and we navigated the mild late morning traffic and headed south towards the Globo-Care office. We reached it about four and a half minutes later to find it looking just as deserted as Fiona had said it would be. The sign was still on the front of the building, but behind the glass facade loomed a dark, deserted office. I tried the door and found it locked and was instantly wishing I had brought my lock pick set along on this trip. With no other alternative, I looked around for an unlocked window or back door, hopeful that they might not have been too careful when they vacated the building. I tried one after another until spying a partially open window on the back corner. I reached in and tried to open it the rest of the way, but I was surprised by the sudden appearance of a rather stern looking woman. She was attractive, tall, athletically built, and had ashen blond hair and strikingly light blue eyes. Still, none of her positive physical attributes took away from the fact that she was not happy to see me.

"Do you mind if I ask what the hell you're doing trying to break into my building?" she asked.

"Not at all. I'm just trying to get into the Globo-Care office."

"Through the window?"

"The door was locked."

"For a reason. Why would you want to go in there?"

The woman was obviously assuming I was an unsavory character, so I decided to use good old fashioned honesty.

"We're trying to find Mark Blake, and we're hoping there might be some kind of useful clue in there as to his whereabouts."

"In case you didn't know, Mark Blake is in custody, and the government pretty much confiscated everything else left in that office as evidence."

"Well then, you'll be interested to know that Mark Blake was released this morning but disappeared shortly thereafter."

The woman looked confused.

"Excuse me, but did you say he was released?" she asked.

"Yeah, I was able to secure his release, but for some unknown reason he did a runner, and now we desperately need to find him, as he's officially been labeled an enemy of the state."

"So, who are you, and why do you care?"

"The name's Finn, Tag Finn, and I'm working with his sister."

She looked me over, as she was obviously wondering if I were full of shit.

"If you don't believe me, you can ask Deputy Ambassador Stansfield here or Mark's sister Fiona."

The woman looked from Tim to Fiona then smiled.

"I can see the family resemblance. You and your brother have some pretty amazing genes."

"Thank you, but how do you know my brother?" Fiona asked.

"I'm Mark's landlord. My name is Johanna. It's nice to meet you," the woman said.

"I'm Fiona. It's nice to meet you too," she said.

"Well, since you're family, I guess I can let you in," Johanna said, as she pulled out a ring of keys.

She went to the door, unlocked it, then stepped aside, and we entered the office to find it looking as though it had been deserted quickly—almost as if there had been some kind of natural disaster that forced its inhabitants to flee in a hurry. The chairs were pulled back from the desks, and any computers they had were long gone. The file cabinets were empty, and most of the drawers were left open, and, oddly, the place looked more like the scene of a burglary, but I was guessing its current state was related to the investigation of Mark and Globo-Care. I set off around the room, ever hopeful to find some kind of useful clue that might hint at a reason why Mark chose to stay on Malkarta and perhaps even point me in a direction to start my search.

"So, why did Mark disappear after he was finally freed?" Johanna asked.

"No idea, which is why we're here," I said.

"I can't believe he did this to all of us. Especially you, Tag. I mean—you called in a favor from the vice president of the United States for Pete's sake."

Johanna looked at me skeptically with one eyebrow raised in disbelief.

"You know the vice president of the United States?" she asked.

"I know what you're thinking. You look at me and say to yourself—there's no way in hell this wonderful, honest, well-meaning guy would have anything to do with a scumbag politician, but what can I say? I saved his life, and he owed me a favor, so I thought it was worth it utilize my connection to the underbelly of society."

Johanna looked from me to Fiona, as I imagine she was probably assuming that I was joking.

"Believe it or not, everything he just said is mostly true, except that the vice president is an amazingly nice and upstanding person and not a scumbag," Fiona said.

"Good to know that at least one politician isn't."

"Yeah, no shit," I said, as I moved around the room looking for clues.

I moved to the far wall and tried to imagine what the place was like when it was bustling with people.

"Can you tell me which desk was Mark's?" I asked.

"That one over there by the window," Johanna said.

I went over to the desk and searched through the drawers but didn't find anything more interesting than a number of pens and paperclips. I felt all around in the drawers then looked at the underside of the desk in the hope that he might have taped some important note or object to it, but that kind of luck had only ever happened once in my career as a private detective—namely during my last case concerning the infamous Mr. Pickles. It turned out that the bad guys had taped a flash drive full of confidential information under the lip of a file cabinet, and my super hot Asian lawyer girlfriend had managed to find it. Fuckinzee. This time I wasn't quite so lucky, and I decided to take a step back from the desk and see what I might instead learn from Johanna.

"Johanna, do you happen to have any idea where Mark might have gone or who he might be with?"

"I'm afraid not. There were a lot of people coming and going from this office, so I have no idea."

Oh well, it was worth a try. I therefore turned my gaze back to the desk area, or more specifically, the cork board that resided on the adjacent wall. There were still a number of pieces of paper tacked to its surface—specifically a couple of business cards and a few post-it notes, but there was an empty spot with a thumb tack holding a tiny shred of the edge of a picture that used to hang there. A strong breeze blew in through the window that I was going to use to get into the office, and, as I stood there, I watched the rustling papers and visually traced the path of the breeze to see where the flow of air traveled as it moved through the office. It seemed to resolve over in the corner by a file cabinet. On a whim, I walked over and inspected the area and spied what I believed might be the missing picture. It was behind the file cabinet, and all it took was a little yoga and a long arm, and I was holding the picture and gazing at the missing edge to verify it was indeed the correct one. I couldn't help but smile as I looked at the faces of the two people in the photo. Sometimes good detective work was about luck, but all too often it was about seeing details that others might miss—something that came quite naturally to someone with an obsessive compulsive personality.

"I believe I have a pretty good idea why Mark might have stayed on the island," I said.

"What is it?" Fiona asked.

"What generally governs most men's actions?" I asked.

"Your penises," Fiona suggested.

"Exactly!" I said, holding up the picture for the others to see.

Everyone moved closer and saw that the two people in the picture were Mark and a very beautiful woman.

"That's Princess Anna De Vries!" Johanna exclaimed.

"Interesting. How do we get a meeting with this woman?" I asked Tim.

"We go to the embassy, and I make a few calls," he said.

"Perfect, and while we're there I'll call Globo-Care and see if they have any useful information," I said, feeling excited that we were making some progress.

"Oh, Mark's apartment is upstairs if you want to have a look at it," Johanna said.

"Any chance he's up there right now?"

"Afraid not."

"I guess I'll leave it be for the moment, though I might come back later depending on how things go. Well, I guess we'll be on our way, so thank you for all of your help, Johanna."

"You're welcome, and I hope you find Mark," she said.

We left the Globo-Care office and arrived at the American Embassy a short time later and drove past the Marine guards and parked within the walled compound. It was a beautiful piece of real estate with stately gardens and an amazing three story structure painted a soft shade of yellow. We exited the car and followed Tim inside and went up to his office, which resided on the second floor. It was large and well-appointed, though not as stately as Jan Akker's. Still, it would be more than pleasant for the task at hand. He set me up at his desk, where, with Fiona's help, I compiled all of Globo-Care's various contact numbers, with the first and foremost being those for Mark's number two person—a young man by the name of Ben Fletcher. I dialed, and he answered after the second ring, and if I wasn't mistaken, he sounded a little buzzed.

"Ben, here," he said.

"Yeah, hello, Ben, my name is Tag Finn, and I'm a friend of Mark Blake's, and I'm here on Malkarta."

"Oh yeah, I know who you are! You're the guy getting Mark out of prison. How's it all going? Are you guys celebrating?" he asked.

"Not at the moment. Unfortunately, Mark pulled a runner at the courthouse."

"Wait, what? I'm not sure that I heard you correctly. It's a little noisy here."

I heard the background noise diminish as he left what was likely a bar or restaurant.

"OK, what was that?" he asked.

"I said that Mark did a runner on us at the courthouse, and now he's officially a fugitive."

"What the hell?"

"Exactly, and now I have a week to find him before he faces some serious trouble with the law here."

"Well shit. How can I help?"

"I need to know who Mark's main contacts were on the island—specifically who he was working with directly."

"That's easy. His main contact was Anna De Vries, as she's in charge of Malkarta's social services and therefore the primary person he worked with."

Again, I had to smile, as my initial suspicion was starting to pan out.

"So, Ben, anybody else come to mind that Mark might be close with?"

"Other than the people themselves—I'd say she's your best bet."

"Well, thank you for your help."

"You're welcome, and good luck bringing our man home safe and sound."

"I'll do my best. Ciao," I said, hanging up.

I waited until Tim finished his call before giving him my news.

"It appears that we're definitely on the right track, as Anna was his primary contact here."

"Interesting."

"Yeah, so what more can you tell us about the princess?"

"Well, she's the King's only child, drop dead gorgeous, and is in charge of Malkarta's social services."

"Any idea how she feels about the island's political situation?"

"We've talked on many occasions, and it's fairly well known that she's a progressive thinker and, unlike her family, is all for social reform—especially education."

"I'd say that we have a great place to start. Any luck getting us an appointment with her?"

"I sure did. She'll see you as soon as you can get there."

Tim wanted to take us himself, but his afternoon was booked full of meetings, so he arranged for us to take an embassy car. I was actually excited about this eventuality, because I preferred getting behind the wheel rather than being chauffeured around. Five minutes later, Fiona and I were leaving the Embassy in a white Ford Focus that was equipped with GPS, though we wouldn't have a problem finding the royal palace, as it was visible from pretty much everywhere on this side of the island. We made our way along the quaint streets and soon reached the waterfront highway, and, up in the distance, the Royal Palace of Malkarta loomed large over the surrounding buildings. It was a beautiful structure that dated back to the middle sixteen hundreds, and, according to the brochure in our hotel room, it had originally been both a fort and a home to the royal family. Nowadays, it was still a home, but it also held all the major offices of government, and, most important for our purposes, the Ministry of Social Services. I pulled up to the imposing front gate, and a uniformed officer approached the car, checked my identification against his list, then made a quick call before allowing us through. We parked alongside a beautiful white Bentley Turbo that I imagined belonged to a member of the royal family. Nothing said royalty like a Bentley. We left the parking lot and ventured over to the main entrance and were formally greeted by a serious looking security man. He nodded, opened the door, and we were suddenly face to face with the woman from the picture. She was stunning in person—statuesque, blond, and likely somewhere in her late twenties, and she had perfect skin, full lips, and a figure that was athletic, though still shapely.

"Hello, I'm Anna De Vries, and it's very nice to meet you," she said, as she smiled and held out her hand.

"I'm Finn, Tag Finn, and this is Fiona Blake. It's very nice to meet you too."

Anna looked at Fiona and smiled.

"Fiona, you are as beautiful as your brother is handsome."

Interesting. Anna apparently thinks Mark is handsome, which was yet more evidence that something existed between them.

"Oh—well—thank you," Fiona said, taken aback.

"You're welcome. Now, please follow me," she said.

Anna led us through a door at the end of the hallway,

and we passed her rather stern looking assistant then entered her official office. It was equal in size to Jan Akker's, but it was less opulent and seemed to be more about the work and less about the prestige of its occupant.

"Would you like anything to drink? Coffee, tea, or water?" she asked, as we all took a seat.

The Princess was particularly polite and surprisingly outgoing for a royal, and, so far, I liked Anna De Vries.

"No, thank you. I'm fine," I said.

"I'm fine too, thank you," Fiona added.

"So, how can I help you?" Anna asked.

"I'm not sure you've heard, but Mark Blake was released from custody today, and before we were even out of the courthouse, he mysteriously did a runner and disappeared."

"Yes, I'm afraid I heard that news."

"Well, as you may or may not know, the government has been nice enough to give me a week to find him before he is officially declared enemy number one on Malkarta and ruthlessly hunted down. Apparently, the agreement he signed for his release was also an admittance of his charges, and it nullified his constitutional protections, and, in more literal terms, means he's completely and totally screwed if I don't find him and get him the hell off this island."

Anna looked worried, and it wasn't the kind of worry that people had for colleagues or associates. It was real emotion—the kind someone had for family, friends, or perhaps even a lover.

"I'm afraid I hadn't heard all of that yet. It's terrible

news."

"Yeah, and certainly not the happy ending we'd expected."

"So, how can I help?" she asked.

"Obviously, I need to find Mark, and, since you were his primary contact, I was hoping that you would have an idea where he might be or who he might be with."

Before she spoke, she pulled out a piece of paper and wrote something down and handed it to us.

"I'm sorry, I wish I could help, but I have absolutely no idea where he might be," she said, as Fiona and I looked down and read the note.

It said that she couldn't speak freely within the palace, and that we should meet at a restaurant called *De Partij* on the other side of the city around six-thirty PM. I nodded that I understood, so it looked as though we had what would be my first date with a princess.

"Well, thank you for your time. If you can think of anything, please call me. We're in the presidential suite at the King William Hotel."

The door to her office suddenly opened, and Maas Groot walked in with a warm smile on his face. Anna made a point to cover the note with another file that was sitting on her desk, though I couldn't be sure if Maas had been observant enough to see it. He gave Anna a hug and a kiss on the cheek, which seemed like an unusually warm greeting, but I suppose they were both European, and Europeans were more touchy feely than the average American. He then turned his attention to us and shook my hand and kissed Fiona's. Sweet mother of goats did his lips get around.

"I see you've met our lovely Princess Anna."

"Yes, I have, and she is indeed lovely," I said.

"I appreciate your kind words," she responded.

"So, Anna, were you able to aid Mr. Finn in his search?" Mass asked.

"No, I'm afraid I wasn't very helpful," she said.

"That's too bad," he said.

"Yeah," I added.

"So, Finn, any other news since we parted the morning?" Maas asked.

"Afraid not, but I'm working on it. Now, I suppose we should be going, as time is obviously of the essence," I said.

"Yes, well, good luck and God speed," he said, with a nod.

We said goodbye to Maas and Anna then made our way out of the palace and back to the car.

"She seems nice," Fiona said.

"Very—and I could see a man risking it all for her."

"You think she and my brother have a thing?"

"I'm certain of it, and I'm pretty sure she can lead us to Mark."

We left the royal palace and drove back to the hotel and returned to the ever majestic presidential suite. No one was home, so I was guessing that Brett was out sunning himself, pursuing the ladies on the beach, or perhaps even browsing the dental hygiene aisle at the local pharmacy. I dropped onto the couch, took off my shoes, then threw my feet up onto the coffee table, and Fiona joined me a second later and let out a long, sad sigh.

"I guess we aren't leaving Malkarta just yet," she said.

"Apparently not."

"Well, I'm really sorry about all this."

"It's not your fault, and, don't worry, I just see it as a working vacation in paradise, and face it, it's better to be here than freezing our asses off back home in the Bay Area."

"True, but what do we do now?"

"Not much until tonight, so we might as well enjoy ourselves while we can. Feel like hitting the beach?"

"Sure."

We rose and adjourned to our rooms to change, and I put on a pair of board shorts then returned to the living room to wait for Fiona. She appeared a moment later and looked stunning in a skimpy red two-piece bikini that instantly brought my mind back to the events of the previous evening. Feeling a distinct spring in my step and a hearty hi-ho silver in my loins, I grabbed us towels, and we headed to the beach to spend the day frolicking in the waves. There, Fiona literally bounced about, with her marvelous breasts providing a tantalizing testament to the frivolity of female appendages. I certainly liked her boobs, though I also liked her firm, round backside, long muscular legs, angelic face, and stunning blue eyes. Still, they were just a small part of the whole picture that also included the fact that she was smart and a sincerely good person, which were two qualities that were easily capable of eclipsing any of her breathtaking physical attributes.

Done with our fun in the sun, we retreated back to the room to relax, bathe, and get ready for our dinner meeting with the princess. I started by making a fresh pot of coffee then filled a cup and headed into my room for yet another maintenance dump. It would be nowhere near as formidable as my morning deuce, but it would make sure that I'd be lean and mean and ready for dinner and any potential late night sexual hijinks with Fiona. I hit the porcelain, took a sip, and voila—*dumpage*! Actually there was more than I had anticipated, which was probably a result of all the fine food and drink I'd been consuming, though swimming in the waves burned a lot of calories and kept the metabolism up, which probably also played a major role in giving me a solid double deuce. Feeling frisky and free to frolic, I flushed and went straight into the shower to wash away the sticky residue of salt water. I applied shampoo and soap then had a nice long rinse and dried off and applied all the after shower goodies before heading out to my room to get dressed.

Now, I faced an interesting dilemma, which was what in the hell I was going to wear tonight. Island outings always tended to be on the casual side, but we were meeting a princess. I therefore went with khaki board shorts, but dressed it up with a short sleeve khaki button up shirt, which I left comfortably un-tucked. I looked in the mirror and decided I looked like a hybrid of island chic and the movie Out of Africa. Oh well, it would have to do. I walked out of my room, took a seat at the bar, and soon heard the front door to the suite open, and I turned and saw Brett and Ayu entering.

"Well, hello, strangers. Where did you two happen to meet up?"

"The beach bar," Brett said.

"Yeah, he looked kind of sad and lonely, so I took him on a little tour of the island."

"Lucky you. I assume you've heard that we're not leaving just yet?"

"Yeah, Tatyana called me as soon as they got word."

"I can't say that I'm not too bummed about spending a few more days in paradise."

"Agreed," I said.

My satellite phone started ringing, and I raced to my bedroom to answer it, figuring it had to be John calling with some kind of news concerning our current situation. I checked the screen and realized that it was indeed the fabled Sasquatch, so I hit the answer button.

"What the fuck do you want?" I asked.

"Is that really how you think you should address one of your oldest, dearest friends, let alone the current vice president of the United States?"

"Yeah, pretty much."

I heard a laugh in the background and realized that John wasn't alone. Oops.

"So, I'm here with Matthew Hill from the State Department, and he's just given me an update on the Malkarta situation, and I can't say that we aren't a little embarrassed."

"Yeah, sorry about that. I had absolutely no idea we'd have a runner on our hands."

"Not your fault—though still your responsibility," John said.

"Oh, well that makes me feel a lot better—not."

"Hello, Mr. Finn, It's Matt here, and I'm sorry to say that I believe we have a bit of a sticky situation."

"Yeah, one week to find our guy and get him un-stuck."

"Exactly, and we've been speaking with the Malkarta authorities, and Mr. Blake now faces some serious consequences. By signing those papers, he more or less admitted guilt to his charges of sedition, and their constitution is pretty extreme on the subject of crimes against the state. If he's not found within the week, he will become public enemy number one, and they will use any and all means to secure his capture, which means no guarantee for his safety."

"Yeah, Jan and Maas explained all that to me, but, I do have good news. I've met with the person he worked with here in Malkarta, and I'm pretty sure that she has a good idea where he might be hiding."

"Any idea why he bolted?" John asked.

"Have you seen a picture of the princess?"

"I have, actually. You think he's doing all this for love?"

"We can't be sure, but I do know that I've had a semi

ever since I met her this morning."

"What's a semi?" I heard from behind me.

I turned to see Fiona walking in, and she looked absolutely incredible in a short flowery evening dress.

"Oh, you'll find out in about three seconds when my semi turns into a full on raging boner and tears out of my shorts."

"Oh yeah, duh—semi—I get it. Wait, who in the hell are you talking to about semis?" She asked.

"John."

"Oh, I should have known."

"Can you hit the speaker phone button?" John asked.

I hit the button, and now Fiona was part of the conversation as well.

"Hello, Fiona. John, here, and I'm sorry about your brother."

"No, I'm sorry. I can't tell you how embarrassed I am."

"Don't worry, we're blaming Finn."

"As usual," I said.

"So, needless to say, Finn, we need you to find Mark Blake and get him the hell out of there before we have a real international incident on our hands."

"International incident? Isn't that a little dramatic?"

"Well, as you may or may not remember, I said that we had some kind of deal brewing with Malkarta. Well, it turns out that it's a little bigger than I thought. It seems that they are in the process of granting the US permission to build a new Naval base on their island."

"Yeah, Stansfield told me."

"Then I assume you understand it means Malkarta would have a nice influx of funds from the United States, and we'd have strategic placement of our military assets. So, having a very public disagreement over the treatment of one of our citizens could have dire consequences on negotiations, and, in turn, national security."

"That's wonderful. Any other things you want to pile on my plate?"

"No, that's it for now, though what fun would it be if there weren't dire consequences riding on your success?"

"I'm feeling so inspired by your words that I'm thinking you might want to give up politics and become a motivational speaker."

He laughed.

"There are a lot of people in Washington who'd probably agree with you."

"OK, Sasquatch, I'd better get going, as right now it's time for me to go have dinner with the princess."

"Well, give her my love, if you know what I mean," John said.

"Am I to assume you're implying that I should only put it in about two inches?" I asked.

"Well, only if that's all you've got, and, if so, you might want to make up the difference by stuffing in your balls."

"Well, if it's a true vice presidential re-enactment you're hoping for, then I'd just use my pinky and forget about the balls entirely."

"Dude, I'm talking about a true reenactment here of my magnificent manhood—and that would entail you probably having to use your forearm and a couple of large pink grapefruits to double as my testicles."

"Yeah, and if I did do that, it would basically be me simulating you simulating my enormous cock and balls."

At that point, Fiona grabbed my phone out of my hand.

"So, if you children are done talking about humping the princess, then I'd like to ask a more important question—namely, how are things with Jessica?"

"You'll be happy to hear that it's going extremely well. In fact, she's here in Washington."

"No shit?" I asked.

"No shit."

"Well, tell her we both say hello."

"I will, now go have fun with the princess and bring us a happy ending that leaves all parties equally satisfied."

"Don't I always?"

"No, so let's make sure to keep the international incident level down to about a two."

"As in two inches, which brings us nicely full circle back to your penis."

"I think you mean your penis."

"No, obviously, I meant..."

At that point, Fiona unceremoniously hit the end button.

"Goddammit! You let him win!" I complained.

"No, technically I kept two adolescent idiots from continuing the most stupid game of penis one-upmanship I've ever experienced, and, honestly, you really shouldn't talk like that to the vice president of the United States."

"To me, he's just John, the president's lackey."

We headed back out to the living room to find Brett and Ayu were at the bar enjoying a cocktail.

"Did you make enough for everyone?" I asked.

Brett filled us each a glass with the white icy concoction, and I took a sip and realized that he had made some damn fine Pina Coladas! It was a perfect drink to start our evening, and, after a few more sips, I was starting to feel a real optimism about the night ahead.

"So, Ayu, have you been to *De Partij*?"

"Yeah, why?"

"Well, we're going there tonight on business, and I was wondering if I was dressed properly."

"You're fine. It's island casual, so half of the people there are in swimsuits and thongs."

"As in shoes or bikinis?"

"Both, actually."

"Well shit—this sounds like the beginning of a beautiful evening."

CHAPTER TWENTY-TWO
A Royal Escapade

I looked at my watch and saw that it was seven fifteen and therefore about time to head off to dinner. We finished our cocktails, said goodbye to Brett and Ayu, then made our way out to the front of the hotel, where a valet left to retrieve our car. While standing there, I noticed Sten sitting behind the wheel of a white government jeep that was parked a short distance away, so I walked over and stood at his open window.

"Evening, cowboy. Still watching me?" I asked.

"Yep, orders still stand to keep you safe."

"You hear about this morning?"

"Yeah, pretty fucked up."

"No shit, but if all goes well, I'll find him and get him the hell off the island."

"Let's hope so."

Our car arrived, and I said goodbye to Sten and walked over and joined Fiona, who had already taken a seat. I typed the address to *De Partij* into the GPS then set off towards the main road that would take us across the city. Evening traffic was light, so it was easy to keep track of Sten, who stayed back about five car lengths. Part of me wanted to see if I could lose him, but there wasn't any point, as he was just there to help keep us safe from Malkarta's negative elements. Ten minutes later, we turned onto a smaller two lane road that led towards the water and were soon pulling in to *De Partij*, which I suspected translated as The Party. We found a parking place then walked into the crowded restaurant and had to wait in line in order to eventually speak with the beautiful young Asian woman manning the hostess stand.

"Welcome to *De Partij*, do you have a reservation?" she asked.

"Kind of, the name is Finn, but we're meeting Princess Anna De Vries."

"Oh, I'm very sorry, sir. Please come this way."

We followed the woman through the crowd and up a small flight of stairs to an elevated lounge that had an excellent view of the downstairs bar and dance floor. The music wasn't as loud up here, but I imagine that Anna had chosen this spot because it afforded a certain amount of ambient noise to cover our conversation. There were only six tables, and Anna was at the one in the farthest corner, and she was looking stunning in a tight fitting black cocktail dress. She saw us approaching and stood to exchange the typical European kisses on the cheek, before we all took a seat.

"Thank you for coming," she said.

"Thank you for inviting us."

"Yes, and I'm sorry I couldn't speak back at the palace, but, as they say, the walls have ears, unfortunately."

A waiter arrived, and we all ordered cocktails, with Anna choosing a Gin and tonic while Fiona and I went with Mai Tai's. The waiter returned quickly with our drinks, and Anna held her glass up to toast.

"To Mark," she said, a little sadly.

I had a sip of my drink then took a minute to look at Anna. She appeared to be fairly composed and had the hint of a smile on her face, though there was some unease behind her eyes that made me believe it was merely an attempt to appear stoic. She had a quick look around the room, then leaned forward and kept her voice low as she spoke.

"Things are not as serene as they appear on Malkarta. It's probably hard to see it here in New Leiden, but, when you go north, you can feel that there is real unrest in the air."

"Actually, I felt a little of that unrest last night on the beach."

"Oh, what happened?"

"The kitchen staff from my hotel didn't like me hanging out with one the waitresses, and we had a little bit of a tussle on the beach."

"I hope you're OK."

"Oh, I'm fine, but there wasn't much in the way of

breakfast the next morning. Now, enough about my travails. Please continue," I said.

"So, this unrest has been brewing for some time, but Globo-Care's arrival seemed to have intensified things, and, honestly, your brother and his foundation have brought real hope to this place, but hope means change, and that's something that the government doesn't want."

"Not if it cuts into profits."

"Exactly, but there's a lot to go around, and, even if they only diverted a small percentage, it would make a huge positive change in the quality of life here."

"I take it that you have a different perspective than your family."

"Yes—my views differ very much from my family, as I would like to see my home become a first world nation, where it's people have access to proper education, healthcare, and a higher standard of living."

"So, when you say that trouble is brewing are you implying the possibility of some kind of revolution or coup?"

"Yes, and while Mark's presence helped stimulate the fervor, he was actually emphatic in working with the MDA to convey to the people here that they could achieve it through peaceful reform rather than violent insurrection."

"I assume that doesn't include the MSA?"

"Definitely not. They would be happy with an armed and bloody takeover."

"So, both the government and the MSA probably don't like Mark very much."

"Definitely not, but the rest of the people here see him as a savior."

"And what do you see him as?"

"The same—and more," she said, taking a sip of her drink and suddenly looking a little lost in thought.

"I hope I'm not being too forward, but I get the impression that you might be more than just friends with Mark."

Anna smiled.

"Yes. You are correct, though I would say that we're a lot more than that."

"So, I'm getting the feeling that you two are a couple of love bears."

She couldn't help but smile.

"Correct, and we'd like to get married."

"Does your family know how serious your relationship is?" I asked.

"I suspect they do, which is obviously part of the reason behind the sedition charge."

"How lame would it be if your parents were so powerful that they could imprison or deport your boyfriend?"

"Extremely lame, I'm afraid," Anna said.

"Which makes it even more critical that I find him and get him the hell off Malkarta."

"Yeah, but even if you do find him, I think it will be hard to get him to leave, as he really loves both me and the people here."

"You could both leave and work in exile."

"Perhaps, but I know that neither of us wants to do

that."

"Well, then perhaps we can come up with another solution, though that obviously can't happen unless we find him before the week's up."

Anna sighed, and I could see the conflict behind her eyes.

"I'll help you, but that means going to the people who are sheltering him."

"Fair enough. How and when do we meet them?"

"Tonight. He's staying in a village up to the north that was one of the key places that he worked, and there's a local man who is very close to Mark."

"Then we'd better eat fast."

We ordered dinner and had a pretty decent meal, and, while the food, like many nightclubs, was good, it wasn't superb, as the primary objective of the place was to get its guest's drunk and dancing. We paid the check and exited the building via a side door that opened directly out to where Anna had parked her white Land Rover. It was the Defender model and would be perfect for the island terrain of Malkarta. We climbed in, and I again took the backseat and gave Fiona shotgun.

"Make sure you buckle up. The roads can be treacherous up in the north," Anna said.

"Always do," I responded.

She pulled out, and we left New Leiden and headed north along a two lane road that was named, not too coincidentally, the William De Vries highway. How odd would it be to have your family name on every major landmark? It certainly wouldn't do much for instilling a sense of humility in the future generations, though Anna seemed far removed from her title. I suppose even royals, in spite of their often overprivileged childhoods, had a chance at becoming well adjusted adults.

I glanced over my shoulder and looked behind us to see if Sten had been sharp enough to see that we had left in a different car, but the large number of headlights behind us made it impossible to be certain. I turned my attention back to the road ahead just in time to see we were coming upon a small and rather plain looking town with most, if not all, of its businesses closed for the night. The only lights were coming from the windows of the surrounding homes, which didn't look to be full of poor huddled masses, but then we were still pretty close to New Leiden, and not even absolute monarchies put their dirty little secrets where tourists might run into them. We continued beyond the town, and my thoughts moved on to a question that had been simmering in the back of my mind.

"What do you think of Maas Groot?" I asked Anna.

"I like him. Why do you ask?"

"Well, I was just curious. He seems like a nice guy, so I was wondering why you made such a point of covering up the note you had written to us in your office."

"Habit mostly, but, as his allegiance is ultimately to my father, I decided it best to keep him out of the loop. That way, if we get up to no good, then he doesn't have to take sides or get into any trouble."

"I wonder if the situation on Malkarta is difficult for him," I asked.

"Perhaps, but he's a military man at heart, and his life is about following orders rather than questioning them. Of course, he's always been extremely kind to me."

Of course he was kind to Anna, as Every man tended to be a little kinder to a beautiful woman. It was all part of our deep seated psychological male programming, and, not too surprisingly, psychologists had discovered that both men and women, even those not following their biological imperative, were generally more drawn towards their comely brethren, often seeing them as being nicer, more honest, and generally friendlier, whether or not they really were. It also explained how people became infatuated with celebrities, and it was, in my opinion, actually quite a sad testament to our ever deepening descent into superficiality, though I suppose evolution wasn't prepared for the entertainment industry and places like Hollywood.

"So, he's just nice in a friendly way. Not in a romantic way?"

"Of course not. I mean, I've known him since I was a child."

She might believe that, but I got a slightly different impression when I saw the way he looked at her, and it's not as though an older man has never had a thing for a younger woman—well, that and the sudden need for a red convertible sports car.

"So, Maas is obviously extremely loyal to your father," I said.

"They're like brothers, so it's hard to tell where my father's opinion ends and Maas's begins."

"And what is your father like? Is he stubborn when it comes to upholding the traditions of his ancestors?"

"Yes, though I know that he's a good man at heart."

"The same man who threw your fiancé in prison."

"Yes, but he can't help it. He has a hard time accepting change and anything outside his control."

"So, he's like every other parent on the planet."

Anna looked back and smiled at me then set her eyes back to the road ahead, and we continued on through several more towns, and each one was progressively more rundown than the previous. Next we came upon one of the many spice processing factories, and it kind of reminded me of Hawaii's once thriving sugar cane industry. There were massive fields of crops, and off to the side was the obligatory processing plant that was belching smoke and subsequently creating more wealth for the powers that be.

Anna started to slow as we came upon another quiet small town, though this one had a bar, and it appeared to be popular, considering the number of people who were milling around outside. Anna parked in the back, then we walked around to the front of the building, and each person we passed gave us a particularly unpleasant glare. Clearly, this was a locals only kind of place, and three *bulès* stuck out like three very sore, very unwelcome thumbs.

"So, Mark's friend will be here?" I asked.

"Yes, it's his place, so he's usually tending bar."

We ventured inside to find the place had the typical dim bar lighting, and there was music playing from some unseen stereo system. The air had that old musty smell of spilled beer and sweat, and its worn and weathered tables were all full of curious onlookers who stared at us as we navigated the crowd. We reached the bar, and the bartender stepped closer and nodded at Anna before turning his discerning gaze to Fiona and me. He was an interesting looking character, likely of Indonesian and European descent, and he sported a neatly trimmed beard and glasses that made him look more like a scholar than a bartender. I hadn't seen many Indo-Europeans thus far, but with this being an island and a limited gene pool, it was only natural that ethnic mingling would occur—regardless of a racist and elitist aristocracy.

"How can I help you?" he asked, in perfect English.

"I'm looking for Mark Blake."

"Alexa, turn off the music," the bartender said, which meant that Amazon had made it to Malkarta.

All eyes in the bar turned to us as the place became eerily silent, and the only sound was the buzzing coming from the flies circling just above our heads.

"Is there a problem?" I asked.

"What do you want with Mark?" he asked.

Interesting, he referred to him as Mark, which confirmed Anna's statement that they were friends. Our princess had made a wise move in bringing us up here, or so I thought until the people around us all pulled out knives, machetes, and clubs. Then, like a great army of zombies, they started moving closer, making it abundantly clear that our princess had made a rather un-wise move in bringing us up here tonight.

"I think that you all have the wrong impression about us. We're here to help Mark," I said.

Anna stepped forward.

"It's OK, Itari. He's telling the truth."

"I trust you, Anna, but how can we be sure about this man?" he asked.

"Look, this is Fiona, Mark's sister," Anna said.

The man squinted as he scrutinized Fiona.

"I can see a resemblance, but it doesn't prove that your other friend here isn't a government spy."

Itari spoke something in Indonesian, and two men who were standing nearby started walking in my direction, probably with the intent to search me, so I quickly stepped back and pulled out my gun.

"Hands to yourselves, boys. I'm only here to help Mark," I said.

The crowd froze, and it appeared we had a Mexican standoff, even though there wasn't a Mexican within a ten thousand mile radius of our current location. There was a sudden commotion off to the side of the room, and I looked over to see Mark Blake walking through the crowd.

"People! Put down your weapons! This man is a friend."

"Alexa, turn the music back on," Itari said.

The music came back on, and the tension instantly dissolved as the bar patrons put away their various weapons and returned to their seats. It was suddenly as though nothing had happened, and Mark immediately hugged Anna, then his sister, before holding out his hand to me.

"Nice to see you again, Tag. Sorry about this morning."

"Oh, I understand completely—now that I've met Anna."

He smiled.

"So—what brings you up here?" he asked.

"Oh, you know—typical tourist stuff. We'd heard this was a lovely place to get a drink and mingle with the locals."

"Yeah, as you can see, Malkarta is a bit of a tinderbox at the moment, which is another reason why I couldn't leave."

"I assume you understand that the paper you signed this morning was basically an admittance of guilt in exchange for your release, and it means that you are now officially a fugitive. The good news is that the government granted me one week to find and remove you from the island before you're officially hunted down as an enemy of the state."

"I understand, but I can't leave."

"They will have the authority to bring you in by any means necessary, and that also includes bullets."

"It doesn't matter. I can't leave."

"Can't or won't?"

"Both, I suppose."

"Couldn't you and Anna leave together? Start a new life

somewhere else?"

"We could, but we won't. Our work here is far too important. You wouldn't believe how the majority of these people live. Someone needs to stand up for their rights."

"Couldn't you continue the movement in exile?"

"Maybe, but if I leave, things might deteriorate into an all out armed conflict. Thousands would be needlessly hurt or killed in the crossfire."

"I guess it's not easy being the good hearted type who's out to save the world."

"Definitely not, and this island won't save itself," he said, gravely.

Suddenly there was a commotion, and a man came running in, looking frantic and out of breath.

"Itari! Mr. Blake! Malkarta Security Forces just arrived outside!"

Mark exchanged a nervous glance with Itari, then both turned to me.

"Don't look at me. I came here with Anna," I said.

A second later, a voice came over a loudspeaker.

"Mark Blake, we know you're in there. You will exit the building immediately with your hands up."

"I thought you said that you had a week," Mark said.

"I do—or I did. Maybe someone changed his or her mind. God only knows at this point."

"What do we do?" Mark asked.

"We use the princess as a hostage," a nearby man said.

"Never. I'd turn myself in before that happened."

The voice came over the loudspeaker again.

"You now have exactly one minute to exit the building or we come in."

"OK, we need to get the fuck away from here and buy some time, so I can call Washington and find out what our options are. Is there another way out of this building?" I asked.

"Yes, just for these kinds of occasions," Itari said.

"Mark, tell them that you're coming out, but you want to allow the other people to exit first. It'll buy us some time and make sure none of these people get caught in any kind of crossfire."

Mark went to the edge of the doorway and yelled out his request, and a second later, the man man's voice came over his loudspeaker thankfully agreeing to Mark's demands.

"OK—everyone start leaving, but keep it nice and slow with your hands up. Don't spook them and give them any reason to shoot. Itari, can you take us out the alternative route?"

"Yes, this way," he said, gesturing at the floor.

"Down?" I asked.

"Yes, it's a tunnel."

"Sweet buttered hens! I knew I liked you the moment I first saw you!"

We walked behind the bar, and Itari lifted a hatch in the floor and pointed to an old ladder that led down to some kind of underground storage room.

"There is a tunnel down there that leads behind the

building and out to the back parking lot, so, hopefully you should be able to leave unseen," he said.

"Thank you, Itari," Mark said.

"Stay safe, and get in touch when you can," he responded.

We descended the ladder and emerged into a dimly lit storage cellar, and just ahead was a corridor lined with old wood planking. We followed it until it came to another ladder which likely led back up to the surface. I climbed up and lifted the metal hatch a small crack and peered outside. We were in the back parking lot and about twenty yards from Anna's Land Rover. Perfect! As I opened the hatch the rest of the way, a pair of shoes stepped into view and, more alarmingly, I heard the click of a round being chambered in a pistol.

"Come out," said an oddly familiar voice.

We all climbed out and assembled in the back parking lot to find Sten standing there with a smile on his face. He also had a pistol in his hand, and Mark and Anna looked at me nervously, so I smiled to put them at ease then turned my gaze back to Sten.

"Fancy meeting you here," I said.

"Yeah, I thought you'd lost me at *De Partij* until this call came through," he said, as he holstered his weapon.

"So, someone apparently knew where we were going."

"Yeah, and it wasn't me. I only just got here."

"Interesting—and what brought you back here?"

"They asked for someone to cover the back, so I vol-unteered, as I figured you were a sneaky fucker and would likely come out this way."

"So, what are our options at the moment?"

"Well, option one would be for me to take you all into custody while option two would be for you to get in Princess Anna's Land Rover and go like hell. If you go with that option, I'll stall as long as possible before reporting you've escaped. It would give you a decent head start, but you'd be on your own from here on out."

"I'll take option two."

"I figured you would."

"Thanks, I owe you one."

"Yes, you do, so be careful and stay safe, so that you can pay up when this is all over, and, just so you now, I hear they can be a little trigger happy in matters of national security," he said.

We left Sten and headed for Anna's Land Rover, and, as we walked, Anna leaned in close and whispered in my ear.

"How, after only one day on the island, did you manage to befriend a member of the Malkarta Security Services?" she asked.

"What can I say? I'm a people person."

CHAPTER TWENTY-THREE
Up Country

We reached Anna's Land Rover and had some quick tactical decisions to make, with the first being who should drive. I was trained in escape and evasion driving, but Anna had the home field advantage, and, after a brief discussion, I was nominated driver and slid behind the wheel. I eased out of the back parking lot and onto the main road but kept the lights off for the moment. When we were about a hundred yards away, I turned on the lights, hit the gas, and gunned the Land Rover. I glanced in the rearview mirror, and, for the moment it was clear, so I turned my attention to our immediate problem, which was where in the hell we were headed.

"So, you two are the experts. Any idea where we should go?" I asked Mark and Anna.

"Farther north, though we want to steer clear of the MSA."

"So, head northeast?"

"Yeah, if we can," Mark said.

We rounded a turn, and the road opened up into a long straightaway, and, just as we reached the far end, I checked the rearview mirror and saw a dense group of headlights coming up quickly behind us.

"Shit, we have company closing fast. What kind of vehicles do the Malkarta Security service drive?" I asked.

"Subaru WRX's. Why do you ask?"

"Just curious how hard I'm going to have to drive to outrun them."

"Oh, are they comparable to my Land Rover?" Anna asked.

"Yeah, so everyone needs to make sure their seat belts are good and tight, because things are going to get a lot worse before they get better."

"Wonderful," Mark muttered.

I glanced in the rearview mirror at our pursuers and did some quick calculations.

"How well do you guys know the roads up here?" I asked.

"Not well," Anna said.

"What about you, Mark?"

"I've spent a fair amount of time up this way, but it's been mostly during the day, and I was usually with a local, so at night, I'd have no fucking clue where we are."

"Well, as usual, I guess we'll have to wing it."

We cleared the straightaway, and headed into a series of curves, where less than a quarter of a mile up the road, I could see the lights behind us were getting closer. It was, therefore, time to leave the main highway. After a particularly sharp right, I turned left onto a smaller dirt road. It had rained recently, and it was slippery, but the Land Rover held firm, and its four wheel drive made the going a lot easier. Still, the back end swung out to each side, and it forced me to corrective steer, and we ended up drifting through the turns like a rally car. After a mile of tense driving, I saw a fork in the road, and I slowed down and came to a stop.

"Any suggestions?" I asked.

"No idea," Anna said.

"Should we flip a coin?"

Before anyone could answer, lights appeared behind us, so I gunned it and sent a rooster tail of dirt shooting up from behind the car as we headed to the right. The Land Rover accelerated quickly, and its big V8 engine roared as we flew down the dark, bumpy road, whose surface was dotted with deep ruts and holes that sent everyone bouncing around in their seat. Still, the pride of Britain's four wheel drive vehicles made easy work of the challenging terrain. A tight right hairpin turn came up, and I hit the E-brake and sent the back around then hit the gas and accelerated into the following straight. At the end there was a dogleg left, and I took it at full speed, and everyone in the car gasped as we went sideways for the entirety of the turn.

"In case you haven't noticed, we have a pretty steep drop-off to our right," Mark said, nervously.

"Thanks, I'll try to avoid it."

Our pursuers were falling behind, and, if I could just

maintain the lead until we reached another fork, we had a pretty good chance of losing them and getting away. We came upon an S-turn next, and the back end came dangerously close to the edge, but the tires held firm, and we reached another straight. I gunned it but then had to brake hard as we navigated yet another sharp turn. Just ahead, we came to a small rise, and on the other side there was a side road leading into the jungle. Perfect! I hit the E-brake and sent the rear out ninety degrees then accelerated up the road and quickly stopped and killed the lights. The pursuing cars appeared a moment later and sped past, but they suddenly came to a skidding halt, which was a bad sign. If they decided to turn around and come this way, then we'd be thoroughly fucked, as we'd forfeited our lead in the hopes of hiding. Suddenly, the cars continued on, and the noise of their straining engines disappeared into the distance and left us alone in the hot and humid Malkarta night.

"I guess we've lost them for now," I said.

"Thank God! Any more of those high speed turns and I'll likely puke my guts out," Mark said.

"I understand, as I'd be feeling the same way if I were in the back seat, so slow going from now on, I promise."

"Where should we go now?" Fiona asked.

"Well, I say we stay in the middle of the island and far away from any main roads until we can find a place to hole up for the night. Any lovely bed and breakfasts up here?" I asked.

"None that I know of, and the roads can be extremely

treacherous at night." Anna said.

"It's OK, we'll take it slow and see what we can find."

I started the car, and we continued on for about a mile before arriving in a small valley with a number of buildings just off the road.

"It looks like an old deserted workers camp," Anna said.

If it was indeed deserted, it would probably be a decent place to spend the night.

A sudden rain squall blew in and engulfed the car and road in a deluge of water.

"Shall we drive over and have a look around?"

"Absolutely. It looks a lot more inviting than the weather and the jungle at the moment," Mark said.

I pulled off the main road, and, in order to keep our Range Rover hidden from the view of any passing Malkarta Security Services, I parked around behind one of the buildings. We climbed out and did a quick recon of the camp, and the first structure turned out to be some kind of large kitchen and dining hall, and strangely it still had power, water, and, perhaps if we were extremely lucky, some leftover food stores. We moved on to the next structure and found a sort of bunkhouse that had a series of beds, and a number of them were even made up with blankets and pillows. It seemed pretty unusual for a deserted workers camp to be this homey, and I was suddenly feeling a little like Goldie Locks, though I was ever hopeful that we wouldn't meet the three bears who actually lived here. On the far side of the building, was a bathroom, and it wasn't exactly as nice as the one back in the presidential suite, but it would be better than squatting behind a bush or tree when the inevitable number one or two came along.

"Home sweet home. Feel free to get comfortable, and I'll head back to the kitchen to forage around and see if there are any food or beverage items."

"I'll come with you," Fiona said.

We walked one building over to the dining hall and made our way into a large pantry. Inside, the shelves were stocked with all manner of canned and packaged food, but, more importantly, on the very top shelf, there was a case of beer and four bottles of Oban Scotch. Nobody left these kinds of goodies around without intending to return and consume them, but all we needed was one night. I grabbed a bottle of Oban and four glasses, then Fiona and I headed back to the bunkhouse, where I poured everyone about three chubby little fingers worth of Scotch.

"Here's to the revolution," I said, raising my glass.

"To the revolution," everyone responded

I finished my drink, but before having another, I decided that I should check in with Matheson. I pulled out the satellite phone, put it on speaker, then hit call, and we waited only two rings before he answered.

"Well, if it isn't Mr. Shit Storm himself," he said.

"Don't worry, I haven't toppled the government or sabotaged your precious military base just yet."

"Yet being the operative word."

"Yeah, so keep your bra on, number two, and remember

that it's people like me out in the field who keep people like you in cozy little offices in Washington."

"Don't be ridiculous. My Washington office is huge."

"At least something is."

"Yeah, otherwise I'd have no place to pull out my enormous penis."

"It's strange, but whenever you say the word penis, all I can think of are those tiny little cocktail wieners."

"That's called projecting," he responded.

"Oh—so that's what your doing."

"Anyway—you mind giving me a sitrep?" he asked.

Sitrep was military speak for a situation report, and I suspect he changed the subject because I had a slight lead in the penis joke department.

"You'll be happy to hear that I found Mark, but for some reason the authorities here changed their mind about the one week reprieve."

"Who did you piss off?"

"I'm not sure, actually, but we had to take our little party on the run."

"Wonderful."

"Yeah, but the upside is that I'll get to utilize all my special operations and CIA escape and evasion training."

"So, I guess I was correct when I called you Mr. Shit Storm."

"Absolutely, and I suppose I should tell you about another little development."

"I'm listening."

"I have Fiona and Princess Anna here with me as well."

"Jesus, Finn, you've dragged a member of the royal family into this mess?"

"I have, and it's probably a good time to make official introductions."

John was quiet a moment.

"Um—are we on speaker phone?" he asked.

"Yep."

"So, everyone has been listening to us talk shit?"

"Affirmative."

"Goddammit, Finn!"

"What? I think government should be transparent."

"I don't think the world is ready to hear about our respective exploits, least of all those involving my penis."

"I think you mean our penises, and I'd have to agree, so, let's move on to a new subject. First, I'd like to introduce you to Princess Anna De Vries. Anna, this is John Matheson, vice president of the United States and a man very obsessed with his penis."

"Hello, Mr. Vice President. It's nice to meet you—and your penis."

John laughed out loud, as I imagine he never suspected a princess would officially acknowledge his penis, and it was, in my opinion, yet another justification of why Mark had risked his life to stay on Malkarta.

"It's nice to meet you, and please call me John."

"John it is."

"And now, Sasquatch, I'd like to introduce you to the

man of the hour. Mark Blake."

"Hello, Mark, it's nice to finally meet you, though I wish it were under different circumstances."

"Yeah, I'm really sorry about screwing up everything you did to get me released."

"Well, having just met Anna, I can kind of understand now. There's nothing on this earth quite as powerful as a good woman to make us menfolk do crazy things."

"Indeed," I said, looking at Fiona.

We were all quiet for a moment, so I figured it was about time to finish up our call.

"Well, Sasquatch, that's all the exciting news I have at the moment. Any final words of encouragement?"

"Good luck and stay safe. I'll do what I can from my end then get in touch as soon as I have anything. Oh, and in case you didn't already figure it out, you're in good hands with Finn. There's no one else in the world I'd trust more with my life."

"Thanks for the vote of confidence, Sasquatch," I said.

"You're welcome, Shit Storm."

The phone went dead, and a quiet moment followed until I felt eyes on me and turned to see Mark staring curiously.

"You seriously talk like that to the vice president of the United States?" he asked.

"Yes, he does," Fiona interjected.

"It's kind of a tradition. We go way back."

"Finn saved his life, so he's apparently earned the right

to give him that much shit," Fiona said.

"Yeah, but to be perfectly honest, I gave him that much shit long before I saved his life."

I filled everyone's glasses then looked around at my unusual assortment of bunkmates and had to smile. When was the last time I had cocktails with a humanitarian, a centerfold, and a princess?

"What shall we drink to? A better tomorrow?" I asked.

"How about a better today," Fiona suggested.

"Indeed, why put off to tomorrow what you can wish for today?" I responded.

We clinked glasses then drank and enjoyed our predicament as best as we could, and, had we been in another part of the world, it would have just been four friends getting out into the country for a little fun and relaxation. Our circumstances were obviously different, but there was no reason not to make the best of it. Three drinks later, we were hearing about how Mark and Anna met and fell madly in love the very minute they laid eyes on each other. It sounded like the opening to a storybook romance and made me understand all the more why he bolted from the courthouse.

But, beyond their love, they shared a noble purpose. They were both willing to risk everything to help the people of Malkarta, and, in Anna's case, it wasn't just another empty promise that I would expect from the typical bureaucrat. She really seemed to care, so, riding high on a scotch buzz as I sat amongst these noble few, I vowed that I would help them complete their task. Their problems would be my problems, and together we would find a way to bring lasting peace and prosperity to the island of Malkarta. Or, perhaps it was just the booze filling me with the romantic optimism to become a real life Indonesian version of Don Quixote, and my efforts would be no more meaningful than tilting at spice factories. Still, I sincerely believed my enthusiasm would remain fully intact in the morning.

Before any of that could happen, however, we had a bottle to finish, and a short time later, we were all drunk, tired, and ready to say good night to what had been one hell of a day. Fiona had an extra toothbrush in her purse, and she gave it to Mark and Anna while I shared hers. We used her little travel toothpaste, and after some vigorous brushing, we were all minty fresh and heading to bed, though we had a final issue to address—namely privacy. Mark had been in prison for the last few months, and I was guessing that Malkarta didn't allow conjugal visits, so he and Anna probably wanted to make some serious love. I looked around at our surroundings and decided that the easiest course of action would be to hang a blanket between us. It wouldn't be sound proof, but people on the run had to make concessions. I found a line and strung it across the room then hung two of the dull green woolen blankets between our respective beds to convert our accommodations into a two bedroom of sorts. I turned out the light, and the room came alive with the soft blue starlight that was shining through the windows and creating a perfect ambiance for the lovers to hump to their heart's content.

Fiona and I undressed to our most basic undergarments and settled into our tiny, though cozy, bunk, where, in order to properly fit, the two of us were forced to spoon. We only had the sheet to cover us, as the blanket was obviously serving as a barrier, but that was fine because the sheet was more than enough cover in the balmy eighty degree tropical night. I had my arm around her, and, as I used my finger tips to gently caress her nipples, she subtly wiggled her lovely backside against my groin. Her efforts were causing my manhood to grow, and it was only a matter of seconds before it was hard and straining painfully against my underwear and in turn—Fiona. As if mother nature herself were mirroring our growing passion, another rain squall blew in, and the sound of the deluge of raindrops filled the air. Fiona abruptly rolled over and kissed me, and there, not three feet from her brother and the princess, we began making out like a couple of teenagers. We did our best to keep quiet, but the bunk had a tendency to squeak whenever we moved, and not even the rain could provide adequate cover. Soon, the same noise was coming from the other side of the curtain, and my assumption that Malkarta didn't allow conjugal visits was appearing to be valid, and there were officially two very obvious sets of horny bears roaming these woods.

Oddly, the lack of privacy did nothing to quell our growing desire, and instead it seemed to work quite the opposite by subconsciously promoting the excitement of the fact we were breaking some kind of unspoken social rule. Every second that passed, our passion grew, and our kisses became more desperate as we explored each other in this unlikely moment of passion. The tiny bunk, however, was quickly becoming an obstacle, so I sat up and threw my legs over the side of the bed, and Fiona straddled me and threw her legs over mine. We were now facing one another as we returned to our previous activity, but this position was a lot more comfortable and made it a hell of a lot easier to enjoy ourselves. I pulled her close and brought her lips to mine then moved on to her neck and kissed it before delivering a playful bite and working my way up to her ear. This only served to fuel her desire, and soon I was pulled back to her lips to find her tongue laying in wait. She slipped it between my lips and penetrated my mouth so that we could engage in a war of tongues in which the outcome was our ever increasing libido.

With our mouths otherwise engaged, I decided to extend the battlefield by reaching down and pulling off her shirt. This exposed a bounty of exquisite flesh, and I ran my hands down to her breasts and used my fingertips to trace a path around her areolas until they contracted, and her nipples grew hard and elongated in a very real cry for attention. I heard their desperate pleas, and I leaned down and teased them with my tongue until Fiona moaned and arched her back. I leaned down and kissed her stomach then pulled her back up because I already missed her lips. As our mouths reunited, I felt her hands move down past my chest to where they happened upon my gentle woodsman, who was quietly straining against the fabric confines of his cotton domicile. Fiona, aware of his plight, freed him then ran her agile fingers slowly up and down his length, though each time she gave his tip a quick twist of the thumb. Not one to be left out, I slid my hand down to her maidenly valley to find it was a hot, moist, and alluring refuge in this storm of passion. I gently ran my fingers over her clitoris, and, as we continued to kiss and explore each other, it was feeling a little like our mutual masturbation session, only this time we actually got to touch each other. As if on cue, we both stood and shed our remaining clothing items then dropped back down onto the bed, though Fiona cleverly maneuvered her hips in order to mount my hard manhood. As we reached full mount, the pleasure was so intense that we both let out a loud lustful moan that was cut off when we remembered that we had immediate company. We exchanged a knowing smile, then she started rocking up and down on me with a slow purposeful rhythm.

I placed my hands on her buttocks and helped guide her efforts, and, even with the rain pounding on the roof, I could still hear our roommates on the other side of the makeshift curtain. It made me worry that they might become even louder, which would be more than a little disconcerting for Fiona, as there probably wasn't anything more disturbing than listening to a family member have sex—unless, of course, you were from some backwater inbred town that approved of incest, which meant that the sex you heard was happening between you and the family member in question. Either way, I would have given any-thing for a little more noise.

As if heaven were blessing our coital union, thunder and lightning began filling the air, and, with a little extra noise, I turned back to my beautiful companion ever aware I was seconds from sweet release. It was therefore tantamount to limit our in and out movement and instead focus on more of a circular grinding motion, as it put more stimulation on the female side of the equation and upped my staying power and, in turn, the chances of a mutually assured climax. As our pace quickened, however, so too did the noise from the bed and, in turn, the bed next door. It was almost starting to feel like a race, and the oncoming orgasmic tide swept all delicate thought and social nicety from the room, as both parties began calling out in proud unabashed delight. Unable to hold back any longer and feeling that Fiona was equally close, I took hold of her breasts and played my fingertips over her taught nipples. The entirety of our world dissolved into the existential playground of our shared sexual experience, and, as we powered into a climactic climax, I was feeling ever thank-ful that our neighbors had reached the same eventuality. Sweet orgasmic relief filled the air until the room eventu-ally grew quiet, and Fiona dismounted, and we snuggled up together in the tiny bed. A moment later, Mark spoke from the other side of the curtain.

"Promise me that we won't ever have to do anything like

this again," he said.

"Camping? I think it makes for an excellent couples retreat," I responded.

"You know what I mean," he said.

"Don't worry, this was the first, last, and only time we share a bedroom this way," Fiona said.

"Tonight, anyway," I added.

Everyone laughed.

"Good night, all," I said.

"Good night," the others responded.

Thus, I closed my eyes and drifted off to sleep, thereby bringing to a close my first time of ever having sex in the same room as a princess, a humanitarian, and a centerfold.

CHAPTER TWENTY-FOUR
A Night to Remember, A Morning to Forget

I awoke and checked my watch to see that it was a little after seven in the morning. It was earlier than I liked to wake up, but we had all gone to bed at a reasonable hour, so I was ready to get up and face the day. The others were still asleep as I padded into the bathroom, brushed my teeth, and headed out of the bunkhouse and over to the building with the dining hall. I foraged around the pantry, and there on the third shelf was some canned coffee. Not bad. I found a coffee machine and soon had a lovely pot filled with the great elixir of caffeinated godliness. I found some powdered creamer, grabbed four cups, the pot, and put it all on a tray, before heading back to the bunkhouse, where I found Fiona awake.

"Oh my God! Coffee! Would it be awkward if I were to propose right now?" she asked.

"No, but I think you should know that I'm an old fashioned boy, so I expect a ring."

"How about felatio instead?"

"Interesting, I suppose that your lips forming a ring around my penis would be close enough."

She took a cup, then we clinked mugs.

"To the greatest man in the world," she said.

As we took a sip of our coffee, we heard a groan from the other side of the makeshift curtain.

"Ugh—waking up to my sister talking about oral sex is pretty much the worst alarm clock ever," Mark said.

"Never mind that! Do I smell coffee?" Anna asked, sounding a little groggy.

"You do indeed."

A minute later, the divider blankets were pulled down, and we could see that Anna and Mark were both looking surprisingly better after a night of sex and sleep. I passed them coffee, and by the time we had all started into our second cups, we were looking and feeling human again. Now, all we needed was to figure out some kind of breakfast. Anna said that there was an abundance of native fruits, and that we could probably just pick our breakfast from the trees, so she and Mark went outside to forage, while Fiona and I returned to the dining hall. Fifteen minutes later, Anna and Mark returned with an armload of mangos to add to the breakfast that we had rustled together. It consisted of powered eggs and spam—the breakfast of champions, though more likely champions of high blood pressure and obesity, if eaten too often. Again, I had to wonder about the abundance of supplies that were housed in this otherwise deserted camp, and I was starting to think that it might not be as deserted as we believed. People didn't stock camps they didn't use, so we had probably over stayed our welcome and should get on the road to find a new hiding spot.

Sated and properly caffeinated, we returned to the bunkhouse to perform the big three: shit, shower and shave. I told the others to go first, as I believed that it would afford me more privacy, because, in theory, they'd be done with their business and less likely to barge in on me. Anna went first, then Mark, and each of them took a good ten minutes before emerging looking refreshed. Fiona then told me to go next, which was fine since I was already having contractions and only seconds from berthing a full term dump. I closed the door and found that it didn't have a lock, but I didn't have time to worry about it, as I was only seconds from release. I hit the cool, plastic seat and unloaded an entire day's worth of waste, and I was ever thankful that I was on a real toilet. I'd shit in the woods plenty of times but never once enjoyed the experience. It always seemed as though my turds had a mind of their own, and, as they exited my backside, they would apparently get homesick and curl back in towards my pants, which were inconveniently bunched up around my ankles and therefore in the drop zone. On more than one occasion I found myself using a stick to redirect a precocious turd in order to make sure it hit the ground rather than my pants. Spending a dump as a traffic cop negated any and all pleasure from the process, which is why this bathroom experience, though not entirely secure, was far and above the alternative.

Finished, I washed my hands and saw that the others had been kind enough to leave out a disposable razor, soap, and shampoo. I grabbed the goodies and entered the farthest of the two showers, and the entire experience felt a bit like being back in college—minus, of course, the hot water. This water was cold, but the air temperature was such that it didn't matter, and soon I was sudsed up and feeling a whole lot better. A second later, the door opened and in walked Fiona.

"Sorry, I couldn't wait," she said.

"No problem."

"You wouldn't say that if you knew why I was here."

"Meaning?"

"You'll see."

I had a bad feeling as I watched her settle onto the pot and deliver a nervous smile. Suddenly it hit me—it being the smell. She was dropping a formidable deuce mere feet away from me, and I was forced to retreat under the rush of water and hold the soap just under my nose.

"Jesus, I guess Playmates really do shit," I said.

"Indeed we do, so let this be a lesson to you. Everybody shits."

I could never be so bold as to shit in front of someone so readily, and I had to admire Fiona's acceptance of her bodily functions, though this was one area where I didn't mind keeping the mystery alive a bit longer. We were barely a week into the relationship, and even more strange was that this was the first time that I had shared a number two with the opposite sex in recent memory. A moment later, she joined me in the shower and began shampooing her hair while I soaped up my face and used the disposable razor to shave. It wasn't great, but I managed not to knick myself and emerged from the shower unscathed and looking pretty damn civilized for a man on the run. Anna and Mark had found towels and left us two. I grabbed one, dried off, got dressed, and was soon joined by Fiona, who also was looking lovely as usual and ready for the day. We exchanged a pleasant kiss then walked out to the main room to join the others and discovered a rather unpleasant sight. Around us were a group of seven men, and all of them were wearing ratty looking military fatigues and carrying AK-47's. Sitting with this ragtag group were Anna and Mark, and neither looked particularly happy at the moment. My thoughts instantly returned to Fiona's untimely intrusion, and I wondered if perhaps an interrupted shower carried the same potential for doom as an interrupted deuce. If so, we were seriously fucked.

"I see the three bears brought four friends along," I said.

"Yeah, and these bears are MSA," Mark responded gravely.

"Those aren't the good bears are they?" I asked.

"Nope."

"Be quiet," the man next to Mark said, striking him in the ribs with the butt of his pistol.

He was obviously the man in charge and appeared by all accounts to be an asshole.

"What brings you all by?" I asked.

"We had reports there were some high profile targets up in our territory," he said.

"Word travels fast on an island."

"Yes it does."

He pointed to the gun and satellite phone sitting on the bed in front of him then looked at me.

"Are these yours?" he asked.

"Why?"

A guy closer to me stepped forward and went to swing his rifle at me, but I trapped it at the last minute, twisted it out of his hands, then quickly turned the weapon around and struck him in the face with barrel. Another guy moved in, but I front kicked him and sent him backwards over a bunk. Just as I turned and brought the weapon to bear on the main man, I saw that he had his pistol resting directly against Anna's head.

"Drop the weapon or she dies," he said.

Shit, this was a live to fight another day moment, so I did as instructed. The guy whose weapon I had taken, picked it up and decided to return the favor by striking me in the ribs with the butt of the rifle. I was expecting the hit, so it wasn't as bad as it could have been, though I pretended it was more effective than it was and buckled over and called out. It made it more likely that he would believe he'd made his point and wouldn't hit me again, though it was hard to tell, as these guys seemed like supreme assholes.

"I'm going to ask you again. Are these your things?"

"And I'm going to respond again with why?" I asked.

He walked closer, smiled at me, then turned and slapped Fiona across the face. I was instantly overtaken by an uncontrollable rage and raced forward and shot my hands into the collar of his shirt and applied a front choke. Unfortunately, his men reacted quickly and stepped in and struck me with the butts of their rifles. I was taking a pretty good beating, but rage was winning out over pain—that is until one of them placed his gun barrel against my temple, and rational thought made a hasty return. I therefore released my grip on the asshole and watched as relief flooded his eyes. A front choke was highly unpleasant yet very effective and usually only took about six seconds before the victim went night-night. I only had it applied for about four seconds, so he was able to recover, and, upon regaining his composure, he smiled and again slapped Fiona. Psychologically, it was a good move on his part, because he knew I wouldn't pull any more shenanigans if the victim was going to be Fiona rather than me.

"Are these your items?" he asked again.

"Oh, you're referring to those items. Yeah, they are. Why do you give a shit?"

"Because I think you work for the American government. Perhaps you are CIA come to spy on us."

"Hardly, I'm just a scientist studying indigenous flowers."

He smiled.

"With a silenced 9mm pistol?"

"It's for the mosquitos."

"Make your jokes, but we'll find out eventually. Now, come along. It's time to leave."

They herded us outside and onto a large military transport truck, and we took up residence on one of the two long perpendicular bench seats that resided on the back. The leader and three of his men stayed with us, two piled into the cab, and the last man climbed into our Land Rover. The leader called out a command, then our two vehicle procession started driving northwest along the same road we had come in on last night, but, now, in the bold light of day, I could see the extent of the surrounding jungle. It was dense with all manner of tropical greenery and flowers, and beautiful waterfalls dotted the hillsides. Actually the place looked a lot like Kauai's Eastern shore and would have been quite pleasant had it not been for our present company.

We were heading north, and the farther we moved into MSA territory the harder it would be to escape, which meant we desperately needed a plan and some luck, but, ultimately, it was all about opportunity. That meant I needed to know everyone's mental and physical state, and that included friend and foe alike. I looked around at the men in the truck and saw that they weren't exactly perfect specimens of military discipline and fitness. I knew for a fact I could overtake or outrun any one of them, but there were three more variables in this equation—namely Mark, Fiona, and Anna. I could easily get free of the truck and escape into the jungle, but it would be a lot more difficult with all four of us, so, for the moment, I had to bide my time until the right opportunity presented itself.

The road reached the end of the valley, and we started climbing up along a treacherous dirt road that skirted a steep canyon which had obviously been formed by the river that now resided several hundred feet below. Escape here would be instant death, so I sat back to bide my time, ever hopeful that our driver stayed true to the road and avoided the very real possibility of accidentally killing all of us. Every so often he would veer uncomfortably close to the edge, and I could see that even our captors were looking a little nervous.

"Do you guys feel comfortable with that jackass at the wheel?" I asked.

The nearest guy started to answer, but, before he could speak, the main man glared at him, so he remained quiet though not exactly calm. Thankfully, the road left the canyon and descended into a dense jungle, and a heavy rain squall blew in and drenched everyone. It was miserably wet, but the rain brought welcomed relief from the oppressive heat and humidity. The deluge departed as quickly as it arrived, and soon our clothes were rapidly drying in the hot tropical sun. At last, we came to a settlement that was populated, as far as I could tell, entirely by men, so it stood to reason it was some kind of training camp. It had the obligatory firing range, improvised obstacle course, and a short distance away were the housing and dining facilities. At the moment, the obstacle course appeared to be the main attraction, and it was rife with activity, and men were busy climbing up ropes, going across monkey bars, and running through tires. There was an unmistakable intensity in their training, and it made me think they were preparing for something big, which was probably not a good omen for the people of Malkarta.

The truck stopped in front of a building that looked as though it had once been a barn. The main man issued an order, and we were hustled into the structure, and I quickly realized my summation had been correct. The floor still had smatterings of hay and smelled of animal waste, and one side of the building had been converted into a sort of holding area, though holding area was probably too grandiose a term. Mildly secure shithole might have been a more accurate description, as inside lay two funky old cots and a bucket that was presumably the toilet. Lovely.

"I hope you like your accommodations," the leader said, as he appeared at the doorway.

"How could we not? We've got the honeymoon suite," I responded.

"I'm happy to hear you've got a sense of humor—because I think you're going to need it."

"Why? Are you a comedian?" I asked.

"Not exactly, but as you've probably already guessed, I am the leader here, and you may call me Pemimpin. Please, make yourselves comfortable," the man said, without the slightest hint of irony.

He and the guards exited and locked us in, and we waited until they were well out of earshot before speaking.

"What the fuck kind of name is Pemimpin?" I asked.

"It means Leader," Anna said.

"How boring yet appropriate."

"So, what do we do now, Finn?" Fiona asked.

"I'm afraid I'm still working on that answer."

I went to the far wall, peered through a thin opening between boards, and saw Pemimpin walking towards a lone cabin, probably his command center. He was carrying my gun and the satellite phone, and those were the two things I desperately needed to get back, but at least I knew where he was taking them. I turned and went to each of the other two outward facing walls and looked through the cracks and tried to get an idea of the camp's size and population. Odds were good that the MSA was a sort of reservist kind of entity where its people would come and train then return to their lives and families until called upon by their fearless leader. If so, it meant that the camp wouldn't have very many inhabitants at any one time, and it would theoretically be a hell of a lot easier for us to manage an escape.

"So, how many people make up the MSA?" I asked.

"We estimate anywhere between five and fifteen thousand," Anna said.

"That's a pretty large spread."

"The numbers can change weekly depending on the state of affairs. If the Monarchy increases work hours, the number of MSA recruits also increases. Build a new school or hospital and the numbers diminish. Why do you ask?"

"I'm trying to figure out how many people we're up against—both in this camp and in general."

"This will be just one of perhaps ten or more similar camps spread throughout the northwest. Our security forces might find one and destroy it, but it's only one of several. Compartmentalizing their assets is actually one of the smarter things they do.

"That's not something your average third world rebel force is generally capable of, so someone in the MSA has some pretty good organizational skills. Does the government have any idea who the brains behind all this might be?"

"No, or he would already be in custody."

"Or she," I added.

"True," Anna said.

Mark looked at me with a worried expression on his face.

"So, Tag. Are you still in the CIA?" Mark asked.

"No—why do you ask?"

"I assume you were trained for these kinds of situations, so I'm obviously wondering if you think you can use your spy skills to get us the hell out of here."

"You bet your ass I'm going to get us the hell out of here. Do you think I'm going to take a shit in that bucket with all you in the same room? Fuck no."

"That's my man," Fiona said.

I continued scanning the outside and came to the conclusion that we had roughly fifty or so men onsite, and all of them were armed and potentially dangerous, though that last designation would have to wait until after I saw them actually firing their rifles—though preferably on the range, rather than at us. Next, I turned my attention closer to home—namely our cell. It wasn't exactly Fort Knox, so I rustled around the various boards and soon found a large slightly bent nail sticking out. It had probably been used to hang some kind of farm implement, but now it would serve as my official wood tester and potentially a weapon if and when the time came. I managed to pry it free then worked my way around the room, methodically checking each board only to find that all were in excellent shape. The walls were made of a pretty solid hardwood and therefore fairly resistant to the extreme heat and humidity of the tropics. A lesser wood might have already rotted and offered a possible means of escape, but such was not the case with this shitty old barn, and that wasn't exactly a great start.

Another thirty minutes passed, and we heard a vehicle enter the camp. I looked through the gap in the wall and saw that it was a black Land Rover. It parked over by the command hut, and a fairly well-dressed Indonesian man stepped out of the vehicle and entered the little command building.

"What do you see?" Mark asked.

"A guy who looks like he comes from farther up the food chain just entered Pemimpin's hut."

Ten minutes later, we heard another vehicle enter the camp, only this one came from the other direction and was only partially visible as it was parked on the far side of the building behind some dense shrubbery. Still, I caught a brief glance and was fairly certain it was a white Land Rover identical to Anna's. I heard one of its doors open then listened as the new arrival entered Pemimpin's command shack.

"We have another visitor," I said.

"Any idea who it is?" Anna asked.

"No, but I'm guessing it's another MSA muckity muck."

Anna stood up and walked over to peer through the crack.

"Did you get a look at him?" she asked.

"Not exactly, but I could see he entered Peminpin's house."

"What do you think it means?" Fiona asked.

"Not sure, but it probably concerns us."

Fifteen minutes later, the white Land Rover left, then five minutes after that, Pemimpin, two of his guards, and the driver of the black Land Rover exited the command hut and started walking in our direction.

"We're about to have some company," I said.

My three companions gazed at me nervously.

"So, what do we do?" Mark asked.

"I'm not sure yet."

The door to the room opened, and all four men walked in, with the man from the Land Rover in the lead. He was a little thick in the middle, and his clothes hinted that he clearly lived quite a bit higher on the food chain than the others in the room. If I had to guess, I would say that he was some kind of middle management in the MSA. He stepped forward and introduced himself to Anna.

"It is very nice to meet you, Princess Anna, my name is Gabir," he said, with a smug self-satisfied smile.

"Sorry, Gabir, but I can't say that it's nice to meet you."

"Understandable, though I'm sure you will be happy to know that I will be taking you and the other woman away from here immediately."

"And going where?" Fiona asked.

"That is not your concern at the moment," he said, as he ran his eyes over her body and licked his lips.

"I beg to differ," she said.

He reached over and ran his delicate, almost effeminate fingers down her face and towards her breast, and she re-coiled at his touch and slapped his hand away. He smiled then punched her in the stomach, and the blow made her gasp and hunch over. I stepped closer ready to return the favor, but the nearest guard pointed his weapon directly at my head, and it drew Gabir's gaze back to me.

"Tut tut, Mr. Finn. It's best you refrain from any heroics.

No need to die any sooner than you have to."

He turned his attention back to Fiona, who had already recovered and was now standing tall and looking stoically resilient in spite of being in the company of a world class asshole. She was quite a woman, and now I had even more reason to be attracted to her.

"You American women obviously don't know your place. Still, I hate to leave a blemish on such beauty, as we're going to make a lot of money when we sell you. Of course, that'll be after my boss has sampled the merchandise," he said.

"You mean tried to sample the merchandise," Fiona said.

"No, he'll definitely get his way, but you do have a lot of spirit. My boss will like that, because it makes it that much more exciting when he finally breaks you."

Gabir motioned at the guards that he was ready to leave.

"Well, it was nice to finally meet you in person, Mr. Blake. And you too, Mr. Finn. I've never been in the company of an official member of the Central Intelligence Agency, and it might have been interesting to have heard some of your spy stories, but unfortunately for you, we won't be meeting again."

"I wouldn't exactly say that's unfortunate."

"You're a funny man, but you won't be funny for long. The reason we won't be meeting again is because you and Mark are going to be executed this afternoon."

My three companions appeared stunned by this news.

"You can't be serious!" Anna said, angrily.

Gabir smiled.

"Oh yes, I am."

"But why? Killing them doesn't serve any purpose."

"Neither does letting them live."

"Don't worry. A lot of skilled and dangerous people have tried their best to kill me, and all of them were a lot more capable than Gabir and his army of beach bums. By this time tomorrow, all of us will be sipping rum drinks and laughing about this little adventure—well, all of us except Gabir, as he'll most likely be dead or dickless and crawling around on two broken legs."

"Americans—you're as ridiculous as your movies. Always so optimistic, even when it is clear that you are not long for this earth. Well, goodbye, gentleman. It's time for us to leave."

The two nearest guards stepped forward, but Anna and Fiona fought bravely to keep them away and swung hard at the men's faces. One got angry and shoved Anna and knocked her to the ground. Mark went to her side and helped her up, but he was rewarded with the same man hitting him in the back with the stock of his rifle. It knocked him onto his knees and left him looking dazed. The guard decided to hit him again while he was down, but I wasn't about to let that happen, and, as the man drew back his rifle to deliver a second blow, I moved in on his blind side, grabbed the stock, then elbowed him in the throat. He released his grip, and I used the rifle like a battering ram to jam the stock into his solar plexus, and it knocked him onto his back and gave me the breathing room I needed to bring the rifle to bear on Gabir. Everyone froze in place, as they were unsure what to do with their glorious leader in jeopardy, but Gabir, however, was unfazed and smiled cruelly.

"Go ahead and shoot. The minute you pull that trigger, my men will kill you."

"If I'm theoretically already going to die, then why not take you with me?"

"Because once they are done with you, they will avenge my death by raping and beating your women," he said.

"I think you mean the women. Where I come from we don't own the opposite sex."

"Either way, I don't believe you would like that outcome. Now, Mr. Finn, put down the rifle."

"What makes you think I won't be able to kill you and your men? I am supposedly a CIA agent after all."

"I know you Americans. You talk a big game, but when it comes down to it, you don't have the stomach to pull the trigger. You are all soft and weak."

I looked around the room to gauge the sentiment of his words, but more importantly, to do a little visual sweep of the position of the guards. Having gotten the angles and my targets firmly in my mind, I turned my gaze back to Gabir and smiled.

"Apparently, you don't know Americans very well," I said, as I pulled the trigger.

CHAPTER TWENTY-FIVE
Lock, Stock, and One Un-Smoking Barrel

Click. All I got was the dull sound of the hammer falling on an empty chamber. Apparently, the guard had forgotten to chamber a round, and now I was paying for his incompetence. Had it fired, it might have been the catalyst I needed to get our escape plan into action. Instead, it left us looking just as helpless and lame as we had been only a moment ago. As I tried to salvage the moment by quickly chambering a round, Gabir pulled out a knife and slithered behind Fiona and pressed the blade to her neck. I guess he finally figured out that I wasn't the spineless American he'd expected.

"Drop the gun, or she dies Mr. Finn!"

I took a moment to weigh my great desire to kill Gabir

against the possibility of accidentally shooting Fiona. Unfortunately, Gabir's new found paranoia was making him stay well behind his human shield.

"Think carefully! I will not hesitate to kill her. She is nothing more than an interesting little plaything for my employer, so her life has little value to me."

"Fuck you," Fiona said, as she tried to struggle free from his grasp.

He pressed the knife harder into her throat, and a trickle of blood formed where the blade was digging into her skin. Fuck it, and fuck Gabir! It was better for everyone to give up this moment in hopes of living to fight another day, so I dropped the gun and watched as Gabir smiled cruelly at his little victory.

"You Americans. How quickly you crumble—and all for a woman," he said, with a real disgust in his voice.

He released Fiona and shoved her roughly into Anna, and it caused both of them to stumble towards the door. They both stopped and turned to gaze at me and Mark with a profound anguish in their expressions.

"Don't worry. We'll come for you. I promise," I said.

Fiona stared into my eyes, and something in her expression changed, and I could see that she suddenly understood that I meant what I said, and no matter what happened, I would come for her. Gabir and his men led the girls out the door, and the room was suddenly feeling very empty and very quiet. I went to the crack in the wall and looked outside.

"Now what the hell is going on out there?" Mark asked.

"A lot, unfortunately. The girls are leaving, and, judging by the men I see heading towards the practice range, I have a feeling that they're probably setting up a firing squad especially for us."

"It just gets better and better."

Every person has a breaking point, a time when they have been pushed past their limit, and were no longer willing to take another ounce of shit. That moment had technically arrived several minutes ago, but I hadn't been in a place where I could act on it properly. I'd had four lives in my hands—my own, and those of three innocents, but now, as luck would have it, I was only responsible for two. Gabir, in his own unintended way, had opened the door for me to finally take adequate action. Now that we were a smaller force, there was a hell of a lot less chance of collateral damage when the bullets started flying—and fly they would.

"Mark, I feel that I should warn you that the shit is going to hit the fan very soon, and if I say down, you better get down."

"OK, I understand, and I'm ready. Let's do this."

"Good—now get down!" I yelled.

"What? Now? Seriously?" he asked, looking confused.

"It was a test, and you just failed. Next time, you better drop your ass down."

I went back to the crack and looked outside to see what was happening in the camp and saw eight men lining up to fire at human shaped cardboard targets. Their leader gave a signal, and they started shooting, and I turned back to Mark to see him looking particularly worried.

"I take it that's not a good sign," he said.

"Actually, it's both good and bad."

"Care to explain?"

"Yeah, while those idiots are practicing to kill us, it'll be a lot less obvious that I'm killing their colleagues."

"You can't be serious."

"Deadly serious. Getting out of here is going to get ugly, but it's the only way we're going to be able to rescue the girls. Being the smaller force, we need to exercise overwhelming violence of action against our foes, and, more importantly, extreme assholes need to be taken down with extreme prejudice."

"Jesus Christ."

"He might understand, though he probably wouldn't approve."

I heard voices and looked out to see a group of five men walking over from the command hut. This was likely our escort, so it was go time. I looked around the room and tried to form a quick strategy, and soon settled on a stupid, yet simple idea. I needed the element of surprise, but that wasn't going to be easy in a converted barn. It was mostly open space, and the only cover consisted of the two cots and the shit bucket, so I had to think vertically.

"Mark! Quick, give me a boost up to that rafter."

"Are you crazy? This has been done in about a million movies!"

"Yeah, so they'd never expect me to be stupid enough to try it.

"Its a bad idea, They'll see you the minute they walk in!"

"Fret not, humanitarian, for people often have limited perception, and they generally see what they expect to see, and by the time they notice it'll be too late. Now, come on, it's our only hope."

He grumbled his disapproval but made a cradle with his hands and hoisted me to the beam, and I pulled myself up and waited for my prey. The door opened, and four of the five men walked in, while the fifth remained outside to watch for any tricks, so I'd have to worry about him later. As expected, it took a moment for them to realize that I wasn't in the room.

"Where is the other man?" the lead man asked nervously.

"He left," Mark said.

The man became even more agitated and shoved Mark back against the wall and prepared to strike him with his fist.

"Where is the other man?"

"I told you. He left."

All four guys were bunched together and ripe for the picking. If they were smart, they would have fanned out and properly covered the room, but that's what you got with an all volunteer terrorist trained army. The main guy was getting more agitated, which meant it was time to act. I leapt from the beam and landed on all four men but only managed to take three completely to the ground. The fourth man was knocked a few feet away and stumbled onto his knees. He was therefore, my first problem. I struggled to climb from atop the heap of guards and closed in on my straggler. He recovered quickly and stood up and did his best to bring his weapon around to fire at me. That was his first mistake. Close quarters combat was a learned skill, and one where you needed to make split second decisions if you hoped to survive. He was stressed and suffering from tunnel vision and therefore focused on his rifle rather the proximity of his opponent. Every weapon had its place and time, and what he really needed was a pistol. Sure, his AK-47 was a deadly and impressive weapon, but only if you had room to shoot. In this situation, it was kind of like trying to swing a spear in a closet.

With his focus more on his rifle than me, I managed to close the distance, redirect the weapon, and deliver a lovely oblique kick to his left knee. With a sickening crunch, it brought his head down and into range of my elbow which I slammed into his temple. This allowed me to take control of his rifle then slam it into his throat, sending him gasping for air as he stumbled backward and fell to the floor. I turned to face his three comrades just in time to see the nearest one was trying to stand up. I front kicked him in the face and split his nose and put him out of action. The next guy made it to his knees only long enough to receive a solid hit from the stock of my rifle. It connected with his jaw, and he too went down. Doing a quick three hundred and sixty degree look around the room, my attention was suddenly diverted when I heard the familiar metallic click of someone chambering a round in an AK-47. I turned to discover guard number five had obviously heard the commotion and decided to crash the party. Unfortunately for him, I didn't particularly like party crashers, least of all the armed kind.

"Down!" I yelled to Mark, as I dove to the floor at the exact moment that shots rang out and imbedded into the wall behind me.

I rolled left and delivered a quick burst of return fire that took out unlucky guard number five, and before his body even hit the floor, my attention was already back on the other guards. The one I had yet to follow up with after my glorious tackle was on his feet and about to pull the trigger. I rolled back to my right just as he squeezed off a burst, and his bullets barely missed me. I completed my roll then pulled the trigger, and one of my bullets tore into his thigh and nearly knocked him off his feet. He cried out in pain, and, as I adjusted my aim and tried to fire again, I came to the sickening realization that my weapon had jammed. I was left particularly vulnerable as I lay out in the middle of the floor, but I was lucky that my enemy was too preoccupied with his leg wound to fire back. I used that brief reprieve to try and clear my weapon, and, when I pulled back the slide, I discovered a bent round had failed to enter the firing chamber. I clawed at it with my fingers but quickly realized it would require more time than I currently had. The wounded man's adrenaline and natural painkillers were kicking in and bringing his attention fully back to the person responsible for his misery—namely *moi*. His pant leg was red with blood, and his eyes were burning with rage as he limped over and hovered over me and smiled maniacally as he prepared to fire.

"Time to die, *bulè*!" he said, through gritted teeth.

Life was often about luck and coincidence, but sometimes you could improve both of those factors with a little preparation. Take, for instance, my earlier sweep of our cell and, more specifically, the fact that I had found what would become a very useful tool—namely the large bent nail I had pulled from the wall. Now, it was my ace in the hole if I could just get it out before he pulled the trigger.

"Hey, what are you so mad about? It's not like I shot you in the heart or anything. Assuming I missed your femoral artery, you'll probably survive."

"Yeah, but you won't."

"Look, I'm a trained medic and probably your only real hope of adequately treating that leg wound. What say we let bygones be bygones, and I help you out."

While I was talking I had secretly slipped the nail out of my pocket and now had it firmly in my right hand.

"Fuck you, *bulè*! I don't want your help," he said, with a menacing sneer as he prepared to fire.

"OK, suit yourself."

The time for chitchat was over, and I jammed the nail into the man's foot, and it elicited a terrible scream of agony. I used that moment to twist and hook my left foot behind his ankle, and, from there, I drove my right heel straight through his knee joint and it snapped, and he crumpled to the ground. Now that I had him down at my level, I slammed my heel down into his groin, and the added shock and pain were enough to allow me to rip his rifle out of his hands. With the weapon in my control, I used it as a club and slammed it into his head and knocked him unconscious. I got up and did a quick threat assessment of the situation then noticed Mark was staring at me with his mouth slightly agape.

"So, you say you *used* to be in the CIA—as in past tense?" he asked.

"Yeah."

"So, what in the hell have you been doing in the meantime?" Mark asked.

"A lot of soul searching and a lot of yoga. Why do you ask?"

"Oh, no reason," he said, shaking his head as he gazed at the carnage around the room.

I stood up and grabbed the closest man's AK and checked the clip to make sure it was fully loaded, as it was basic gunfight reasoning—reload when you could so that you always had a full clip when you needed it most. After that came the search for provisions, which, in this case, meant ammunition. I searched the other guys and took their clips as well as one extra AK for Mark. Before handing it over, I quickly showed him the basics of the rifle. It was a pretty straightforward weapon in spite of having been designed by Mikhail Kalashnikov to emulate several other more complicated weapons—specifically the M1 Carbine and the German StG 44. The Soviets, however, were a practical people, so his creation had to be equally practical. That meant anyone could maintain and use it, regardless of age, intelligence, or stature, which was also why it was so popular amongst terrorists and third world armies. Mark didn't appear too thrilled with any of the information, but he listened closely and took hold of it when I finally handed it over.

"It's heavier than it looks in the movies," he said.

"Yeah, that's because it's fully loaded. The 7.62 mm round is pretty big and heavy and one of the reasons America prefers to outfit its troops with the M16 and M4. They use the 5.56mm NATO rounds which are smaller and lighter."

"Isn't that a disadvantage?"

"Not exactly. They make up the difference in mass with kinetic energy, and having smaller and lighter rounds means a soldier can carry a lot more ammunition."

"Well, thanks for the rifle lesson, though I hope I don't actually need to fire it."

We heard a stirring and looked over to see one of the guards was groaning.

"That guy's still moving. What do we do?" Mark asked.

I saw the man he was referring to slowly climbing onto his knees.

"This," I said, delivering a solid kick to the man's jaw

that knocked him out cold.

"That was a little extreme."

"Maybe, but we can't worry about pleasantries right now, as each and every one of these assholes was prepared to kill us, and every minute we fuck around worrying about their welfare, the love of your life and your sister are getting farther away. You have to keep all of that in perspective so when, and if, the time comes, you'll be prepared to pull the trigger of that rifle. It's either us or them, and we need to survive if we're going to rescue Anna and Fiona.

CHAPTER TWENTY-SIX
No More Mr. Nice Guy

We moved through the door and into the open area of the old barn, with me in the lead and my eyes and the barrel of the gun sweeping the room as I looked for targets. It was thankfully empty, so I moved to the doorway, where I could survey the camp. The men were still on the firing range practicing their little hearts out, so it appeared that no one had distinguished our shots from their shots.

"OK, we need to go to the command hut."

"Why? Wouldn't it be smarter if we just hightailed it out of here right now?"

"Normally I'd agree, but they have my gun and, more importantly, my phone."

"Can't you just get new ones?"

"In theory, yes, but in reality—no. The gun has sentimental value, and the phone is our only direct line to the vice president of the United States. Trust me—when we get out of this shit storm, we're going to need that phone to get out the much bigger shit storm that is Malkarta."

"Can't you just call the White House and ask for the vice president?"

"Have you ever tried to get through the White House switchboard? You'd have better luck reaching a live customer service representative at AT&T."

Mark thought for a moment then nodded, as he obviously had experience with the communications giant.

"Nuff said. Let's go get your shit."

There was a fair amount of open space between here and the command hut, so we needed to move cautiously and use the ground cover and buildings as best as we could. I gave Mark the signal, and we moved out and around to the back of our building but paused at the far corner. Seeing it was clear, we continued on past some kind of storage shed and eventually reached a dense cluster of ferns that sat directly across from the command hut. As we crouched there, I heard the sound of people walking in our direction, so we ducked down and slithered deeper into the ferns and remained motionless as we waited. Two men came walking up and stopped only a foot away, and I was worried they might be pausing to pee. This was the jungle, after all, and every bush or tree could double as a urinal. Thankfully, they only paused long enough for one of them to stub out and discard his cigarette, which was nice, as it spared us from the indignity of a golden shower or huffing any of his cigarette smoke. It did, however, reveal that the MSA were chronic smokers and, worse still, litterbugs. With the area now clear, we had an unobstructed view of the command hut, and I could see there were several people inside.

"Alrighty then, Padawan. We need to get my shit back, but it's also very important that we find out where they took the girls. That means we have to keep at least one asshole alive, hopefully Pemimpin himself."

Seeing the coast was clear, we slipped out of the ferns and moved quickly across the open road and stopped and squatted down below the window of the command hut. I stood up and briefly glanced inside to get an idea of the layout and location of the bad guys. Pemimpin was sitting at his desk, and there was one man in the chair opposite him as well as another standing in the corner. With the reconnaissance completed, we were ready to storm the hut, but the entrance was around the other side. The two of us slipped along the edge of the building, but I signaled for Mark to pause, for, just a few feet away around the corner was a sentry standing guard. He was smoking a cigarette and stupidly had his rifle uselessly slung over his shoulder. He wasn't exactly a shining example of MSA efficiency, but that's what you got with an unpaid rebel army full of weekender slacker idealists.

I slid back around the corner then made a "pssst" noise. Sure enough, the guy appeared, and his dull eyes never even had time to register the butt stock of my rifle as it caught him full in the face. It was a lucky hit, and it knocked him out cold, and he went limp and dropped to the ground, with his cigarette now bent but still drooping out of the side of his mouth. I used my foot to knock it free then stubbed it out.

"Any particular reason you took the time to stub out his cigarette?" Mark asked.

"Second hand smoke is deadly."

"As are you, my friend."

I reached down, grabbed the guard's rifle, then moved towards the door but paused and raised three fingers to Mark and began silently counting down. At one, I opened the door and entered the hut.

"Afternoon, assholes," I said.

The man in the corner reached for his rifle, but he was too slow to react before I swung the AK for the base of his jaw. It impacted with a loud thud, and his eyes glazed over and closed as he sunk down onto his knees. I front kicked him hard in the face and sent him the rest of the way to the floor, where he crumpled into a heap. The guy sitting across from Pemimpin started to reach for his weapon, but, like his friend, he was just a hair too slow, and it gave me plenty of time to swing my rifle like a baseball bat and nail him in the side of his head and send him sprawling onto the floor. In spite of being dazed, he made a valiant effort to reach for his rifle, but by that time I had my AK resting firmly against his temple.

"Move and die. Hold still and live."

He stopped, set down the weapon, then raised his hands.

"Good choice," I said, twisting my rifle and hitting him yet again with the rifle stock, though this time it knocked him out cold.

"I wouldn't exactly call that a good choice," Mark said.

"It's better than dying."

With the underlings out of the way, I turned my attention to Pemimipin, who was sitting calmly at his desk.

"Do you really believe you have any chance of escaping an entire camp of armed men?" he asked.

"We've made it this far."

He continued to sit there and smile smugly, and it made me like him even less than I already did, and it didn't help that he had one of those faces that begged to be punched.

"So, Pimp, I'm going to need my pistol and phone."

"All I have is your pistol. Gabir took your phone."

"Speaking of Gabir—I need to know where that piece of shit took the girls?"

"Unfortunately for you, I don't know."

"I'm pretty sure you do."

"Well, I'm pretty sure I don't, and I certainly wouldn't tell you if I did."

"We'll see about that."

I reached down and took hold of his pinky finger.

"Do you happen to play guitar?" I asked.

"A little. Why do you ask?"

"Well, what I'm about to do will drastically limit your ability to play seventh and ninth chords."

He looked confused for a brief moment, but then his

expression turned resolute as he spoke.

"I am a martyr to the cause. There is nothing you can say or do to make me give up any information."

I bent his pinky back but paused when it reached its maximum stretch.

"Are you sure about that? Because after this little piggy decides to go to the market, you're only going to have nine little piggies left. After I get to them, there won't be a single piggy left to go wee-wee-wee all the way home."

He again smiled smugly, so I jerked his finger back and dislocated it from it the joint, and it caused him to scream in agony.

"Where did he take the girls?" I asked calmly.

He remained quiet, so I moved to the next finger and gave him one of my own smug smiles.

"I guess this little piggy is also going to join his friend at the market."

I wrenched it back, and he again cried out in pain, though this time tears appeared in the corners of his eyes, which meant Pemimpin was getting closer to his breaking point.

"Only eight more piggies to go. Got anything to say?"

"No," he said, without a lot of conviction.

Now we were on to his middle finger.

"It's funny. This is the point where I imagine that you'd love to give me the finger, but in a different way, if you know what I mean."

"I don't understand."

"It's a joke. In America, giving someone the middle finger is the same as saying fuck you."

"I see," he said, raising his middle finger and smiling.

He was a complete asshole, but I had to give him credit. It took some balls to make a joke at a time like this. Still, it did nothing to keep me from reaching over and taking hold of the finger, and I watched as his expression quickly turned to fear, and beads of sweat started to drip down his forehead. I had barely pulled it back before he suddenly broke the silence.

"Wait! I know where he took them!"

"I'm listening."

"Friesland. It's on the northern most part of the island. There is a large estate on the outskirts of town."

"Sounds vague," I said, bending his finger back.

"No! You can't miss it. It sits at the end of Soest Avenue. The owner is a man named Budi Kusuma."

"What do you think, Mark? Is he lying?"

"I've been to that part of the island, and there is a large estate out there."

It was time to make a judgment call. Had I broken Pemimpin's will, or would I need to break another finger? Without a lot of time, I would just have to trust that the martyr to the cause wasn't actually that much of a martyr.

"OK, where's my gun?"

"Here, in the top drawer of my desk."

He started to open the drawer, but I stopped him and opened it myself and found my gun and four clips inside. I checked the action to make sure it was loaded then stuffed the extra clips in my pocket.

"Just so you know, we don't hit women where I come from."

"What?" he said, looking confused.

I hauled back and proceeded to punch him so hard that it knocked him unconscious.

"Jesus," Mark said.

"Oh come on! He had it coming."

"Yeah, I suppose he did."

"Alrighty then! Let's get the fuck out of here."

I pulled Pemimpin out of the seat, bound his hands and feet with an electrical chord, then headed for the door.

"If we're lucky, we'll just slip out of here nice and quiet with no one being the wiser."

I stepped out of the command hut and took a look around then motioned for Mark to follow as I walked towards what appeared to be their motor pool. It was a large metal sided structure that resided just west of the command hut, and, at the moment, it was deserted except for a lone man sitting and smoking a cigarette on the hood of an old Toyota Land Cruiser. We had yet another smoker, and it made me wonder what why all these MSA guys had such an obsession with unhealthy habits. Apparently, socialist rebels believed their twisted ideals made them immune to lung cancer, though the upside is that their smoking would eventually start to cull their numbers. We slipped a bit closer, then I paused to talk strategy.

"OK, I'm going to take down Smoky McPot over there as quietly as I can, so I need you to watch my back and don't let anyone sneak up behind me."

"Are you going to kill him?"

"Not sure, but if you're morally opposed to the idea, we could we could wait another twenty years until he dies of lung cancer."

"Very funny. What happens if I see someone?"

"Shoot him," I said.

"Seriously?"

"Yeah, we need to rescue Anna and your sister. This time it's personal, so you need to man-up and put on your big boy pants, because we're going balls to the wall here, Mother Theresa."

"Any other euphemisms you want to throw in there?"

"Not at the moment, but if I think of any more I'll be sure to relay them to you. Now get your head in the game and let's do this."

"That's officially two more, not bad."

"Yeah, because I'm on the spectrum—of awesome."

I left Mark and moved closer, though I was careful to take the time to place every step on a piece of ground where it wouldn't make a sound. It was an art that I had learned at a young age from my eccentric karate sensei, and I had actually managed to put it to good use during my time in special operations and the CIA. Now, I would use it to remove the last obstacle between us and freedom. I got within a few feet of the man, and the acrid smell of his cigarette became reason enough to remove him from the earth. He finished his cigarette and tossed it aside just as I closed the final distance and looped my arm around his throat and started dragging him backwards into the structure. His hands immediately went to my arm, and he frantically tried to pull it free. Fortunately, I had a good grip and continued to keep his neck tight within my grasp as I waited for him to pass out. Suddenly, he reached into his pocket and pulled out a knife. It was one of those folding models, and with a flick of this wrist it was open and heading for my forearm. Shit. I released the choke and shoved him into the side of the Land Cruiser, and he quickly turned around and smiled cruelly.

"Now you gonna die, *bulè*!"

"We'll see, Smoky McPot."

I looked down at the knife to see his grip. You could actually tell a lot about a knife fighter by the way he held his weapon. Blade up or reverse grip would mean that he was experienced, while blade down—the way you cut into a steak, usually meant that the knife wielder used it to cut up food items and not other people. This guy held his reverse grip, which meant that he might just know what he's doing, and it also meant that I needed to find some kind of weapon if I hoped to have any chance of walking away unscathed, as I never forgot my sensei's cardinal rule that everyone gets cut in a knife fight.

I glanced at the workbench beside me and grabbed a toilet plunger. It wasn't an ideal weapon, but it would do for the moment. With the plunger at the ready, I turned back to face Smokey. He had his left hand forward and his knife hand back, as he was probably hoping to perform some kind of grab and stab. He moved in and out and threw a few exploratory slashes, probably hoping to get a feel for my hand to hand skills while also trying to get me a little off balance. I stayed calm, however, and kept my awareness on the weapon and watched for any kind of mistake that I could use as an opening. Suddenly, he switched his grip to blade down then came straight in at my stomach, but I swung the plunger down and hit the back of his hand, and it elicited a pained grunt. Smoky wasn't deterred and immediately brought the knife up and around in a back handed motion in an attempt to go for my face. Luckily, I was ready and twisted the plunger clockwise and sent the tip up, and it impacted his forearm and stopped the blade only inches before it could pierce my cheek. I delivered a left elbow to his floating rib then reached up and took hold of the knife hand while simultaneously throwing a front kick to his opposite knee. It buckled him over, and I segued into a basic Filipino stick fighting technique that entailed flicking the plunger with my wrist and striking him in the face. It wasn't devastatingly damaging or painful, but it served as more of a distraction while I wedged the end up under his throat and barred the middle over the radius bone of his forearm. It created a hold that martial artists called a figure-four, and it could impose a lot of pain on the opponent's arm, shoulder, and neck. I slipped my foot behind his, and used the leverage of my three points of contact to take him backwards down onto the ground. There, I torqued his wrist past ninety degrees, and the pain caused him to open his hand and let me take hold of the knife.

"I'm afraid this *bulè* isn't quite ready to die," I said.

Just as I was about to apply a choke and finish the job, I heard Mark yell out from behind me.

"Tag! Look out!"

I turned to see that another MSA asshole had arrived, and he was currently standing about ten feet away and aiming a pistol directly at my head. Mark had his rifle pointed at the man, but he wasn't pulling the trigger.

"Mark, shoot him."

Mark stared at the man, and his hands visibly started shaking as he contemplated his actions.

"Mark, he's going to kill me. Shoot him!"

The man gazed at Mark then turned back to me.

"It appears that your friend doesn't have the balls to pull the trigger," he said, with a smile.

"He's killed a lot of people today already, so his balls have reached their daily quota."

The man didn't appear to like my joke and proceeded to cock his pistol and give it a hair trigger. As if I didn't already have enough shit to deal with, I now had a humorless rebel with an itchy trigger finger.

"Drop the weapon and let go of my friend!" he ordered.

"Easy there, turkey tits. I was just doing a little acupressure to help your friend quit smoking. The Chinese have been using this technique for thousands of years, so believe me when I say it works," I said.

"Drop your weapon or I shoot!"

"No problem," I said, immediately dropping the plunger.

"I was referring to the knife," he said, with a sneer.

It was official. The guy had absolutely no sense of humor.

"Oh, you mean this weapon," I responded innocently.

Bringing a knife to a gunfight was never a good idea and now served as a sad testament to the direness of my situation. I therefore did the only thing I could do, which was throw the knife. Had it been a movie, it would have impacted perfectly, blade first, into the bad guy's chest and killed him instantly. The real world was not so perfect, however, and the knife hit handle first and bounced off the guy's forehead. It wasn't exactly life threatening, but it did manage to throw off his aim when he attempted to shoot me at that very moment. The bullet went high and whizzed over my head, thereby allowing me to step sideways, draw my own pistol, and return fire. I put two bullets in the man's head then turned my attention back to smoky, who was in the process of trying to slink away. He immediately threw up his hands and started pleading for his life.

"Don't kill me! Don't kill me!"

"What happened to the guy who just said, you gonna die, *bulè*! Is he still around—because I'd really love to shoot that guy."

"No! I'm sorry! Don't kill me! I have a wife and children who need me."

"Yeah, they need you to be a better person. The kind who quits smoking and doesn't blow up restaurants, plot armed revolutions, or kill innocent people."

"I'll change! I promise I'll change!"

"Sorry, Smokey. I don't know if I believe you."

He closed his eyes and started to weep, as he had no idea that I had no intention of killing him at this point, but I wasn't going to let him off easy. Instead of pulling the trigger, I pistol whipped him in his left temple and knocked him out cold. Mark, meanwhile, came over and joined me, and he looked guilty as he averted his eyes.

"I'm sorry—I couldn't pull the trigger. I just—couldn't."

"It's OK. The world would probably be a better place if there were more men like you—men who couldn't pull the trigger."

At that moment, we heard shouting and looked towards the other end of the camp and saw men from the firing range running in our direction. Apparently, they had taken some kind of break and heard the commotion and were coming over to investigate. Lovely.

"We need to get the fuck out of here! Mount up," I said.

Mark did as I asked, then the two of us jumped into Anna's Land Rover. Thankfully, the MSA had been thoughtful enough to leave the keys in the ignition, and I started the engine then threw it in reverse and backed out towards the oncoming group of men. Not expecting us to drive into them, they were too shocked to shoot, and instead, jumped to the side and scattered like flies as we passed through. Once clear, I spun the wheel and performed a bootlegger to bring us around one hundred and eighty degrees. Now pointed in the opposite direction, I jammed the car into second and tore out of the camp and headed east. The men started shooting, and bullets were chewing up the ground around the vehicle, and a lucky few impacted into the back of the Land Rover with a dull thudding sound. Two hundred yards down the road, the shooting stopped, and it appeared we had, by some miracle, managed to escape unscathed. Mark looked back then turned to me and smiled.

"I can't fucking believe it! We made it out of there alive!" he said, excitedly.

The road continued on into a long straightaway, and about a quarter of a mile down the road, I looked in the rearview mirror and spied two Land Cruisers full of angry MSA rebels in hot pursuit.

"Well—we've made it this far, anyway," I said.

Mark looked for himself then turned back to me.

"Fucking fuck," he said.

"Fucking fuck indeed. I guess the old saying is true. Never count your chickens until those fuckers hatch, grow up, and have been fried and thrown on the plate beside the corn and mashed potatoes."

"Agreed, Colonel Sanders."

"Yeah, and if we don't lose those pricks, then we're finger licking fucked."

CHAPTER TWENTY-SEVEN
Death Race

Now it would come down to luck, skill, and potentially the direct intervention of a divine being, but, no matter what, I would do my best to see that we survived so that we could rescue the girls. I hit the accelerator and pushed the Land Rover to its performance limits, and the excessive speed made us break loose as we went from one curve to the next. When we reached a fairly long straightaway at the bottom of a valley, our pursuers made up ground, and shots were soon coming our way. I swerved ever so slightly left and right, though, judging by their aim, or lack thereof, we might have been safer maintaining a straight course. We came upon a series of sharp turns and managed to enjoy a little respite from their firing, but, on the next straightaway, the shooting resumed, and a lucky shot imbedded into the pillar behind my head.

"Mark, you're going to have to shoot back. Can you handle that?"

"I think so."

He pulled out one of the AK's and leaned out the window and steadied the rifle before firing off a quick burst.

"That's it. Just fire enough to let them know that we mean business, and hopefully they'll stay back. We just need some time to reach a more populated part of the island, and they'll likely give up the chase."

"He fired another short burst, and our pursuers hung back a little farther, and their return fire stopped for the moment."

Up ahead, we were coming to a fork in the road, but their was a fallen tree blocking the way to the right.

"I guess we're going to the left," I said.

"Good, the farther east we go, the less likely we'll run into more MSA."

I went left, and we entered the shadow of a large mountain that made the weather become decidedly wet. The road became even more slippery, and I battled the wheel and did my best to keep the Land Rover under control, but eventually I was forced to slow down in order to keep from sliding off into the dense foliage. The road was getting a bit thinner while the surrounding greenery was getting thicker, and I was starting to worry that it might eventually come to an end, and we'd be forced to continue on foot.

"Have you ever seen the movie Romancing the Stone with Michael Douglass and Kathleen Turner?" I asked Mark.

"I have, actually. Why do you ask?"

"If we have to abandon the Range Rover and go traipsing through the jungle, it'll feel a hell of a lot like a contemporary re-imagining," I said.

"Yeah, I suppose, but who's going to be Kathleen Turner's character?"

"You, obviously."

"Which means that if we slip and go sliding down a muddy hill, you're the one who is going to end up face first between my legs."

"Shit—maybe I should be Kathleen Turner's character."

We laughed then turned our attention back to the road ahead, and, as we came around the next bend, there was another fork in the road, but the lane going off to the right was blocked by yet another fallen tree. We headed left, and, about a quarter mile later, we came upon a massive barricade that was blocking our way. I slammed on the brakes, spun the wheel, and was barely able to stop in time to avoid hitting the mass of felled trees, twigs, and branches.

"Shit! I can't help wondering if these roadblocks are deliberate, and, if so, it would mean that the MSA have allied themselves with the fucking beavers!" I said.

"Beavers? Oh—I get it. The barricade is like a dam."

"Yeah, and now we don't have a damn direction to go."

"What do we do?"

"I guess I'll turn around, and we'll go see if we missed a turnoff."

Just as I put it in reverse and turned my gaze out the back window, I could see the two MSA Land Cruisers about a half mile up the road.

"Shit. Those fucking MSA assholes just won't give up! We need to vacate the vehicle and hoof it the fuck out of here!"

We grabbed the rifles and all the ammo we could carry and climbed over the barricade and continued on down the road, with the goal being to gain as much distance as possible before cutting into the jungle, where our progress would be markedly slower. Two hundred yards down the road, I could hear our pursuers and gestured to Mark that we should make a hasty retreat into the foliage. We were stuck moving at a snail's pace, and the various trees and plants delivered a brutal onslaught of annoying scratches and abrasions to every inch of exposed flesh, but it was definitely better than getting shot.

"This is a real buttfuck," I said.

Mark laughed.

"Yes. Yes it is, so hopefully we'll reach some kind of clearing," Mark responded.

"Technically, I'm looking for a river."

"Seriously?"

"Yeah, it's one of nature's highways, and, once we find one, we'll be able to travel a hell of a lot faster than this."

As with any place in the tropics, Malkarta experienced a lot of rainfall, and all that water carved out excellent paths as it made its way to the sea. To that end, we continued down the lush hillside until the ever increasing sound of rushing water brought us to a steep section of mountain that overlooked a sizable river. We had our expressway to freedom.

"So, Tag, I've been meaning to ask you how in the hell you happened to meet my sister and get yourself dragged into this whole mess."

"That's one hell of a story."

"Well, then I've got to hear it."

"OK, but some of it might be a little unsettling."

"After everything I've experienced today, there's very little that would shock me."

"Alrighty then—here it is. A couple days ago, a boat with a gaggle of strippers on board hit a rock near Alcatraz, and it started sinking."

"So, was my sister on this boat?"

"Yeah."

"Why?"

"She was the main attraction."

"Meaning?"

"Meaning she was stripping to raise money for your legal defense fund."

"And she was the main attraction?"

"Yeah."

"I know she's attractive and all, but how did that happen?"

"Well, she also happened to do a spread for *Playboy* and became Miss October, which she obviously did as a last ditch effort to raise money for your legal defense fund."

Mark looked particularly bothered as he contemplated

this.

"I had no idea things had gotten so desperate."

"Yeah, and she's quite a woman and clearly loves you a lot."

"Fuck—I'm her older brother. It's my job to protect her. Not the other way around."

"Everyone needs a little help sometimes."

I could see that Mark, like Fiona, was also very proud and not comfortable accepting help from others.

"I can't believe my situation on Malkarta drove her to reveal her body to the entire world."

"Yeah, but at least you can take solace in knowing that a lot of amazing women have bared it all on the pages of *Playboy*."

"I suppose."

"Honestly, I think it's about time the world woke up to the fact that nudity isn't a bad thing, and no one should ever be ashamed to show their body—centerfold or not."

Mark regarded me a moment with a questioning look on his face.

"Pervert or philosophy major?" he asked.

"Probably both, though I was a philosophy minor, and in spite of being a pervert, I'm actually kind of serious. We are who we are, so why hide it?"

"Yeah, I suppose America is still a bit entrenched in its puritanical roots. European women don't think twice about going topless at the beach while women doing the same thing in American would get arrested for indecent exposure."

"Exactly!"

"But what about guys?"

"Honestly, I'd rather not see their wieners and saggy balls, but if they want to air their pork products then so be it. Of course, on the other end of that I wouldn't mind banning men from going out in public in fucking overalls or sweatpants with gathered ankles."

"Of all the weird-ass clothes in the world, those are the ones you single out?"

"Absolutely, and let me tell you a little story about sweatpants with gathered ankles. There was a crazy motherfucker back home in Sausalito—a character I called Sweatpants Guy."

"And let me guess—he wore those exact kind of sweatpants."

"All the fucking time, and never wore anything else."

"Maybe that's because they're comfortable."

"Comfortable if you happen to be crazy. He ended up killing his landlord with a hammer then later killed himself while he was in jail."

"And you think the sweatpants were a contributing factor?"

"Hard to say, but either way they were an excellent indicator of his state of mind."

"Seems like a pretty weak correlation to me and still doesn't explain the overalls thing."

"Overalls creep me the fuck out, because I watched the

movie *Deliverance* at a young age."

"Ah—squeal! Squeal like a pig!" Mark said.

"Tell me that scene with those overall wearing hicks wasn't disturbing."

"OK, I'll concede the overalls, but I'm holding firm on the sweatpants."

"Assuming we make it out of here alive, take a little time to look at the people wearing those fucking sweatpants, and you'll see the world in a new light, my friend."

"You are a strange man."

"Strangely insightful, now come, padawan—let's get our asses down to the river, so we can get the fuck out of here and go save Anna and Fiona."

I glanced down the steep slope then back to Mark.

"You ready, Joan?"

I was obviously referring to Kathleen Turner's character from *Romancing the Stone*.

"Ready when you are, Jack."

I smiled that he remembered Michael Douglas's character.

"Good memory," I said.

"It's a classic."

I started my descent only to realize that the slope was incredibly wet and slippery, and it only took one more step before I was down and sliding on my ass and picking up speed. I tried to used my hands to steer, but I still took two medium sized ferns right in the Jack Johnsons. The ground suddenly disappeared below me, and I went airborne and flew a good ten feet before coming to rest in the shallow slow moving edge of the river. Just as I stood up, I heard a scream and turned around just in time to see Mark flying through the air towards me. His legs were open, and I didn't even have time to raise my arms before his groin impacted my face and the two of us flopped into the water. He clambered off me, stood, and both of us burst out laughing as we realized that we had indeed inadvertently done a decent re-enactment of the famous scene from Romancing the Stone.

We continued to stand there and laugh like idiots until we heard a noise, and both of us looked upriver to see the MSA rebels moving in our direction. Unfortunately, they saw us as well and immediately began firing their weapons. I ducked down and motioned for Mark to do the same, and we began following the river—stopping only long enough to return fire when necessary to cover our escape. At last, we got to a deeper, faster flowing section, and we moved into the middle and began swimming. The shots temporarily subsided, and we swam on in silence until eventually reaching a bend, where we climbed out onto some rocks, and I had a moment to sneak a peak at our pursuers. They were split into two teams, one on each side of the river, and each one was about two hundred yards away. I took aim at the group on the right and squeezed off a burst and sent them scrambling for cover. I did the same to the group on the left, then Mark and I set off jumping from rock to rock until we came to a choke point where the river turned into a massive waterfall. We moved right out to the very edge and stopped and looked at each other.

"I guess this is it, Sundance," Mark said.

"No, there's always a way."

"I don't know. It's looking pretty grim."

I leaned out over the edge and saw that it was at least a thirty foot drop into the pool below. In theory, the water would be plenty deep, as the river had been constantly carving away at it for thousands of years. Of course, that same river might also have loosened up some boulders that could be lurking just below the turbulent surface.

"I say we jump," I said.

"Can't we just fight it out? You're a former CIA operative for fuck's sake. Aren't you trained for these kinds of situations?"

"Says the pacifist."

"I'm starting to re-evaluate my principles."

"Look here, Mr. I Found my Inner action hero—I might be able to kill some of those assholes, but we could just as easily jump. If we make it down, there's no way in hell they'll follow us."

Shots started coming from behind, and bullets were churning up the water and ricocheting off of the surrounding rocks. I turned and fired a quick burst, then turned to Mark.

"Time to hump or jump!" I said.

"Fine, I'll take the latter."

We walked to the edge and looked down before glancing at each other for moral support. Another fusillade of shots rang out, and it gave us all the final motivation we needed to make the leap. Everything suddenly became silent, and it seemed as though an eternity passed before I felt the hard slap of my shoes hitting the water. The rest of my body quickly sunk deep into the cool turbid waters, and I started swimming upward, though the rifle in my hands made the task a hell of a lot more difficult. I finally surfaced and started looking for Mark, and he popped up a second later looking harried.

"Fuck! I lost my rifle," he said.

Suddenly bullets started tearing up the water, and I looked up to see our friends above us taking pot shots. I dove down and pulled Mark with me, and we swam to the side of the river then took cover behind a large boulder. I leaned out, took aim, and fired off a short burst, and one of the men screamed as he reached down and clutched at his leg.

"Hot damn, you hit one!"

"Play with the bull, you get the horns," I said.

I fired one more time, and it sent them diving for cover, and we used the opening to run and gain some precious distance. We made good time and traveled nearly a mile downriver without a single bullet being fired at us, and all was looking good. The valley was thinning, however, and I feared we might run into another choke point. We continued to trudge over rocks, sand, and water, and our shoes were wet and heavy. I was used to this kind of punishing long distance foot travel, but I had to admit that Mark, for a civilian, was keeping good pace, and not a single complaint escaped his lips. Not many people could put aside all their aches and pains and buckle down and keep going in a situation like this, and I had a new and profound respect for my companion. I could certainly see that tenacity was indeed a quality that ran deep in the Blake family.

We reached another choke point and saw that it led to a series of steep cascading waterfalls, and we now had some serious choices to make. We could work our way down or climb up and around, but both would be slow and extremely dangerous and potentially leave us out in the open and vulnerable to our pursuers—assuming they hadn't yet given up the chase.

"Any thoughts?" Mark asked.

"Yeah, let's call an Uber."

"If only you had your precious sat-phone."

A noise came from behind, and we both turned to see our asshole pursuers trudging down the river and getting closer by the second.

"I guess they decided to jump," Mark said.

"They aren't quitters."

The rebels once again separated into two groups, and each took a side of the river as they began closing in quickly on our position. About a hundred yards away, I fired a quick burst, and they scattered for cover. Then, they actually did something smart. One group fired at us to pin us down behind the rocks, while the other moved forward. They repeated the process and used it to move ever closer, which meant that it was only a matter of time before they were upon us, and all would be lost. Suddenly, over my shoulder, I heard the sound of footsteps, and I turned to see armed men emerging from behind the nearby rocks, trees, and bushes, so this had apparently been some kind of very elaborate trap.

"We're officially fucked," I said.

The men all raised their weapons, and I spoke a silent prayer as I knew that I was about to spend the next five or so seconds of my life emptying my clip and taking as many of these motherfuckers with me as I could. I gave Mark a nod, then slid in a fresh clip, pulled back the slide and pre-pared to die—albeit gloriously.

CHAPTER TWENTY-EIGHT
Shiny Happy People Holding Guns

Just as I aimed my weapon and prepared to fire, a familiar man stepped from a thick grove of ferns. He, like the others, was carrying an AK 47, but, unlike his peers, he was smiling. Mark reached over and gently pressed my rifle down before standing up and approaching the man. Holy shit—our visitor was Itari the bartender.

"I have never been happier to see you, my friend," Mark said.

"And I too am happy to see that you are safe and sound. We were all very worried when we got news that you had been captured by the MSA. Luckily, we had watchers in the hills above the camp, and they informed us of your escape, and it allowed us to mobilize our men and facilitate this little trap and your subsequent safe return."

"So, you know about the guys behind us?" I asked.

"Of course, it was all part of the plan."

Mark and I shared a confused look until recognition dawned on me.

"So, you're the beavers who created those roadblocks," I said.

"Damn right."

I had to smile at his clever pun.

"It was the easiest way to lead all of you into this part of the river," he added.

"I take it that you're more than a clever wordsmith and bartender."

Mark smiled.

"Finn, I'd like to properly introduce you to my good friend. This is Itari Behrendt, part-time beaver and full time leader of Malkarta's Democratic Alliance."

"It's nice to officially meet you, as we didn't have much time for introductions back at the bar. My name's Finn, Tag Finn."

"Nice to officially meet you as well, and I'm sorry about our first meeting, but we have to be especially careful these days."

"I understand, though do you mind if I ask a slightly personal question?"

"Not at all."

"Is Behrendt a Dutch name?"

"Yes, my father is Dutch, and my mother is Indonesian."

So, my earlier summation that he was both Indonesian and European had been correct. My thoughts were suddenly interrupted by the sound of gunfire and shouting upriver. It would appear that our MDA friends were taking care of our little problem—namely the contingent of MSA that had been pursuing us for the last hour. A few moments later, we looked upriver to see the MSA rebels being led down to our position. The guy I had shot had a makeshift bandage wrapped around his leg wound, and he was making a very obvious point of glaring at me. Of course, I fully understood his feelings, as I would have been doing the same had the situation been reversed. He walked closer and stood before me with a vicious scowl on his face.

"You Americans are the scourge of the world!"

I was trying to think of a clever response, and instead came up with an oddly nostalgic one—well, nostalgic for me, anyway.

"You rebel scum!" I responded, in a low affected sounding voice.

"Wait, dude—was that seriously a Star Wars reference?" Mark asked.

"Yes, which means there are at least two Star Wars nerds on the island of Malkarta."

Itari cleared his throat.

"Excuse me, but technically a more specific answer would be that it's a Return of the Jedi reference," he said.

"I take it back. There are apparently three Star Wars nerds on the island of Malkarta."

Itari motioned for us to follow him, and we found ourselves on a well hidden path that crisscrossed up the mountain until reaching what I presume was the same road we had been on earlier. We loaded into Land Cruisers and started driving east towards the coast.

"So, what happens to the MSA assholes?" I asked.

"Nothing, they will be held until we can figure something out, as their greatest crime sadly is ignorance and, in some cases, full blown stupidity," Itari said.

"But not a lack of perseverance," I added.

"Judging by your little chase, I'd have to agree."

"So, I assume that you know that the MSA have Anna and Fiona," Mark said.

"No, I did not. Do you have any idea where they are being held?"

"Supposedly at a large estate up on the northeast shore. The owner is a man named Budi Kusuma."

Itari nodded.

"I know of the estate and its owner. Once we're back at my house and you two have had a chance to freshen up, I'll tell you more about Budi, and we can figure out how we're going to rescue Anna and your sister."

We loaded up in Itari's Land Rover and traveled along the dirt road until reaching the William De Vries highway. We made a left and headed north for about twenty minutes before turning right onto a small paved road that headed towards the ocean. We arrived at a large, though somewhat weathered, two story house that sat beside a picturesque beach. It had a well-kept garden, and there was even a stable and plenty of open space. Itari pulled up in front of the garage, and we stepped out to be greeted by a black lab that was curious about the new arrivals.

"This is my dog Willy," Itari said.

I reached down and petted Willy, though I was referring to Willy the dog rather than the willy in my pants that I'd been petting since puberty, and the amiable dog followed me inside the house and licked my face when I leaned down to remove my shoes. I scratched his back down near his tail, and he wiggled appreciatively, and I realized that I now had a new best friend for life. There was nothing more loyal or loving than a dog.

"My daughter Grieta will show you to your rooms, and you can get cleaned up. Once you're done, I'll be waiting for you in the library."

Grieta stepped forward and smiled.

"I'm Grieta, nice to meet you," she said.

She was in her early twenties, beautiful, and had long brown hair, deep brown eyes, and bronze skin that was obviously a combination of her genetics and a life in the tropics. She also happened to be wearing a rather skimpy two piece bikini that made a point of revealing her lithe though strategically curvaceous figure, and I was worried it would make me have to work especially hard to maintain proper eye contact.

"I'm Finn, Tag Finn. Nice to meet you too."

"Follow me," she said, as her full lips formed into an inviting smile.

We left the kitchen and followed her onto the stairs,

which presented us with a lovely view of her pert bottom as it swayed from side to side with each step. I tried not to stare, but her bikini bottom showed more than a polite amount of her buttocks, and I found my eyes inadvertently returning back to it every couple steps. I turned to see that Mark was equally distracted, and we christened our moment of weakness with a silly smile. As I turned back around, I was shocked to see that Grieta had paused at the top of the stairs, and I did my best to make an emergency stop, but I ended up stumbling and fell forward with my face on a collision course with Grieta's backside. I instinctively reached out to catch myself, and my hands landed on her hips as my face slammed into her butt cheeks. Mark immediately burst out laughing, and I pulled my face free and stood up, only to have Grieta turn around and look at me with a large questioning smile on her face.

"You know, Tag, if you wanted to kiss my ass—all you had to do was ask," she said.

I smiled embarrassingly.

"Sorry, it was an accident. I got distracted and tripped."

"Oh, and what distracted you?" she asked, knowing full well the answer.

In a mild panic, I had a quick look around and noticed there was an abundance of interesting art on the surrounding walls.

"I was—um—just looking at..."

"My ass?" she interjected.

"I would be lying if I said I hadn't noticed it, but in this instance I was going to say the art."

My comment had been intended to save face, but I really did think the art was impressive.

"Oh, really?"

"Yeah," I said, as I stepped past Grieta and stood before a painting that depicted a beautiful young woman sitting by the ocean's edge.

The brushstrokes were bold—as was the use of color, and I liked it.

"Do you seriously like the painting?" Grieta asked.

"I do, actually, and if I'm not mistaken, the style seems to be an homage to post impressionism and a touch of Fauvism—perhaps inspired by Matisse?"

"Very good! You have quite an eye, Tag. Are you also a painter?"

"Unfortunately, no, but I took a few art history classes in college."

"You obviously know your art," she said, as she smiled at me.

"Well, I know what I like, and I really do like these paintings."

"As much as my ass?"

Now I was smiling and feeling a bit embarrassed, but I decided I might as well be honest.

"It's hard to imagine anything that compares to your ass, but these paintings come pretty darn close."

"Well, good, because these paintings are all mine."

"Seriously?"

"Yes."

"You've got real talent."

"Thank you, though my father hopes I'll keep it as a hobby."

"What does he want you to do?"

"Stick to biology."

"Oh, did you study it in college?"

"Yeah, I got my degree at the Australian National University, though I wish I could have just gone to college here."

"Do they have a college?"

"Afraid not."

"Well, hopefully change is coming."

We continued down the hall, and I was led to a large bedroom with a queen sized bed, bathroom, and a view of the ocean. The furniture was all wicker, which made sense considering the salt air and humidity. She left and took Mark to his room then returned a few moments later and announced her presence with a knock on the doorframe.

"If you give me your clothes, I'll put them in the laundry."

"Better service than the King William Hotel."

"Certainly less attitude," she said, as she stood there waiting, which was making me feel a little uncomfortable.

"So, you want me to take off my clothes right now?"

"Of course. They aren't going to get clean if they're still on your body."

I took off my shirt then paused before removing my shorts.

"Um, should I, perhaps um..."

"Don't worry, I'm just fucking with you," she said, as she smiled and turned around.

I slipped off the shorts and tossed the entirety of my clothes across the room, and they landed at her feet.

"There you go," I said.

She bent down and picked them up but unexpectedly turned around at the last moment and eyed me from head to toe in my full glorious nudity. I stood there feeling incredibly awkward, though a small part of me was still guilty for head butting her butt cheeks, so I thought suffering a little reciprocal humiliation was the least I could do.

"Meow! Somebody has been going to the gym," she said.

"Yeah, but only when I'm not too busy shoving my face into random women's butts."

"So, I'm not your first butt?" she asked, feigning sadness.

"No—but you're probably my favorite so far."

"Good to know, but next time I might mix things up by walking up the stairs backwards."

I had a second to think about the implications of her statement and couldn't help but smile.

"Good one. I'll be looking forward to it."

She held her gaze a bit longer then left and closed the door, and I was left naked but thankfully alone. I decided to check out the facilities and ventured into the bathroom to find a traditional western style toilet, which meant I would be able to take a good old fashioned dump when the time came. For the moment, however, I was more concerned with the shower and cleaning up after the day's crazy events.

I turned on the taps, stepped inside, and stood under the rush of hot water and felt the stress and filth being washed away from my body. I grabbed some shampoo then soaped up before rinsing off and leaving the solace of the aquatic sanctuary. There was a fresh towel, and I used it to dry off before wrapping it around my waist and stepping out into my room, where I was wondering what I would wear until my clothes were clean. There was a knock at the door, then it opened, and Grieta was standing there holding a small stack of garments.

"Here are some shorts and a shirt from my father."

"Thanks."

She stood there, and I wondered if perhaps she was hoping for another show. After yet another long awkward moment together, she gave me a little smile then headed out of my room but paused at the door.

"We'll be waiting downstairs in the library when you're ready," she said.

She left, and I got dressed in khaki shorts and a light blue shirt before heading into the hall, where I ran into Mark, who was, coincidentally, wearing the exact identical outfit. Apparently, Itari didn't vary his wardrobe too much, and now Mark and I looked like fraternal twins.

"Nice outfit," I said.

"You too."

"Did Grieta watch you undress?"

"Not this time, but she has in the past, so, don't worry—she just enjoys fucking with new male visitors."

"Interesting girl. I suspect they don't get a lot of guys out here."

"Apparently not."

We continued downstairs and entered the library to find it was well-used, and the Persian rug on the floor had probably seen better days, as it was now inhabited by a number of bare spots where time and travel had dulled its colorful surface. Residing on it were two weathered leather couches and a coffee table, while around them were floor to ceiling shelves loaded with books. I took a moment to browse some of the titles and saw that there were texts that covered everything from philosophy and economics texts to microbiology and chemistry.

"Pretty heavy reading for a bartender," I said.

"The bar is more of a pastime and place to conduct busi-ness—if you know what I mean."

"I understand, and the American Revolution would have never happened without the aid of pubs. Every cause needs a good place for its champions to drink and ruminate."

"Yes indeed."

"So, I take it you have interests beyond bartending?"

"Not to take away from my other profession, but I also happen to be a professor of economics. I got my PhD at the Australian National University then taught there for a few years before returning back to my home, where I hoped to found Malkarta's first University. The wealthy here could afford to send their children abroad, but the poor were lit-erally trapped in ignorance. The only chance for Malkarta's population to grow intellectually meant bringing education to the people, but, needless to say, my efforts were soon quashed, as the powers that be preferred a cheap uneducated workforce. I therefore set about working for change in a different way, which was greatly enhanced when Mark and his Globo-Care arrived. With international aid and attention, we were starting to make real progress, but then Mark was arrested. As in the case of many revolutions, however, the effort to quell it can often be the spark that ignites it, and it's brought real unrest to this island, and some people are even willing to fight for it—as is the case with the MSA. The obvious problem with that is that they have no qualms about using particularly violent means and don't care who is caught in the crossfire. We in the MDA are hoping for non-violent change, though that is growing more unlikely by the moment."

"I might be able to offer some help. I happen to have the ear of the vice president of the United States, and I know they want to put a base here. Stability makes that more possible, and if change helps achieve that, I imagine you might be able to get some serious foreign support from good old Uncle Sam."

"It certainly wouldn't hurt," he said, nodding enthusiastically.

"Yeah, and oddly our immediate problem is also related to our long term problem. The same man who has the girls also has my satellite phone—which happens to be my only direct line to the vice president at the moment. Once we have it and the girls back, we can hopefully do something about Mark's outlaw status and perhaps even get some outside help with the political situation here on Malkarta," I said.

"That would be excellent, so, let's get to it. Now, the man holding the girls, Budi Kusuma, is an extremely successful businessman, and, as you know, he lives on a vast estate just to the north. Strangely though, he is by all accounts a capitalist, so I find it particularly interesting that he might have ties to the MSA."

"I suspect that he has more than ties. The leader of that camp was downright reverential, and I had to dislocate two of his fingers before he gave up Budi's identity. You don't have that kind of loyalty unless the person in question is very important, very powerful, or both."

"Well, no one has officially come forward as the leader of the MSA, so anything is possible, though Budi is a bit of an enigma. He, like me, was born with mixed heritage, but, in his case, his father was Indonesian, and his mother was Dutch. That being the case, he faced different kinds of problems growing up. A Dutch man taking an Indonesian wife was more acceptable than the reverse, so Budi faced more challenges—specifically discrimination. Still, he managed to get a formal education and attended the Dutch Royal Military College before serving in the Dutch Army."

"Interesting. Perhaps he has a touch of the Stockholm syndrome."

"Perhaps, as it made absolutely no sense that a boy would

grow up and become a part of the institution that was the vehicle of oppression for both himself and his culture for the last four hundred years."

"If you can't beat them—join them," I said.

"It would appear that strategy worked, because upon returning to Malkarta, he somehow managed to amass a great deal of wealth and slowly bought up land and spice manufacturing facilities before diversifying into media. Now, he owns the local telecom company, the radio and television stations, as well as the island's only internet service provider. Beyond that, he's officially become the second largest private landowner on the island, which is no easy feat for a non-Dutch citizen."

"So, I imagine he's seen as kind of an Uncle Tom in the eyes of the locals?"

"Exactly, so how and why would such a man be the leader of a Socialist uprising? It doesn't make any sense."

"No it doesn't, but perhaps he bought his place within the MSA. Even socialist rebels need money."

"Anything is possible, I suppose."

We had a moment to think, then I decided it was about time we address our primary objective.

"So, how do we breach this fucker's estate?"

"Well, the first problem is getting there. There is the road, of course, but it will obviously be under a lot of surveillance—both human and electronic."

"Does the estate border the ocean?"

"Yes, and the main house sits at the waters edge on a

beautiful private beach."

"You sound like you've been there."

"I have. Back when I was trying to raise funds for the university, we held a fundraiser there, because I thought an island native would recognize the need to bring education to Malkarta. He had been to college and therefore knew what opportunities it would bring to the people here, but, as it turned out, his support was all a lot of hot air, and our university idea was shut down. Since that time, it is fair to say that I do not enjoy the company of Budi."

"What's the wave action like on the beach? Any chance of a water born insertion?"

"This time of year, it's still as bathwater."

"Can you get me a boat—preferably an inflatable?"

"Of course, you can use mine. It's a twelve foot Zodiac with a fifty horsepower Mercury outboard."

"Well cover me with butter and roll me in flower! Now, I just need for you to draw me a floor plan of Budi's estate with as much detail as you can possibly remember."

"No problem. Plus, I also have pictures from the night of the fundraising dinner that will also give you a better idea of some of the interior details."

Itari, went to his desk, grabbed paper and a pencil, then went to a shelf and pulled out a photo album before returning and setting everything on the coffee table. He then set about drawing out a floorpan while I went through the album and looked at pictures from the infamous night. It was obviously a pretty big affair, and Malkarta's most elite citizens were in attendance, which, of course, included Maas Groot and Anna.

"So, you and Anna have known each other for some time?"

"Yes, and oddly it was she that introduced me to Mark."

"Bartender, professor, statesman, and even matchmaker. You're quite a Renaissance man, Itari."

"It's too bad I was born four hundred years too late."

"Yeah, but it means you're here tonight."

A half hour later, I had a rough idea of how and where I would breach the estate. Now, it was a matter of timing and assembling a team. It was essentially a hostage rescue, but I didn't exactly have a crack group of people at my disposal. Instead, I had myself, an academic, a humanitarian, and whoever the hell else Itari could find on short notice. I would therefore be the point man when we entered the house while the others would remain as my backup. With the planning mostly done, we adjourned to Itari's dining room to wait for nightfall by enjoying an informal dinner of chicken satay and *Nasi goreng*—a delicious Indonesian rice dish.

By the time dinner was finished, the sun was dropping over the horizon, and we walked out past Itari's back deck and across a short stretch of white sand beach to reach his boathouse. Upon stepping inside I saw his Zodiac sitting on a small trailer, which obviously served as the means to roll it into the water. I stepped closer and examined the interior and was pleased to see that it had a small steering console, which was a shitload more convenient than sitting on the back and having to manually turn the outboard motor.

"This is exactly what we need for tonight's mission!" I said.

We rolled it out and into the water until it floated free, then Itari tied it up to the old dock that extended about twenty meters into the small bay.

"It's already got a full tank of gas, so now all you have to do is figure out what you need to bring, then we'll pack it in the raft and leave when you're ready."

"What kind of moon do we have tonight?" I asked.

"Sliver, and it won't be appearing until after midnight."

"Perfect, if all goes well, we'll already be back here by then! OK, folks, I'm going to do a quick weapons check, then, when it's zero dark hundred, we'll storm the castle."

We left the dock and ventured back into the house, and I went up to my room and disassembled all the weapons before reassembling them and checking their action. Next, I went through the various clips and carefully loaded each magazine to make sure every round was perfectly seated. The only silenced weapon we had at the moment was my Pistol, so I was hoping that any shooting would come from me. The AK's stolen during our escape from the camp would only be used if we needed to shoot our way out.

I looked out the window and saw the dying light of the day and thought about the writer Dylan Thomas and his oft quoted poem. I would indeed rage, though not against the dying of the light, but rather against the unfortunate man that held our women. I packed up the weapons, and, as I was about to leave the room, Itari appeared in the doorway, and he was carrying an HK 94 submachine gun. I knew it because I too owned one, and Itari's, like mine, had all the bells and whistles—namely a silencer, laser sight, and flashlight.

"Holy shit! I own one of those beauties as well," I said.

"Then you're a lucky man, as it's truly the Rolls Royce of submachine guns."

"And the coveted weapon of every S.W.A.T. and hostage rescue team the world over. Where did you get it?"

"It was a gift from a friend, and I figured it might come in handy tonight. It's yours if you need it."

"Hell yeah! Bring it along. We can use all the help we can get."

Mark appeared a moment later, and his eyes grew wide when he saw the HK.

"Jesus! Where the hell did you find that?"

"It's Itari's."

"I thought you were a pacifist," Mark said.

"I usually am, but tough times call for tough measures, and tonight I'm feeling a bit more proactive," he said.

"Proactive perhaps being an understatement if you're pulling out weaponry like that," I responded.

The three of us gathered up all the weapons and headed downstairs and out to the little boathouse, at which point Itari walked over to a cupboard and smiled as he opened it to reveal it was full of boxes of 9mm ammo.

"Well hello, Santa Klaus!" I said.

"Merry Christmas," Itari said, pulling out several boxes and placing them into a black nylon dive bag.

We loaded the guns into a similar bag then walked out into the darkness towards the end of the dock, where a person sat quietly waiting in the raft.

"So, who is the fourth person going on this mission with us tonight?" I asked.

"That's a good question and one I spent a lot of time considering. I have several people that would be of use, but I decided to keep our little team closer to home."

"Which means?"

"You'll see."

As we got closer, I saw that it was Itari's daughter.

"Grieta will be our driver tonight," Itari said.

"Are you sure you're comfortable with that? We really have no idea exactly what we're facing, and it could get dangerous."

"We need someone to stay with the raft and have it ready to launch if everything goes to hell. I know she's young, but, believe me, Grieta is more than capable."

"From what I've seen thus far, I'd have to agree."

We climbed aboard, and she turned the key and brought the Mercury outboard engine to life. Meanwhile, Itari untied the bowline, and we pulled away from the dock and headed out into the bay.

"Well, my friends—next stop, the Kusuma Estate," I said.

CHAPTER TWENTY-NINE
Panic Room

Grieta pushed the throttle all the way forward, and the Zodiac literally jumped out of the water and leveled off onto a plane and flew over the smooth ocean at what I would guess was about thirty five or so knots. That translated to nearly forty miles per hour, which was pretty fast for a twelve foot Zodiac with four people aboard. We left the safety of the little bay, and the water became slightly rougher, though it was by no means a bumpy ride, as the boat cut through the chop and made light work of the small waves. A little over ten minutes passed, and I could see a section of land up ahead that extended well out into the sea, and at its northern most point was a lighthouse. Itari saw where I was looking and leaned in close so that he could be heard over the rushing wind.

"That's the William De Vries Lighthouse, so Budi's house is just beyond it in the next cove."

"Sweet fucking Jesus, what isn't named after William De

Vries on this fucking island?"

"The poverty?"

"I suppose, though that fucker is responsible for it."

"Too true," Itari said.

We continued on, and the Mercury engine effortlessly pushed the Zodiac along at full speed until Grieta throttled down as we rounded the point. The boat came off of its plane, and our stern wave caught up and sloshed against the transom of the raft. I looked ahead and, even in the darkness, could see a long beautiful stretch of white sand beach, while just beyond it resided a massive well-lit house that stood out in stark contrast to the dark countryside. Now, that we were motoring along slowly, I could get a better feel for the wind direction. Wind was important to consider on an operation like this, because it was extremely effective at carrying sound over the water. Tonight, however, we were lucky because we had a nice offshore breeze that would hopefully carry the noise of our outboard down the coast and away from the estate.

We still had some distance to cover, so I decided to use the time to go over basic hand signals that would allow the three of us to communicate silently once we were near the estate. I showed them freeze, hostage, OK, and go prone, leaving out the other thirty-nine in the interest of time and minimizing confusion. Fifteen minutes later, we were moving towards shore, and all of us were keeping low in the raft to minimize our profile. We decided to hit the beach about two hundred yards south of the estate, and, when the bow touched sand, we slipped over the side and pulled the raft just far enough ashore to keep it and Grieta from floating away.

"Are you going to be OK here on your own?" I asked.

She held up her AK-47 and smiled.

"I'll be just fine."

"Alrighty then—we'll see you in a little bit."

We moved inland and formed up just inside the tree line, and I did a few tests of our communication signals to make sure my earlier lesson had been understood. Everyone seemed to have it down, so we continued up the edge of the beach but kept in the shadows and took it slow in order to make sure we didn't accidentally overtake any sentries. There was also a chance they had passive listening devices, but the sound of the ocean would theoretically have made them almost useless, so odds were in our favor that humans were our most likely obstacle.

Fifty yards from the fence line, we paused, and I used a pair of binoculars to survey the main house. It was a massive three story structure with lots of glass, and the bottom floor housed the kitchen, dining room, and main living areas while the second floor housed the guest rooms. The very top floor was, not surprisingly, where the lord of the manner resided. Below all this and bordering the beach was a massive deck with a pool, Jacuzzi, and even a small cabana hut that I would bet good money was a bar. Budi, like the Dutch citizens, certainly lived well beyond the humble means of the average Malkartan.

I scanned for security people and found two standing together on the periphery of the deck. One was smoking while the other was speaking animatedly and utilizing a number of hand gestures to accompany his words. God only knew what he was so excited about, but it was a fair bet to assume the topic was either sports or women. My theory was proven correct a moment later when he cupped his two hands in front of his chest, so he was indeed referring to women or, more specifically, breasts—likely large ones. I also took this as a good omen that they might be talking about Budi's latest houseguests, and that meant we were clearly in the right place.

"OK, so far, I only see two guards on the deck, and, if I can take care of them, it'll be the easiest way to enter the house."

At that moment, a man walked out onto the deck and joined the two men, so I trained the binoculars on the new arrival and was pretty sure it was Budi.

"Itari, you mind taking a look at the new guy and telling me if I'm correct in assuming that he's the lord of the manner?"

"Not at all," he said, taking the binoculars and peering at the man.

"Yeah, that's him. You can tell by the cloud of smugness that's emanating from his body."

Itari handed me back the binoculars, and I returned to gazing at Budi. He appeared to be in his middle forties, had a full head of brown hair, and wore a white linen suit that made him look like the head of a South American drug cartel. He talked to the men for a bit longer then disappeared from view as he headed back inside the house.

"Let's move out," I said.

We continued along the beach, and the gentle lapping of the waves was the only sound other than our labored footfalls as we made our way across the soft sand. Soon, the tree line came to an end, and we had a long, open expanse between us and the house. We could either stick to the beach or move inland onto the grounds of the estate, and I decided to go with the estate, as it afforded more cover with its finely pruned hedges, flower beds, and palm trees. The first barrier was a low fence and a hedgerow, but we managed to slip in through a small access gate and took cover behind a great topiary trimmed to look like a team of unicorns. It was an odd theme for a man's garden, and it made me wonder about Budi's mental state. Were we dealing with a rational adult or someone with the eccentricities of a thirteen year old girl?

We moved on and passed a small coy pond then paused behind a grouping of palm trees. There, I took another look at the deck to check on our two guards and noticed that they had separated, with the smoker now making his way out and along the edge of the grounds. That was actually good news, because it was a pretty fair indication that they didn't employ noise sensors around the estate, and instead relied on human based reconnaissance.

Once the smoker was well out and away from our position, we moved forward to the edge of the deck then fast crawled around its edge to the access stairs. There, I stood up to take a quick look for the remaining guard, and, strangely, I found him by the sound of clanking bottles. He was over in the cabana hut pouring himself a large glass of scotch, so it would appear that my earlier theory that it was a bar was correct. He proceeded to gulp down the entire contents of his glass then poured himself another before meandering over to the pool to take a seat in one of the deck chairs. That was some pretty lax security, though I imagine his lack of vigilance meant that they didn't get much excitement on this shift. Still, I imagine he timed this little lapse in protocol to correspond to his friend's segue out onto the grounds, and, as long as he sat in that chair, it was a good indicator that his friend wouldn't be returning anytime soon.

I looked around for an entry point, but everything in the vicinity entailed walking past the boozer, so I told Mark and Itari to wait while I crawled over to take a look at the other side of the house. As I came around to the kitchen, I inadvertently triggered a motion sensor, and the entire outdoor patio was suddenly bathed in light. The door opened a moment later, and another guard stepped outside, but I managed to quickly duck back behind the built-in barbecue grill. The man scanned the area then shook his head and looked mildly annoyed.

"Fucking cat," he muttered as he turned and headed back inside.

I had flushed out the presence of yet another guard, though this made me wonder what culinary delights Budi kept in his kitchen if he needed to post a sentry. Judging by the unicorn topiary in his garden, I wouldn't be surprised if he had a Holly Hobbie oven and a stash of red velvet cupcakes, but that little piece of information would have to remain a mystery for the moment, as I had two distressed damsels desperately in need of rescue. Using the barbecue as a shield to keep from triggering the sensor yet again, I moved into the shadows of the nearby shrubbery and made my way back to the others.

"Anything exciting happen while I was gone?" I whispered.

"No, but our guy did go back for another drink."

"Three in a row. A couple more and I'll be able to just walk right past him."

I turned my attention to breaching the house, and my gaze soon fell upon the second floor, as it had a massive deck that overlooked the ocean. The second floor was almost always the greatest lapse in home security and a favorite among cat burglars, because people often felt safe leaving those windows and doors open. In a hot climate like this, it was almost a certainty that I'd find at least one point of entry, but the problem would then be getting up there. The house's sides were as smooth as butter, and there wasn't any strategically placed lattice that I could use as a makeshift ladder, so this would come down to some Jackie Chan-esque kind of maneuver.

I nodded at my compatriots then slithered onto the deck and moved quietly along through the shadows until reaching the little cabana. I slipped past it and the boozing guard then stepped up onto a chair before jumping and grabbing the edge of the upper story's deck. From there, I swung my legs up and onto the ledge—all the while trying to abstain from making any excess noise. I was about to pull myself up the rest of the way, but I paused when I heard a noise from below, and I looked down to see that the boozer was going for yet another drink. I froze and prayed that he didn't glance up to see the idiot hanging from the deck above. He walked to the cabana bar then returned with a fresh drink but paused directly underneath me as he took a sip. I silently hung just above him and kept my breath completely silent, with the only movement being a bead of sweat that was slowly making its way down my forehead. It soon passed my cheek, and I swatted at it with my tongue but missed, and it went tumbling down and landed on the boozer's forehead. He was ever so subtly startled, so I readied myself to drop down and take him out.

"Fucking rain," he finally said, before continuing on his way.

A moment ago I was a fucking cat, and now I'm some fucking rain, so I was apparently a lot of fucking things to Budi's security people, but I took this all as a sign that there might indeed be a merciful divine being overseeing all of my shenanigans tonight. The guy returned to his seat while I climbed up and slipped over the railing and onto the deck then started checking windows, hopeful to find at least one open. I got lucky on number four, which turned out to be a sliding glass door, and I slid it open and stepped inside then took a moment to let my eyes adjust to the darkness. A large room came into view, and I could see a four poster bed with a shape lying in the middle. Wonderful—the room was occupied. It could be one of Budi's staff, or, if I were incredibly fortunate, either Anna or Fiona. Unfortunately, there was only one way to find out, and I pulled out my pistol and quietly slithered to the far door then turned on the light. To my surprise, I saw Anna handcuffed by her right hand to the bed, and she opened her eyes and looking particularly startled until recognition set in, and she relaxed and breathed a sigh of relief.

"Thank God it's you! Wait, how the hell did you get in here?" she asked excitedly.

"The sliding glass door. Are you OK?"

"I'm fine, but it's Fiona I'm worried about."

"Do you know where she is?"

"I'm pretty sure that she's up in Budi's bedroom—something to do with her being a Playboy Playmate, I suspect."

"Wonderful."

"I do have some good news at least. I saw your sat-phone downstairs in Budi's office."

"Excellent! But we'll worry about it after I free you and Fiona. Any idea where the handcuff key is?"

"The guard keeps it in his pocket for when he has to come set me free me to use the bathroom."

"I think we can work with that. How about you call him in here, and we can kill two birds with one stone—so to speak."

She didn't appear to be all that thrilled with my suggestion, so I told her not to worry as I took a quick look around the room to find something heavy. My eyes quickly fell upon a small bust of Socrates sitting on a corner table, and I smiled to myself as I pondered the irony of using the physical visage of one of the great thinkers of history as a blunt weapon. But, in my mind, it was perfect choice, as the great philosopher had also been a brave warrior and fought in three major campaigns of the Peloponnesian Wars. I grabbed the statue, turned off the light, then hid behind the door as Anna called for the guard. The door opened a moment later, and light spilled in from the hallway as he peered into the room.

"What is it?" he asked.

"Bathroom."

"All right," he said, turning on the light and walking towards the bed with his hand already reaching into his pocket for the handcuff key.

I moved up behind him and bashed him hard across the back of his head, and it sent him flat onto the floor. Thankfully, the blow knocked him out, and he went down without a fight. I grabbed the key off the floor then freed Anna, and she joined me in the task of lifting the guard up onto the bed. Once we had him properly in place, I handcuffed his hands to the frame then tied a gag over his mouth to make sure he didn't alert his friends when he woke up. The final detail entailed pulling the blanket up to his chin in the hope that anyone glancing in would assume that he was Anna.

"Time to rescue Fiona and deal with this Budi character," I said.

"Speaking of which, how in the hell did you figure out where we were?"

"I used a little physical coercion on Pemimpin."

"Good—I hope it entailed inflicting a lot of pain on that asshole."

"Oh, it inflicted a lot of pain, but not on his asshole. Instead, I stuck to his fingers, so, depending on which hand he uses to wipe, I suppose it'll eventually have ramifications on his asshole."

She smiled at my stupid joke.

"Well, whatever you did to cause that fucker pain will definitely make me happy," Anna said.

"So, do you have any idea what the easiest way to the master bedroom might be?"

"The main stairs."

"Do you think he'll have more guards up there?"

"Not if he's doing what I think he's doing."

We left the room and continued on to the stairs, where I stopped dead in my tracks to gaze in awe at the majesty of Budi's home. I could appreciate fine architecture, but this was ridiculous and made me feel as though I had wandered into a Roman palace. The main stairway resided at the center of the house and was at least twenty feet wide and made of blindingly white marble that glowed brilliantly beneath a massive crystal chandelier.

"Any chance Budi is related to your family?" I asked, in reference to the lavishness of his home.

"Definitely not, though he obviously lives as though he is."

We reached the top of the stairs and paused before huge white doors adorned with tacky gold trim that was probably actual gold rather than just paint. We heard a muffled scream then glanced nervously at each other as we moved closer to check the handles. Both were locked, so I inspected the doors in the hope that I might be able to bust them open with a strong kick. Unfortunately, they appeared to be pretty solid, and it was probably a good idea not to make too much noise. We therefore needed another way into the room and set off along the top floor hallway and found a large walk-in linen closet that had a window. I opened it and was pleased to see that I could easily climb out onto the slanted roof.

"Do you want to wait here, and then I'll let you in once I get into Budi's room?" I asked.

"Fuck that. I'm coming with you."

She was pretty ballsy for a princess, and each moment I spent with Anna made me understand all the more why Mark had chosen to stay on the island. We climbed out and crawled along the roof to reach the master bedroom's deck then moved towards the open sliding glass doors. As we drew closer, we could hear the man of the house chatting away, though the strange thing was the lack of any coherent response from his guest other than a few muffled grunts. We paused at the doorframe and were at last able to see in the room, and what we saw was utterly unbelievable. Budi was standing there wearing nothing but red silk g-string underwear and had an obvious, though unimpressive, erection pressing at the small patch of fabric in the front. In one hand he held a martini, and in the other he held a glittery gold colored leather flail, and he was standing menacingly in front of Fiona, who was also standing, though she was naked and spread eagle with her hands and feet secured by four pink fur-lined handcuffs that were attached to the massive carved wooden bedposts at the foot of the bed. Adding to her indignity was the fact that her mouth was gagged with a red silk scarf, though its presence at least explained the strange muffled cries we had heard from outside. This was fifty shades of crazy, and I felt as though we had stumbled into a really twisted softcore movie set—except this was all very real and happening before our eyes. Budi, meanwhile, was still oblivious to our presence and took a sip of the martini then slowly dragged the flail across Fiona's bare breasts, where he appeared to be relishing every moment with his beleaguered captive.

"Who would have ever thought I'd actually have Miss October right here in my bedroom?" he said.

"Not me," I said, stepping into the room and pointing the barrel of my pistol directly at Budi's erection.

He instantly cowered and jumped back and dropped

both the flail and the martini.

"Shame to waste a perfectly good cocktail," I said.

"Who the hell are you?" he muttered angrily.

"The name's Finn, Tag Finn, and my companion I believe you already know," I said, gesturing at Anna.

Recognition dawned on Budi's face, and he smiled.

"Nice to meet you, Finn, though I certainly hadn't ever expected to see you—alive that is."

"Yeah, your friends back at the camp seemed pretty intent on killing me."

"How lovely that you escaped. Now we can have a nice little chitchat."

"Yes indeed, and the first thing I'd like to ask is what the hell is an adamant capitalist doing fraternizing with a bunch of socialist rebels?"

"Interesting question, though the answer is a bit complicated, so do you mind if I pour myself another drink?"

"Go ahead."

He reached down for a new glass, refilled it from the pitcher on the table beside him, then took a sip before looking over and smiling at me. He was definitely a creepy little man, but I had to give him some extra points for extreme composure in the face of adversity. Not many men caught unaware in red g-string underwear could appear so calm and composed.

"I like to think of myself as a capitalist first and situational socialist second."

"And opportunistic rapist third?"

Clearly Budi was no different than any other asshole capitalist, socialist, or communist. When they acquired wealth and power, they would do or say anything to keep their ill gotten gains. Anna, unable to contain her displeasure any longer, stepped forward and looked utterly shocked.

"Budi, I would never have imagined you capable of this much depravity in a million years. To think that I sat next to you at those State dinners."

"Oh, tut tut. Everyone has their secrets. Now, to the more relevant question, which is what makes either of you think that you can get out of my house alive?" he asked.

"We got this far, didn't we? How do you know that all of your security personal haven't already been incapacitated?"

I cocked the pistol then returned my aim to his dwindling erection. There was just something about having a gun pointed at your manhood that killed the mood.

"Wait! There is no need to act impulsively. I am a wealthy man, and I could pay you quite handsomely to forget this matter and let me live."

"Sorry, I don't need the money, and the only things I value in this entire house are currently in this room—one standing beside me and the other handcuffed to your bed."

"Be real. Everyone has a price."

"Not me."

"Believe me. You don't to want kill me! I have information that would be very useful," he said, starting to get anxious.

"Don't worry. I have no intention of killing you. The

worst I might do is leave a little scar little," I said, gesturing at his penis.

He glanced around the room with his nervous rodent-like eyes then started backing up towards the corner. Suddenly, the little fucker clapped his hands, and the room went dark. Sweet mother of innovation! The scantily dressed swine had a Clapper! Apparently, Budi, among his many pursuits, was also a purveyor of gimmicky late night television products. I clapped, and the lights turned back on just in time to see the creepy lord of the manner disappearing through some kind of trapdoor in the nearby wall. I raced over and found the subtle outline of the hidden door and slipped my fingers into the edge and tried to pry it open but it wouldn't budge. My final effort was to deliver a solid kick before concluding it was a lost cause.

"That slippery little motherfucker managed to escape!" I said, giving the wall a final hit of frustration.

Suddenly, Budi's voice came through the speaker system in the room.

"You didn't think I got this far in life without planning for just these kinds of contingencies did you?"

"Are you referring to the contingency of having another man point a pistol at your genitals while you're cavorting around in ladies' undergarments?"

"Such a poor attempt at levity, Mr. Finn, but I'm afraid you won't be making your little jokes for long, as now it is all of you who are at a disadvantage," he said, with a maniacal cackle.

"What the hell is that supposed to mean?"

My question was answered shortly thereafter when vents on the ceiling started making noise, and I could feel moving air. Lovely—it was probably tear or sleeping gas, so it would appear that Budi had a panic room behind the wall and had installed some tricky options. We therefore needed to free Fiona and find a way out of this house of horrors. Using the handcuff key from earlier, I freed Fiona's hands and feet then removed the scarf from her mouth, and she immediately threw her arms around me and held me tight.

"I knew you'd come," she said.

"If I'd known you were going to be naked and cuffed to the bed, I would have *come* a lot sooner."

She smiled and kissed me.

"Save that thought for when we make it out of here alive," she said, letting go of me and grabbing a robe that was sitting atop the nearby dresser.

She had a pretty good attitude for someone who had just suffered through the beginnings of a sexual assault, and I was thankful we had gotten here in time to keep anything worse from happening. Unfortunately, however, the room was rapidly filling up with gas, so we needed to vacate it as soon as possible. I went to the main door but found the lock mechanism had been electronically overridden, so I tried to ram it with my shoulder. It held firm, and I tried a kick but had no luck, which meant our situation was becoming quite dire. As if it couldn't get any worse, Budi's voice come over the speakers yet again.

"Time is running out, and soon it will be you who has a gun pointed at your genitals, Mr. Finn," he said, before delivering another round of manic laughter.

Sweet Lord! Budi was like a bad guy character from a James Bond movie.

"Back to the deck," I said.

The three of us ran towards the deck only to find that the sliding glass door had been remotely closed. This night was just getting better and better. I threw a solid front kick at the glass but only achieved minor cracks for my efforts. Fuck, it was tempered and reinforced. Anna coughed then looked at me nervously.

"I think I'm starting to feel the gas," she said.

"Me too. What a revolting development this is," I said.

The girls looked at me, and the fear in their eyes was growing with each second we spent in this fucking room.

"Don't worry. Where there's a will, there's a way—out that is."

CHAPTER THIRTY
Little Pink Handcuffs for You and Me

The windows and sliding glass door were obviously a bust, so I turned my attention back to the main entrance. Sometimes when people reinforced a door, they didn't always bother with the wall around it—hopefully anyway. Instead of kicking the door, I kicked the wall just to the side of it, and I hit something solid, which meant they had reinforced part of the wall, but I was hoping they had gotten lazy and ended their efforts there. Moving my aim over about sixteen inches, the usual distance between studs in a wall, I threw another kick, and this one sailed right through the wallboard and into a wad of insulation. I kicked again, but this time I aimed higher and my foot went through the outer layer of wallboard, and the hallway was now visible. Salvation! I threw a couple more kicks then used my hands to tear an opening big enough to send the girls out. I followed directly behind, and we reformed in the hallway and took a moment to consider our next move. This also gave me some unintended time to have a long, hard look at Fiona and her lovely state of undress created by the mostly sheer robe.

"I like the outfit, by the way. It really goes along with my less is more philosophy of fashion," I said.

"You get us all out of here alive, and I'll take it a step further."

"Point taken. Let's get the fuck out of here!"

I led the way down the stairs to the second level but paused when I heard men approaching from the bottom floor. Apparently, our little thonged menace had sounded the alarm, and now all of his security people were converging on his room.

"What do we do?" Anna asked.

"Fuck it! Let's hide out in your room. They'll all be going up to rescue Budi, so all we have to do is wait for them to pass then slip downstairs."

"Good thinking!"

We ran down the hall, reentered Anna's room, and saw that the guard was groggy and coming awake. His eyes soon came to rest on the scantily dressed Fiona, and he continued to stare with dull, albeit lustful, abandon. Leave it to a man to get knocked out cold and the only thing he can focus on when he wakes up is a beautiful half-naked woman. I suppose I couldn't blame him, as I would probably be doing the same thing. I turned my attention back to the hallway and listened to the heavy footfalls of several men on their way upstairs then took a quick glance out the door to make sure it was clear before signaling for Anna and Fiona to follow me downstairs.

"If I remember the floorpan correctly, I believe the office is on the northern side of the main level," I said.

"Yes, it's over there," Anna said, pointing across the vast space that made up his living room.

We headed off at a brisk pace and ventured past Budi's rather opulent furniture, which was brash and bold and reeking of new money. As we passed his lovely oak and glass coffee table, I managed to steal a quick glance at his magazines and saw the October issue of playboy sitting on the top of the pile. I started to reach for it, but Fiona smacked my hand away and delivered a fairly chastising glare as she spoke.

"Don't even think about it! You get to see the real thing whenever you want."

"Fine," I said, feeling a tad bit dejected having thought it would have made for an interesting memento.

We continued on and thankfully found Budi's office empty, as all of his men were obviously up in his love nest on the top floor. I headed for the desk, and, along the way, had a look at the various art and mementos that hung on the walls, as I was curious what kind of picture it painted of our unusual host. There was the obligatory stately portrait of Budi, done in oil on canvas, and it depicted him standing beside a lion as he gazed out with a deeply self-satisfied smile on his face. To a normal person it would have been funny and ironic, but I suspect he sincerely saw the lion as his animal spirit. Beside it, and even more prominent due to its shiny gold frame and specialized lighting, was his diploma from the Dutch Royal Military Academy. Clearly, he was proud to have been a part of his alma mater. What was it with guys never letting go of their college years? I did a quick sweep of the other walls and came to the very obvious conclusion that he was the typical egomaniac, though nothing in this room could explain that fucking red g-string. I flushed my mental toilet of thoughts of Budi's neurosis and went to his desk and had to look no further than the top drawer to find my phone.

"Time to leave," I said, motioning towards the sliding glass door that conveniently opened onto the main deck.

Just before we reached it, the door slid open, and, there, looking just as surprised as us, was Gabir. Before he could react, I grabbed him and dragged him inside and slammed him against the nearby wall. It elicited a pained grunt, but he recovered quickly then stood there in utter panic and looked like a cornered animal.

"Ah, Gabir! It's really nice to see you again. Do you happen to remember what I said to you earlier today?" I asked.

"No," he said, nervously, though his expression obviously told another story.

"You made fun of my American optimism."

"I don't remember doing anything of the sort."

"Well, then let me refresh your memory. I said that by this time tomorrow, we'd be sipping cocktails and laughing all about this entire experience. You, of course, thought that was a lot of hot air. Any of that ring a bell?"

"Not really."

"So, you also don't remember that I said you'd be either dead or dickless and crawling around on two broken legs?"

"No, definitely don't remember that either."

"Well, I suppose it doesn't really matter anymore, because I was wrong. You see, it's not yet tomorrow, and you'll be happy to learn that I've decided to be the bigger person and not break your legs or kill you."

"Thank you, Mr. Finn and please except my sincerest apologies. I was only acting on Budi's orders."

"Yeah, but you still put a knife to Fiona's throat, and that I can't forgive."

I chambered my leg and delivered a forward thrust kick straight into his groin, and the blow buckled him over and brought a grimace of horrible pain to his face.

"Fiona, is there anything more you would like to say to our friend Gabir before we leave?"

"Yeah, this," she said, stepping forward and punching him so hard on the jaw that she knocked him out cold.

"Well done, my scantily dressed pugilist! I believe he'll remember this moment for a long long time," I said.

"Yeah, and I'm glad we didn't actually kill him, because it wouldn't have been a humiliating enough experience to properly atone for his sins."

A man carrying a pistol suddenly came into the room, and, just as he opened fire, everyone dove for cover. I had been his primary target, but the bullets missed me as I dropped down behind the couch. I moved to the other side and popped up and fired back two quick shots, and both hit him center mass, but, judging by his reaction, he was wearing a bullet proof vest. The impacts had merely knocked the wind out of his lungs, and he staggered backward a step then looked as though he might fire again, so I plugged him two more times in the chest, and it knocked him to the ground. I closed the distance and stepped on his wrist to force him to release his pistol, and I picked it up to make sure he didn't use it again. Now, the man was staring up at me with terror in his eyes, as he was afraid I was about to end his life. Instead, I decided to be the bigger man and let him live.

"Don't worry, I'm not going to kill you, but it's still going to hurt."

"I don't understand," he said, meekly.

"You will," I said, as I pistol whipped him across the jaw and knocked him out cold.

I looked around the room and did a quick threat assessment and was happy to see we were finally free and clear of Budi's security assholes.

"Alrighty then! Let's get the hell out of here before anybody else comes into this fucking office," I said.

We slipped out onto the deck, and the boozer was still in

the same chair, having drunk himself to sleep. We made our way past him and down to the lawn, where Mark and Itari were eagerly awaiting our arrival.

"Thank God you made it out alive! We heard all the commotion and had no idea what was happening inside!" Mark said, excitedly.

"Yeah, we made it all right, but the shit is definitely hitting the fan and about to fly all over the place, so we need to get the hell out of here."

The five of us tore out across the lawn and ran past the trees, flowers, and hedges until again encountering the unicorn shaped topiary. Sweet Lord! Everything about Budi's estate, inside and out, was a bizarre physical manifestation of his deep inner crazy. We finally slipped through the outer gate and crossed onto the beach, but headlights came shooting through the darkness and illuminated the entire area, and I looked back and saw men on ATVs racing towards us at breakneck speed. Shots started ringing out behind us, and we all dove to the sand then crawled towards the tree line for cover.

"OK, I think you should all continue on to the raft while I'll slow them down."

"I'm not going anywhere without you," Fiona protested.

"Me neither," Mark added.

"Believe me. This isn't a suicide mission. I'll be right behind you. I promise."

"No," Fiona said.

"It's the only way. Now, go on! Get moving!"

Itari handed me his beloved HK.

"Here, you might need this," He said.

The others ran their hearts out along the tree line while I turned, chambered a round into the HK, then set the selective fire switch to burst mode. That would limit it to three rounds at a time and would conserve my ammo and improve accuracy. The HK-94, even with its butter smooth action, tended to rise up a bit on full auto. Next, I took up a prone firing position and sighted in on the ATVs, which were rapidly approaching. I needed to slow them down, so I pointed the HK at the one on the left and aimed for the spot I imagined to be the location of one its bulbous tires then squeezed off a three round burst. The vehicle suddenly swerved and began tumbling end over end, so I had obviously taken out at least one of the front tires. I had one ATV down, but the other kept coming and, worse still, its driver fired another round of shots. Bullets peppered the sand around me with hot lead, so I rolled right into a new firing position and squeezed off another three round burst but only managed to hit the headlight. More shots came, but I had already rolled back to the left when I returned fire. This time I placed my aim higher and managed to hit the driver, and the little ATV slowed and coasted to a stop only a few yards away.

The man was slumped over the handlebars, and I shoved him off of the vehicle then climbed aboard, hit the gas, and sent up a rooster tail of sand behind me. I might have been riding for my life, but it still didn't take away from the fact that it was incredibly fun blazing along over the beach on the ATV.

"Home free," I said, aloud to myself.

Or so I thought until I heard engine noise behind me, and I stole a quick glance over my shoulder to see at least three more ATVs racing up the beach. How many fucking security people did that asshole have? Shots rang out, and, a fraction of a second later, bullets whizzed past me, so I aimed the HK behind me and squeezed off two bursts. They security assholes kept coming, but thankfully I had reached our insertion spot and saw the marks of where the raft had been dragged back into the water. I slammed on the brakes and skidded to halt then turned my gaze out towards the ocean, but I was unable to see any trace of the raft.

"Hey! Where are you fuckers?" I called out.

There was no response, so I called out again.

"Hello? Where are you fuckers! It's me, goddammit!"

"Me who?" Fiona yelled back.

"Me, the guy who's going to be giving you sexual healing if we make it out of here alive!"

"Oh, that me."

"Yeah, so why the hell didn't you guys answer?"

"Because of the ATV, dumbass! We thought you were one of Budi's security assholes."

"Well, I'm definitely not, but, as you can see by the approaching headlights, they're more assholes coming this way."

"OK, we're coming in for you."

I hazarded a quick glance at my pursuers to see they were ge
close, and I realized I needed to buy some extra time by creat
diversion.

"Don't bother, it's safer if I come out."

I searched the vehicle and found a Velcro strap on the rear
and I wrapped it around the throttle and sent the ATV merri
its way farther down the beach. With my decoy set in moti
immediately entered the sea but managed to keep all my wea
above the surface by utilizing a modified version of the old co
sidestroke. It was a very efficient Navy SEAL swimming tech
similar to the traditional sidestroke, but, in this case, I was usir
left arm to hold the weapons aloft. It made the process a bit le
ficient, but I managed to reach the raft without any of my go
dipping into the corrosive sea water.

I handed the weapons to Fiona, but, as I climbed aboard, C
gunned the engine and turned the boat quickly out to sea. I h
climb in as the raft bounded along over the choppy water, and
a lot like some drop-off and pickup training I did with the SE
Sweet siren of the sea! I couldn't help but think that Grieta
want to consider a career in the Navy piloting fast attack boa
mere seconds, we were well offshore and officially victorious
made our way back towards the Behrendt's beachfront home. I
still, we had escaped without any injuries, though we would sur
scarred by the memories of Budi in his red g-string. In anoth
minutes we were idling up to Itari's dock, and everyone climbe
so that we could haul the raft up onto its little trailer and roll
the boathouse.

Finished, we went inside Itari's house to celebrate, and eve settled into couches except Fiona, who went upstairs with Grieta to find something to wear. A few minutes later the girls reappeared, and Fiona was in a cute island style dress that adhered to her ample curves in a way that tickled my pickle and made me relish the idea of ejaculating. Just when I though the moment couldn't get any better, Itari appeared with a tray full of cocktails, and he proceeded to hand everyone a drink then held his glass aloft.

"What shall we toast to?" he asked.

"To the eventual trial and imprisonment of Budi Kusuma—purveyor of skimpy red g-string underwear and a character I will forever remember as the man with the golden flail," I said.

Everyone clinked glasses, but Mark, Itari, Grieta, and Riya looked particularly confused by my toast, so I decided I should tell them about the sordid details of our experience inside Budi's bedroom. When I was done, everyone quietly pondered the bizarre events of the evening and appeared thankful to be safely back here and well away from their peculiar neighbor to the north.

"I'd heard that Budi was a bit of a pervert and is always trying to lure local girls back to his home. I guess the rumors are true," Grieta said.

"Afraid so."

"I've been to so many official functions with him, that it's still hard to believe what I saw."

"So, what the hell is actually going on here on Malkarta? First, the government violates the five day window they gave me to find Mark, then the biggest capitalist on the island turns out to be the leader of the MSA. None of this makes any sense."

"Anna, who would have the authority to override that grace period?" Itari asked.

"Good question. I suppose it would be limited to my family, a few senior ministers, and possibly even Maas Groot," Anna said.

"Except Maas was the one who managed to get me that week, so it wouldn't make sense for him to go back on it."

"Well, the other possibility would be someone who has my father's ear, which could be just about anyone in his inner circle."

"I get the impression that you and your father don't exactly see eye to eye," I said.

"Not since I returned from college with new opinions about the policies of my home, and the only reason he made me minister of education and social services was just to keep me placated and out of his hair."

"Well then, it looks as though we have a good old fashioned mystery on our hands," I said.

"Afraid so," Anna added.

"Perhaps we'll get some good news when I speak with the vice president in the morning. Malkarta wants that base as much as the US does, so we still have some real leverage, and, if all goes well, we'll get some kind of amnesty for Mark and gain a little time to get a handle on what the hell is actually going on here."

"I certainly hope so. The people here are ready for change, and, if we can't find a way to peacefully transition this island into a better future, that change will come with bloodshed, and many innocent people will pay the price for a few men's greed," Mark said, finishing his drink.

"Same as always," I said, somberly.

We ended up drinking two more pitchers, but the conversation thankfully moved onto more jovial matters—namely tales of life on the island of Malkarta. Itari's wife Riya went and grabbed us all slices of fresh fruit for dessert then began telling us about her unusual upbringing. She, like Itari, grew up on Malkarta and also managed to go to college in Australia before coming home to become a teacher at the local school. Her most humorous tales, however, were a little closer to home and concerned the difficulty of living with a stubborn husband and an obstinate daughter. This of course made me realize that the world was the same no matter how far you traveled from home. The relationships between people, especially husbands, wives, and their children were universal.

We also heard more about Mark and Anna's first meeting, and, while Anna had told us a bit at dinner that night, we were now getting all the juicy details. Apparently, he went into her office expecting a stuffy aristocrat, and instead he found the very beautiful, very caring, and very empathetic girl of his dreams. She, in turn, had been expecting a smelly hippy, and instead she discovered the very handsome, very caring, and equally empathetic man of her dreams. It was like the beginning to a Disney movie in that he was a commoner and she was a princess, and, regardless of what happened in the coming days, they would at least always know that they had found one of life's greatest rewards—true love.

Midnight rolled around, and everyone retired to their respective rooms feeling buzzed and relieved that the night had been successful, and everyone was safe and sound. Fiona and I decided to take a shower, and we enjoyed having some alone time in a proper bathroom, as our last shared shower had been in the camp. We used shampoo then switched to soap and washed each other thoroughly before rinsing off and adjourning to the bed.

"Quite a fucking day," I said.

"Yeah, and being here now, it's hard to believe it all really happened."

"No doubt."

I turned off the lamp beside the bed, and the room came alive with the soft blue light emanating from the sliver moon that was shining in through the bedroom window. Fiona was glowing like an angel, and, as we touched lips and joined tongues, she ran her hand down my chest and into my waistband, where she began stroking the tip of my manhood. Every second was stoking the bonfire of my libido and making me long to explore, so I slid my lips down her neck towards her breasts to find that her nipples were already hard and just begging for some attention. I ran my tongue around each areola then finished up with a gentle nibble that caused Fiona to arch her back and gasp in pleasure. As I was about to move on, I had a sudden tinge of guilt as I considered that Budi's revolting assault might have left her not actually wanting physical contact. I therefore stopped and looked up into her eyes in order to get a feel for her true psychological state.

"Are you sure you're ready for this—considering everything that you went through tonight?" I asked.

"Oh, I'm sure. There's no way in hell that I would let that little fucker get to me, but I am sincerely touched that you would be concerned enough to ask."

"Well, sex is only good when both parties are fully committed."

"Don't you worry about that, because I am fully committed—even more so now. Our time on this earth is just too precious to waste, and besides, I managed to grab a little memento from tonight that I was hoping we could use tonight."

"Oh, so it's OK for you to grab a little memento?" I asked, in reference to her putting the kibosh on my attempt to nab the Playboy from Budi's coffee table.

"Yeah, because my memento is for both of us," she said, pulling a pair of Budi's pink fur-lined handcuffs from under the pillow.

"You didn't happen to grab an extra red g-string as well did you?"

"Sorry, there wasn't enough time. We'll just have to use our imaginations," she said, as she threw her arms up to each side of the center post of the wooden headboard.

"And what about the key?"

"It's under the pillow, but you won't be needing it just yet. Now, stop fucking around and have your way with me."

I was definitely facing an interesting ethical quandary. I desperately wanted to make sweet love to Fiona and had no problem with handcuffing her to the bed, but I would only do so if she were truly comfortable with the experience. As a psychology major, it was clear to me this was some kind of response to her trauma.

"Are you really sure about this? Trauma can manifest itself in a number of ways and..."

"Am I going to have to handcuff myself to this bed?" she interrupted.

Fuck it. Sometimes you just had to go with flow, so I reached up and clicked the cuffs over her wrists and secured her firmly to the bed, where she lay there gazing up at me expectantly, with her breasts rising and falling with each bated breath.

"I feel like a kid in candy store," I said.

"Good, because I'm open for business."

I decided to start at the top and work my way down, with the first stop on my itinerary being her lips, where I was eager for another run-in with her dubious tongue. I discovered my hot and slippery little friend laying in wait, and it darted forward to part my lips like a hot knife through butter. Our tongues became entwined, but remained in constant motion like two dancers encircling one another.

I eventually had to part ways, and I ventured south and again kissed her nipples, all the while treating them in accordance with the foreplay rules set forth in the Geneva Convention. That entailed making sure both were awarded an equal amount of tongue action and continuing to do so until Fiona wriggled with pleasure. Leaving them dangerously hard, I moved down her stomach until I was hovering above her labial range and preparing to make landfall at my next stop.

"Last chance to turn back," I said.

"Do you hear me complaining?"

I made a quick pass and ran my tongue down over her opening, before making a cruel leap to her inner thigh to give it a gentle bite that made her moan in anticipation. I bit the other thigh then finally moved back to the midlands, where I touched down dead center and moved slowly upward and took my time to reach her clitoris. Fiona was practically shaking in anticipation as I slid ever closer, and she wrapped her legs around me and attempted to pull me in, but I held firm and teased her with the torture of withholding sexual gratification. At last I relented and slid my tongue up and over her pleasure button then made slow, deliberate circles that made her entire body so tense that the chain of the handcuffs was making an audible rattle as she pulled against the bed frame. I increased the pressure and speed ever so subtly, and the motion inspired her to open her legs and press her pelvis upward.

With each pass, Fiona cried out a little louder and drew

closer to an unavoidable collision course with an impending climax, and, merely a breath away, I lessened the pace and cruelly ran my tongue down and inside her essence before returning yet again and starting anew. I continued repeating this cycle until she could stand no more, and she all but begged for release. Hearing the longing in her voice, it was officially time for the pièce de résistance, and that meant sliding each of my hands around and under her buttocks, so that I could pull her entire pelvis to my mouth and make her clitoris a prisoner to the whim of my tongue. It drastically intensified her pleasure, and she immediately started into the throws of a violent orgasm, and her entire body began to shake as she rode each successive wave of pleasure with her hips involuntarily spasming until she at last came to rest and had to take a moment to catch her breath.

"Feel better?" I asked, as I leaned back and smiled up at her.

"Yeah, now stop fucking around, and make love to me," she said.

I moved forward and slid my knees under her thighs and steered my hard member to her opening then slowly ran the tip up over her clitoris before dropping back down to taunt her with the promise of penetration. She gasped and strained against the handcuffs, but they held her firmly in place.

"Oh for fuck's sake—you're killing me here. Will you just fucking fuck me!" she pleaded through gritted teeth.

"Believe me, this is a lot harder on me than it is you," I

said.

"Then do us both a favor and…"

At that moment I quelled her complaints by pressing in until our hips came together at full mount, and both of us uttered a lustful gasp. I set about plying the warmth of her female essence by thrusting in and out, and I found myself racing uncontrollably towards release and had to summon a will exceeding that of any mortal man in order to slow down and hold back the spilling of my seed. As we caught our breath, I changed positions and slid my knees back, so I could engage in the oft used missionary position. It may have been mundane, but done properly, afforded an ample amount of clitoral stimulation, and, better still, brought her lips back into proximity of mine. I leaned down and kissed her then pressed my hips into hers and focused on delivering a circular motion rather than going in and out, as it served to limit my own hair trigger while drastically intensifying her pleasure, thus creating a delicate balance that would prolong our union.

Time and reality became meaningless as we hovered on the edge of release, but eventually sheer force of will could no longer hold us back from the inevitable, and we began our approach to the intersection where heaven met earth. I pressed my hips to hers and began thrusting and grinding with every ounce of my remaining strength, and both of us began crying out as we tumbled into the great orgasmic vortex. The sum total of our existence became that moment, and we floated together in ecstasy until emerging back into the world feeling spent as we basked in post coital bliss. At last, we stopped, and the sound of waves rolling in over the nearby beach slowly came back into our awareness.

"Sweet mother of God! I believe that's exactly what I needed," she said.

"Glad I could help," I said, as I un-cuffed her hands.

She rubbed her wrists then wrapped her arms around me and pulled me in for a long kiss before taking a moment to gaze up into my eyes.

"I have to admit that I was pretty scared back at Budi's place tonight," she said.

"As you should have been. No one should ever experience that kind of horror, least of all from a man wearing a red g-string."

"That'll be a tough image to forget," she said.

"For all of us."

We had a moment of quiet introspection before my inner psychology major came out.

"So, I'm assuming the handcuffs were obviously part of a little psychological test."

"Yeah, and I figured it was a quick and easy way to prove to myself that he hadn't gotten to me, and that I could still trust another person."

"Coming to terms with the items of your torment is very insightful, though I think it should be pretty obvious that no silly asshole in a red g-string brandishing a golden flail will ever be able to break your spirit."

"I certainly hope not, though I guess you were right. We

all need a little help sometimes, so, thanks for coming for me tonight."

"My pleasure, and I think you should know that I'm more than happy to come for you as often as you'd like."

Fiona let out a playful groan.

"You know that's the second time you've tried to use that joke tonight."

"Yeah, but don't worry, the third times usually the charm."

"Let's hope so," she said, with a smile.

She gave me a final kiss then placed her head on my chest, and I ran my fingers through her hair as she drifted off to sleep. Now, I was alone with only my thoughts for company as I lay there in the stillness of the night, quietly pondering the peculiarity of the day's events. Some time passed, and I felt a distinct vibration and heard some muffled moans coming through the wall. Clearly, Mark and Anna were also enjoying themselves this evening. I smiled to myself, for I was happy that I had managed to help some people today and achieve something good in this all too often bad world. With that final thought, I closed my eyes and drifted off unto the realm of dreams feeling optimistic that the dawn would bring a better day.

CHAPTER THIRTY-ONE
Citizen Finn

The morning, as I hoped, brought with it a fresh and optimistic outlook for the day ahead, and I rolled over and looked out the window to gaze upon the calm waters of the Banda Sea. The sun was out, and Grieta was looking alluring as ever in a two piece bikini as she walked along the beach and played with Willy. She was indeed a lovely girl though also ballsy, and I imagined that she would go far in life. I rose from bed, hit the bathroom, then took an epic morning horse piss and accidentally let loose one particularly long fart that caused me to giggle to myself.

"You having fun in there?" I heard Fiona ask from the other side of the door.

"What do you mean? I'm just peeing."

"And farting. I heard it from here, thunder pants."

Fuck. I needed to remember not to let my guard down, because, aside from the fact that we had masturbated in front of each other, experienced a dump-shower crossover, and played with some fuzzy pink fur-lined handcuffs, we clearly hadn't crossed the fart barrier yet—well not until now, anyway. I moved to the sink to brush my teeth, and Fiona appeared a moment later, fanning the air.

"Whew, what did you eat last night?" she asked.

"You."

She smiled, but then she had to, because it was technically true.

"I'm going to forage for some coffee. Do you want some?"

"Do you really need to ask?" she responded.

I left the bathroom, threw on some shorts and a T-shirt, then headed downstairs to find Riya in the kitchen. She had already made coffee, and she poured two cups and handed them to me before I could even ask.

"How did you sleep?" she asked, with a knowing smile.

"Very soundly."

"I imagine you did—once you actually went to sleep."

Grieta walked in with Willy at that moment and poured herself a cup of coffee before turning to me.

"Good morning," I said

"Yes it is, and probably even grander after such a good evening," she said, delivering a smile very similar to her mother's.

I was getting the distinct feeling that the walls of the Behrendt house weren't all that soundproof.

"Well, I'll be back down in a bit. I'm going to bring Fiona some coffee."

"Fiona is a very lucky girl," Grieta said.

"She is indeed," Riya added.

Feeling a little awkward after having been double teamed by the Behrendt women, I left with the two cups of coffee and headed back upstairs to find Fiona sitting by the window, where she was gazing out at the sea. When she heard me enter the room, she turned to me and spoke with a hint of sadness in her tone.

"This place is so beautiful, it would be tragic if they don't figure out how to move forward in a way that doesn't cost any innocent lives."

"All too many times throughout history, humanity almost always errs on the side of violence," I said, handing her a cup of coffee.

"Hopefully it'll be different this time."

We sat and drank in silence until about a half of a cup later when I felt a very familiar pressure in my lower abdomen, which meant it was time to use my behind to leave a little bit of myself behind.

"I'm going to hit the head," I said.

"Will you trust me enough to leave the door open?"

"Not likely."

"How about unlocked?"

"I'm not sure I'm ready for that step either."

"I let you handcuff me to the bed."

"That's different."

"You leave it unlocked, and I promise not to disturb you. How about that?"

"I think I'd rather have you handcuff me to the bed."

"Come on, man up and do it."

"Fine."

I went into the bathroom, set my cup on the sink, then instinctively turned to lock the door, but paused and stared at the knob, as I desperately wanted to press the center lock button. I ignored my impulse and sat on the toilet before reaching over and picking up my coffee to take a long sip. I took a moment to relish its flavor then swallowed and exhaled in an effort to try to will myself into a state of optimistic calm. Three more deep breaths and I was ready to tempt fate. I took another sip of coffee and proceeded to literally and figuratively lay waste to the porcelain kingdom. The first salvos went by easily, and, after another sip of coffee, I released the second movement. It wasn't as grand as the first, but it was still satisfactory, and I was starting to feel all warm and fuzzy inside as though I were approaching a bathroom epiphany—something I had only experienced once before on a toilet at a gas station in Switzerland. Maybe, just maybe, I could learn to have a morning movement like a normal person—one without anxiety or fear of karmic retribution from a cruel and unmerciful universe. Perhaps Fiona was right, and I needed to learn to trust fate. She had, after all, been brave enough to let me use Budi's instrument of torture on her last night, so why couldn't I do the same? Interesting. Was this how the moment of enlightenment manifested itself? I closed my eyes, yet felt as though I could finally see. A bright light was forming in my consciousness, and I was feeling yet another glorious wave of release. Suddenly, I heard the doorknob squeak, and I looked over to see it turning and felt the warm light of enlightenment slipping into the dark black hole of regret. My heart nearly stopped, and my sphincter clamped down and violently closed the door on my remaining fecal traveler.

"Goddammit! You promised!" I protested.

"Quit your bitching! I'm just checking to see if you kept your word."

"Same difference. Now, step away from the door!"

"You can relax, princess. I'm not coming in."

The joy was officially gone as I took a moment to relax, catch my breath, and release my final fecal refugee. Finished, I rose from the pot, flushed, and entered the shower and felt like one of James Bond's martinis—shaken, though in this case, a little stirred. Shit. Did that count as an official bathroom incursion? Was it a harbinger of some kind of imminent doom, or was it a simple hiccup in my morning routine? Only fate knew for certain, so I decided to err on the side of optimism and continued with the task at hand—namely enjoying a refreshing morning shower. I poured out a dollop of shampoo and relished the fresh floral scent as I massaged it in and basked under the torrent of water. I heard the door open, and I peeked around the curtain and saw Fiona walking in with her coffee in hand.

"Are you coming to join me?"

"Not yet."

"Then what are you here for?"

"Sorry, but I really need to use the bathroom."

"Wait a minute. One or two."

"Two."

"Not again."

"Afraid so, but you should be used to it by now."

"One dump does not a pattern make."

"Don't worry, I'll open the window."

"Seriously? You can't wait?"

"No, and this is what you get for waking me up with a fart," she said, as she took a sip of coffee and dropped onto the toilet.

"Aren't you the least bit afraid of killing the romance?" I asked.

"Do you have any less desire to fuck me because I'm taking a shit?"

"At this exact moment—yes, but in the bigger picture—no," I said, in a slightly dejected tone.

"Well, there you go."

Fuck, she was right, but I still retreated behind the curtain and grabbed the soap as a kind of scented lifeline as I awaited for the inevitable armageddon. Strangely, there were no explosive farts or great fecal splashes, but I could envision the process nonetheless. I therefore tried to breath through my mouth, and it was appearing to work, as no traces of her morning business were reaching my olfactory awareness while I cowered like a cornered animal. She abruptly finished and flushed the toilet, which of course gave me no warning to try and make it out from under the water before it turned scaldingly hot.

"Dildo Baggins's burning balls!" I yelled, as I jumped back and away from the shower head.

"Oh sorry, I always forget how the toilet affects the flow of cold water to the shower," she said, as she joined me a moment later.

The water temperature returned to normal, and she edged me out of the way and proceeded to wet her main of long hair.

"Anyone ever tell you you're a shower hog?"

"Would you rather bathe alone?" she asked, as she pressed her slippery breasts against me and took hold of my manhood.

"Not anymore."

"Good. Now quit your whining and hand me the shampoo."

I handed it over, and she lathered up her hair while I grabbed the soap and did the same to her body, paying special attention to her breasts, thighs, buttocks, and sensitive lady bits. Once we were both good and soapy, we stepped under the water, rinsed, then exchanged a kiss that quickly grew in intensity until we were full on making out. I pulled her close and our mingling of bodies inspired a real growth spurt in my gentleman region. Fiona felt it pressing against her thighs and took hold of it and managed to get it good and hard before abruptly turning and exiting the shower.

"Cocktease," I muttered.

"Sorry, I just decided that I wanted to make sure you had

something left for later."

"Oh, don't you worry—there'll be plenty."

"Good to know," she said, as she exited the bathroom.

I turned off the water, grabbed a towel, and dried off before heading out to the bedroom. We both dressed then headed downstairs, and, annoyingly, I could still feel a real longing still present in my now diminished manhood. Cruel indeed were the women of this world. We arrived at the table, where everyone was waiting patiently though expectantly, and I sat and placed the satellite phone beside my cup while Riya, the best hostess in the world, came over and poured me more coffee before taking a seat beside Itari. I added cream and took a sip then looked down at my plate and smiled. Riya had also made scrambled eggs, sausages, and fresh fruit for breakfast. I dug in feeling ever happy to replenish all the calories I had burned in both the rescue operation and the sweet-ass lovemaking session with Fiona. When I was finished, I took another sip of coffee then picked up the phone, dialed John, and hit the speakerphone button before placing it in the center of the table.

"Well, here we go," I said, as I looked around to see everyone looking a bit nervous.

"I hope something good comes from this," Mark said.

"Yeah, and I think I should warn everyone that the vice president and Tag have quite a history together and tend to use some colorful language," Fiona said, directing her warning to Itari, Riya, and Grieta.

John picked up on the second ring.

"About fucking time, Shit Storm," he said.

"You sound cranky. Did we interrupt your mid-morning high colonic?"

"Yeah, but it's not the same without you here to hold the hose and the bucket."

"It never is."

"So, anything exciting happen since we last talked?"

"Not much, except we were captured by MSA rebels, and Mark and I had to make a daring escape from one of their camps only minutes before they were planning to execute us."

"Ha! If only I had a nickel for every time someone was planning to kill you and you survived."

"Yeah, yeah—you'd probably have a fuckload of nickels, so be happy that I'm still alive and only making you wealthy in the metaphorical sense."

"So, where in the hell were Anna and Fiona during all this?"

"They were being held prisoner by the Man with the Golden Flail, but we managed to pull off a hostage rescue mission late last night, so everyone is safe and sound, and I should also mention that the people who helped us pull that off just happen to be with us at this very moment. First up is Itari Behrendt, a man who is also the leader of Malkarta's Democratic Alliance, and next is his lovely wife Riya as well as their beautiful and fiery daughter Grieta."

John was quiet for a long moment before letting out a long, pained sounding sigh.

"Are we by chance on speaker phone again?" he asked.

"Of course. How else could I introduce you all to each other?"

"Goddammit, Finn! Would you mind warning me next time!"

"I'll try—but I just get so excited when I hear your voice that I get all flustered and forget."

"I'm sorry, everyone. My colorful language was intended only for Finn's un-delicate ears. So, what say we move on to more important matters—such as proper introductions. It's nice to meet you Mr. Behrendt, as well as your lovely wife Riya and you're beautiful and fiery daughter Grieta."

Fucking John had a memory for names that bordered on super human, which was probably part of why he had done so well in politics. Of course, he also had bucketloads of genuine charm—with the case in point being that Itari and his family were now exchanging giddy smiles at having been officially addressed by the vice president of the United States.

"I'm very pleased to finally meet you as well, sir, though I wish it were in person and under better circumstances," Itari said.

"Yes indeed, so, Finn, what news do we have on our situation over there?"

"I'll leave that up to Itari, as he's clearly the expert in this area," I said.

Itari explained the current social and political situation in Malkarta and the fact that the island was on the verge of serious change and possibly even a violent coup if the MSA continued to gain favor.

"And you're sure about this?" John asked, with legitimate concern in his voice.

"Absolutely. Change is coming, and the best hope for nonviolent reform means getting the monarchy to work with us in bringing this island into the modern world. That means bringing about equal rights and privileges for all of its citizens and not just the ruling class. Anything short of that and we could be looking at armed insurrection."

"We certainly don't want another civil war or rogue regime on our hands, least of all, when we need a staging area for anti-terrorist operations in that part of the world. Assuming you can achieve some kind of working relationship with the existing government or even form one of your own, would you be in favor of our plans to build a base?"

"I can say with absolute certainty that the MDA would be completely in agreement—assuming we could actually get that far, of course."

"Well then, Mr. Behrendt, you have my word that I'll do all I can from my end."

"Of course, we have to face the fact that my father will not accept change very easily," Anna added.

"It appears he'll have to—one way or the other," I said.

"Good point. OK then, friends, I'll see what I can do and get back to you as soon as I have anything."

"Thank you, Mr. Vice President," Itari said.

"Yeah, thank you again for all you've done," Mark added.

"You're welcome, everyone."

"OK, Sasquatch, we'll talk soon," I said.

"Well?"

"Well what?" I asked.

"You know what."

"Fine, I'll say it first. I love you," I said.

"I love you too," he said, before hanging up, which now left the room completely silent.

Riya was the first to speak.

"You certainly have a rather close relationship with the vice president," she said, with a chuckle.

"Finn saved his life when they were in the military," Fiona said.

"Well that certainly explains the camaraderie," Itari added.

"So, now I guess we have nothing to do but wait," I said.

"And hope the Malkarta Security Forces don't find us in the meanwhile," Mark responded.

"Or the MSA," Fiona added.

"No need to worry. I posted sentries throughout the area, so we'll have plenty of warning if anyone comes our way."

"Well, in that case, we might as well clean up and hit the beach," I said, bringing my plate to the sink, where I started washing it.

"I'll get that," Riya said, trying to pull it from my hands.

"No way. You've been a gracious hostess, so I want to help."

My mother always taught me to be a gracious guest, so

I figured helping to clean up after breakfast was the least I could do to help repay the Behrendts for their kindness and generosity.

"No, let me clean up! You are a guest in my home!" she pleaded.

"Exactly!" I said, maintaining my grip on the plate.

"OK, fine. You wash, and I'll dry."

She turned her scrutinizing gaze to Itari.

"You know you could learn a thing or two from Tag," she said.

Grieta laughed, which inspired Riya to turn to her next.

"You too," she said.

When Riya turned back to the sink, both Grieta and Itari gave me a mild look of annoyance. Oh well, I always found it to be a good idea to be in favor with the lady of the house, because they often had the real power. I turned back and set to work on the sink full of dishes, and ten minutes later we had the kitchen cleaned up, so we decided to head out to the beach. I changed back into my board shorts, and Fiona and Anna borrowed bikinis from Grieta. They weren't exactly a perfect fit, but they were good enough for a little fun and sun, and the ever so subtle lack of material in their swimsuits made it all the more interesting for the menfolk. We set our towels down on the deck then stepped out onto the warm sand to gaze at the beautiful expanse of bright blue ocean. First to step into the water was our hostess Riya, who looked quite nice in a bikini, and I could see where her daughter got her fabulous figure. Next was Fiona, then Anna and Grieta, and the sight of all four of them frolicking in the waves was far too enticing for any sane man to resist, so Mark, Itari, and I joined them shortly thereafter.

We played in the ocean, swam, snorkeled, and had what amounted to an unbelievably calm and wonderful morning considering the storm of potential anarchy that loomed just over the horizon. After several hours of joyous abandon, a unanimous decision was made to get out and take up residence beneath the large canvas awning that hung over the Behrendt's beachside deck. Conversation filled the air, and it felt as though we were just a group of friends enjoying a proper day on the beach, until the sat-phone rang, and everyone's eyes turned to me as I hit the answer button then pressed speakerphone, so that all could hear.

"What's the latest, Sasquatch?" I asked.

"Don't you mean Yeti?"

"No, but I'd settle for Bigfoot."

"More like Bigcock."

I, of course, giggled, but John took this as an ominous sign, and there was a pause, and all I could hear was his breathing until he came back on the line.

"Are we on fucking speakerphone again?"

"Of course, Bigcock. Any other nicknames you want to put out there?"

"Yeah, how about we call you Little Asshole."

"I can live with that."

"Good, so how about we switch to a subject people actually want to hear about?" John responded.

"Good idea," Fiona said.

"Alrighty then, let's hear it," I said, desperately hoping John had pulled off some kind of diplomatic miracle.

"OK, but I suggest everyone sit down."

"Meaning?"

"Meaning, I've managed to get Mark a decree of temporary amnesty."

Everyone erupted with cheers.

"There's more. I've also managed to get you a meeting with King Jacob De Vries today at one p.m., so you'll have an opportunity to relay the direness of the situation on Malkarta."

"John, you're a miracle worker."

"I know, and that's why I'm in politics."

"I always thought it was for the money, power, favors, and women."

"Well, that too, but it feels nice to actually do a little good now and then."

"Thanks again, Sasquatch."

"You're welcome, but don't be celebrating too much just yet. A happy ending here ultimately comes down to your ability to convince the King that his cooperation in bringing about positive change is the only way to save his kingdom."

"Don't worry, I have all the confidence in the world that Itari and Mark can do that once we're face to face."

"All right then. Good luck, everyone," John said, before hanging up.

I hit the end button and noticed that Mark was looking

particularly concerned.

"You OK?" I asked.

"Yeah, just a little nervous thinking about all that's riding on this meeting today. I could be deported or imprisoned, and the same could happen to Itari since we're all technically dissidents."

"That's true. The MDA are looked upon just as unfavorably as the MSA," Itari added.

"Of course, the much bigger problem is that Malkarta could end up in a full blown civil war," Mark said.

"Buck up, campers. We've gotten this far haven't we?" I said.

"I suppose," Mark responded, trying to sound hopeful.

He was justified in worrying, but such thoughts wouldn't help anyone at the moment. What we needed most was a positive outlook, as it would be more likely to give us the strength to face a very stubborn and rigid man whose family had owned and controlled this island for the last four hundred years. King Jacob De Vries was our final, potentially insurmountable obstacle and the key to a better life for thousands of people—six of them sitting right here on this very deck.

CHAPTER THIRTY-TWO
Back to the Future

We gathered up our things and headed inside to get ready for the big meeting, and Fiona and I again shared the shower, though she at least refrained from any more of her cocktease hijinks, and it allowed me to exit clean and free of blue balls. I got dressed, and, at the last minute, slid my silenced pistol into the small of my back, where I made sure it was covered by my unbuttoned shirt. I doubted I would need it, but I still wasn't sure how to interpret the morning's *dumpus-interruptus*. Was it an omen of impending doom or a false alarm? Only time would tell. We went downstairs and found Itari in his office, and he was looking very serious as he talked on the phone, so Fiona and I waited patiently until he finished his conversation.

"Important call?" I asked, after he hung up.

"Very much so, and possibly even the difference between life and death."

"Was it your proctologist?"

He laughed.

"Yes, and he said I was full of shit," he responded.

Now I was the one laughing, though I was still a little curious about Itari's mysterious phone call. The others soon arrived, and we piled into Itari's Land Rover and headed south towards New Leiden. The drive would take about an hour, but the weather was lovely, and I enjoyed a first class tour of the entire upper eastern side of Malkarta. It was beautiful, and the hills were covered by dense jungle, and every inch was rife with flowers, wildlife, and picturesque waterfalls. As we traveled farther south, we came to the open fields where they grew the various spices, and I could see the armies of workers toiling away in the hot Malkarta sun. Soon thereafter, we passed Itari's bar, and, thirty-five minutes later, we were on the outskirts of New Leiden and navigating the light midday traffic before pulling into the royal palace. Itari stopped in front of the guard station, and Anna leaned forward and told him we were expected. The guard immediately recognized Anna then waved us through, and we parked directly in front of the main entrance. We exited the vehicle, and everyone was looking particularly anxious as we followed Anna inside to the main lobby. I noticed that they had a metal detector, and I realized it would surely uncover the fact that I had a gun on my person. As I tried to think of a way around this unforeseen obstacle, Anna led us around the metal detector and up the large center staircase. Phew! As I looked around, I realized I probably didn't really need to worry, as there weren't any guards in attendance at the moment, but this made me wonder where they might be. Was it a shift change, or had they just been posted elsewhere?

We reached the top of the stairs and made a left onto a grand hallway that ended at a large set of oak double doors. Anna knocked then opened them, so that all of us could enter the official royal office. The interior was stately, and the walls were adorned with portraits of the De Vries ancestors while the center of the room was occupied by royal blue colored European style couches and matching chairs that formed a fancy conference area. A short distance away and sitting in front of the windows was the king's oak desk, though it was unoccupied at the moment, as King Jacob De Vries and Queen Isabella were sitting on one of the couches. Maas was also there, but he was in one of the nearby chairs, and he was looking quite content as he sipped coffee from a fine white china cup. There were also two security people standing off in the corners of the room, and one was my old buddy Sten while the other was a man I didn't recognize. All eyes turned to us, and Jacob and Isabella, looking ever relieved to see Anna safe and sound, proceeded to stand up and come over.

"We've been so worried about you, dear. First you disappear without a trace, and then we hear that you had been captured by MSA rebels," she said, as she hugged Anna.

"It was quite an ordeal, but you can thank Tag, Mark, and Itari Behrendt and his family for my timely rescue."

Jacob and Isabella turned their attention to us, though

Isabella spoke first.

"It's good to see you again, Mr. Behrendt and you too, Mark, and I must say it's a pleasure to finally meet you, Mr. Finn."

"It's a pleasure to meet you as well and please call me Tag."

"Tag it is."

I took a moment to gaze at Isabella, and I now understood where Anna got her looks. Isabella was truly beautiful—tall, blond, and statuesque with blazingly bright blue eyes and a smile that could melt men's hearts from across the room. She smiled then stepped back to made room for Jacob, who came forward to make his official introductions.

"So nice to see you again, Mark," he said, with his tone free of any hint of malice.

Mark waited until they were already shaking hands before responding.

"And you as well," he said, trying his best to sound sincere.

Jacob moved on to Itari, but he gazed at him for a moment before speaking.

"Wow, it's been a really long time since we've seen each other, Itari," he said, shaking his hand.

"Yes, I believe the last time was during the fundraising dinner for the university I wanted to create."

"It's too bad that didn't pan out," Jacob said, though I didn't know him well enough to detect if he was being sincere or just talking out of his ass.

He then turned his attention to me and offered his hand, and I had a close look at the other half of Anna's excellent genetics. He, like his wife and daughter, was good looking as well as tall and imposing, but, his gruff demeanor seemed to subtly diminish his attractiveness.

"It's very nice to meet you, Tag," he said.

"You too, your majesty, and might I say you have one hell of a daughter. Not many people could have kept such a stiff upper lip in the face of adversity."

"Yes, though that same trait also makes her quite difficult at times."

"Jacob!" the queen protested.

"Oh relax, my dear. It's a father's prerogative to complain about his daughter. Now, would someone please introduce me to this lovely young lady!"

"Of course, father. This is Mark's sister Fiona Blake," Anna said.

Interestingly, Jacob appeared to recognize her as he took hold of her hand and kissed it, which made me suspect that he too might be a fan of Playboy Magazine. Men will be men—royal or not.

"A pleasure to meet you, my dear."

Now, it was Maas who stepped forward and shook everyone's hand before hugging Anna and looking relieved to see her safe and sound.

"Now that we've all been properly introduced, I'd like to thank all of you for delivering Anna from harm and back to us. So, with that, I suppose we should get this meeting underway, as I'm curious what you wanted to speak to me about. Vice President Matheson was incredibly adamant though decidedly vague," Jacob said.

"That's probably why he's only managed to make it as high as vice president," I said.

"Funny—because one thing he did say was that I shouldn't be too surprised if you poked fun at his job title."

"The vice president and Tag have been friends a long time," Anna interjected.

"I got that impression, now, please come have a seat," Jacob said, gesturing for us to follow him over to the circle of chairs and couches.

Everyone took a seat and quietly waited for Jacob to start the meeting.

"All right, who would like to begin?" Jacob asked.

Interestingly, Jacob made no mention about the fact that my one week grace period had been unceremoniously recalled then reinstated, and it made me wonder if it was a deliberate omission or the simple fact that he just didn't give a flying fuck. Oh well, I suppose the fact that we had gotten this meeting meant we should forget the past and move on. Mark and Itari exchanged a look, then Mark started giving a detailed account of his work over the last two years and the overwhelming discontent the people were voicing about the government—some of it even going so far as to hint that armed rebellion was being planned by the more radical factions such as the MSA. At this point, Mark passed the torch to Itari to take over the conversation, and he cleared his throat and provided a more detailed account of the actual number of people known to have joined the MSA as well as the fact that armed insurrection was indeed brewing. Itari was an excellent speaker and delivered his words with such passion and sincerity that it left Jacob looking quite upset as he rubbed his chin and tried to process the information.

"I just can't believe that the people are really this close to armed insurrection. Maas, what do you think?"

"Well, your majesty, our intelligence services have been reporting increased MSA activity."

"We can definitely confirm that fact having just experienced it first hand at one of their camps. Those men were definitely training for something big," I said.

"I always assumed the MSA were a bunch of armchair revolutionaries," Jacob responded.

"They might have been in the past, but now they're becoming a halfway a decent force with their capitalist leader Budi Kusuma running things."

"Excuse me? Did you just infer that Budi Kusuma is associated with the MSA?" Jacob asked sounding incredulous.

"I'm not inferring anything. I'm telling you straight up without a doubt that he's their unofficial leader. I take it that no one has told you he was the man holding your daughter captive?"

"No," Jacob said, turning to look at Maas.

"It's ridiculous, your majesty. Budi is a respectable citizen of Malkarta, and, as such, he would no sooner be involved with the MSA or kidnapping than you or I."

"Sorry, Maas, but your resident Uncle Tom is a two faced piece of shit—and a bit of a pervert to boot."

"But why would he kidnap Anna?" Jacob pleaded.

"I'm afraid only Budi could answer that question, but, ultimately, he's only a small part of the problem. The real thing to worry about here is that the MSA is gaining traction with the general populace, and the longer the people remain feeling disenfranchised the more likely that they will turn against the government," Itari said.

Jacob sat there thinking, and deep worry lines became visible on his forehead.

"Your majesty, I've been all over the world and seen a lot of governments, big and small, fall prey to the whim of an angry populace, so I can tell you without a doubt that change is coming whether you like it or not. You can either embrace it now and be a part of it or ignore it and be a victim to its whim," I added.

Jacob took a moment to think, and there was a real uncertainty growing behind his eyes.

"My family has ruled this island for four hundred years. I was born to serve Malkarta, and it's all I have ever known in my life. You may not believe it but, I love this island and its people. I just can't give it up and walk away."

"You aren't walking away from anything. This is about you facing it head on by embracing change. Be the one to reform this island. All the people need to quell their anger is for you to let them know positive change is real and it's coming, and let's face it, Malkarta's spice industry generates enough income to make this island a first world nation with excellent education, fair wages, and a bright future. Is that really so crazy in this day and age?" Itari said.

"But what about my legacy to this office—to this family?"

"You will always be king, but the important thing is to be a good one, and that entails improving the lives of your people. You have an opportunity to make history—to use your title and position to do something good," Mark interjected.

"Father, you have to see that what he's saying makes sense."

Jacob sat there and had turmoil behind his eyes as he processed all the information he was hearing. Honestly, I kind of felt bad for the man. It wasn't his fault that he was born into this existence, so who would blame him for being afraid of change. When it came down to it—we were all afraid of change. Fear was the single most limiting factor to our growth as human beings, though I could see the look of fear on Jacob's face as a sign that he believed that the winds of change were blowing towards this palace at this very moment. Mark, sensing an opening, continued the conversation.

"Your Majesty, you have a daughter, so you therefore understand what it means to want for a decent life for your child. Anna has had all the things that a person deserves—loving parents, a good life, and a good education, so is it so crazy that your people want the same for their children?

Done right, Malkarta could be the cultural jewel of Indonesia."

Jacob sighed, and his expression was weary as he rubbed his hands over his forehead. Fear was a heavy burden on the soul, and I was witnessing its effects first hand. Still, a little fear might be enough motivation to help him to see the path to a better future.

"I just don't know what to do," he said, turning his gaze to Isabella then Maas, who shrugged as he was unsure how to comfort his king.

As Jacob sat there pondering the fate of Malkarta, I realized I was excited to be a witness to this incredible meeting, and it made me think about the founding fathers of the United States and what it must have been like to be around at the beginning of a great political and social change. Itari also appeared to be excited and decided to step in to take up the charge.

"I understand your trepidation, your Majesty, but mind you, no one expects this to happen overnight. We can ease into reform, make it work for everyone—you included. The most important thing we need to do right now is avoid armed insurrection, and the easiest way to do that is to let the people of Malkarta know that you care. All you have to do is acknowledge that you're willing to initiate reforms—anything to quell the anger."

As Jacob was about to respond, shots started ringing out in the nearby courtyard, and everyone dove for cover. Sten and the other security man both pulled out pistols and moved to the window, then Sten dropped back down and turned his attention to Maas.

"Um, sir, you might want to come see this," he said.

Maas joined him at the window and glanced outside before dropping back down, with his expression anxious as he regarded everyone in the room.

"I believe things may have reached the boiling point they have been telling us about," he said.

CHAPTER THIRTY-THREE
No Country for Old Men

I moved to the window and peered out at the courtyard below to see a large number of men in fatigues pouring onto the grounds, and they were firing their AK forty sevens as they made their way closer to the royal palace. Apparently, the MSA we saw in the camp had indeed been training for something big—namely a coup. The Malkarta Security Forces were returning fire, but the larger number of the aggressors appeared to be allowing them to make headway and move closer to the palace. At that moment, a stray bullet impacted the building just above me, and I decided it was time to get the fuck away from the window. I dropped back down and saw that Maas was now on the other side of the room, and he was pacing back and forth as he spoke animatedly into the radio mic on his lapel. He finally stopped and took a minute to listen, then Jacob, looking dire as he held Isabella in his arms, turned to Maas.

"What's happening?" he asked.

"MSA rebels are storming the palace, my Lord."

"Can you call in more troops?"

"I'm trying," he said, turning his attention back to his radio.

Several tense sounding conversations occurred before he turned back to Jacob.

"Reports are coming in that all of our forces are otherwise engaged with multiple attacks taking place all over the island."

"Maybe we should check the local news," I said.

It was a common phenomena that intelligence agencies often got their news from the same places as civilians, so I figured it wouldn't be a bad idea to get a feel for the scope of the attack. Jacob grabbed a remote control off his desk and turned on the flat screen television that resided on the far wall. A moment later the screen turned on, but it only showed a static logo that said the channel was off the air— probably not a good sign.

"I take it that's the channel for the local news station?" I asked.

"Yes," Jacob said, gravely.

"Let's try the internet."

Maas went over to the king's computer and brought up a browser and typed in the URL for the local online news site and got an error message.

"If they have taken over all of the media, then they've

likely already taken control of most of New Leiden," Maas said.

The shooting outside seemed to be coming closer, and everyone tried their best to get as far away from the window as possible. Not being the kind of person to sit idly by, I did the opposite and crawled closer, so I could take another look for myself. Popping up to take a quick peak, I realized that things were pretty much exactly as we thought—utterly fucked. Judging by the sound of gunfire, the Malkarta Security men were obviously holed up on the lower floor of the palace trying to fight off the MSA, who were spread out around the adjacent grounds. My little battlefield analysis was interrupted a second later when a fusillade of shots came through the windows and elicited a number of screams as shattered glass flew across the room. Maas got back on his radio and frantically issued orders until his gaze turned grave, and he turned to Jacob.

"Your Majesty, I'm afraid we have to try and get you and everyone else out of here right now!"

The other security man and Sten moved towards Jacob and Isabella, then the entire entourage started moving towards the door. Maas, who was listening intently to his radio, suddenly paused.

"It's too late. They have taken control of the bottom floor of the palace," he said.

"Isn't there another way out?" I asked.

"We could try the fire escape. It's accessible via the adjacent anteroom," Maas said.

Just as we reached the door to the anteroom, the shooting outside abruptly stopped.

"What do you think is happening?" I asked Maas.

"No idea."

He got on his radio and asked for a situation report then listened intently and looked visibly shaken as he turned his attention to the group.

"My men are holding at the stairs, so, apparently, we are in a bit of a standoff, and the MSA have requested a meeting. I'm going to go talk with them and see what I can do. Nils, you and Sten stay here and guard the royal family with your lives if need be."

"Yes, sir," Nils and the Sten responded.

Jacob looked more confused than terrified as he stared back at Maas.

"You can't be serious," Jacob said.

"Your Majesty. I will personally do everything in my power to see that you and your family are not harmed. If I do not return, may I say that it was my greatest pleasure serving you."

With that, he turned and left, and the room became eerily silent, and I looked at Mark and Itari.

"I guess you guys were right about that whole unrest thing."

"Sadly, yes, though I wish we had been wrong," Itari said.

"What happens now?" Fiona asked.

"Hard to say. This is obviously what the MSA were training for at the camp and probably the reason they wanted

Mark dead."

"This can't be happening!" Jacob exclaimed, with his voice a mixture of anxiety and anger.

"Don't worry, your majesty. We're all going to get the hell out of here one way or another," I said.

I decided to have a little strategy talk with Sten.

"What do you make of all this?" I asked.

"Not sure yet. We had absolutely no idea this was coming."

"I see you don't have a radio mic like Nils and Maas."

"Afraid not. I was called in directly from home and didn't have time to grab all my gear."

Five minutes later, there was a knock, then the double doors opened, and Maas walked in with his expression grave.

"What is it, Maas?" Jacob asked.

"Your Majesty, I have negotiated a temporary surrender and have good news and bad news."

"Meaning?"

"They have agreed to let you live if you abdicate the throne and leave Malkarta immediately."

"And what about my family?"

"They may also leave."

"What if I refuse?"

"Then they will likely imprison and eventually kill us all. There really isn't any choice, sir. Stay and die or leave and live to fight another day."

"And what about the rest of us?" I asked.

"You may leave as well, and the sooner the better. Things are extremely tense, and I fear the situation could change at any moment."

Jacob stood and paced back and forth, with his eyes lost in thought as he obviously pondered the end to his family's empire. He turned and looked at Isabella and Anna, and his expression was grim as he realized that he had only one decision left to make as the King of Malkarta.

"Maas, please make the necessary preparations for us to leave immediately," he said.

Maas left the room, and Jacob went and sat at his desk—very likely for the last time. He looked like a broken man as he took a moment to look around at the visages of his various ancestors, who all gazed back from their stately portraits. I too looked at the walls and saw the years of history laid bare in the form of pictures, paintings, and medals from various wars. There was even a picture of Maas looking young and proud in his uniform. Fiona came over and stood beside me and took my hand in hers.

"Think about what this means to the people of Malkarta," she said, her voice filled with sadness.

"Yeah, it's terrible. An MSA regime will be even worse than life under the monarchy."

Jacob, who was standing nearby scowled at me.

"Sorry—no offense intended," I said, to him.

"None taken."

It was an unintentionally funny moment to me, though obviously not to Jacob. Oh well, humor is what people needed during moments of extreme stress. Our awkward moment was interrupted a moment later, however, when the door opened, and Maas appeared.

"I have been ordered to take everyone out of the palace, so that we may be escorted to the airport."

Maas walked over and stood beside the King and Queen as they began their slow, sad progression towards the door, and everyone fell in behind them a moment later. As I stood there watching the events unfold, I suddenly felt my *scrot-sense* tingling. There was something nagging at the back of my mind, but I couldn't put my finger on it. I let my thoughts drift as I looked at the people in the room, and, for some reason, I became fixated on Maas and his incredible composure during such a difficult time. Next, I glanced at the picture of him on the wall yet again, and there it was—the answer, and I was surprised I had missed it before this moment.

"Wait a minute," I said, to everyone.

They all came to a stop and turned to look at me.

"Your majesty, I don't think that you should be leaving just yet."

"Why?" Jacob asked.

"I believe that this entire affair is a very sophisticated plot to remove you from office."

"Well, of course it is, though I would hardly call it so-phisticated."

"Oh no, it definitely is, sir."

"I don't understand," Jacob responded.

"I believe that your friend Maas here is working directly with the MSA and has very likely co-engineered this entire coup."

"Don't be ridiculous! He's my head of security and oldest, most loyal friend and confidante."

"Really, Finn, you're being ridiculous and putting everyone's life in danger," Maas said, angrily.

"Well then, care to explain what you were doing at the MSA camp where Anna, Mark, Fiona, and I were being held?"

Maas looked uncomfortable and averted his eyes momentarily, which inadvertently confirmed that my suspicions had been correct.

"Did you really see Maas there?" Anna asked.

"Yes, though I was keeping that little fact a secret until the right time—which, as it turns out, is right now," I said, clearly embellishing and playing a hunch.

"I don't believe it," Jacob said.

"Well, you will once I explain it to you and reveal how it all goes back to our resident capitalist Budi Kusuma."

"But what the hell does that have to do with Maas?" Jacob asked.

"I believe the two of them are working together and have been for a long time, with this coup being the culmination of years of careful preparation. Now, take a look at this picture and see for yourselves," I said, pointing at the picture on the wall.

Everyone turned their gaze to the picture.

"It's just an old picture of Maas from when he was in the Malkartan unit in the Dutch military," Jacob said.

"Yes, but it's also what I suspect is the beginning of a lifelong friendship. You see, I believe Maas and Budi are army buddies, old friends, and, more importantly, business partners."

"Ridiculous!" Maas said, angrily.

"Not ridiculous at all. In fact, if you look closely, you'll see a young Maas, and there behind him in the next row is a young Budi, as they were both in the Malkartan unit of the Dutch Army," I said, pointing out Budi.

Maas was starting to look uncomfortable.

"Yes, we were both in the army together. It doesn't mean anything. Clearly, Finn has no idea what he's talking about," Maas said.

"Oh, I believe I do. You see, Maas and Budi go back even farther than that—namely the Dutch Royal Military Academy. When I first met Maas, I noticed his tie clip with the academy's crest, and, as we already know, Budi attended the academy at the same time as Maas."

"How could you possibly know that?" Jacob asked.

"Itari told me, though I also saw Budi's diploma on the wall of his office when I was rescuing Anna and Fiona."

"Again, that doesn't mean anything," Maas countered.

"Oh I think it does, as everyone knows that school ties run deep, and I suspect that it has been this friendship and connection between you two that has allowed Budi to build up such an impressive empire here on Malkarta. That's no easy feat for a non-Dutch person, so he would need help from the inside—help that you were more than willing to give in exchange for a piece of the pie. But wealth is only one part of the equation, while the other half is power. I imagine that you were also tired of working for the man and decided that you wanted to be the man, and that meant getting rid of Jacob and his family."

"Maas, please tell me this can't be true!" Jacob pleaded, looking sincerely confused.

Maas puffed up a bit before he spoke.

"It's all a bunch of lies, your majesty. Clearly Finn has some other agenda here."

"Yeah, an agenda to find the truth."

I had a moment to think about the entirety of my time in Malkarta, and more pieces started coming together to complete the puzzle.

"It all makes perfect sense!" I said.

"Would you mind sharing?" Jacob protested.

"Your majesty—who rescinded my one week amnesty to find Mark?" I asked.

"No one."

"Really? Then why did the Security Services follow us to the bar last night and try to take Mark into custody?"

Jacob looked confused as he turned to gaze at Maas.

"Just as I suspected. You see, Anna told me Maas was your eyes and ears, which means he is very capable of controlling what you know—or, in this case, what you don't know. He decided it was better to eliminate Mark, and he used me to find him, so I'm guessing he had a tracking sensor on Anna's Land Rover."

"Seriously now, Finn, you're starting to sound like a crazy conspiracy theorist," Maas said.

"Well, initially I thought you might have seen the note on Anna's desk, but then I remembered you needed glasses when you signed Mark's release documents. You therefore couldn't have possibly read her note from where you were standing, so that meant you needed another way, and what's more simple than a tracking device?"

"If that were the case, then why did we give up the chase? We could have easily picked all of you up last night!" Maas said, angrily.

"So, you know by not denying it that you just admitted to canceling Mark's amnesty?"

"No, well—yes, but I only did so in the interest of getting him back into custody for his own safety."

"Nice try, but the real answer is that you realized the easiest way to get rid of all of us was to use your MSA buddies for a little wet work. You knew damn well that we were hiding just off the road, but you decided to call off the chase, so that we could be captured the next morning. That way, you'd look completely innocent to the rest of the world when all this came to light. It also explains how the MSA found us in that camp and how they managed to follow Mark and me when we made our glorious escape. The only constant was Anna's Land Rover."

Maas stood there looking conflicted until something

changed in his expression. It was the look of determination—the look of a man who had a plan and would do anything to see it through, and all of a sudden he reached into his jacket and pulled out a very large Sig Sauer forty-five caliber pistol then pointed it at Jacob's head.

"Well, your majesty, I had hoped to achieve this in a far less violent manner. Unfortunately, Mr. Finn's revelations have changed all that."

"Maas! You can't possibly mean that!"

"I'm afraid I do."

"What do you plan to do?"

"I was hoping you'd all leave quietly, but now I'm afraid you all have to die."

"You can't expect to kill us all and get away with it," Jacob protested.

"Oh, I can—and just like Finn said, I'll blame it all on the MSA rebels who stormed the palace."

"But then you'll have America to deal with," I said.

"Exactly, but I'll be the hero of the hour when I retake Malkarta from the rebels."

"That's ridiculous," Jacob said.

Maas was a serious asshole, but he was also a seriously clever asshole.

"More like ingenious," I responded.

Everyone looked at me.

"It's true. Think about it. To the outside world, Maas will be a hero. No one knows that he and Budi control the MSA and used them to engineer this entire coup as a very clever act. Once all of you are out of the way, they'll have everything—the industry, the money, and even the contract with the United States to put in the Naval Base."

"But, General, you can't be serious about doing this. It's cold blooded murder," Sten said.

"I am, and you would be wise to follow me. You and all my men stand to do very well in my new government, and this will be your repayment for serving your country well."

"How can you do this to us, Maas?" Anna asked.

"Well, to be truthful, I would have preferred to spare you, my dear. You see, I have always liked you, though I can't imagine any relationship forming after what I'm about to do to your parents and friends."

"Definitely not, so I guess you'll just have to kill me too," she said.

"Too bad. I shall miss you dearly."

I glanced at Anna.

"I told you he had a thing for you, and it's probably why you were being held at Budi's estate," I said.

"Once again, Mr. Finn is correct, but that's neither here nor there at the moment, for I believe it's time for all of you to die and me to ascend to the seat of power."

Suddenly there was the sound of gunfire and shouting outside, and Maas looked around nervously then clicked his lapel mic to ask for a situation report. Hearing no response, he paced nervously while he waited for any kind of news. Hearing no response, he abruptly stopped then cued his mic.

"This is Maas. Report, over!" he said.

Again there was no response.

"Having a little trouble, Maas?" I asked.

"No, obviously our frequency must be overloaded by radio traffic."

"Maybe—maybe not."

Frustrated, Maas walked over and pointed his pistol at Jacob's head.

"Well, I'm sure it's just a small glitch, so there's no reason to prolong the inevitable. Goodbye, your majesty."

I made eye contact with Sten, and he nodded, which I hoped meant he was on our side. I then signaled that I had a pistol and pointed my finger at Maas, and he did the same but pointed his at the other security guy. In theory, we had an unspoken plan, and each of us would take a target, though only time would tell if I could indeed trust my new friend. I extended three fingers and proceeded to count down, and, at two, I could see that Maas had hardened his resolve and was ready to fire, so I pulled out my pistol and cocked it to give it a hair trigger. As I counted one and prepared to fire, Itari unexpectedly cried out and lurched at Maas.

"No!" he bellowed, as he took hold of Maas's gun hand and drove it up and away from Jacob's head.

A chaotic fight ensued, with the two men falling onto the ground, where they clambered for control of the pistol. Maas yelled for his men to shoot Itari, but Sten was on our side, and the other guard couldn't get an adequate shot with his target rolling around on the floor with his boss. Maas was desperate, however, and continued to yell the same command over and over.

"Shoot him! Shoot him Goddammit!" but the man still couldn't get a clear shot.

Itari finally got hold of the pistol, but Maas managed to land an elbow to his midsection that sent the pistol flying. With that opening, Maas rolled free and made Itari an easy target, but, as the other guard prepared to fire, Sten was quicker and fired twice, and both impacted the man center chest and knocked him to the floor. He was wearing a vest, so the bullets only managed to incapacitate him, but it was good enough for the moment. Movement brought my attention back to Maas, and I saw that he had managed to get ahold of the pistol, so I brought up my weapon and fired at him. My bullet tore into his right forearm, which happened to be the exact spot I had been aiming. It was a risky shot, but I hoped to take him alive, so that he could atone for his crimes in a much more humiliating way than dying. He dropped his gun and crumpled onto his knees and writhed in pain as he clutched at his forearm. As I moved in, he saw me approaching, and he scrambled for the gun and managed to grab it with his other hand.

"If I shoot your left hand, you won't have a single hand left to wipe your ass. That won't be a fun way to live in prison," I said.

He dropped the gun then leaned back against the wall and looked like a broken man. With our immediate problem averted, I turned my attention back to the sound of gunfire and shouts, which seemed to be drawing closer to our position. I took a quick look out the window and saw there were even more men than before, and they appeared to have formed a pretty solid perimeter around the entire palace. Lovely.

"What's going on now?" Sten asked.

"A lot unfortunately, and it's making me wonder if Maas's partner changed the plan and decided to take it all for himself."

"Wouldn't that be typical," Anna said.

"I take it there isn't any kind of underground secret escape tunnel out of here?" I asked Jacob.

"The only ways out are the door and the fire escape," he responded.

"Then I guess we'll have to make our stand right here. Everyone, take cover behind the desk and stay low," I said.

The group crowded behind the desk, which was thankfully substantial and made of oak, though it was doubtful it would completely stop AK bullets. Still, it was our only cover, and Sten took one side while I took the other, and all of us quietly stared at the door. I took a moment to make my peace with the world and readied my pistol and felt as though I were standing at the OK Corral about to go out in a blaze of glory. The doors burst open, and Itari immediately jumped up and stepped into the path of the intruders.

"Hold your fire!" he yelled frantically.

The large contingent of armed soldiers lowered their weapons and walked into the room, and I was relieved to see that they were obviously friends of Itari's and very likely some of the same men who had met us up at the river. Itari was now smiling, and his gaze made me think back to the phone call he had made right before we left. He had described it as the possible difference between life and death, and, as it turned out, he couldn't have been more correct. Whoever he was talking to had been part of his own backup plan, and it was good thinking and yet another sign of his wisdom and prudence.

"So, Itari, which one is your proctologist?"

"Obviously the one with the delicate hands and confident smile."

"So, it's clearly the man in front."

The man laughed.

"I might be confident, but these hands are far from delicate," he responded.

Itari smiled and went over and patted the man on the back.

"You're just in time, Eko. How are things elsewhere in the city?"

"What do you mean?" Eko asked, looking confused.

"Maas said the MSA were attacking multiple targets all over the island."

"No, just the palace and the airport. Whatever he told you was obviously part of some kind of deception."

I thought for a second and had to smile as yet more puzzle pieces fell into place.

"Of course! It's so obvious now! All they had to do was

make us believe the MSA were mounting attacks all over the island."

"I'm not sure I'm following you," Itari said.

"Who owns and controls the communications networks like radio, television, and internet?" I asked.

"Budi Kusuma! It's just like the movie Wag the Dog," Itari said, instantly understanding.

"Would someone please explain what the hell is going on?" Jacob asked, sounding frustrated.

I turned and looked at Jacob.

"In order for Maas and Budi's plan to work, all they had to do was make you believe the island was being taken over. Turn off the television, radio, and internet for a few hours then stage a few gun battles, and you'd have willingly left in order to save your family. It's so simple it's brilliant."

Jacob turned his gaze to the men at the door.

"So, who are all of you?" he asked.

"Excellent question, and now, your majesty, I'd like to introduce you to the good guys. This is the Malkarta Democratic Alliance, and if you haven't already guessed, Itari is their brave and fearless leader," I said.

"Honestly, I'm quite shocked. I've always thought of you as an academic and not a man of action."

"Or the kind of man who'd put himself in harm's way to save his king?" I added.

"Frankly no, but I'm happy to say I was wrong," Jacob said, as he stood and walked over to Itari.

"Thank you, my friend," Jacob said.

"You're welcome, your majesty."

"Itari, I'll forever be in your debt and will do whatever I can to repay your act of bravery," he said.

"Well, I suppose it would be as good a time as any to reopen the discussion on the state of affairs of our beloved island. As you have witnessed today, there is real unrest on Malkarta, but positive non-violent change is entirely possible if we act now."

"What would you have me do?"

"We, as your people, have come to your aid—and therefore, now ask for you to come to ours. We need to bring this island out of the dark ages, but that can only be achieved if we work together, and, as an educated man, I understand this can't happen overnight and will take time and patience on everyone's part. So, what I'm asking you at the moment, your majesty, is if you will officially decree the beginning of positive social and economic reform in the hopes of building a new Malkarta, a better Malkarta—one we can all be proud to be a part of."

Jacob looked at the people around him for a long time then gazed at the various portraits of his ancestors around his office. When he was done, he closed his eyes and let out a long sigh before opening them back up to gaze at Itari. Everyone in the room was now silent, knowing that Jacob's next words would either signify a great move forward, or a potential plunge into rebellion and bloodshed. At long last, he cleared his throat and spoke.

"Change is—difficult, and I'll admit that I've been resisting it my entire life. I would have to be blind not to see the inequity and subsequent discontent that has existed for so many hundreds of years. Of course, I am a product of that system and have been content to maintain the status quo, but, after what I experienced today, I see the error of my ways—of my family's ways, and therefore, hereby declare that from this day forward, Malkarta shall move towards political and economic reform in hopes of creating a nation where everyone shall have equal right to life, liberty, and education. We will have a new Malkarta!" he declared as he stood up.

Everyone in the room erupted in cheers, and I exchanged a smile with Itari and Mark, who came over and swept me up in a group hug. As we parted, Mark put his arms around Anna and kissed her, and their happiness was so intense that it seemed to radiate out to everyone in the room.

"Will you marry me?" he yelled.

Everyone grew instantly quiet, and all eyes turned to the couple, but, before Anna could answer, Jacob slammed his fist on the desk and spoke.

"Absolutely not!" he bellowed.

There was a gasp of disapproval, and the joy in the room instantly dissipated.

"But, father!" Anna said, looking heartbroken.

"I forbid it until he has properly asked my permission. You are a Princess for God's sake."

Mark approached Jacob.

"Sir, may I have your permission to ask for your daughter's hand in marriage?"

Jacob thought a moment and scrutinized Mark before speaking.

"Very well. You have my permission, young man, but I think you should know that if you ever break my daughter's heart, the sedition charge will be immediately reinstated."

"Jacob!" the queen protested.

"Oh, don't worry, I'm just kidding," he said, to Isabella before mouthing to Mark that he was serious.

The room once again erupted with cheering, as we now had two reasons to celebrate—namely a new Malkarta and a wedding! Fiona turned to me and delivered a long, passionate kiss, then she smiled as she gazed into my eyes.

"You helped make a lot of people very happy today, Tag Finn."

"What can I say—I like happy endings."

CHAPTER THIRTY-FOUR
A Happy Ending

My work on Malkarta was officially done, but I was sticking around for another two weeks, as I had two very important errands to complete. The first was to deliver testimony against Budi Kusuma and Maas Groot, who would likely be spending some serious time behind bars, which, of course, beckoned the question as to whether or not Maas had a problem with a roommate who wore g-string underwear. Of course, the other more important errand was that I was going to be Mark's best man at his and Anna's wedding. That was still a week away, however, as Royal weddings took a lot of planning, but I was perfectly happy to wait, because, at the moment, Fiona and I were back at the King William Hotel, and we were sitting on the beach sipping Mai Tai's as we enjoyed gazing out at the beautiful after-noon sun as it dropped ever closer to the horizon.

Fiona rose from her chair a moment later and regarded me.

"Need a refill?" she asked.

"I do. Want me to go?"

"No, you've done enough. Just sit there and relax. I'll be right back," she said, as she turned and headed off for the bar.

I leaned back in my beach recliner and wiggled my toes in the sand then closed my eyes for a moment of deep relaxation. Some time later I felt a shadow looming over me, and I opened my eyes to discover a person standing in front of me. I tried to see their face, but the sun was obscuring my vision.

"Excuse me. Can I help you?" I asked.

"Don't you remember me, *bulè*?" he asked.

I leaned forward and shaded my eyes with my hand, and now I could recognize the stranger's face. It was Gori, one of the guys I had tussled with on the beach that night.

"Actually, I do. How's your jaw feeling?"

"That's part of why I'm here."

Lovely, all I needed was a fight to ruin the calm of an otherwise perfectly peaceful afternoon. I decided I better get out of my seat and moved my feet to one side of the recliner.

"You don't need to get up."

"OK," I said, feeling a little confused.

"I heard about what you did for the people of Malkarta, so I'm here to apologize. I was acting like a *bajingan* the other night.

"Which means?"

"Asshole."

"I'll have to remember that."

"I want you to know that I was wrong, and I won't ever again judge a man by the color, or should I say lack of color of his skin."

"Apology accepted. Care to join me for a drink?"

"Maybe later, I'm still on the clock."

He reached out and we shook hands, though now we were friends. He said goodbye and walked back up to the hotel, and I had to wonder if perhaps this was an omen of things to come. If Gori and I could make amends then why not all of Malkarta? I smiled to myself and realized that I had been a part of something important—something great—the likes of which were only read about in history books. Better still, I had helped change people's lives and made a small, though significant, place in the world a hell of a lot better. I felt eyes on me and looked over to see Fiona had returned and she was staring at me with a puzzled expression on her face.

"What are you smiling about?" she asked.

"Life and shit. Why do you ask?"

"Well, I was thinking you might have forgotten that it's your turn to wear the handcuffs tonight."

"Of course, I haven't forgotten, which is obviously the reason I was smiling."

Such was life in paradise—a good drink, some good friends, and if you were lucky, a good woman and a pair of pink fur-lined handcuffs.

TAG FINN WILL BE CONTINUING HIS ADVENTURES IN

POI PREDICAMENT

Tag Finn is in Hawaii to be the best man at the wedding of his good friend John Matheson—who just happens to be the current vice president of the United States and a very likely candidate to become the next president of the United States. It's all about fun, sun, and two people coming together in holy matrimony until Finn awakens on the day of the wedding to learn that there has been a murder, and the future first lady is the number one suspect.

With only a week, he must unravel the perfect crime and thwart a ruthless group of conspirators if he hopes to save his friend's marriage and political career. Sex, intrigue, danger, and indeed the potential fate of the United States and the free world are all on the line as Finn does his best to save the date.

THE MANTASY SERIES:

SOFT TACO ISLAND

TOPLESS AGENDA

GORDITA CONSPIRACY

MR PICKLES

STRIPPER BOAT

POI PREDICAMENT

CHALUPA CONUNDRUM

PROMETHEUS PROTOCOL

ACKNOWLEDGEMENTS

I suspect every writer has a large list of people who make their work possible, and mine begins with my wife, who hears every one of my idiotic ideas and gives her opinion freely and without fear that I might get offended and stop helping with the housework. Next, would be my editors, Ruth A. Bright, Chris Cooper, and Aria Pearson who have generously given their time to comb the book for mistakes and keep me grammatically, if not politically or morally correct. After editors, comes my army of proof-readers, namely Matt Zeeman, Chris Imlay, Bob Horton, Katherine Gundling, and Jason Bright. Following them is my family, especially my father Fred Christie, who has always believed in my artistic endeavors and supported them both figuratively and literally. Next would be my mother Jane Christie (Posthumously), who definitely played a roll in my odd sense of humor. Also in the family category, is my pushy sister Sheree Wilson who helped get me into a posh New York Literary Agency, as well as my less pushy sister, Shelly Hall. From there, it continues on to two special friends who helped in a very unusual way, namely securing the Macbook Pro laptop that I would use to write while incarcerated at Stanford Hospital. Those two generous souls, inadvertently responsible for the proliferation of the Mantasy Genre, are Michele and Dan Scanlon. Next is my oldest friend and layout expert Chris Imlay followed by Dianna Woods, Jimmy and Jodie Woods, as well as Robert O'Brien and Elizabeth "high-beams" Machado, all of whom have been willing to suffer through early drafts, mistakes, inaccuracies, and a vast number of unusual sexual metaphors.

Another special thank you goes out to Greg Owens, good friend and international man of business acumen, who passed on the following advice from his mentor George Leonard—take the hit. Which means: should you ever be sidelined with something such as five years of cancer treatment, do something positive with the time—in my case writing a bunch of escapist, erotic, adventure novels.

I'd also like to thank Mike Rowe and his *Dirty Jobs* show, Tom Selleck and the creators of *Magnum PI*, Jeremy Clarkson, James May, and Richard Hammond and their show *Top Gear* (which is now more or less the *Grand Tour* on Amazon), and, last but not least, J.K. Rowling and her *Harry Potter* book series. All four would make an unbearable time more bearable, and, in the case of when I finally left the hospital, I had a new immune system and more or less was the equivalent of an adult newborn and therefore had to avoid the public and its various viruses, bacteria, and germs. To that end, I was home all day every day, and the only way to keep from going totally bonzo when I was writing was to have a show on in the background. With *Dirty Jobs* I found the perfect everyman in host Mike Rowe, whose filthy exploits and double entendres kept me feeling connected to the "dirty" world beyond my room. *Top Gear* and its wacky hosts and scenic locations kept me fully entertained and desperate to get well and make it back out to the world at large. *Magnum PI*, however, was a different experience, for it brought me back to one of my beloved childhood shows, and its characters and setting served as a kind of comfort food during the anxiety filled hours of treatment. In the early stages of treatment, however, I started reading J.K. Rowling's *Harry Potter*. Nothing was better at taking my mind off the chemo drip, and it was actually the void I felt after finishing the series that helped inspire me to create my own literary world in which to escape—though mine would obviously be for adults and contain a shitload of profanity, humor, and sex. We often underestimate the value of entertainment and its unique ability to take us away from our problems, and so, to all four entities and all those involved—you have my gratitude!

My final word of thanks goes out to my vast martial arts community, all of whom helped keep me alive and well throughout the dark days of cancer treatment. At the top of that group, and requiring special thanks, are Matt Thomas, Rick Alemany, and Margaret Alemany whose wisdom and teaching helped inspire many of the techniques in the book. Beyond them and within our own karate community is Lauren and Rob Sandusky, Thandi Guile, Aria and Daniel Pearson, Tom Jacoby and Jennifer Solow, John Hedlund, Michele & Dan Scanlon, Katherine Gundling, Bob Horton, Sue Fox and J.T. Meade, Mark, Matt, Brad, and Jade Zeeman, Ted Hatch, James Parks, Rob Capps,

Mari Sciabica, Jeremy Holt and the Holt Family, Sabrina Haechler, Jonathan Johnson, Brannon Beliso, Catherine and Eric Engelbrecht, Catherine and Ian Moore, Tamera Blake, the families and students of Christie Kenpo Karate, Michael Mason MD, Natalya Greyz MD, Sally Arai MD, and the Stanford University BMT Unit & ITA. If you don't see your name here, don't worry—there is a more comprehensive list of the karate community on the Thank You page of my website.

To all of you, I say be well—and more importantly—dump well.

ORIGIN OF THE MANTASY GENRE

In 2010, I was diagnosed with Stage 4 Non-Hodgkins T-Cell Lymphoma Cancer, and, with only weeks before my imminent demise, began rigorous dose dense chemotherapy. With an extremely low survival rate, about one in five, I was particularly lucky to achieve a full remission in just over two months. I went on to receive a stem cell, and eventual bone marrow transplant at Stanford University, the last procedure being the most effective treatment for a lifelong cure.

So, what exactly does a person do when faced with extreme isolation and the fear of a potentially premature demise? Well, I started reading Harry Potter and filled many long hours hooked up to a chemo drip, spending my time with the life and adventures of the boy who lived—hoping, in my case, to be the man who survived. There aren't many books more removed from the doldrums of cancer, so it became the perfect escape. The problem, however, was that I tore through them so quickly that I was soon on my own again—desperately in need of something to fill my long, anxiety filled days.

I tried several popular novels and authors I liked but couldn't find anything to adequately fill the endless hours of isolation. Of course, I could have wallowed in self pity, but I really didn't want the months of downtime to be meaningless. If I was forced to sit around like a piece of shit, then I wanted to do something with the time. I immediately decided that I should turn my screenplay writing skills into the ultimate, tell-all cancer book, but, five pages in, I realized the topic was too depressing and decided to instead write a novel. It was going to be the book I desperately wanted to read and would include all the things I lacked at that moment—namely sex, alcohol, adventure, travel, and privacy in the bathroom—the key elements for a truly rewarding existence.

I finished chemo at Kaiser then headed south to the Stanford University Hospital and quickly realized that I would have nothing but a window and the internet for a companion in the coming months. Worse still were the medical horrors that would soon become a part of my daily existence. My morning nurse, concerned about the debilitating physical effects of intense chemo, entered my room each day with the following words:

"What would you like me to check first? Your balls or your butt hole?"

"Um—neither?" I responded.

At that point, all I desired went into my writing, first and foremost being a little privacy in the ol' baño. The nurses had an annoying habit of always wanting to weigh my stools—something to do with keeping track of fluid and food intake and the subsequent amount of release. My bathroom contained what I called the cowboy hat, a plastic insert to catch waste entering the toilet. Peeing in the little urinal was enough indignity, so whenever possible, I woke up early and dumped before they could make their rounds. Every day that I sent a number two un-accosted down the drain was a small, though cherished victory. I felt like a prisoner—a veritable Count of Monte Cristo, though my prison was a hospital and my battles were waged over porcelain.

Continuing with the theme of writing about all I lacked meant that the book would sizzle with sex, adventure, and humor. Three months later, I would complete book one and within the year, finish two more—completing what I called at the time, The Mantasy Trilogy—the word Mantasy, being the combination of Male and Fantasy. The following year, I managed to write five more follow ups, all with the same character and eccentricities but with new and exciting storylines and locations. Now, I had a Mantasy Series. Or, if I wanted to follow in Douglas Adam's foot-steps, I would say—books four, five, six, seven, and eight in the Mantasy Trilogy. I'm currently finishing books nine, ten, and eleven.

Writing has always been one of my great loves but sadly, it took a life threatening illness to bring us back together full-time. I have written a number of screenplays and had two optioned for motion pictures, but traditional writing is more complicated and requires a hell of a lot more work. It is, however, more rewarding because you have the ability to deliver your story directly to an audience, whether it's your friends, the woman at the Post Office, or the thousands of potential readers trolling the online eBooks. It doesn't need a fifty million dollar budget, a production team, distribution, and funding for it to reach an audience—and that is pretty awesome.

ABOUT THE AUTHOR

Lyle Christie was born in San Francisco, raised in Marin County, and attended the University of Kentfield, San Francisco State University, the Academy of Art College, and Dominican University, where he majored in film and social psychology, and minored in Philosophy, Anthropology, and Human Sexuality—all of which gave him the diverse educational background to become a writer and director. In addition, he holds a fifth degree black belt and teaches Kenpo Karate, Jujitsu, Arnis, and Wing Chun. During his lifetime in the martial arts, he has taught civilians as well as police and military personnel and has the unique pleasure of training with elite members of the United States and international defense and intelligence community.

He also teaches firearms, swords, sticks, and knives, though he is equally deadly with the nunchaku, machete, goat, tether ball, and skin flute—the last perhaps being his greatest skill set. Above all else, he maintains excellent, if not grey, hair and lives aboard a yacht in Sausalito with his wife, French Bulldog, and Miniature Dachshund. When he's not writing, directing, teaching martial arts, or training with the real life James Bonds of the world, you'll find him fighting injustice, cherishing a number two, working out, or riding his mountain bike through the scenic hills of Marin County.

You can learn more at www.lylechristie.com